UNLUCKY IN LAW

"Intriguing . . . the most interesting of the Nina Reilly series so far." —*Dallas Morning News*

"This is a quick-moving novel of modern-day legal issues. . . . You'll enjoy any of Perri O'Shaughnessy's novels, but *Unlucky in Law* is one of the best."
—*Somerset (PA) Daily American*

"[A] potent blend of dramatic court scenes, intelligently written characters, and highly suspenseful and fascinating plot. This is simply superb storytelling at its best. . . . Another score for O'Shaughnessy, and as usual we're left eagerly anticipating the next in this furiously engaging series." —*New Mystery Reader*

"The courtroom drama in *Unlucky in Law* is intensely absorbing, the forensics fascinating, the mystery unusual, and the investigation suspenseful. . . . Don't miss this one."
—*Romance Reviews Today*

"Nina is always fun to spend a few hours with. . . . O'Shaughnessy proves once again that she has built a strong brand with plenty of scope to grow."
—*Orlando Sentinel*

"O'Shaughnessy has with Nina Reilly created one of the more interesting criminal defense attorneys presently on the bookshelves . . . [a] fine series."
—*Bookreporter.com*

"Entertaining . . . O'Shaughnessy fans will be pleased with this addition." —*Booklist*

"A great read with a convincing defendant . . . The end is beautifully executed and is not easily deduced."
—*Romantic Times*

PRESUMPTION OF DEATH

"Nina Reilly is burning up the courtroom again . . . a fiery read." —*Entertainment Weekly*

"The protagonists are well-rounded and engaging . . . and the pace is relentless. *Presumption of Death* virtually demands to be read in one sitting."
—*BookPage*

"Counselor Nina Reilly keeps on . . . getting better. . . . Generous heart, steel-trap brain, elegant looks: great fun to read about." —*Kirkus Reviews* (starred review)

"A very good and exciting legal thriller [that] is also so much more . . . Perri O'Shaughnessy will appeal to readers who love John Grisham."—*Midwest Book Review*

"Nina Reilly['s] pedal-to-the-medal approach to cases provides armchair thrills on just about every other page. . . . Perfect summer reading fare."—*Fort Worth Star Telegram*

"A vivid read." —*Houston Chronicle*

"Well-rounded and likable characters [are] set against a richly developed backdrop of some of the loveliest country in the world." —*Publishers Weekly*

"Stylish and elegant . . . the story is compelling."
—*Cleveland Plain Dealer*

"By far the most intriguing and complex mystery in O'Shaughnessy's Nina Reilly series."
—iloveamysterynewsletter.com

"[Perri O'Shaughnessy has] a track record that is hard to beat. [Her] readers have come to expect a terrific plot inundated with exciting twists and turns. . . . This book is a winner and a perfect summer sizzler. Enjoy!"
—Bookreporter.com

UNFIT TO PRACTICE

"Here's to a lawyer with as much heart as brains. Bottom line: a winning case."
—*People* (Page-turner of the Week)

"Nina's eighth may be her most irresistible to date."
—*Kirkus Reviews*

"This fast-paced novel, filled with legal maneuvers and courtroom drama, once again proves Nina Reilly to be an intriguing heroine."
—*Chattanooga Times*

"Scenes of gripping courtroom drama, coupled with a gut-wrenching, action-packed conclusion . . . will keep O'Shaughnessy's numerous fans happy."
—*Monterey County Herald*

"Nina Reilly seems to have hit her stride. . . . O'Shaughnessy furnishes believable characters and well-drawn

courtroom scenes, but what really gives this legal thriller its appeal is the genuinely unusual premise."
—*Booklist*

"Will keep readers spellbound until the case's dramatic wrap-up . . . O'Shaughnessy's knack for infusing her stories with a darkly suspicious atmosphere makes for satisfying reading, and the novel really does seem to speed toward its finish. . . . Her grip remains tight on both her characters and their story." —*Book Street USA*

"Nina Reilly [is] one of the most popular legal heroines ever called to the legal bar. . . . Read the book or face the music." —*Ottawa Citizen*

"A suspenseful ride . . . Malice becomes murder in this drama that shifts from a tension-filled courtroom to the secret recesses of a woman's heart."
—*Denton Record-Chronicle*

"A lightning-paced read, highlighted by the fascinating cases Nina takes on . . . suspenseful."
—*Romantic Times*

"O'Shaughnessy gets better and better with every new title. . . . There is not a quiet moment in this cleverly woven tale. . . . It is nearly impossible to put the book down. . . . A delightful series of mysteries."
—*Rainbo Electronic Reviews*

"The story rolls forth without a hitch . . . intense."
—*Deadly Pleasures*

"With every book Perri O'Shaughnessy gets better and better. I am continuously surprised by the twists and turns

that this book takes.... I loved this book and as soon as I finished it, I opened it up and read it again."
—*Mystery News*

WRIT OF EXECUTION

"O'Shaughnessy [has] crafted yet another crackling courtroom drama featuring a strong yet believably human female lead. Move over, John Grisham."
—*BookPage*

"Captivates with its scenes of wily courtroom negotiation."   —*Publishers Weekly*

"A tense and fast-paced legal thriller . . . O'Shaughnessy delivers on every front."
—*Tampa Tribune & Times*

"Satisfyingly complex, *Writ of Execution* is a twisty legal thriller that cuts to the edge."
—*Romantic Times*

"They entertain with the best."
—*Kirkus Reviews*

"O'Shaughnessy deals readers a winning hand—the seventh in the series of Reilly adventures is another jackpot."
—*Orlando Sentinel*

ALSO BY PERRI O'SHAUGHNESSY

PERRI O'SHAUGHNESSY

UNLUCKY IN LAW

A DELL BOOK

UNLUCKY IN LAW
A Dell Book

PUBLISHING HISTORY
Delacorte hardcover edition published July 2004
Dell mass market edition / April 2005

Published by
Bantam Dell
A Division of Random House, Inc.
New York, New York

Library of Congress Catalog Card Number: 2004047840

ISBN 0-440-24088-3

Printed in the United States of America
Published simultaneously in Canada

www.bantamdell.com

OPM   10   9   8   7   6   5   4   3   2   1

IN MEMORY OF BEN MCGOVERN AND DEDICATED
TO ALL THE OTHER CHILDREN STILL FIGHTING
BLOOD-RELATED CANCERS

THEY DESERVE A CURE.

AND FOR JANE FULLER OF OWEGO, NEW YORK

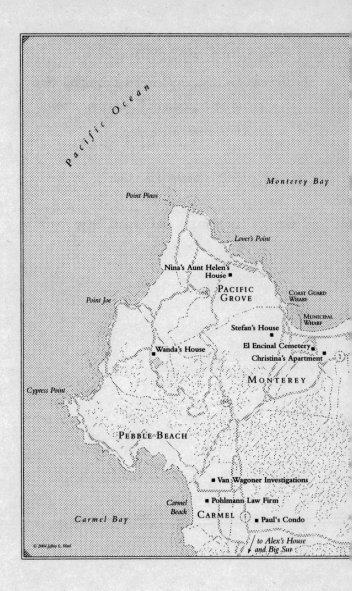

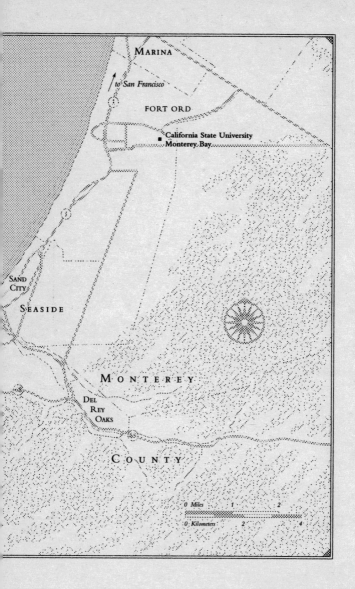

UNLUCKY IN LAW

PROLOGUE

Christina's Story
Monterey, California, 1966

HER FRIENDS CALLED THEIR FATHERS "DAD" or "Daddy," but he wanted Christina and her little brother to call him Papa because he had called his father Papa. His mustache drifted below his mouth at the corners, tickling her when he kissed her cheeks. When he was sick and lying on the couch in his study, he liked to sing to her. At bedtime he read her stories, like "Masha the Bear," which was a lot like "Little Red Riding Hood," and the story of "The Crow and the Crayfish." Sometimes she persuaded him to read her favorite.

" 'The Snow Maiden' again, Papa."

He groused and teased, finally pulling out a tattered book and finding the page. " 'Everyone else was building snowmen. "Why not build a snow maiden?" the old lady asked. And so they did. When they were finished, they stepped back to admire her.' "

"She came to life," Christina said, excited. "Like Pinocchio!"

" 'She smiled!' " he read, " 'and she began to move her arms and legs. How her grandparents doted on her. White as the snow was Snyegurochka, with eyes like blue beads. Blonde hair dangled all the way down to her waist. She had no color in her cheeks, but cherry red lips made of shiny ribbon. She was so beautiful!' "

He read on. Finishing the story, he leaned over to touch her cheek. "You, my little princess, have pink cheeks, nothing like this pale girl made of ice who melts in a bonfire."

"Why did she jump over the fire?"

"She didn't want to hide by the icy river anymore. She forgot she was made of snow, and dreamed she could be something she was not."

"I'll be like her. Brave. Jump over the fire."

"No," Papa said. "Remember, she lost her life for this dream."

He shut the book. "Tomorrow, I will play some music for you, something you will like."

"What is it?"

"Music for the snow maiden, based on the story you love so much," he said, "by a man named Rimsky-Korsakov."

"Okay." Her eyes drooped. "Papa?"

"Yes, my princess."

"I can't sleep."

He kissed her forehead. "One last story," he said, "the true story of a boy in Russia. Then if you can't sleep, you will have to count sheep." He thought for a moment. "I warn you in advance, it's tragic."

"Does the wolf tear the goat to bits?"

"Yes and no," he said.

"Is it sad?"

"Yes, some of it is sad."

"Put your blue egg in the story, the one you keep in your study."

"All right." He laughed.

"Does anyone die in it? I don't want them to die."

"In true stories, people die, Christina."

"Not me!"

"Everyone."

She digested the information silently, then said, "Tell me your story, Papa. I promise not to cry."

1

Monday 9/1

SEVEN A.M. ON THE FIRST Monday morning in September. Nina Reilly and Paul van Wagoner snoozed in his king-size bed in the sole bedroom of his Carmel condo. As the sun came through the shutters, striping the rug with light, Paul kicked off the covers on his side and, as Nina opened her eyes, turned over so all his long naked backside was displayed: the blond hair, smooth, well-muscled back, strong legs, and narrow feet.

As if he felt her attention, he turned to face her. Eyes closed, he grabbed her around the waist and pulled her tight to his body.

Nina was naked, too, the way Paul liked her. Herself, she favored expensive silks or shabby cottons, but since she had gotten involved with Paul, she had learned to appreciate what he called his simple needs. He liked skin, he liked the smell of her, he wanted nothing to come between them, so nothing did, at least not when they were in bed together.

This time with Paul was precious. Her son, Bob, fourteen, had spent the previous night with his grandfather. She had "freedom," in the way all mothers had freedom, meaning contingent freedom, but at least Bob was safe enough for the moment. She stretched in Paul's arms so her toes reached his calves, and kissed his stubbled cheek.

"Mmm, coffee time," Paul said, smiling, eyes closed.

It was her turn. She didn't have far to go in the compact condo. When she came back with the mugs, Paul was sitting up in bed, legs crossed.

"I feel suspiciously elated, considering it's Monday morning," she said.

"Ben Franklin would call us slackers. He would have been up since five, making a kite."

"Progress means we get to do whatever the hell we want this early in the morning," she said.

Nina had moved to the Monterey area from Tahoe in early summer to be with Paul, just to see how things would play for them. She had gone to law school here, at Monterey Peninsula College. Her father lived here, and she had other old ties. But now, after her move from Tahoe and after a brief vacation of sorts, she had signed on for her second murder case in three months.

Her part started today, though the poor client had been counting the days at the Monterey County Jail for four months. A new case, a new chance to test herself and show her stuff, was always a thrill. So she felt good right now, enjoying the smoldering looks she was getting from Paul.

"Get back in here," Paul commanded. He patted the bed beside him.

"Be polite or you won't get this coffee. Triple-strength fresh-ground French roast. You'll never get better."

"All right, I'm begging you, please, get back in here. Or is the plan for me to admire you standing there with your hip cocked like that?"

She climbed into bed and pulled up the sheet, and they both sipped their coffee. Paul seemed to have something on his mind, so she held back the impulse to jump up and throw her clothes on, waiting to hear it. He ran a very successful investigation and security business. Selfishly, she hoped he was worrying about work and not anything that would slow her down.

He set his cup on the bed stand and drew her close. "Back to the grind for our girl. I hope Klaus is paying you a whole lot to compensate you for putting your life in such an uproar."

"I'm just glad to have a paying gig again, even though I'm coming in so late. It's going to be very demanding. But I've got you, and I've got Sandy to back me up, so I'm wallowing in a pleasantly fuzzy false sense of security."

"What about this case snagged you? You told me you weren't going to accept any more work until you made some decisions about the things that really matter. Remember?"

She knocked back some of the coffee left in her mug, remembering a distant time when she made decisions with only her own future to consider. But she had Bob to worry about, too. "Klaus called. He needed my help. And then the case . . ." She stopped. "I don't know much yet, but Klaus is ready to go all the way with Stefan Wyatt. He says Wyatt is accused of stealing a skeleton and strangling a woman in Monterey named Christina Zhukovsky. I'm going to meet the client today and start going through the files."

"Fine," he said, so absorbed in his own thoughts he probably hadn't heard hers. "But what is it about this case that has you looking so damned"—he paused to run his hands through the tangle of her long brown hair—"gorgeous?"

She laughed and hit him with a pillow. "That's your eyes giving you trouble. I've heard that happens as a man ages."

"You don't fool me," he said, pulling her into a full-bodied kiss. "You like distinguished. Aged red wine; ripe bananas; men with faces that show they've lived a life of excess and pleasure; flaky cheeses . . ."

"Shall I compare thee to a flaky cheese? Do you really want that?"

He laughed. "Anyway, have you considered this? Maybe this case will lead to a partnership opportunity. How would you feel about that?"

"Would you like that?" She knew the answer. She asked to avoid answering.

"Yep. You know I'd love to tie you down right here on the Monterey Peninsula. I'm always on the lookout for opportunities."

She smiled at him. "I guess I'll deal with a partnership offer when and if the time comes." Life felt easy here in his arms. Protected. But she was starting to notice something after this time she had spent away from work and from her own solo practice at Tahoe. She felt smaller, younger, less able.

Criminal defense work had always been her big place, her New York City. Good at her job, getting better all the time, she helped the hapless, damn it. She had a calling to go out and save miserable souls who could not save themselves, help them through the labyrinth, make sure the rules were followed and that they had their defense, even if they were guilty. She liked a large life. She wasn't sure yet how big her life could be with Paul.

He looked at her now, considering something, stroking her hair. Then he reached beyond her and pulled open a drawer to the bedside table. "Maybe the time has come," he said.

"What? Nobody's made me a partnership offer," she said.

He pulled out a small, ornately decorated enamel box. "Oh, but I have."

"Ah." She pushed her hair out of her eyes and looked at the box.

"Right. Marriage."

"We should have talked about this last night, at dinner, when we had time."

He shook his head. "Last night was chaos."

She remembered. Bob had decided he needed their dog, suddenly, for reasons known only to him, but he had been so insistent on her bringing Hitchcock that they interrupted their dinner date to drive back to her house to get him and then drove to her father's to deliver him. Paul had done it all so patiently, even though she had been fuming.

"Anyway, I don't want to talk, Nina. We've said it all and now's the right time for this. Mornings with you are so beautiful." He took her left hand and turned her to face him, popping open the box to reveal a twinkling square diamond ring, with two tapered baguettes flanking it.

He had asked her to marry him before, but the ring was a new, serious development. Nina held up her side of the sheet, gazing at the ring, her lips parted. The band, a sleek platinum, held the big stone between elongated prongs so that the light could dance around it in all directions.

"It's called an azure-cut—four equal sides. It was my grandmother's," he said. "A bluestocking in the early 1900's, I'm told. Seemed like the symbolically perfect thing for you."

"It's gorgeous," she said, stammering a little.

He took the ring from its box. "Nina, will you marry me?"

He had been patient with her. He deserved an answer. "I think . . ."

"Don't think."

She took her hand out of his, and covered the hand

holding the ring with both of hers, feeling tears coming to her eyes. "I really love you!" she said.

"Then say yes."

"Marrying you means what? Staying here? Or would you come with me back to Tahoe?"

"I want you with me, Nina, forever and ever." Blond hair fell over his forehead, and his bare flat stomach creased delightfully at the waist.

"There's Bob," she said.

"He's a kid. He'll adjust."

"My work. Matt, Andrea, their kids. My whole life is in Tahoe."

"Unless it's here with me." He pulled the ring out and turned it in the sunlight, watching it twinkle. "Wear it?" he said. "Be mine?"

"I am yours."

"Yet, I get no answer." He said it lightly, but she could hear his disappointment.

"I just . . ."

"Okay. Bad timing, trial comin' up. So here's what we'll do. You try it on for size. See how it feels on your finger. Take some time. Think if you must. Sound like a plan?"

She let him slip the ring on her finger. She liked the way it felt, and how pretty it looked there.

They kissed for a long time, languorous, loving.

"Maybe I should wear it on a chain around my neck," she said, "or everyone will assume we're engaged."

"Wear the ring. Maybe you'll discover you can't take it off."

She glanced toward the clock on the bureau. Well, if she was a little late, so be it. Her client wasn't going anywhere. "Paul, I have questions."

"Okay."

"Being together," she said slowly, "what's that mean to you?"

He leaned back and laughed. "I don't want a Stepford wife, okay, or why pick you? There's a babe out there somewhere who is ready to bake a rhubarb pie for me, and even wash my dirty laundry once in a while as part of the deal. I hope you will sometimes. Maybe I'll do the same for you, in a pinch. I'm willing to go untraditional. I just want us to take the next step. It would be beautiful to marry you."

She rubbed a finger against his rough morning cheek. "What I'm trying to say is, how about a counteroffer? I don't see why two people who love each other, two strong people, have to . . ."

"Marry? It's not a bad word. Go ahead. You can say it."

She nodded. "Marry. It's not as if—you always said you don't want kids."

"I do say that."

"So that's not an issue. I mean, you have such a fine life here, your business, friends. And I've got another one up in Tahoe. I miss it. I think all the time about my little house and my brother's family, and I check the weather up there every day. When it's foggy here, I think about how sunny it probably is in the mountains. When it rains here, I wonder if they're getting snow."

"Is this a no?"

She shook her head. "Just, I have questions. Isn't what we have good enough? Isn't it excellent?"

"I don't know what to expect. I don't know if you're coming, going, staying."

"I'm not sure I know what you mean by 'marry.' "

"Enough discussion, okay?" He fiddled with the ring on her finger, centering the stone so that it glittered. "You know what I mean when I ask you to marry me. You know. Don't start quibbling. Now come closer, you're making my brain ache with all this talk."

Her thoughts whirled. Only his touch brought them to a screeching stop. "Is this close enough?" she asked.

"No."

"This?"

"No."

"You always know exactly what you want and you aren't afraid to make your wishes known," she murmured. "I have to get to work. I have a meeting."

"Fifteen minutes."

"I really can't. Five."

"Five isn't enough for what I have in mind."

"Okay, ten, if you can convince me you'll make it worthwhile."

"Damn lawyers! Everything's a negotiation."

Later, his body wrapped tightly around hers, he said, "Nina?"

She was busy covering his neck with tiny kisses. "Yes, Paul?"

"I love you."

"Ditto," she said.

"And I await your final verdict."

2

NINA WALKED DOWN THE HALLWAY at the Salinas jail behind the guard and went into the cubicle he indicated. Featureless, windowless, worn, it held one scarred chair, a wall phone, and a shelf under the large window through which her new client would soon spill his secrets.

As soon as she had pulled the chair up to the window and placed her briefcase on the floor, the door on the other side of the glass opened and a hesitant young man entered. Stefan Wyatt had a soul patch on his chin and enormous biceps developed during, or maybe due to, his months of imprisonment. He wore the usual jail-issue orange jumpsuit, and tripped over the chair that faced Nina through the window before sitting down. The deputy, just closing the door from his side, reflexively reached for his weapon at the sudden movement.

At this first meeting with her client, Nina examined him as severely as she would a new pair of shoes, checking for hidden defects. Sometimes clients brought a smog of evil into the room along with their stories, and she knew right away: here's one who could have done it. This one didn't strike her that way.

"It's all right, man," Wyatt said to the deputy, who

relaxed, seeing there was no harm intended. Fumbling with the phone, twisting the wire straight, he said, "Hello, there." Twenty-eight, tall, a college dropout with a spotty employment history—odd jobs, bartending, almost a year at a moving company, and six months on a fishing boat— he had blue eyes, an average IQ, and a great smile that indicated a nature so sunny even this dungeon hadn't stolen his spirit.

Nina showed him her State Bar card and smiled back, saying, "How are you?"

"Fine?" He shook his head as if uncertain of the truth of his own words. The blue eyes on her were wide open, bewildered.

Had Klaus forgotten to mention her during his visit the day before? "Er, I'm Nina Reilly."

"Right. You're working with Klaus. I'm Stefan. I guess I didn't expect . . ." He paused, smiling. "I guess I thought you'd look like Klaus."

Nina raised an eyebrow. "I probably will, at his age."

"Nooo. Not ever."

"Ready to settle down this morning and do some work?"

"Sure. Absolutely."

"Like Klaus, I'm your attorney, and you have the same privilege of confidentiality in talking with me as you do with him. Do you understand that, Stefan?"

"You can't tell anyone what we talk about. I know."

"I'm here to ask a few questions. You probably understand that I'm coming in late to your case and need to hear it all."

"Klaus didn't explain everything to you?"

"Short notice."

"Okay," he said amiably. "What do you need to know?" She was already forming more judgments about the young man in front of her. Sane, at least oriented to reality at the moment. Engaging. Nice mouth, set of beautiful teeth, a healthy fellow but passive and awkward, the big body not quite coordinated. His eyes held a hangdog eagerness. He looked anxious to please. A certain kind of woman would want to take care of him.

Klaus had said this divided room wasn't bugged. They could talk safely, he believed, so she would put her doubts aside and ask for the whole story.

Uncapping her lucky Mont Blanc pen, Nina wrote the date on her yellow legal pad.

"It's not like I know who killed that woman," Stefan said. "I was in the wrong place, just trying to help someone and make a few bucks I really needed."

"All right," Nina said. "I'm listening. Tell me what happened right up to your arrest."

"Everything?"

"Everything. What you were thinking, not just what you did."

Stefan began to talk, his story coming out in spurts as if he were still coming to terms with some of the things he had done. As he spoke, Nina looked up from her notes now and then and watched him, gauged him, weighed the words.

"It was April, cool at night."

"What day in April?"

"The twelfth. Right into the next morning, April thirteenth. Lucky thirteen, ha, ha."

"Go ahead."

Stefan had waited for the sun to sink low, so he could get it over with. He didn't want the job; just thinking about it made him feel like some grisly comic-book character.

But he had already delayed one night on account of rain and a minor drinking binge that sent him to bed early instead. Alex might be angry about that, and he didn't like disappointing people. Still, if anything could wait, in a weird way, it was this. After all, the old man had been dead for decades. He wasn't going anywhere.

Yet.

But now, if he was going to do this thing, tonight was the night. He would go light on the brewskis and be primed for action later.

He couldn't tell Erin, which put a strain on what should have been a great Saturday night. He had made a solemn promise to her never to break the law again, and here he was preparing to break it just this one last time. Feeling guilty in advance, he took her out for fish and chips at her favorite place at Fisherman's Wharf, the Captain's Gig, where, stoked on caffeine, she talked fast—happily, it seemed to him, though as usual she looked longingly at the shops across the street that carried wind chimes and sea otter statues and that gnarled burlwood furniture they couldn't afford. And jewelry, beautiful rings . . .

While Stefan listened with one ear to a guy ranting through a microphone across the plaza, who actually said a few things Stefan agreed with about working people and how important strong unions were, Erin got on the topic of her family and how much they would like him once they got to know him.

Stefan knew what this meant: What they had heard of him made them not like him. They had heard he had a record. Erin wouldn't lie about that to anyone. He didn't feel ready to meet them until he had his life in better order. But he loved Erin, so he listened to her as they walked home, hoping she wouldn't raise the issue of meeting her folks again.

When they got home, Erin drank the shot of tequila he poured for her in the kitchen. Flushed and beautiful, she sidled up behind his chair to give him a kiss and back rub.

Shit, Stefan thought, heaving a sigh, pouring himself a beer. How he would prefer to be pulling that yellow sweater over her head and taking advantage of her mood. But that had sabotaged him the night before. Tonight he couldn't let it happen. Erin showed no signs of slowing down, and he needed her asleep, so he pretended to keep pace with her while discreetly tossing his own Coors down the kitchen sink. He drank most of one first, to be honest.

They sat down at the kitchen table. "My favorite place, if you're gonna talk about places worth noticing, is that spot between sleeping and waking. Like after good sex?" Erin nudged him with her knee. "You float around like you're in a boat."

"Uh-huh." He stuck his nose into her neck, getting a whiff of her warm smell.

"You tickle." Smiling, she pushed him away a little and put her hand on his leg, then she slid it up and started messing with his fly.

He really did not want to leave.

His brother Gabe called Erin "dim" behind her back, but Stefan didn't know what that was supposed to mean. She was hard to read sometimes. But if Gabe meant brights, well, Erin was brighter than Stefan. Gabe wouldn't think that was saying much, but it meant something to Stefan. He respected her. He liked the surprises that came out of her. "Deep" fit her best. Her politics were naive to nonexistent, but she had something he didn't have. She had connection, to people, to the earth.

He touched her and listened to her, staring beyond the window curtain to the darkening trees.

Thinking: Where is that shovel?

And: I wish to God I didn't have to do this.

Erin's chin sank to her chest as she nodded off. He led her into the bedroom, took her clothes off, and tucked her into bed regretfully. Her eyes closed instantly. "Stef," she mumbled.

"What?"

"Stef," she said again, and then just breathed.

Dark had gathered outside. Yellow lights brightened in the mist. He leaned down to Erin and stroked a strand of hair back from her forehead.

"Forgive me for this," he whispered. "Never leave me."

He put on a warm jacket, located the new gardening gloves he had bought, and stuffed them in his pocket. Outside, he pulled tools from the shed where Erin stored things for her landscaping jobs: a shovel, a pick, a few other things that he thought might come in handy. He tossed them into the trunk of his Honda Civic.

A few cars passed, and every one made him jump. One slowed down as it passed, and he regretted not making sure the light had been out above the shed, but in the dark, he couldn't make the car out, and in the end, he decided it didn't matter. What he had to do was macabre, yeah, but not wrong, exactly.

Who was there to care about an old man dead for decades? The only people who might care didn't, as far as he could tell.

Stefan patted the wallet in his pocket. He needed this money. Erin wouldn't have to pay the rent again this month, and with what was left over, plus what was to come, he could buy something for her that he had wanted to buy for a long, long time.

He took Del Monte Avenue as it curved around the bottom of the bay, passing the wharf and the Doubletree Inn right in the middle of Monterey, then drove north along Lake El Estero and turned toward the two main town cemeteries. The narrow gates at both entrances to the

Cementerio El Encinal were closed, and beyond the wrought iron the green grass looked gray.

Driving around the perimeter of the cemetery, he looked for a hidden place to park nearby. The cemetery boundaries didn't include any good private places, so he pulled into the lot at Dennis the Menace Park. No brightly lit ball games at the field next to the park, the kids in bed, the old locomotive engine at the entrance to the park a dark volume against the thin night. All good.

Stefan checked his watch, discovering it was just past midnight, then pawed through the back seat until he found the flashlight. From the trunk he pulled out the shovel and pick, which he pushed into the army-surplus duffel bag he had brought. Walking along the boundary of the cemetery, the bag slung on a long strap over his arm, he watched for cops, taking in the sounds of the night, amazed at how vivid white clouds looked against the black sky. In spite of his black jeans and black polo shirt, he felt bright as a peacock.

Avoiding the gate with its pointed metal shafts, and the open side around the corner that had no wall but seemed too exposed, he threw the bag over the six-foot wall, listening for the soft clank as it hit ground on the other side. He cast one last look at the street. Bums and dopers sometimes hung out at the picnic tables across the street, but he couldn't see anyone. Still, he definitely felt watched.

The ghosts aren't happy to see me, he thought.

He had meant to cheer himself up, but this joke had the opposite effect. Childish fears woke up and started working on him.

Maybe this wasn't illegal. Was it? It was trespassing, sure, but was it more? He didn't want to break any laws, not only because he had promised Erin, but because he always got caught. He was a poor risk. Whether you believed in the system or not, there was power behind it, and you were the little guy getting squeezed like a juice box if it took hold of you.

He fingered the little Buddha Erin had given him to wear around his neck, saying it might help avoid the bad luck that followed him around everywhere like an evil little brother.

Stefan had always had bad luck. If he used a meter, it expired before he could finish his business, and the meter maid would show up in a bad mood. If he so much as palmed a ballpoint pen after signing a credit-card receipt at the store, the clerk ran after him to get it back.

Five hundred dollars in my pocket, he told himself. More to come when the job is done. Now, that's good luck.

Grabbing a tree limb, he got his boots onto the rough wall and dropped into the cemetery, landing on wet grass. He was on the end near the corner, roughly in position. Turning the flashlight on, he skulked off the path among the graves, hunting for the headstone he had scoped out two days before. At first he stepped gingerly between the stones, but then he loosened up, thinking, The people aren't under the stones. They're stretched out in front of their stones, right where I'm walking.

Some of these flat stones were a hundred years old. The groomed green grass and silk flowers kept the place—well, not pretty, but kind of sweet during the day, but in the dark, they became brown blobs that could trip him if he wasn't careful.

He looked for an odd marker, one with two straight parallel boards at the top and, below, a crooked, slanty one. He flashed on the headstones, on the strange names and lettering. Why did so many Russian people come to Monterey, he wondered, enough of them to rate their own neighborhood of the dead?

After what seemed like forever, he found a funky head-stone marking the right name. Unlike most of the graves here, this one had a concrete rim and contained just muddy dirt and gravel instead of a grass surface. Opening his case, he pulled out the pick, swallowing hard. He swung it back and when it hit dirt it buried itself right up to the shaft in the damp ground.

Stopping, he looked around. The nearby graves did not open. No bony fingers pushed up the stones. He could smell the kelpy waters of Monterey Bay on the breeze, hear the street traffic, but he couldn't shake the feeling that some things didn't sound natural. Standing with the shovel poised over dirt, he listened hard, heart pounding even though he hadn't even started digging.

Dead means dead. Don't start thinking about it.

Working furiously, Stefan assaulted the soil next to the complicated gravestone. As he dug, his body warmed up. The *chunk-chunk* of the shovel covered up what the wind did to the trees and bushes around him, and to his heart-beat.

Once his eyes adjusted, not daring to leave his light on for long, he turned it off and went mostly by feel. He dug as fast as he could, which wasn't very fast.

When they were both young, he used to dig holes with Gabe. He remembered trying to dig to China, and ending up with a shallow hole in the grass, and his mom pitching a fit.

He had a few good memories mixed in with the bad ones. When his brother had gotten sick, that was bad. Gabe would lie in bed, pasty white, listless, while their mom rushed around to doctors looking for hope. Sometimes Mom looked at Stefan, and even though she tried to hide it, he saw her outrage that it was Gabe who had gotten sick, and not him. Gabe was her favorite, born loved and deserving of success, with Stefan the sidekick goofball who slipped on banana peels when there weren't any.

But Gabe got cured, and Stefan was proud that he had been able to help him with that. Now look at Gabe, Mom's gold-star boy, making decent money and taking her out for Mother's Day next month to some fancy restaurant in San Francisco. And check out her younger boy, out here in the cold, digging up a dead body, getting a rhythm going, panting, liking the exercise and finding the work remarkably easy. This dirt wasn't hard; in fact, it was strangely uncompacted, considering the guy had been buried for over twenty-five years. That heavy rain last night must have softened the ground a lot.

Gabe would never have agreed to do this. Mom always said Gabe got the smarts and Stefan got the muscles. Stefan didn't necessarily agree. He had ideas, lots of them, as many as Gabe. He would like to start a business someday, where he could work outside. He thought he could do better, now that he had Erin. He had someone who respected him, who thought he came first.

Yes, he would have a business, and then they would have kids, and that was fine by him. He wanted that. He wanted to create a happy family with her. His childhood wasn't happy, with his mom always treating him like second-best after his brother, her hero. A chronic, infernal worry about money had hung over their lives like a bad moon. His mother and brother both loved him, he believed that, but being poor didn't help family relations. He would love his kids equally. He would take them camping, be the good father he had never known.

His thoughts went back to Erin. He would buy her a new bed, with a pillow-top mattress, and an aquarium for her birthday. Erin liked goldfish. And after tonight, he could finally afford that ring, the one in the window she pretended not to notice, the one that made her look hungry.

Something in the dirt stopped the shovel. He looked into the open grave. Dirt, blackness, wet. A shiny patch? He probed at it, around it. Six feet deep, that's how deep the old man was supposed to be, so how come he'd only dug a couple of feet and the shovel was hitting something?

He scraped around the obstruction, trying to figure out where the edges were in the big hole. Because he felt fear overtaking him, he put the shovel aside for a moment and, head up, listened to the wind, which was stirring up the plants and getting loud. Dude, didn't anybody else notice? No, they wouldn't. They were dead!

He laughed, his nerves tingling right down to his fingertips. Eucalyptus and the scent of the local pine mixed unpleasantly with the damp old dirt in the air, hanging around him like mildewed walls. Working the soil again, he couldn't locate any edges to the thing, whatever it was, in the grave, so he gave up with the shovel and put it on the ground beside the hole. He jumped in with the pick, staying close to the edge, but rubbing up against the dirt. He had worn canvas shoes so that they could be washed later.

Flipping on his flashlight, he reached down with his gloved hands and felt around inside the hole. Smoothing away another layer of dirt, he could see what was there: a couple of big plastic garbage bags all wrapped together and tied with loose rope. Trash? An old Christmas tree? He tried to lift the bundle. No, too heavy, and all one piece. Had a relative tossed in a bag of the old man's possessions at the funeral in 1978? Did Russians do that? Had they buried the old man in a bag?

Then his breath caught as he thought, It's a body that got out of its coffin! The shape was right, the length and size of the thing in there—did they even have plastic trash bags in 1978? The bags didn't look twenty-five years old, either.

Scrambling out of the hole, he shivered. The urge to get out of there was so compelling that he had to plant his feet harder on the ground to keep himself from leaving the whole shebang behind and running like hell.

Think.

He stomped his feet a few times, got back in, and shined the light carefully all around the bags. Just more damp dirt, harder underneath.

He scratched his head, heedless of the dirt. *Okay.* Open the freakin' bag. He took out his buck knife and slit through three layers of black plastic, and . . .

An arm fell out. He shined the light on it, saw what it was, and stumbled back against the dank soil wall he had dug, half in and half out of the grave.

"Shit!" he shouted. He looked anxiously around but saw nobody. Wind flowed in from the sea and lifted his hair.

The thin female arm, ending in painted nails, wore a plain watch with a black leather band. Crouched right there, a foot from the bag, Stefan looked at the arm for a second. She might be alive! He reached out gingerly to touch the cold, dirty hand. He lifted it, feeling for a pulse.

He was ready for the thing to start twitching, to grab at him. But the hand was dead, and so was its owner. He pushed the button on the watch and the backlight flashed on, ticking, time accurate to the minute.

Now he should slit the bag and look at her, but he did not want to see her face, maybe see the evidence of some wasting disease or car-crash injury. He didn't want to dream of a dead face for the rest of his life. She was none of his business! No—*he* was none of *hers*!

Momentarily stifling his fear, anger flashed through

him. Somebody was playing with his head. He should go right now, gather up his stuff and just bolt.

He reconsidered. Maybe the gravediggers often threw someone in on top of another coffin. Weren't there double tiers sometimes? The cheap seats. The bunks. He didn't smile at the thought. He had gone through all that worry, dug until his back was killing him, and now, by God, he would find the old man and get what he came for.

All the hard work was done. He pulled his gloves up tight, then lifted the body in the trash bags. Her body, heavy, flopped around like a beat-up stuffed toy. He found it hard to hold on. Horribly, her arm fell against his chest as he laid the body on the ground beside the hole. He cried out.

She's dead. She doesn't care, he told himself, jumping back into the hole. In staccato, powerful thrusts, he struck the ground with the pointed tip of his shovel, rapidly opening up a narrow trench. For some time he didn't think at all. Another hour went by. She became company, his silent witness, rolled over a few feet away and sleeping. Did souls hang around after death? What would her soul look like?

Would he just feel it like a worm wiggling into his ear? Damn these chills running up and down under his parka— he was going to have to quit, he felt sick with fear . . .

"Shit!" Hurting his shoulder, he hit something. He dug harder, deeper, like a crazy man. Not much farther down, the top of a mahogany casket showed up, exactly what he had been told to expect.

"There you are, you damn dead Russian," he grunted.

The clasp, so firm looking, was not locked. Wiping off the dirt, he closed his eyes and opened it.

Swamp air. As squeamish as a tourist on a tossing boat, old food rising in his esophagus like a tide, he opened his eyes and looked at the remains of Constantin Zhukovsky.

Thank God. Just bones in rags. Not enough humanity left to say, Get away from my casket, you son of a bitch.

Pulling the duffel in, Stefan breathlessly stuffed the bones in, everything falling apart as he packed sloppily, like he was going on a little vacation to Hell. Feet. The skull, with hair, the hat falling off. Bits of clothing clinging to the skeleton fell away as he picked up the ribs.

Something small and hard fell into the coffin, and he rooted around until he found it. In the dark he couldn't see very well what he had, but it was made of metal. He ran a grimy fingernail over the blackened surface and saw a golden gleam. The haunts were everywhere, all around him, outside and inside, and his thoughts had gotten disorganized. Fingers trembling, he stuck the metal object into a pocket. Quickly, he pushed the duffel out of the hole and slammed the lid of the casket. Then he climbed out, filthy, not caring, just wanting it to be over.

The dead woman lay in her plastic shroud on the gravel, pitiful, frightful. "Sorry," he mumbled. He felt her wrist one more time—the lifeblood not pumping—tucked her arm back in and rolled her over to the lip. He let her drop and heard the thud. Then he shoveled dirt until his heart pounded with the effort and sweat flicked off his face.

He tried hard to repair the surface so the gravel wouldn't look too bad. He couldn't see well enough to know if he had succeeded. The edges could probably use something to make the merge between the intact and the disturbed earth invisible, but all he could do was stomp the ground and riffle around with the toe of his shoe, hoping things would look okay when daylight came.

Bones, it turned out, weren't so heavy, but they didn't lie neatly in the duffel. They seemed reluctant to give up their structure. He couldn't zip the bag all the way. He carried the partly open thing over his shoulder across the grass and stones, under the dripping trees, then threw it over the fence, climbed over, and skulked back to the car, looking around the whole time, seeing things that just couldn't be there, eyes in the bushes, dark forms of ghosts hiding behind trees.

Trying to open the trunk, he fiddled with his keys, but his hands shook so much, the usual jiggling didn't work. He laid the duffel in the back seat, on the floor, stuffing it down and covering the remains with a blanket.

All he had to do now was drive up Highway 1 and drop the duffel into a Dumpster behind the self-store place in Marina. The guy who had hired him would take it from there, and mail Stefan another five hundred the next day.

Driving slowly along Pearl Street, he struggled with himself, sweating in the cold. Who was the dead woman? Was he meant to find her? Why? On Aguajito he turned at a dignified speed. A few other cars, lights, people. He felt comforted being around the few night stragglers still on the streets.

He turned on some music and sank in to the driver's seat, let out a big breath. All good. He fingered the little Buddha around his neck.

At the corner of Sixth, a red light erupted behind his car, just the silent, turning red light, but he knew right away that it didn't matter that he had driven perfectly.

He should have known. He never got away with anything.

He pulled over.

Telling the story had drained him. "Erin dumped me. She only came to see me once, to tell me she dropped my stuff at my mom's."

"That's rough," Nina said.

"Her parents were already iffy on me because of me being in jail a couple of times before."

Nina nodded sympathetically.

"That's the worst part, losing Erin. But here's what I'm thinking. I go on the stand—whatever you call it when you get up in court to testify—and I tell the jury what happened, the whole thing, spit it out. What do you think are the chances that they'll believe me? Because if they do, she has to. I know she's hurting, too."

"It's an interesting story." He did tell a good story, but then many of her clients did. They all had such excellent motivation for lying, and months in jail to perfect their yarns. If a lie bought you freedom, and telling the truth bought you imprisonment, well, the choice was a no-brainer for most of them. "I'm going to go back to it in a minute to ask you some questions. But I ought to say right now, Stefan—you won't be telling any of this to the court."

"Why not?"

"It's very unusual for a criminal defendant to testify. You have the right not to testify, and a jury isn't allowed to draw any negative conclusions if you don't. If you do, all kinds of havoc can break out. In your case, you have two prior convictions. The prosecutor will make a very big deal out of them if you testify, which automatically makes you look very bad to the jury. Sometimes that's fatal."

"Yes, but how will the jury know what happened if I—"

"The witnesses and the hard evidence have to do the job for you."

Then Nina took him through the whole thing again.

3

Monday 9/1

NINA PARKED A BLOCK AWAY and walked past the flowers and art galleries of the quaint tourist mecca of Carmel to the offices of Pohlmann, Cunningham, Turk. She arrived at the white wood-frame office on the corner of Lincoln and Eighth by eleven-thirty, buoyed by her talk with Stefan Wyatt. The early morning fog had burned off and she had made good time from Salinas, consolidating her thoughts all the way.

Innocent or guilty, at least she liked the client. Some clients were so angry, so distant, or so disturbed that they were an ordeal to sit next to at all. Stefan was a cooperator. The jury wouldn't dislike him on sight. She reminded herself to try to get some young women on it.

Walking up the white-brick stairway to the law offices, she remembered herself in her thick-soled athletic shoes bounding up these same stairs during her law clerk days. Somehow she had managed to take care of Bob as a single mom, work at the Pohlmann firm, and go to the Monterey College of Law at night. None of her subsequent incarnations, as an appellate lawyer in San Francisco and as a sole practitioner at Tahoe, had been as harried, yet she remembered those days, when she had been deeply immersed in learning new things and raising a little boy, as happy and rewarding.

Back then she had assumed that the financial need, her single life, and her direction in law would all be resolved by now. Well, marrying would be a resolution of sorts, but she had lived enough to know that a good life didn't resolve. It offered satisfying moments, new beginnings, and more ir-resolution.

Nina wasn't completely lacking in self-consciousness, but she found thinking about her own life confusing. Other people's lives never bored her, though—their lies, their capitulations, their bad luck, their fates. Other people's situations made her skin vibrate, her heart beat louder, her blood pump harder. She could do practical things, applying her intelligence and rationality to their lives in ways she never could for her own. She could make a difference, and what else was there to live for before you ended up moldering in a coffin, bones, like the poor man in this case?

Love? She held up her left hand and looked at the glittering diamond on her finger. It had a sharp, definite look about it.

Near the top of the stairs, hurrying too much, she paused by the window. One of the secretaries had kept a delicate flower garden going out there in the old days, and the white building that had started its life as a house had blue irises, red geraniums, and a hominess that didn't seem present anymore in the practical juniper bushes and clumps of tall grass waving in the soft gray air.

Nodding at the receptionist, she walked down the short hall and opened the door to her new office.

Nina's secretary from Tahoe, Sandy Whitefeather, filled the brown chair in the compact front office like a lion balancing four legs on a tiny stone. Today she wore a down vest over a black turtleneck over a long denim skirt and burgundy cowboy boots. Sandy's long black hair was pulled into a beaded band that fell down her back. Behind her, a mullioned picture window looked over a courtyard full of stalky weeds and wildflowers.

She hung up the phone, saying, "About time. I see you have new shoes again. You're gonna break your neck one of these days, wearing those torture heels."

"You have new shoes, too. Don't tell me those narrow pointy toes are the shape of your foot. I've seen your feet. I bet they're killing you."

"Yeah, but I like what I see when I look down."

Nina sat down and kicked off the high heels. "Okay, we'll both get bunions. Peace pipe?"

"Hmph. The Washoe people don't use peace pipes. Get your stereotypes straight." She studied Nina. "New shoes," she said, "and jewelry, too. A whole new you."

Nina felt obscurely embarrassed, but she held out her finger for Sandy's scrutiny.

"Big," Sandy said. She wasn't looking at the ring. She was looking at Nina.

"It was his grandmother's."

"Tradition is good."

"No need to fall out of your chair celebrating or anything."

"Congratulations, of course."

"Thanks."

"It's a big step."

"Forward," Nina said firmly.

"How did Bob take the news?"

Bob had spotted the ring the minute she picked him up from her father's house. She tried to explain, but he put up a hand. "I know what a ring means, Mom." His reaction had been mixed, not altogether positive, but not harsh, to her relief.

"He'll need time to adjust to the idea," she told Sandy, realizing she was using Paul's words.

"So you'll be staying here. With the golfers and the retirees."

More assumptions. "We haven't worked out the details."

"Hmm." Sandy turned back to the paperwork on her desk. "I made up the files and left a list of the D.A.'s office and other numbers on your desk. Mr. Pohlmann says the firm's taking you to lunch. He dropped off some of his files for you."

"Great."

They had a month to work through everything, including the upcoming trial. Although Nina had succumbed to Klaus almost immediately, she hadn't actually committed to Stefan Wyatt's case until she had found out Sandy wasn't just available, she was eager to take a break from Tahoe. Solid, matter-of-fact, and smart, Sandy was a friend too, for all her crankiness and obstinacy. With her along for the ride, Nina felt strong and supported.

After finishing up a job in Washington lobbying for more Washoe ancestral lands, Sandy had come down to Monterey County with her husband, Joseph, and established herself immediately with some old friends who ranched near Big Sur, where her son, Wish, was already staying. As she explained it, one of her daughters had shown up unexpectedly a month before at their ranch near Markleeville, kids in tow, husband glaring.

Sandy didn't go into what had brought her daughter home, she just said the tepee up in Alpine County, actually a small horse ranch she and Joseph owned, was feeling mighty cramped these days. Joseph was recovering from surgery and needed fresh air, riding, and "no more of what that girl of ours has to give at the moment." She had accepted Nina's offer of a temporary position at the Pohlmann firm without bothering to ask a single question.

If Nina stayed here in Carmel with Paul, she would lose Sandy. Sandy was rooted to Tahoe deep as the white pines and ancient oaks on her property. The idea made Nina quake. She needed Sandy.

"How did it go with Wyatt this morning?" Sandy asked.

"It's a long story." Nina gave her an abbreviated version. "Could you get my interview notes into the computer today?"

"Sure. Guilty or not?"

"Don't know."

"Didn't you form a first impression?"

"He looks harmless."

"But then so did Jeffrey Dahmer. I heard Stefan Wyatt went to school at CSUMB for a while before he got arrested," Sandy said. Her son, Wish, had also attended California State University at Monterey Bay that summer, picking up more credits toward a degree in criminal justice. "You know their thing, right?"

"No," said Nina. She picked up the top file Klaus had left and scanned it.

"Holistic studies," Sandy said, her voice passing stern judgment.

"Okay."

"Good place for kids with bad attitudes who can't cut it in the real world."

"Wait a minute. Your own son goes there. Wish says he has terrific teachers."

"He's not doing that holistic stuff. He's on the vocational side."

"I think it sounds interesting. And it sure fits Wyatt's style. He's young, loose, in the tearing-down phase politically."

Sandy, shifting in a borrowed chair, black eyes narrowed, expressed the mood of the displaced and dispossessed, saying, "Other people have to be practical about what they study so they can get along after college. Other people settle down, pay a mortgage, keep a business going . . ."

"Without gallivanting around the Monterey Peninsula, grabbing diamond rings, when they should be back practicing law at Tahoe with their long-suffering secretary. Is that what you're saying?"

Sandy put on her poker face.

"I'm not sure I need a hard time from you this morning, Sandy."

"You call this a hard time? Where's the groom?"

"Paul's due in a few minutes. I called him on my way in from Salinas and told him about my interview with the client."

"That Dutchman's a bad influence on you."

"Yeah?" Nina said, putting one report aside and picking up another. "Seems like you always used to promote him as the solution to my problems."

"Did not," Sandy said.

"What are you working on there?"

"Paperwork, to do with your temporary employment here, health insurance forms, tax info. As usual, you generate more stuff to be assembled than a four-year-old at Christmas. Meanwhile, take a look at this."

Nina took the file. "What have we here?"

"When Stefan Wyatt first retained the firm, Klaus hired a detective. This is his report. Read it and weep, while I finish copying the rest for you."

Nina went into her temporary office. Yellowing oak bookshelves covered three walls, mostly full of California codes. The stately blue leather compendiums of yore were quickly becoming obsolete in law firms. She could rely on her computer for most of her research these days.

One wall held a big window to the courtyard with its beach fog, bees, and weeds. She sat down at the unfamiliar desk, into a chair molded to fit some other body. She opened a drawer in the desk she had been loaned for the duration. Inside, lint, dust, and moldy mints had accumulated. Not allowing herself to think of her bright and pleasant office at Tahoe, now in the hands of a young lawyer friend, she shut the drawer, picked up the file, and began to read with concentration this time.

"So?" Sandy asked from the doorway a few minutes later.

"Aside from its brevity," Nina said, "what surprises me most about this report are Klaus's notes about it."

"What notes?"

"Exactly. There aren't any notes. No follow-ups. No signed witness statements. The report itself—this investigator interviewed witnesses, but he gave Klaus a couple of no-content paragraphs on each interview. I question whether he talked to these people in person or just gave them a quick call. Why did Klaus hire this guy anyway? He's known and used Paul for years. Why didn't Klaus call Paul?"

Sandy wore an expression that looked exactly like the first and the last time she had eaten squid in Nina's presence. "Sandy?"

"Mr. Pohlmann did call Paul."

"Oh, no," Nina said. She already knew: Klaus had called Paul, but Paul didn't know; ergo, interception.

"If Bob was in jail, what would you do?"

Sandy's son, Wish, had been charged with a serious crime earlier in the summer. Abandoning her temporary job in Washington, Sandy had come to make sure Nina and Paul were going to keep him out of jail.

"You're telling me that while we were using Paul's office this summer, at his kind invitation, you took a call for him from Klaus?"

"I did answer a few of his calls. Paul was really strapped for time."

"Klaus said he needed Paul's help on the Zhukovsky case but you never told Paul?"

"Triage is what they call it in an emergency," Sandy said. "Caring for the sickest first. So when Klaus called, I told him Paul wasn't available. He was busy."

"That wasn't right, Sandy."

"Yep." Sandy pulled at her lower lip, a sign of deep thought.

"Does Paul know?"

"Nope."

"Okay. I don't like this. We're going to have to help Klaus get organized. Call this investigator and find out if you have all the reports. Find out who he actually interviewed. I'll give you a list tomorrow of the people he should have spoken with. Call them and try to get some appointments for him. Coordinate schedules with Paul, so he's free when we need him. We have to catch up, and there's no time. Paul's going to miss some sleep, and so are we."

"Fair enough. Logical consequences. I'm paying the price." She took the file and picked up the phone.

"If Sandy's paying, I want to be invited," said Paul, poking his head through the door. He wore the forest green cashmere sweater Nina had given him for his last birthday, and tan slacks. Gently, he touched Nina's shoulder, nodding at Sandy.

"Congratulations, Paul," Sandy said. "Such changes."

He grinned. "Thanks. Taking me to lunch, are you?"

"Sure," Sandy said.

He had been joking. Now he looked flabbergasted.

"A big, nice lunch," Nina said. "Sandy was just saying how she's looking forward to working with you again and really wants to treat you today. To one of Carmel's finest restaurants, your choice."

"Sounds great," Paul said, exuding faint alarm. "What time?"

"One."

"I get it. You have some friendly words of advice for me and Nina, huh?"

"Who said anything about being friendly?" Sandy turned back to her desk and got busy.

Paul followed Nina into her office, swept her into his arms, and gave her a delicious kiss on the mouth. "You look fantastic in navy blue," he said. He squeezed her waist.

"That's good, since it's about all you'll see me in for the next month." Nina moved out of his arms and rustled through a steeple of files.

"Maybe I've misjudged Sandy," Paul said, stepping toward the window to peer out. "I admit to occasional midnight doubts that she likes me at all. That's a very generous offer."

"She likes you, all right. And she respects your work more than you know. Take a look at this."

Paul came over to her desk to take the main body of the investigative report. As he read, he scratched his head. "Feeble. I mean, 'Subject said he didn't know anything'? It's like that all the way through. Somebody always knows something. You'll find that on page one of Paul van Wagoner's monograph for the novice investigator."

"If somebody knows something, you'd never know it from this." She tried to keep most of the concern she was feeling from her voice. So far, everything Klaus had given her had been sketchy at best. Where was the promised preparation? Not in this report.

"Why didn't Klaus call me?" Paul asked. "First time to

my knowledge he didn't when he needed some real work done. He around?"

"Not yet." She glanced at her watch. "Our firm meeting's in a few minutes. He's late, ferrying Anna somewhere in that car he loves so much."

"Klaus and Anna are one of those couples where you can't imagine half being left behind." He knocked his hip against hers. "Kind of like us."

"We are all alone. Togetherness is illusion," she said. "All the poets say so."

"Which is why my bedtime reading is John D. Mac-Donald." Paul impatiently flipped the page he was holding and looked at both sides. "Who wrote this damn thing, anyway?"

Nina looked around. The front page had fallen under her desk. She picked it up and handed it over.

He read the sheet. He put it on top, then he took the few pages, inserted them into the blue file folder, straightened the edges carefully, tapping them on the desk. He tossed the folder into the trash.

"Deano." The name came out as if forcing its way past rough terrain in his throat.

She reached down to extricate the file from the plastic canister and read the top sheet. "You know Dean Trumbo?"

"Yeah." A peculiar half-smile lit Paul's face. "You know, I'm surprised I didn't recognize his special touch right away."

"He's done work for you?"

"He's done work on me."

"You don't like him?"

"Actually—I kind of look forward to running into the guy again."

Nina said, "Let's make a list, then." They outlined a sped-up course of action for the investigation.

"We seem to have some blood evidence," Paul said. "Are you bringing Ginger in?"

"Sandy called her already. Ginger's driving in from Sacramento. She's due here at two-thirty."

"Rush, rush, rush," Paul said.

"Klaus hasn't—I don't see any independent defense analysis of the blood yet." Nina put her hand on his arm. "Paul, Klaus doesn't seem to have done much work at all."

"You've worked with him in the past. Does he usually prepare more thoroughly?"

"I don't know. I never worked this closely with him before."

"Well, he did one thing right. He brought you in, honey," Paul said. "Let's start filling in the holes."

4

BECAUSE HE COULD NEVER SIT still, Bear Cunningham sprang up and shook hands with Nina at the door. He hadn't changed at all over the years. He would be a thousand times happier jumping up and down in a hallway than being in a meeting. This was a real problem for an attorney who spent much of every day impaled in a chair dealing with people and their troubles, taking meetings, attending hearings. She could almost see his muscles fighting to escape his skin.

If you wanted to talk to Bear, you walked with him, or you ran with him at noon, or you biked ten miles home with him. You caught him on the fly. He handled the personal injury cases and the business matters. Bear was a smart, cheerful, happily married man, the backbone of the firm by now, she guessed, with Klaus getting older.

The meeting must have started without her, maybe because she wasn't a full-fledged member of the firm and didn't need to know about other cases. Seated in the leather chair by the fireplace which had never, to Nina's knowledge, held a fire, was Sean Eubanks. Nina shook hands with him. "Nice to meet you."

"Delighted." Sean had been with the firm only a year

and had the harried look of the one who usually gets the last-minute court appearances. Klaus had told Nina that he was a Yale Law grad who shared Klaus's passion for the underdog. The youngest lawyer in the office, he was barely thirty and often said he would rather be surfing. His style was classic California lawyer–casual chic, windblown and tanned, friendly on the surface, with the requisite killer instinct lurking below like that big mean fish all lawyers got tired of hearing about. With a special interest in fathers' rights and gay rights in custody cases, he handled family law cases for the firm.

Nina found a spot on the ancient couch along the window. Adjusting his specs from behind his desk, Klaus said, "I realize that I have not reported on the status of this case for some time, so I am kicking two dogs with one foot. The trial date is September fifteenth."

"That's only two weeks away," Alan Turk said. "Even if you're fully prepared, Klaus, Nina will have a hard time catching up." Alan sat next to Nina on the couch, holding his coffee, one leg hooked over the other, slightly cross-eyed behind his glasses and blue tie. His hair had thinned badly, and his back seemed to have bowed as he moved through his fifties. He had given her his usual nod, as if she hadn't been away eight years, and Nina had nodded back.

During her time as a law clerk, she had enjoyed working with Alan. He was methodical, organized, and never lost his temper. "Anal Alan," Bear had once called him in a conversation with Nina, showing the litigator's distaste for the lawyer who sits back at the office generating and responding to the details of law practice.

But as the trusts, wills, and estates man, with a certification in tax law, Alan had always brought in a steady high flow of income to the firm. Without it, Bear couldn't fly his more risky PI's and Klaus couldn't pursue his endless appeals. Alan was currently a bachelor who owned a 2001

metallic blue Ferrari, which, word had it, had cost almost
two hundred thousand dollars. The firm building, in line
with the rustic ambience of Carmel, had only a one-car
garage on the street. Alan kept the Ferrari there under security far superior to the systems for the rest of the building. He also owned two other rare automobiles. Nina
didn't keep track of what kind.

Klaus, Bear, and Alan had all helped Nina get started in
law. Even now, she sometimes dreamed of this office with
its lamps and photos and books, and the old man sitting behind his desk with the little smile. To be here again, her
eyes falling upon Klaus's favorite Meissen figurine on the
mantel, was disconcerting, yet felt as comfortable as a trip
back to the old homestead.

"Of course we're fully prepared." Bear continued to
champion Klaus, as he always had. "Nina, have you had a
chance to review the files?"

"I'm doing that today. I met the client this morning."

"How'd that go?"

"He told me his story. Really, there wasn't enough
time to form an opinion of his chances." Bear, Alan, and
Sean shot smiles around that landed eventually on her.
They seemed to know a few things she didn't. Perfectly
natural. "I have the general outline," she went on. "I'm sure
I can take the second chair, help with the cross-exams
and—"

"Do brilliant work," Klaus said.

"Work hard, anyway," Nina said. She sat up straight,
trying to look like the kind of person who wouldn't let
anything get by her.

Klaus smiled and nodded, his white goatee jabbing the
air. Seeing him the previous week for the first time in
years, Nina had been amazed at how little he had changed.
Perhaps after seventy there is a long, placid evening for
some people during which they finally take on their real

form and stick with it. He still had the twinkly eyes, sparse white hair on his head—which, as he didn't like the cold ocean air, was often covered with an archaic homburg—a black suit, a red tie, and on court days a flower in the buttonhole, tucked in no doubt by his devoted wife, Anna. The only difference Nina saw was that he seemed to be a couple of inches shorter now that he had reached his early eighties.

Klaus had always taken the criminal cases and the appeals. His national reputation dated back from his noisy, contentious teaching days at the University of Chicago and at UC Berkeley. He and his wife, Anna, had come to the United States just before the Second World War from somewhere they refused to talk about in Europe, somewhere German-speaking, Austria, maybe. That one of them was Jewish was all Klaus would ever say, and it had given Nina enough to reconstruct a basic history. Klaus had helped defend Angela Davis and had been a friend of Henry Miller and Linus Pauling in their Big Sur days.

"Our client," Klaus said, "as you will remember, is Stefan Wyatt, a young man in a hell of a pickle. He has not been able to make the high bail and has therefore been in jail for four months. Though I tried to talk him out of it, he was adamant. He wanted a quick court date. He wants out of jail."

"Short amount of time to prepare for a murder case," Sean said.

"An innocent young man is in jail," Klaus said. "Technically, he has a right to a trial within sixty days."

Nina listened, more interested than the others. Any new details to come today were helpful to her. Klaus had told her that he required her assistance and that he assumed she would fly to his side, which she had. He blew off her objections like dandelions. She would play a small role as backup. He had everything worked out, he had assured her.

Klaus had always kept his cases close, maybe because he was the only criminal lawyer at the firm and nobody else could give him much help with strategy. Bear appeared for him now and then in Law and Motion hearings, but he didn't like criminal defense.

"Why was he arrested?" Sean asked. "There was something strange about that." He furrowed his brows, then snapped his fingers. "Bones tucked into the back seat of his car, right?"

"Precisely." Klaus nodded. "And those bones will be key to helping us explain Mr. Wyatt's presence in the graveyard that night. But what concerns us most is the second body the police found in the grave Mr. Wyatt is accused of robbing, the body of a woman, Christina Zhukovsky."

Sean's blond head bobbed up and down. "I remember now, he was stopped because he had a taillight out. And then the cop saw a skeleton flopping around in the back seat. Wyatt sounds like one of those guys who can't jaywalk without stepping in front of a patrol car."

"At least he didn't talk to the police," Alan said. He tapped his fingers on the leather. His nails were manicured to soft pink curves, perfect as shells shaped by a century's tides. Obsessiveness was a good trait in a tax lawyer, Nina reflected. Alan was well known locally as an exacting collector of very rare, small fine-arts objects and sculpture. His office, which displayed only a small but spectacular grouping of jade netsuke, had the organizational rigor of a military locker room.

Years before, Nina had gone to Alan's house for an office celebration and marveled at the elegance of the decor. He pressed a tiny bronze sculpture of a dancer into her hands to appreciate, and told her everything about it for the next twenty minutes. His love of beauty spilled over into the kind of women he married, another form of collecting, Nina thought, but you didn't get to keep all the women.

"Stefan Wyatt has had experience with law enforcement," Klaus said. "He doesn't trust the police, and was wise enough to say nothing and to call us immediately."

"Do we admit the grave robbery?" Sean asked. He didn't ask whether the client had confessed to Klaus. That would be bad form, since they were closing in on a trial at which they would claim the client was innocent no matter what he had told his lawyer in the cloister of their confidential relationship.

"Yes. There is a complication, however. Mr. Wyatt found a medal in the grave and put it in his pocket. The value of the medal makes the charge grand theft, a felony."

"Sounds pretty minor, in the context of the murder charge."

"Ah, but it is not minor, Mr. Eubanks. The young man has a record. Two previous felony convictions. Violent felonies, and he did time for both. The first was for throwing a brick at a police officer at a demonstration. He was convicted of assault and served four months in the county jail. He had just turned eighteen."

"That was bad luck," Bear said. "The birthday, I mean. If he'd been seventeen . . ."

Klaus went on, "While still on probation, at the age of nineteen, he struck another young man with his fist at a neighborhood party. Both young men had been drinking. Unfortunately, the boy he struck fell against the curb and suffered a skull fracture. Mr. Wyatt pled guilty to assault again and was sent back to jail, for eight months this time."

"This is one bad-luck kid," Sean said.

"His victims were the ones with the bad luck," Alan said. "Let's not forget them. Sounds like you've got a client that deserves to go down."

Klaus found the comment unworthy of a reply. "Mr.

Wyatt was released after five years' probation and he has kept himself employed and clean," he concluded. Nina made a note to herself to go into those priors in more detail with Stefan.

"Which makes a conviction for the medal a third-strike conviction, even if he's acquitted of the murder," Bear said. "Mandatory twenty-five years to life, under California law."

"Do we have the resources to handle a murder trial with a Three Strikes complication?" Sean asked. Bear frowned at him, which Nina interpreted to mean, Don't question the old man's judgment, you barking young pup.

"Nina and I will handle it," Klaus said dismissively. You could view Klaus as laudably confident or you could view him, as Sean probably did at that moment, as arrogant.

"We are being paid—how?" Alan reverted to his usual motif, money, using a finger and thumb to neaten the crease in his trouser leg.

"We accepted a ten-thousand-dollar retainer and five thousand dollars as an advance against expenses. We are taking payments from Mr. Wyatt's mother as further fees are incurred. It's hard for her. She had to get a loan. His brother, Gabriel Wyatt, is helping. He was Mr. Turk's client at one point and remembered us fondly enough to refer his brother to us when he was arrested," Klaus said.

"I was called over to the jail right after Wyatt's arrest," Alan explained to the rest of them, apparently not pleased at the memory. "Klaus was down with the flu and you were in depositions in L.A., remember, Bear, and Sean had a trial the next day. I lined things up for Klaus to see him. I only had a consult with his brother, Gabe, so I was surprised when the family called me, but I guess I was the only lawyer they knew. Gabe has a job, but I'm also guessing that you're not charging him full freight. Am I right, Klaus?"

"You are right, Mr. Turk," Klaus said, unperturbed.

"We are charging fifty percent of our usual hourly rate, plus actual expenses."

"Just so everybody's straight on this. At the moment overhead's running sixty-five percent." Alan glanced at Nina.

Kachung. Overhead. Negative balance sheet.

"Is the D.A. offering any kind of plea bargain? Do we really have to try this one?" Sean asked.

"Any felony conviction runs a risk of a Three Strikes enhancement, so we cannot bargain," Klaus said. "The trial will take no more than a month by my estimate. We have had a good year, gentlemen. You all received ample year-end bonuses. Now we give back by helping this young man."

Alan said in ungentlemanly fashion, "I referred him to you because I felt obligated, but I never understood why you took this case in the first place, Klaus. We're mixed up in something—unsavory. There's no new law to be made, no real money in it for the firm, no noble point to his crimes."

Klaus stared at Alan, lips turned down, as if generally unhappy with his attitude toward their client. "Alleged crimes," he corrected softly. "Yes, Mr. Turk, your objections from the start have been noted. However, I did not found this law firm forty years ago to make money. I founded it to seek justice and make law."

"Oh, please," Alan said, rolling his eyes. "The jails are full of guys just like him, probably a hell of a lot more worthy."

"I am shocked at you, Mr. Turk," Klaus said. "Mr. Wyatt's brother was your client, and he needs help."

Silence fell.

Bear said, "Give it a rest, Alan. You have enough money for a thousand years from your parents. The client's family is paying most of the freight. Let's get on with practicing law."

"Somebody has to pay the secretaries," Alan said, but without heat. He had decided not to take Bear on.

"It's good to have you on board," Sean told Nina.

"Thanks. I'm sure we'll do fine," Nina said briskly. "You'll be seeing a couple of new faces around the office besides me. Sandy Whitefeather, my secretary from Tahoe, has come down to assist me. You'll pass her in the hall. You might want to take the initiative with her and introduce yourself. She's a very capable person but, uh, a little shy."

"I ran into her this morning," Sean said. "Shy might not be the right word for her. She's—prepossessing. From the Washoe tribe, she said?"

"Right. Descended from the first inhabitants of Tahoe. Good people."

"Big money in casinos these days," Alan said.

"The Washoe have chosen a different way. Ask her about it. That, she'll talk about."

The meeting had settled back down, to Nina's relief.

"You all know Paul van Wagoner, I think. He'll be taking over as our investigator. And we're bringing in Dr. Ginger Hirabayashi as our forensic pathologist." Nina knew Ginger well and had made the suggestion to Klaus. Although he seemed satisfied with the work that had been done already, she had been relieved to discover that he was willing to go further based on her recommendations.

Klaus broke a smile and pushed his chair back. "And I am happy to repeat that we now have on board this lovely young lady, prepared to stagger us with her energy and legal skill. She will be the saving grace of this unfortunate young man. Let us have lunch and celebrate, eh?"

And so, although time was tight and Nina knew she should work through lunch, they all piled out the door, Nina in the place of honor, walking alongside Klaus at his sedate pace into Carmel's tangy ocean air. They made their way through the tourists to the Alpine Bistro. Klaus went through the door into the heavenly smells waiting inside. As Nina prepared to follow, Bear pulled her aside onto the flower-filled veranda.

"I'm glad you're back, Nina, really happy. Let us know what we can do to help. Anything." The weather-beaten lines of his face shaped a wholehearted smile. "Klaus needs the help."

Through the window, she saw Klaus sit down in the place where he had eaten lunch for forty years. The waitress and the manager stood by, ready to attend him. He caught her looking his way and grinned so widely she could see his gums, as pink as a baby's.

The meeting had disturbed her. It felt as if the other lawyers were indulging Klaus with this case. They hadn't even tried to quiz him about strategy and defenses, questions she would have expected. Why were they all so worried?

Walking into the restaurant she received another unearned smile from Sean Eubanks. He was much too glad to meet her, she thought, sitting down beside him. He acted as if her presence relieved him of a burden. Only Alan, chewing sullenly on a carrot, was a relief from otherwise unalloyed delight.

What had she gotten herself into?

"You're a champ for dropping everything to see me," Nina said to Ginger when Nina finally got back at three. "Sorry I'm late. Lunch ran long."

"I enjoyed the ride," Ginger said. She gave Nina a warm hug, which Nina, surprised, returned. "Sandy and I have been catching up." Encased in soft black leather from head to boot, she smelled of spicy perfume. Her black hair, tipped with white, spiked out like a sunburst, and she seemed to have a couple of new piercings in her ears. She was forty-five and looked a lot younger. She ran her own business now, after a long stint with the state lab in Sacramento, and was one of the top pathologists on blood evidence questions in California, much in demand by both defense and prosecution as an expert witness.

"Thanks for coming all the way down from Sacramento. I know how busy you always are, and I think you know I appreciate it. How are you?" she asked as Ginger took her seat. "It's been a while."

"Good work, bad affair, new girlfriend, bought a glam condo near Oldtown Sac since we last worked together," she said. "You?"

"Left Tahoe, came here with Paul, so old new love," Nina said, attempting the same game and giving up. "Let's just say, after the court case in San Francisco in which my own State Bar tried to take me out and failed, I have been rethinking my life. I'm living too near my father, mostly at odds with him whenever we get together, getting together with Paul, and getting on Bob's case. He's mighty intense these days."

Ginger spotted Nina's ring. She took Nina's hand into her own. "Wow. Fabulous! Art Deco, I do believe." She lifted Nina's hand up and down, as if weighing it. "Heavy commitment, this dazzler." Letting go, she looked into Nina's eyes, questioningly. "You're going to marry van Wagoner and stay here? You won't be going back to Tahoe?"

"I'm trying out the ring for size. Any words of wisdom?"

"He's a pig," Ginger said, "but you know that, and we love him in spite of his flaws."

Nina smiled.

"You're not imagining you'll reform him, are you?"

"Not really. No."

"He's a macho control freak."

"That's a little harsh. Anyway, so am I."

Ginger thought about that. "True. So I don't know where that leaves you."

"Making progress?"

"Right. Well, we're not going to resolve your life or mine, but maybe we can make some headway on this case."

They got down to it.

"What I'm seeing," Ginger said a half hour later, after examining some of the documents the D.A.'s office had provided them, "is that the victim apparently was killed in the kitchen of her apartment in Monterey on Friday night, April eleventh. That's what—nearly five months ago? It's a strangulation. Hands-on, no evidence of a cord or anything like that. There were small signs of a possible struggle—some broken glass. Some of the glass had blood on it."

"Right," Nina said. "And as you can see, it appears from this report that all of the blood samples found at the crime scene have been identified as Stefan Wyatt's."

"Not good. The blood seems to have been reasonably fresh. The amounts were small for a decent analysis, so that's an area we might challenge."

"Does the state lab work look like it will stand up?"

Ginger shook her head. "Too soon to draw conclusions for you, Nina. Did you request samples for independent analysis?"

"You can pick them up this afternoon in Salinas."

"Well, you never know. Maybe they don't know what they're doing. Although Dr. Susan Misumi's supervising, and she's no slouch."

"You know Monterey's assistant medical examiner?"

"Known her for years. We attend the same conferences,

and we're both Asian females in a world of white, whiskery faces. We have some things in common."

Nina nodded. "Here's another tricky aspect of this case," she said. "I told you Stefan Wyatt took bones from the same grave where the victim, Christina Zhukovsky, was found? The bones of her father, a man named Constantin Zhukovsky?"

"Yeah, what's that about?"

"Wyatt says he was hired to dig them up. While he was digging, he found the second body, of the victim, in the grave."

"Sounds like a setup."

"I think so, too. The guy who Wyatt claims hired him is a professor at CSUMB named Alex Zhukovsky. And get this, Ginger—he's Constantin Zhukovsky's son and Christina's brother. He denies he hired Wyatt or had any knowledge about any of it."

"Could he have tipped off the police to do a traffic stop on Wyatt?"

"Good question, but there's no evidence the police were tipped. They stopped Stefan for a silly but legitimate traffic infraction. Anyway, I want you to examine the bones of Constantin Zhukovsky as well as the blood found in Christina Zhukovsky's apartment. Meanwhile, Paul will be interviewing Alex Zhukovsky."

Ginger, surprised, said, "Hasn't anyone talked to Zhukovsky before? If Wyatt is innocent, Zhukovsky must be the killer."

"He's been interviewed before, but barely."

"Where are the bones now?"

"They're still in a morgue locker at Natividad Hospital in Salinas, but Alex Zhukovsky recently demanded their return for cremation. The police are inclined to turn them over to him. The bones don't directly relate to the charges, except as proof that Stefan robbed the grave. And, privately, between you and me, he did. They have plenty of proof, but they didn't even charge him for that crime."

"Why do we want the bones, if the prosecution isn't even bothering to test them?"

"Because Alex Zhukovsky wanted them." Nina propped one of her small, chain-bedecked, pointy-toed shoes on her desk, and wound a finger through her hair. She felt the groove between her eyebrows digging inward, toward unsettling thoughts.

"What kind of tests are we after, with regard to the bones?" Ginger asked.

Nina bit her lip. "I'm counting on you to help me with that question."

"At least a genetic profile, then, if possible," Ginger said, making a note. "I'll look for poison, anomalies, strange diseases, anything that pops up. That okay?"

"If Zhukovsky wanted those bones for a reason, and you can find it by examining them, I know you'll find it."

"So we'll grab a couple of bones for me before he burns them. A femur. The pelvis. Big bones, okay? Those are both impressive enough to be fair bets for DNA even after all this time."

Nina made notes. "You'll get them. But we have to work fast."

Sandy knocked and brought in coffee for both of them. "I thought you deserved better than that ancient coffeepot in the back room, so I went to the coffee place on Ocean," she said.

"You are the best," Ginger told her as she went out again to answer a ringing phone.

Nina leaned back, forcing herself to relax. Her body felt constricted in several places by an invisible but robust nylon rope. She couldn't quite believe how much work lay ahead.

After a minute, Ginger picked up a file and went on,

"Okay, I know what to do on the blood and the bones. Now, let's talk about the murder itself. I've just skimmed the autopsy report, but it's a clear strangulation death. Have you looked at a domestic violence angle?"

"Christina wasn't married, and Klaus's investigator hasn't identified a significant other, but we'll be looking into that. Any thoughts?"

"Strangulation is statistically suggestive of a male killing a female. I mean, someone who goes for the throat is usually passionately angry and you have to be strong to maintain the sustained force necessary to kill."

Nina nodded. "It's a kind of horrible intimacy." Ginger raised her eyebrows, and Nina went on, "In answer to your next question, Stefan Wyatt swears he never knew Christina Zhukovsky. Never saw her, never met her, never heard of her."

"Is he violent?"

Nina said slowly, "He does have a couple of violent priors. I plan to talk to him about them. As far as I know now, he was young, drunk, stupid. Things got out of hand. He really isn't a violent type."

"Oh, really."

"No women, no strangling."

"Still."

"I know. It's possible the priors will come in during the first phase of trial when the jury is considering guilt or innocence. Klaus and I will fight that, of course."

Ginger said, "I was hoping I'd meet Mr. Pohlmann today. He's in charge of the case, isn't he? The four months of investigating and pretrial work so far?"

"He's in charge of the case."

Ginger didn't follow up on that, but her perplexed expression told Nina she was as concerned as Nina about the sparseness of the investigative files. "Okay, back to the body." She gave the autopsy report back to Nina and pointed to one paragraph. "Christina was small. It's possible that a woman strangled her. Too bad there's no sign of drugs. Almost anyone can strangle someone who is already unconscious. Not too much strength needed, you see?"

Nina sighed. "There's so much we don't know."

"I don't see anything about skin cell samples from the neck. Were they taken?"

"Actually, I think I have another sheet on that." Nina gave it to her. "Klaus did make sure samples were saved, but they didn't find any skin cells from Stefan."

Ginger moved on to the police report with its series of crime-scene photos, looking at the black-and-white photos of Christina's body for a long time. "The jury will react to these. Her face didn't hold up well. The plastic bags make the crime seem really depraved."

They both thought about that. Nina looked through the photos for the third or fourth time. Christina Zhukovsky's body had been photographed in various stages as it was removed from the bags. There were close-ups of her neck and face from the morgue. They hadn't closed her eyes first.

If Nina let herself really look at that tragic, distorted face, cut off from the world after only four decades in it, she would not be able to sleep at night. She concentrated on the bruising on the neck, then covered the photos.

"Okay, blood, bones, and body. You got it," Ginger said. "Pass me copies of whatever you have. I've got to stop in Salinas by five and get back to Sacramento."

"I'll walk you out." Out in the fog, Ginger packed her zippy yellow Porsche with the files and got behind the wheel.

"Good luck," Nina said.

"Luck is roulette," said Ginger. "This is poker."

5

MAINTAINING THE VALLEY'S REPUTATION AS California's fresh-food heartland, the breeze around the Salinas courthouse carried along the scent of broccoli. Pulling her new gray wool blazer close around her, Nina walked between the columns and headed toward the west wing under the early morning sky. All along the upper walls of the courthouse building, concrete reliefs of faces from California history that had always looked to her like gargoyles seemed to watch her suspiciously. The entryway doors opened like a maw. Her client waited inside, in the belly of the beast.

The first day of trial is overwhelming, as the first day of a war is overwhelming.

She pulled a case full of heavy files and her iBook, purse securely hung from her shoulder, determined to appear resolute however uncertain she might feel. Button that tailored jacket, girl, she told herself, and keep your eyes open.

As she hurried in, Klaus and Deputy District Attorney Jaime Sandoval were already arguing in front of the elevator on the first floor. "Ten minutes," Klaus was saying. "If you were a gentleman, you would agree."

"Judge Salas will start on time, unless you fully explain why you suddenly need a last-minute consultation with your client, Mr. Pohlmann," Jaime said. The prosecutor's face wore a look Nina had seen before, superficial deference for the old man masking a smirking condescension. He had tried a case opposite Nina early in the summer. With Nina he usually maintained an amiable front, but Klaus had already provoked him out of it.

"Good morning," she said.

"Ah, now we have a real lawyer here. Please tell this man that we need to speak with Mr. Wyatt before the jury comes in," Klaus said. The elevator doors swished open and the three of them entered, Nina in the lead, noticing that since she was wearing three-inch heels, Klaus was actually shorter than she was. He wore a red rosebud boutonniere. Jaime, portly and closely shaven, standing on the other side of her, exuded citrus aftershave and irritation.

Why now, Klaus? she thought. Haven't we already talked to Stefan Wyatt? But since something had apparently come up, her job as second chair demanded that she leap in and support Klaus, so she said to Jaime, "You know he won't be brought in by the bailiffs until the stroke of nine-thirty, and the jury will be in at nine-thirty-one. We just need a couple of minutes."

"Then ask Judge Salas," Jaime said, staring straight ahead at the door.

"He'll do it if you agree, Jaime. You'll need a lot of accommodations, too, over the next few weeks. Is this how you want it to be? No mutual courtesy?" she asked.

"Of course not. But Mr. Pohlmann never lets a deadline go by without challenging it. This is the start of a murder trial. He's had months to talk to his client. Salas is not going to hold things up unless he hears a damn good reason. I haven't heard one."

They stepped out into a milling crowd of lawyers,

reporters, and spectators, the doors to Courtroom 2 still locked, Klaus gesticulating and excited, saying something about how he didn't have to give a reason, but Jaime shouldered his way over to the clerk's office and disappeared from view.

"Mr. Pohlmann, Mr. Pohlmann." Annie Gee from the *Salinas Californian* appeared in front of them just as Nina took Klaus's arm, intending to steer him toward a conference room. "Any comment this morning? Any change in your strategy?"

Nina held on, steering him through the crowd. Over his shoulder, Klaus said grandly, "My client is innocent. He will be acquitted."

"Come on," Nina said, and Klaus let himself be led into a quiet waiting room.

As soon as the door closed Klaus sat down, grinning at her. With his tiny beard and ruddy cheeks he appeared as rested and bright as a little old elf. "We have him on the run already," he said.

"Jaime?"

"He's off balance." He chuckled at the thought.

"What do you need to talk to Stefan about?"

Klaus's white eyebrows raised, as if her question came out of nowhere. "Why, nothing. But it's all Mr. Sandoval can think about right now. We won't really ask for extra time."

"That doesn't seem very—"

"He told me in the last trial I had with him that he thinks I should retire. He thinks I'm a terror. Unpredictable. Why not encourage that kind of thinking? He makes a weaker opponent when he expects weakness."

"O-kay." Nina set her case against the door, looked at her watch, and sat down opposite the old man. Their styles were different, she reminded herself, and this wasn't her case. "We have five minutes," she said. "You were going to show me your opening statement."

Klaus pulled out a sheaf of papers and handed them over. Scanning them, Nina said, "Summarize it for me."

"Well, I greet the judge and jury. Then I talk about what we're going to prove. Yes. Mr. Wyatt's alibi. The fact that he is just a patsy for the interests of the Russians. Then we show how Alex Zhukovsky lies. He probably killed his sister, Christina, not Mr. Wyatt."

Through suddenly parched lips, Nina said, "But we agreed on Friday that we can't use a third-party defense. Zhukovsky denies he ever talked to Stefan, and Paul hasn't been able to prove he did at this point. If we tell the jury we're going to prove something and then can't do it, they'll remember. We'll get into trouble with the judge. It will hurt Stefan."

"Alex Zhukovsky is lying, that's a definite fact. You will prove that."

"Klaus, we're going to cast some suspicion onto Alex Zhukovsky during the trial, but we're in no position to do anything more than establish doubt. It's Stefan's word against Zhukovsky's, and we're not going to let Stefan testify. We've talked about this a dozen times." Panic leaked around the edges of her carefully built composure. "You can't do this," she said.

"You are telling me what I can and can't do?"

Nina tried to keep her tone soft. "But we agreed . . ."

"You are so smart, Miss Reilly," Klaus said, "I think you should make the opening statement." He tapped a finger on the table. "Yes, that is a fine idea. Get your toes wet."

"But . . ." She thought, What is going on here? She picked up the yellow lined papers he had given her and inspected them harder this time. A flowery greeting covered the first page, half-illegibly. The other pages, other than some fountain-penned chicken-scratchings of notes, were essentially personal reminders that could speak only to Klaus.

She rocked back, thoughts racing. Why had he fobbed the opening off onto her? He might mean to toughen her up for the long race by demanding an opening sprint. He might be overreacting to her doubtfulness. Or he had reasons she couldn't yet fathom.

She looked at him. Klaus had lost not a shred of dignity through the years. Though physically small, he gave the overall impression of enormity, which was never so apparent as when he was interviewed or photographed by the press. He was the local legal colossus, as historically significant in his own world of Monterey County as Ernest Hemingway and Franklin Roosevelt were in theirs. He had won cases that couldn't be won and had made law along the way. Who was she? By comparison, she was a pipsqueak mouse skittering in the corners of the courtroom, hardly one to question him. And yet . . .

Calmly awaiting her reaction, he tugged on his goatee.

"We'll reserve our opening statement," she said, summoning her resolve, frightened for Stefan. "We'll present it after the prosecution has put on its case, when we put on the defense." She didn't want to do it, but they had that right. What a shame, and what a mess. She had spent two weeks getting ready for the witnesses, picking up fallen pieces Klaus apparently had not noticed. She had depended on one of his famous, rip-roaring opening statements today.

She pictured Stefan, as displaced from his normal life as an ocean fish plopped into a fishbowl. He had been in jail before and seemed resigned, but she could see the toll the months away had taken. He was beaten down, upset at losing the girl he loved, and taking on the debilitated air of a loser beyond hope. He needed them to do their best work to get him freed and back on track with his life.

"No." Klaus shook his head. "We have to establish a good relationship with the jury. The judge barely let us talk to them during the selection process. You will be fine. I will be right there at the counsel table to advise you." Somberly, contemplatively, he went on. "I have been trying cases for fifty years. I know we will win this one, so please, straighten up. Do not walk into the courtroom like a beautiful partridge in a gun sight, Miss Reilly. Emanate confidence."

"I *was* confident a few minutes ago."

"You will do fine," Klaus repeated, smiling warmly.

"All rise." The courtroom unsettled. The audience in the pews, the spanking-new jurors in their weekday best, and the principals at the counsel table stood up. Judge Salas appeared at his dais.

"Oyez, oyez, the Superior Court of the County of Monterey, Judge José Salas presiding, is now in session." The audience adjusted itself, already sounding like a chorus of critics to Nina, who sat up front at the counsel table nearest the jury box on the left side of the room, Klaus on her left, and nearest of all to those who would judge him, the defendant, Stefan Wyatt.

Stefan wore a sleek suit from the men's store on Alvarado in Monterey. He tugged on his tie trying to loosen it, pulling it tight instead. His shoulders bulged immoderately. He belonged outside, digging up streets in the hot sun, a young workingman who looked so good in his scruffy leather belt and jeans that women wanted to hoot as they passed by.

"The People of the State of California versus Stefan Alex Wyatt. The defendant is present. State your appearances," Salas said in his high voice. He had spent years wangling a judgeship and intended to stay and make the most of it. He liked to preserve all the niceties, and Nina, who had already had one trial before him, believed his rigidity would temper as he grew more comfortable with his position. In the meantime, the wise attorney followed the rules precisely.

She glanced at Klaus, but he was busy winking at a juror in the second row, a well-tanned elderly lady wearing a pink golf shirt.

"Jaime Sandoval appearing on behalf of the People of the State of California, Your Honor." Jaime stood up at his table, voice steady, warm brown eyes sincere. "My designated investigating officer, who will be with me for the duration of this trial, is Detective Kelsey Banta of the City of Monterey Police Department." Salas nodded in a friendly and approving fashion while Detective Banta also stood up for inspection, her hair highlighted golden by the overhead lights, like hair in sunshine. She beamed California health.

Then Klaus rose to his feet. Posture stern, voice forceful, he said, "Klaus Pohlmann, of Pohlmann, Cunningham, Turk, Your Honor. May I present my second chair, Miss Nina Fox Reilly."

"I know Ms. Reilly." Salas inclined his head slightly, formally, not hinting whether he bore any lasting grudges based on their previous skirmish in court. Nina stood, then sat down, tucking her skirt carefully around her knees. Stacked neatly in front of her were the contents of her case: the motion files; the trial briefs, including the one she had whipped out ten days before; her laptop with a fresh battery; research pages downloaded from Lexis, the online research service; and her other lucky pen, labeled "Washoe Tribe Welcomes You."

From the corner of her eye she surveyed the jury of twelve and two alternates. Madeleine Frey, wearing a stiff expression and a black suit, seemed prepared for a funeral but determined in advance not to weep, not a good omen, but the rest of the eight-woman, four-man jury seemed to be in excellent spirits, leaning forward, eyes bright, eager to do their duty.

Their expressions would change, Nina knew, as the trial went on. A couple of the men would reveal their opinions of the proceedings by dozing, eyes open. Some of the women's faces would turn fretful, then later on sour, and would ask, Are you people aware that nobody is doing my laundry? And then there would be one or two eerie metamorphoses as a man or woman flamed up, determined to convict or acquit. The job of the rest of the jurors would become to withstand this fiery certainty when the time came, and to vote on the facts.

"Any new motions?" Salas said. With a loud answering squeak, Klaus pushed his chair back. Jaime held his pen at the ready, waiting for Klaus to move for a short continuance before the trial had commenced, as he had threatened.

Thick silence smothered the courtroom.

"No motions, then. Mr. Sandoval, your opening statement."

Jaime put his pen down and rubbed his mouth as if he were giving it a lube job. Frowning at Klaus for the unexpected switcheroo, he stood up and and walked over to within a few feet of the jury box. Under his sober and appraising gaze, they straightened up.

"On behalf of my office and the State of California, I would like you to know that your services in the pursuit of justice in this courtroom are greatly appreciated," he began. "I know, Judge Salas knows, that it isn't easy for you to put aside all the important tasks of your lives for the next several weeks. Your work is the most important work of all here, and you have my grateful thanks for being willing to help us."

He paused to let those so inclined pat themselves on the back.

"Christina Zhukovsky," he said. "Forty-three years old, she was a woman respected by her peers, a woman of intelligence and conviction. She had lived in the Monterey Bay area all her life, and was a prominent member of the Russian-American community to which she belonged." He looked down, then back up at the jurors, as if pausing for a swift, sincere prayer. "Now she is dead."

Nina thought, Okay, I'm chilled, and that means the jury is, too. Jaime was known for concise but touching opening statements, a characteristic for which he had won praise back when they both attended the Monterey College of Law. She remembered that the defense's opening statement was nonexistent at the moment. Fretting about that, she lost track of the next few sentences.

"We will prove," Jaime was saying, "that between one and three A.M. on Friday night, April eleventh of this year, someone came to the door of Ms. Zhukovsky's home. She let this person in, and together, they went into her kitchen. She was drinking a nightcap, a small glass containing brandy.

"We will show that the visitor attempted to grab Ms. Zhukovsky, and that she fought back—fought for her life, and managed to throw the glass at the attacker, cutting him. We will show that her bravery wasn't enough. She was strangled. Dr. Susan Misumi, the pathologist who performed the autopsy on this unfortunate young woman, will tell you exactly how that occurred. It wasn't instantaneous. Christina had perhaps two full minutes to know she was dying and to suffer the awful helplessness of being the victim of murder."

Nina heard a sort of group exhalation behind her. Jaime Sandoval would never achieve the heroic stature of a

Klaus Pohlmann, but he knew how to move the courtroom to care by invoking the spirit of a dying woman.

"We will show you that the killer had prepared and
planned his actions. He stuffed Ms. Zhukovsky's strangled
body inside several plastic trash bags and wrapped them
with laundry cord. He hid the body, and laid his disposal
plans."

Stefan hadn't gone to the grave site and discovered
Christina's body until the following night. Since nobody
knew where her body had been kept, since they had found
no evidence of Christina's body in Stefan's car, Jaime was
obscuring. Nina made a note to herself to emphasize the
lack of proof that Stefan had hidden Christina's body for a
full day.

"The next night, Saturday, he transported her body to
Cementerio El Encinal, Monterey's municipal cemetery."
Jaime came closer, almost to the bar behind which the jury
sat, and raised his voice.

"Where better to dispose of a body? No one would
look in a grave," he said. "He hoped she would disappear
into the old dust of others who had the dignity of proper
burial, maybe never missed. Maybe missed but never
found." He hesitated, to allow the jurors to consider how
wrenching that would be. "His footprints were found at
the scene. He dug up the grave of her own father, Constantin Zhukovsky, a man who had died more than twenty
years before, and he placed her body in that open hole he
had dug, and then he covered her up and stamped"—Jaime
stamped his foot on the floor—"the earth down." He lowered his voice again, so low the jurors in back leaned forward to hear. "He used his boots to spread the gravel
around, to hide the body he had dumped. There was no
grace, no decorum in her burial, no family there to grieve
her properly, and no attempt made to restore peace to the
grave he had just desecrated. He finished his dirty work."

Klaus leaped to his feet, vigorous as a boy of twelve. "Objection!" he shouted.

Jaime, startled out of the spell he was casting, jerked his head around.

"I object! He is arguing his case, making poetical leaps instead of telling the jury what facts he intends to prove! Ridiculous—"

"Counsel, come forward to the bench," Salas said. Nina began to rise but Klaus waved her back. Jauntily, he stepped up to the side of Salas's dais, where Jaime already stood. They put their heads together and Salas hissed for a full minute. As the judge wound down, both Klaus and Jaime bobbed their heads like marionettes.

Klaus returned and sat down.

"What'd he say?" she whispered.

"He said if I interrupt again in an attempt to force a mistrial he would jail me," Klaus whispered back, and offered her the small smile. "But I was right, was I not, Miss Reilly?"

"I'm not sure," Nina said, voice hushed, courage uneven. "Klaus, please. Don't do that again. He wasn't that bad, and we don't want Salas to get—"

"Oh, I promised to be a good little boy from now on," Klaus whispered, "and I intend to keep my word. Salas doesn't give second chances." He chuckled. "Look at Sandoval, so upset to be tripped in the middle of his showy dance number."

"The objection is denied," Salas said, face impassive. "Counsel, you may continue."

"Thank you," Jaime said. Pointedly turning his back to Klaus, he approached the jurors again. Taking a deep breath, he glanced over some notes in his hand and continued. Unfortunately, when Klaus broke the spell for him, he had broken it for everyone. The emotionally laden graveyard burial had yielded to a procedural mood.

"Officer Jay Millman of the Monterey Police Department will testify regarding a traffic stop he made near that very same cemetery at about two o'clock on Sunday morning, the night of April twelfth into the thirteenth. He will identify for you the defendant over there, Stefan Wyatt, as the person driving the car in question. He will indicate to you what he found in plain view in that vehicle that led to the arrest of Stefan Wyatt for the murder of Christina Zhukovsky."

Interesting style, Nina thought, momentarily diverted from the notes she was making for her own opening. Jaime was creating suspense. Those jurors were in for a nasty shock when they heard just what it was Stefan had in that duffel bag. She had seen Jaime in action before, and she saw the amount of care that had gone into this argument. She also understood that he was pushing the limits of what he could do in his opening statement.

She would do the same, once she had an opening statement.

Another pause, but one that held no nervousness. Klaus hadn't permanently dented Jaime's self-possession. Pacing, arms behind his back, Jaime's lips whitened with the seriousness of his purpose.

"What Officer Millman saw falling out of a duffel bag in the back seat of the car driven by Stefan Wyatt, ladies and gentlemen, were bones, human bones. Those bones, we will show, were all that was left of a man named Constantin Zhukovsky after twenty-five years of peaceful rest."

Well, Nina thought, Klaus was right. Jaime was getting more fanciful than he should, but she understood the impulse. He wanted to give the jurors a framework for thinking his way, and he also couldn't resist exploiting the more bizarre facts of the case.

She made a note to herself. She came after he did, and

that position held inherent strength. She needed to use it to mitigate his every harm.

"We will prove that the defendant declined to make any statement about how he could legitimately be in possession of human remains. A thorough search of nearby cemeteries undertaken by the Monterey Police Department resulted in the discovery of the disturbed grave of Mr. Zhukovsky, who had died in 1978, with the surface sloppily restored but not intact." Jaime wet his lips, giving everyone a chance to hearken back to Stefan's callousness.

"When that grave was reopened, Christina Zhukovsky's body was discovered on top of Mr. Zhukovsky's casket, which had been tampered with. We will present testimony from our forensics investigator, Detective Kelsey Banta, showing that Christina's apartment was then searched and blood samples collected from pieces of glass found on the kitchen floor. We will show that subsequent DNA testing matched those blood samples with the blood of the defendant, Stefan Wyatt." A few of the jurors turned to eyeball Stefan, who yanked at his necktie until Nina quietly suggested he stop.

"Detective Banta will testify as to another significant fact. When Mr. Wyatt was searched in the early morning hours of Sunday, April thirteenth, his pocket contained a medal. A small Russian military medal," Jaime went on, showing them a size with his hands, "very old, a gold medal which had been buried with Constantin Zhukovsky.

"Very briefly, then, this is what we will prove to you in the course of this trial, ladies and gentlemen. One: that Miss Zhukovsky was strangled by a killer who premeditated the crime. Two: that in fighting for her life Miss Zhukovsky wounded the defendant, who left his blood behind in her apartment. Three: that the defendant was stopped soon after the murder, driving away from the cemetery with remains from a grave in which her body had been buried. And four: that the defendant had in his pocket a medal stolen from the same grave.

"There are many other facts which we will prove in the course of this trial, ladies and gentlemen. We will prove, for instance, that the defendant actually left his footprints at the grave site. But I have found that it is best to have in mind the ones which irrefutably must lead to a finding by you that this defendant killed this lady.

"This isn't a complex case. The defendant was sloppy enough to drive around with his taillight out. All you need to remember right now are three facts about the defendant: bones were found in the back seat of the defendant's car, an unusual medal was located in his pocket, and he left blood at Ms. Zhukovsky's apartment."

Jaime steepled his fingers and held them to his mouth. "It is a serious responsibility," he said, "to sit in judgment on another human being. Yet you have accepted this awesome duty and I know you will carry it out with diligence and fairness. Thank you."

The jurors, heads inclined toward Jaime Sandoval as if bent by a powerful wind, nodded, every last one of them. What a fine, upstanding prosecutor, their expressions told Nina. He's only after fairness for this poor lady who that bastard—sidelong looks at Stefan—probably killed.

Somebody needed to correct that impression. Klaus, unruffled, ostentatiously examined his fingernails. Nina had been trying to write down Jaime's main points, trying to keep the flood of anxiety down.

"Miss Reilly will make the opening statement on behalf of the defendant," Klaus said.

"It's customary for lead counsel in a trial to make the statement," Salas said, thick eyebrows knitted over his reading glasses.

"We are an equal-opportunity defense team," Klaus said, on his feet again.

"What's that supposed to mean?" Jaime asked.

But Klaus, now seated, was enjoying a sip of water. Nina rose and looked down at the notes she had taken while Jaime was making his statement, which seemed so grossly inadequate she had to look up again, swallow, and read them one more time.

Flowery greeting. Right. She introduced herself and Klaus, and presented Stefan, who looked seriously at the jury, biting his lip.

She blanked her mind and waited for the words to flow like magic, unsummoned. This had happened to her many times before. In fact, she could almost rely on the trick, but apparently it only worked when she had already stuffed her unconscious with a prepared statement. Nothing came out, so she walked over to the jury box, put her hands in the pockets of her jacket, took them out again, and put them on the railing, clammy with fear. She forced herself to think about what the jury would want to hear and need to hear.

"Ladies and gentlemen of the jury, you have already gone through a long process in which you yourselves were judged. You have filled out a questionnaire. His Honor Judge Salas, Mr. Sandoval, and Mr. Pohlmann have each talked to you and asked you questions. Many of the people who were called to jury duty did not become jurors, but you did.

"You were selected because you have demonstrated an ability and a willingness to listen with open minds to the testimony you will hear. You can be jerked left and right, but ultimately, your minds are open and you are thinking and weighing, and coming to the conclusion that fits the evidence you will hear. You have also shown us that you will be able to come to your verdict based on the legal standards that must be followed.

"There may even come a time when you don't want to follow some of those standards. Like, for instance, the most important of those standards: the weighty burden borne by the prosecution—to show guilt beyond a reasonable doubt. Please remember throughout this trial—you cannot convict Stefan Wyatt of the charges against him unless you find that he is guilty of them *beyond a reasonable doubt*." She stopped to let the words gather their full effect. She knew the jurors had heard them a thousand times before, but here was a solemn context, a court case, a life at stake.

No, don't get into the law any further, she told herself. Salas had begun to fidget on the bench. She anticipated the interruption forming in his mind and changed direction.

"I am not here this morning to talk to you about the specifics of the law, however." She just had. She hoped she had gotten that all-important standard etched into their brains. "I'm here to tell you about the factual case which is about to be presented to you by the prosecution, and about the defendant's case.

"Let me explain first that Stefan Wyatt will not be testifying in this case. He has the right not to testify, and later the judge will tell you that his failure to testify cannot be held against him by you." Nina swiftly continued as Salas again opened his mouth and she moved out of line. "He will not testify in this case. It is up to the prosecution to prove its case, and Mr. Pohlmann and I will be responding to each and every point Mr. Sandoval makes.

"Before I tell you what some of our responses will be, let me point out important issues that will not be explained by Mr. Sandoval: no evidence, no facts, no witness will tell you that Mr. Wyatt, the defendant here, knew the victim in the case." Pause. "No evidence will prove that he hid the body for a full day before burying it. No witness will tell you that they met or had a relationship, or that they had an argument and that there was bad feeling. Mr. Wyatt and Ms. Zhukovsky did not know each other. You cannot speculate that they did.

"Ask yourselves throughout this trial, Why would Stefan Wyatt kill this woman? He didn't know her. You will learn that valuable goods and gold jewelry were left untouched in the apartment. In short, you will not hear that this murder occurred as a result of a robbery.

"Why, then, would this defendant kill this woman?" Nina held out her hands and shrugged, but the effect was lost when Jaime, behind her, said, "Approach the bench?" to the judge. It was payback time for Klaus's interruption of Jaime's opening statement. Salas motioned to her and, willy-nilly, she was pulled from the picture she was drawing for the jury.

Nina walked up to the bench, heels clacking.

"We don't have to prove motive," Jaime said. "Motive isn't a required element. I request a corrective instruction so the jury sees this is all smoke and mirrors."

He should talk about smoke, mirrors, and dirty work, but tit for tat, he had to object in order to keep the point count even, and she had to deal with it. "I am sticking to fact," Nina said. "The prosecution has no idea why this woman was murdered. They can't link the defendant to the victim. It has nothing to do with motive, it goes to the basis of the prosecution's case, and we have a right to mention it."

So no enterprising reporter could read his lips, Salas hid his mouth with his fingers, saying, "Stick to the facts. You're arguing the case. I know what's going on. You take your cues from the old man. You're arguing the law and trying to prejudice the jury from the get-go. Listen. I won't stand for it. You understand? Talk about what you're going to prove and then sit down. Is that clear?"

"Thank you, Your Honor," Nina said, hoping she sounded truly grateful. The old game was afoot. The jury must think the judge approved of her whenever she could pull it off. Salas waved them away, and she went back to the witness box.

"Er—as I was saying . . ." What had she been saying? Something that had got her slammed against a wall—talk about the facts—take control, be bold . . .

"Four facts," she said. "The prosecution claims that four facts will show Mr. Wyatt committed this murder. Well, three of them do link Mr. Wyatt to a grave in Cementerio El Encinal." That got the jurors' attention.

"Mr. Wyatt's footprints were indeed found near the grave. Mr. Wyatt did indeed place the remains of Constantin Zhukovsky in his car. When stopped by Officer Jay Millman of the Monterey Police Department, Mr. Wyatt did in fact have a medal in his pocket which had been buried with Constantin Zhukovsky in 1978. Those facts link this defendant to that grave, the grave where the body of the victim in this case was found.

"The evidence also will show that Mr. Wyatt, who had been unemployed for the previous three months, had five hundred dollars in his pocket. It will be up to you to draw a factual inference as to why Mr. Wyatt had that money and whether it was related to disinterring the remains of Constantin Zhukovsky."

Right, keep the fact that he dug up an old man's bones and stuck them in a grubby duffel bag at a distance by using words like "disinter."

Hmm, the forewoman's face said.

"Digging up a grave for someone is not murder," Nina told the jurors. "Someone paid five hundred dollars. Who? Who else knew Mr. Wyatt would be digging up the grave that night? Ask yourselves that question as this trial progresses."

Nina stopped. She could not accuse Alex Zhukovsky of anything outright, because Stefan Wyatt wouldn't be testifying to say he had hired him in the first place. Zhukovsky denied he had hired Stefan, and all the defense had was five hundred bucks floating around in a pocket that never otherwise sported such riches to show Stefan hadn't acted on his own.

She had said all she could on that topic. "Ask yourself this, too," she went on. The inner logician reappeared, unexpectedly. She wasn't thinking ahead of the words that came out. Silently, she applauded that part of herself that worked in the background, a silicon chip, amassing information, collating, and on top of that, doing the work of a creative artist, figuring out how to adapt the information to best effect. "Where was Mr. Wyatt taking those bones? What earthly use could he have for them? If he just murdered a woman and went to hide the body in a grave, why pick Christina Zhukovsky's father's resting place? Why make a spectacle of himself, driving around Monterey with a taillight out and a set of human remains in his car?"

The jurors appeared flummoxed.

Excellent. As the trial progressed, somebody would have to come up with a coherent theory about Stefan Wyatt and that duffel bag full of bones, and it better be Jaime. Thank goodness that wasn't her job. The burden of proof was on the prosecution. Sometimes the defense's main job was to sow confusion, and that was the one thing she felt absolutely qualified to do in this case.

"Now, you will also be presented with blood evidence, ladies and gentlemen," Nina said. "A forensic technician will testify for the prosecution that some small amount of blood found in the victim's apartment turned out, after all kinds of newfangled DNA testing, to be similar to Mr.

Wyatt's blood. It's always tempting to accept what a scientist tells you about a test that's very hard to understand. I ask you not to do that uncritically.

"Instead, I ask you to listen with discerning ears to the testimony of the defense expert, Dr. Ginger Hirabayashi, a top forensic pathologist, who will tell you that—that mistakes can be made." It was weak, but she had to say something about the blood. Actually, the blood evidence would convict Stefan if Ginger didn't come up with an alternative explanation, and she hadn't been able to do that right up to this moment, so . . .

Forget about Ginger. There was something else about the blood she wanted to say, something helpful. She turned toward Klaus, hoping he would be able to mouth some crucial word at her to help her remember, but Klaus simply waved, the king approving of his resourceful lackey.

"Right," Nina said. Someone stifled a yawn in the back, which set the tip of her tongue to tickling. The blood, and oh, yes, where there was blood there had to be . . .

"Mr. Wyatt was arrested the day after this murder, booked, searched, and examined, but please note: here's the evidence. He didn't have a single cut or bruise on his body. He was not wounded. So how could he have bled at Christina Zhukovsky's apartment late the previous night?

"Where did that blood come from?"

Nina put her hand on the railing and asked them the question she had been punishing herself with for the past two weeks. *"How could blood possibly come from Mr. Wyatt when he had not bled?"* She heard Ms. Frey's jaw click as she processed the question. Nina didn't move, holding them in that moment, Stefan's chance.

Finally, Ms. Frey looked away. The other jurors cleared their throats and stabilized themselves in their chairs. Nina stepped back. "Thank you for your time."

"We'll take the mid-morning recess." Judge Salas rapped his gavel.

Nina recovered from the haze of her thoughts to face the bald glare of the courtroom, smelling the sweat of people too long confined and the ordeal of their thinking. She felt worn out, as if she had run a long way on a boiling hot day. Gulping for breath, dry-throated and unable to speak further, she left the courtroom ahead of Klaus, who stayed behind to talk with Stefan. Her mouth tasted of burnt pudding, cinders, dust. Today stood out among the worst days of her life. She had winged an opening statement in a homicide case. She felt angry, relieved, used, and plain confused.

Making the curve outside the courtroom door in record time, she headed for the ladies' room, hoping the reporter Annie Gee wouldn't follow.

She washed her face and hands, got out her brush, bent over so her hair hung toward the floor, and started brushing her hair from the roots up. This ritual blood-stirring always calmed her.

The door opened. Annie's inquisitive eyes reflected brightly in the mirror behind her.

6

"STATE YOUR FULL NAME FOR the record." Tuesday was a new day, and the courtroom smelled of smuggled coffee. The high windows let in a flood of marine light, reminding Nina that the Pacific Ocean, even in inland Salinas, was only fifteen miles away.

The young police officer, a new father whose eyes sagged with lack of sleep, said, "Jay Arthur Millman."

"You may be seated."

Millman, in full uniform except for his weapon, which had been checked, sat in the witness box and looked around curiously, as if unsure where the questions would come from. Jaime didn't get up, but, marshaling his files and his papers, he let his witness know where he was.

Beside Nina, Klaus sat in his black suit, starched white shirt with gold studs, and a blue-on-red tie. Right on time and sunny as usual, he had brought nothing but a leather notebook with a large brass clasp and a fountain pen. Nina had set up the files in front of him. Watching him come up the central aisle as he greeted Paul, the reporters, clerks, and other lawyers, and seeing the affection and respect he received, Nina felt comforted. He was a legend, and there was inherent dignity in acting as his minion.

From the report Officer Millman had filed, they already knew what he had to say. Nina took rapid notes as Jaime whisked the witness through his graduation from the Police Academy and his two years as a patrolman on the City of Monterey police force. Talking about these familiar topics, Millman relaxed. He was shockingly young, twenty-three years old, thin-shouldered under his uniform jacket, his chin scraped clean.

"Now, directing your attention to the early morning of April thirteenth, were you on duty that night?"

"Yes, sir, third watch, twelve to eight A.M."

"What were your duties on that particular night?"

"Patrol the downtown Monterey area, check the patrons at the nightclub on Alvarado when the club closed to make sure they weren't driving away intoxicated, respond to any incident calls at the hotels or burglar alarms going off at any of the downtown businesses. Make traffic stops as needed. Keep an eye out," Millman said. Ms. Frey nodded, apparently liking this fresh-faced young man.

"You were patrolling with a partner?"

"Officer Kyle Graydon. He joined the force last year."

"Did your patrol area include the city cemetery?"

"Yes, and the Catholic cemetery right next to it. The cemeteries are located about a mile from downtown, along Lake El Estero, just across from Dennis the Menace Park."

"And during the first two hours of your shift did you pass by the cemetery? The city cemetery?"

"Yes, sir, once on the Fremont Avenue side and once on the Pearl Street side, where the park is."

"Did you observe anything unusual during those drive-bys?"

Millman thought, then shook his head. "It was a quiet night. Occasionally, we get teenagers climbing the fence into the park to get onto the locomotive at the kids' playground or just to party on the grounds there. Right across from the cemetery there's a parking lot, and a grassy area with picnic tables where people come to feed the ducks in the daytime. Late at night, some come to make drug deals or sit in their cars. But that lot was empty on Saturday evening, April twelfth, and going on into Sunday. Like I say, it was a quiet night."

"What about the parking lot for the city cemetery?"

"There isn't one. You just drive through the gates—which are closed at sundown, by the way—drive through and park along the paved ways by the grave you want to visit. Or there are a couple of spots at the manager's shack in the middle of the cemetery. But we don't ordinarily patrol inside there at night, since the gates are closed."

"Is the lot by Dennis the Menace Park and the municipal ball field closed at night?"

"There are always a few cars there, day or night. I think park personnel leave their cars there overnight. As long as the people aren't hanging around, we don't give them a hard time."

"Did you observe cars in that lot during your shift during the early morning of April thirteenth?"

"Yes, sir. Officer Graydon and I were driving by and we saw an old Honda Civic pull out of the lot onto Pearl. We were just turning onto Pearl off El Estero, and we began to follow the vehicle."

"When would that be?"

"After two in the morning of the thirteenth." He put the time into parlance the jury could understand.

"Why follow the car?"

"The left taillight was out."

"Do you always pull over cars with missing taillights?"

"The driver shouldn't have been in the park lot at that time of night," Millman said primly. "We check things out, try to keep the place safe."

Jaime opened his mouth to continue his methodical

line of questions but Millman jumped ahead. "We pulled him over right at the corner of El Estero and stopped behind him. Officer Graydon remained in the police car to call in the plates, and I approached the driver's door with my flashlight. That was at two-ten A.M."

"What happened then?"

"The driver rolled down his window. I asked for his license and registration. While he was getting it, I shined my flashlight around the interior of the car."

Nina made a note, adding an exclamation point. The exact method by which Millman had discovered the bones had not been thoroughly reviewed in Klaus's files. Paul had tried to interview Millman the week before, but the officer was on a brief paternity leave and hadn't been available. They might have an illegal search and seizure issue. Unfortunately, the time to raise that issue was before trial.

"Why, oh, why didn't we file a 1538.5 motion?" she whispered to Klaus, but he wiggled his fingers at her and kept listening. She pulled out the pretrial motions file and double-checked. Nothing. She had read the preliminary hearing transcript quickly the week before, and hadn't noticed the potential legal issue. Her chest tightened, as if her heart were hardening itself against an assault.

Millman was busy covering that potential issue. "Standard procedure requires that we make sure the area within a vehicle where a driver could grab a weapon is clear."

"You were not looking for anything but a weapon?" Jaime asked.

"Oh, no, just making sure it was safe to be standing there. That late at night you don't want any surprises."

"What, if anything, did you see, using the flashlight?"

Sensing a coming revelation, the jury paid attention. A thought pushed at Nina straight out of evidence class in law school: if you don't object before trial, you can usually still raise it at trial, but if you don't raise it then, the issue's waived, gone forever.

Except, of course, at the legal malpractice hearing.

She didn't have time to get up or to form a complicated thought. She just called out, "Objection!"

Jaime spun around, and she knew he had thought he was home free. Disappointed, the jury frowned her way.

Klaus whispered, "What are you doing?"

"Just one moment, Your Honor," she said. She put her head close to Klaus's, saying, "Why didn't we raise the search issue?"

"What search issue? The flashlight? He's entitled to a light."

"No! No! There's a case!"

"About a flashlight?"

"Klaus, I'm going to make an objection. For the record. Please don't stop me . . ."

"By all means, make your case," Klaus said mildly. "No permission is required."

She stood. "The defense objects to the introduction of any evidence regarding items found in the car on grounds that the search was conducted in violation of the Fourth Amendment, which makes it an illegal search and seizure."

Stuck in a pose in front of the jury, Jaime let out a disbelieving snort. Nina hardly dared to look at Salas, but she nevertheless felt the bullets of disapproval he launched toward her from the bench.

"Five-minute recess." Salas admonished the jury not to talk about the trial. They filed out.

Then he aimed a look at her that told her she had blown whatever goodwill they had started out with. He said, "On the record. You have stopped this trial cold to raise an issue, which, unless I am mistaken"—he looked at the index of old pleadings in front of him—"has never before been raised. Am I correct? Was there a motion filed?"

Nina looked at Klaus, but Klaus just shrugged, and she thought, He has no idea or else he doesn't give a damn.

"There was not," Jaime said.

"Was there a 1538.5 motion filed after the preliminary hearing?"

"No, Your Honor," Jaime said.

"How about a motion *in limine* or any sort of pretrial motion at the time we were hearing motions on issues like these?"

"None was filed, Your Honor."

"I apologize to the Court," Nina said. "I am relatively new to this case, and need time to confirm Mr. Sandoval's statements. I regret that this issue apparently was not identified earlier. However, the defense asserts its absolute right to raise it at trial."

"All these proceedings I just mentioned," Salas said, "they're to prevent just this sort of thing—interruptions at trial, lost jury time, inefficient administration of justice."

"Yes, Your Honor," Nina said. "However, I object to the introduction of any testimony regarding what Officer Millman saw with his flashlight, or any evidence that might have been obtained as a result of the use of the flashlight."

"Your authorities? Do you have a brief to present?"

"I request a continuance of twenty-four hours to prepare and present points and authorities," Nina said desperately. She couldn't remember the case about the flashlight, not now.

"Mr. Sandoval?"

Jaime returned to his table. Leafing through some paperwork, he said, "The officer has testified that it was late at night. He made a legitimate traffic stop, and it is well established that he had a right to make sure the driver didn't have weapons within reach as he approached the car. It's a matter of the safety of our officers.

"That's number one. Number two, Your Honor, I object to any continuance. The defense received the police report outlining the traffic stop and use of the flashlight months ago. It is within the Court's discretion to deny this motion for a continuance in order to conduct this trial in an orderly and efficient fashion . . ." He went on, but the words rushed by, a background torrent in Nina's ears now.

When Jaime finished, Nina opened her mouth and let go of the emotions that batted at her, saying, This will bury Klaus; you are exposing him, the firm, and yourself to ridicule and possibly a malpractice accusation. She spoke to the law. "Your Honor, we should not have waited to raise this. However, if this tainted testimony comes in, there's no way to block it out of the jurors' minds later." Implicit in that sentence was the threat that the verdict wouldn't stand up on appeal.

Salas's face darkened. He loved being on the bench. He exercised good judgment. He abhorred reversals. "You may cross-examine Officer Millman as to this issue, and you may raise it on appeal or do whatever you can with it later. But this Court will not put over the trial a day on a matter that could have been carefully briefed and heard on numerous—numerous—occasions prior to this trial. Is that the extent of your authorities right now? The prohibition in the Constitution against search and seizure? Do you have any California case law to present?"

"Not without time for research," Nina said.

"The motion for a continuance is denied," Salas said to the recording clerk. "The motion to suppress the testimony and evidence flowing from the flashlight observation is denied."

A short silence followed. Then Nina said, "I reserve the right to raise the motion again after cross-examination of this officer." She sat down.

"Bring the jury back in," a dour Salas told the bailiff.

• • •

"A large green duffel bag was lying partly on the back seat and partly on the floor," Officer Millman said. "Looked like it was falling off the seat. It was right behind the driver. Open about four inches."

"Did you see anything unusual?"

"I sure did, a long object about eighteen inches long, with a sort of thick knob on the end. And another knob poking out where the bag wasn't closed. I call that suspicious."

"Why?"

Everybody in the courtroom waited for Millman to say he thought the objects were bones, that they were bigger than anything Colonel Sanders dished out, but Millman surprised them. "I thought they might be weapons," he said.

Bones turned into rifles on that scary, dark night; it was an elegant move on Jaime's part. He had just buttressed his legal-search argument with struts strong enough to support the cathedral at Chartres. The police had more leeway in the law when they thought they were seeing guns than when they thought they were seeing evidence. Nina didn't believe for a second that Millman had really thought about weapons upon seeing a bunch of bones spilling out of a duffel bag.

"What did you do then?"

"I asked the driver to step out. I called Officer Graydon over. Then I asked the driver what he had on the back seat. He refused to answer, so I opened the rear passenger door behind the driver and pulled the bag out onto the street."

The jury leaned forward again. Madeleine Frey threw a quick glance at Nina to see if she would pop up again to deny them their testimony, but Nina had done what she could. She sat there, hoping to express nothing more than a bland nonreaction while Millman said, "The contents fell out on the road. They appeared to be human bones, and pieces of what looked like a man's blue suit."

While a few winced, on the whole this was going to be a tough group—most eyes squinted with interest. A murmur traveled around the courtroom. Millman had the rapt attention of every person there.

"What did you do then?" Jaime asked.

"I attempted to question the driver about the bag. He said he wanted a lawyer, even though I hadn't Mirandized him or arrested him. I told him he was being detained for questioning and I secured his vehicle and the bones, then put him in the police cruiser and took him to the station."

"Did the driver say anything on that drive?"

"No, sir. Not one word then or after, so far as I know. He made no attempt to explain."

"What happened then?"

"Well, Watch Commander said it was okay for him to make a call, so I let the defendant use the pay phone and he called his girlfriend."

"About what time was this?"

"By then—I would say after three A.M. I escorted him into a witness room for questioning, and Detective Banta took custody."

Jaime turned his back on Millman to look at Stefan. "And can you tell us the name on the driver's license you examined that night?"

"Yes, sir, the name on the license and on the registration was Stefan Wyatt."

"And do you recognize the person you took in for questioning early on Sunday morning, April thirteenth, based on the events you have just testified about, here in this courtroom today?"

"Yes, I recognize the defendant over there. That is the

individual I stopped that night." Millman pointed with his finger.

"Let the record show Officer Millman has identified the defendant, Stefan Wyatt," Jaime said. "What, if anything, did you do then in connection with this traffic stop and detention?"

"I was on shift until eight A.M. that next morning. Officer Graydon and I called the two cemeteries right across the street from where we first saw the driver—the defendant. At about four-thirty A.M., I got a call on the radio to return to El Encinal Cemetery. Officer Graydon and I returned there and we met Jim Martinez, a groundskeeper. He took us over to a grave in the El Estero Street side of the cemetery, not far from the gate to Pearl Street. In spite of the dark, I could see some evidence of a disturbance there."

"What sort of evidence?"

"A messed-up surface," Millman said. "It didn't look right."

"What happened then?"

"Jim called in a backhoe operator, who brought floodlights. Oh. I almost forgot. There was a name on the grave. Constantin Zhukovsky. Jim went into the office and called his next of kin on the records and got permission from Alex Zhukovsky, the man's son, to do the digging."

So the potential legal issue that the grave had been searched without authority would go nowhere. Nina crossed off her note and waited. Jaime was covering every bet. His examination was a model of careful preparation. Maybe he would get his way this time, and bring Klaus's distinguished career to a screeching halt. That ought to please Jaime.

"At a little after five-thirty in the morning we—or anyway the backhoe operator—started digging."

"You were present? Who else was there?"

"Jim Martinez, the operator, Officer Graydon, and myself. And cups of coffee all around."

"What happened then?"

"We could just see daylight on the horizon. By six-thirty-five A.M. the operator had dug a couple of feet down. He hit something, a woman's arm, coming out of a trash bag."

Well, the moment had arrived. All Nina felt was relief.

Madeleine Frey, plainly disturbed, retied the bow at her neck. The rest of the jurors chewed on the skin inside their mouths, scratched their heads, or engaged in other activities that expressed disquiet. They had been chosen in part because they were not newshounds, unlike the reporters in back who scribbled furiously.

Stefan faded into his chair as if he could disappear. He kept his hands on the table as Klaus had instructed, but balled into fists.

"A woman's arm was sticking out of the trash bag?" Jaime said, although the words had been quite clear.

"A small arm I took for a woman's. Yes." Millman wasn't an exaggerator, Nina had decided. When he bowed his head, remembering, he needed to do it.

"Protruding from a trash bag about four feet down?"

"That's right. A couple of bags, big, black dirt-covered trash bags with yellow ties."

Jaime put down his papers, screeched back in his chair, and asked, "What happened then?"

"I called into the station and made contact with Detective Banta. She said she would take over. I stayed and secured the premises until she and other officers from Homicide arrived about half an hour later."

"And then?"

"And then I wrote up my report, went off duty, and went home."

"Thank you, Officer Millman. I have nothing further," Jaime said.

"We'll take our lunch recess," said the judge, with the usual words to the jury. Stefan, looking flushed, was led into the back room where the guard would give him his lunch. Klaus and Nina stood up.

"The flashlight—I'm going to do a computer search during lunch," Nina said, feeling unable to avoid the presence of an elephant in the courtroom.

"You think I made a huge mistake there, don't you, Miss Reilly?"

"It's unheard of not to try to suppress traffic-stop evidence in a traffic case," she blurted.

"You think I'm senile?" Klaus said. "You think I didn't give the matter due consideration?" He wore an expression as proud and sure of itself as an American flag. "Well, I am old but my mind is intact. I didn't judge it to be necessary."

Nina stashed the files in her case. When the courtroom emptied, they left, Klaus in the lead, Nina following behind his erect posture and immaculate suit.

7

WEDNESDAY MORNING KLAUS CROSS-EXAMINED Officer Millman, who diverged not a whit from his testimony. Nina fed Klaus a list of questions about the flashlight search, and he read them through reading glasses, putting them to the witness as she requested, along with a few of his own thrown in for good measure. For now, he behaved like a lamb, modulated and meek, but Klaus was no lamb. He never broadcasted his strength in advance but saved his power for the attack, or at least he always had in the past. She hoped to see it again during this case when they needed it most.

Nina had tracked down her flashlight case, which turned out not to be so significant. A flashlight search was legal anywhere an occupant of a vehicle could reach within it. Millman and Jaime must have read the case, too, because Millman practically quoted it line for line. Yes, Stefan could have reached into the back seat of his small car. Yes, Millman had merely flashed the light through the window. No, he did not insert the flashlight inside the vehicle.

After another brief but heated argument out of the hearing of the jury, Salas ruled that the search came under

the Plain View Doctrine. That was that, until the time came
for appeal, if Stefan was convicted. They had lost the skirmish, but at least they had belatedly got onto their horses
and come out jousting, which protected the issue for appeal, and peripherally, but seriously, might protect the firm
from a malpractice claim.

What a close call. Klaus should have raised the issue
long ago, but now they were in the middle of a trial, which
was a bad time for self-flagellation.

At lunch, Klaus placed his napkin neatly in his lap and
stuck it to her again, suggesting she take the cross-exam on
Kelsey Banta.

"I'm not prepared, Klaus," she said patiently. "We
should keep with the plan that you handle it."

"Of course I am ready and able to do that," Klaus said.
He put a leaf of lettuce into his mouth. He went on eating
while Nina chewed on second thoughts.

"Are you tired?" she asked.

"No."

Why was he doing this to her? To conserve his energy?
Because he sensed his powers were fading? Did he believe
she might do a better job? She decided he wouldn't ask if
he didn't need her. "If you really need me, I can do it if you
give me your notes right now."

Without a word, Klaus passed over his legal pad. "Detective Banta," said the tall slanted letters at the top of the
page. What followed was a concise outline of topics to be
covered in Klaus's superbly angular Germanic handwrit-
ing.

Nina began feeling better. "But—if you want me to
take a witness and it's not an emergency or something—
can you please let me know the night before? I could use
more time to plan."

Klaus set down his fork and wiped his mouth with his napkin. "Look here," he said. "Do you know what happens when a lawyer sits up all night memorizing old testimony and reports and concocting long lists and so forth?"

"What?"

"She sacrifices the ability to listen to the testimony as it comes from the witness's mouth. She is so busy checking off items, thumbing through exhibits, flipping through paper, she hears nothing."

"I prepare," Nina said. "That's the way I practice law."

"Then it is time to jump to a higher level," Klaus said, "where you demonstrate your mastery of law, not your practice of it. When Detective Banta speaks, don't look at your notes. Don't think about the next thing she might say. Open up to fresh ideas. What does she tell you with her body, her voice, and only last of all, her words? When does she exaggerate? Watch her when she skids over a topic. Note statements in her direct testimony that don't sound right. Go straight to those things and follow them to where they lead."

"What about this outline you prepared?"

He tapped on it, and she read it. It was unlike any notes preparing for testimony Nina had ever seen. Five topics in capital letters were followed by brief notes in the present tense that summarized the night Stefan Wyatt was arrested and Banta's subsequent activities:

1. STATION
   Millman leaves and Banta takes over
   suspected homicide. Wyatt in an interview
   room asleep in a chair waiting for his lawyer
   (Mr. Turk, who got there at 9 A.M.). Stefan is
   booked and searched. Medal found and
   tagged.

2. CEMETERY
   Arrives 7:00 with her partner—still pretty
   dark (fog)—backhoe has encountered a thick
   clump of black trash bags lying on top of an
   older coffin. She gets in, wearing gloves,
   opens the bag, and sees the victim—secures
   premises—calls investigative team and D.A.'s
   office. Calls Alex Zhukovsky again for
   permission to open coffin—inside, body has
   been removed. Takes statements from
   cemetery security, checks for ID, finds none,
   calls in medical examiner and forensics team.

3. STATION
   Returns to station and meets Alex
   Zhukovsky—he's in a very upset state (still
   doesn't know it's his sister). Takes statement
   re: his father, Constantin's, burial. Shows Alex
   the bones and he says clothes are those his
   father was buried in—but medal is missing—
   describes the medal of St. George.

4. MORGUE
   The medical examiner, Susan Misumi, calls
   to say Christina's body has been taken to
   county morgue. Banta takes bones and Alex
   to morgue where he IDs Christina and
   breaks down.

5. CHRISTINA'S APARTMENT
   Banta and partner now go to Christina's
   address on Eighth. (Alex gave key. Unable to
   attend.) They enter. See very little sign of
   anything at first. Prelim tests for blood on
   kitchen floor are positive. Find glass. They
   bring Forensics in. Talk to D.A. Sandoval and
   decide to hold Stefan on suspicion. Alan has
   been to station. Then they go off-shift.

"That's it?" Nina said.

"Jaime always asks his questions chronologically," Klaus told her. "He is as reliable as the annual monsoon floods in Bangladesh. As for what Detective Banta will have to say on these matters, you will have to listen to find out."

The bill arrived. He pulled out the firm's credit card, leaving a whopping tip on the slip of paper. Bantering with the waiter, he seemed completely relaxed, completely unconcerned. Nina watched, wondering.

Klaus had handled the Millman cross adequately. Maybe he was okay after all, a memory lapse here or there as you would expect from an elderly person, but what about the opening statement? What about the Banta cross? Was he doing this to her on purpose, trying to train her as though she were fresh out of law school?

I have plenty to learn, she thought, looking at the concise notes, but is Klaus still a good teacher?

"What do we want to get from Banta?" Nina said. "Where's a list of discrepancies among the reports? She's a hugely important witness . . ."

"We do not know what she can give us until we hear her," Klaus repeated. "Shall we go?"

"Klaus, I can't work like this," Nina said. "Fortifying in advance—it helps me cope with surprises and contributes to my being able to operate on a more intuitive level during trial. Yes, I go on guts at times, but I arrive in court with the facts well analyzed and memorized. I can be more creative on my feet when I've got my background in place. Plus it keeps the anxiety from turning me into a zombie."

"How long have you been practicing law, Miss Reilly?" Klaus asked without waiting for an answer. "Several years, and in the last couple of years you have conducted major trials. How long do you think you are going to last as a trial lawyer, the way you work? I will tell you. I give you ten years, then you will have to retire into another line, because you are too tightly wound to last any longer. You will give yourself cancer or a heart problem. Look at me, eighty-one years old and I still smoke cigars and my wife and I are still an item." He put his hands on the table and pushed up. "Listen to the witness," he said. "She will invite attack. You will notice it in her voice and in that pinched place between her eyes. You will discern fissures in her testimony, and into those cracks, you must go."

She followed him outside to the old silver Jag. Klaus got into the passenger seat and tossed her the keys. Somehow over the past couple of weeks, in addition to being second chair, she had become the official Pohlmann chauffeur.

"You should have stayed with me," Klaus said, fastening his seat belt.

"That's not fair," Nina said. "I learned a lot from you, but I had to leave to learn other things." She thought for a moment, then said hesitantly, "I'm not you. I don't have your set of talents. I have to work hard to make up for my deficiencies—my lack of experience."

One thing definitely remained: Klaus's lovely, booming laugh. "I'd trade my talents to have the forty years of law you still have ahead of you. Why pay attention to what I say, anyway? You think I'm very far over the hill, in the next valley wandering aimlessly amid the cows and sheep and goats, don't you?"

"No. Of course—"

"Moo-oo-oo!" He laughed again, looking out the window.

Now did not seem the right time to share her fears. Besides, Klaus seemed spookily aware all of a sudden, as alert as ever. She said, "What exactly are you trying to advise me with regard to this case?"

"You cannot treat this case as an intellectual exercise. It

is not. This tragic story holds great mystery and hidden truths we will discover, because our client didn't kill the woman. Somebody else did. We will expose that person, Miss Reilly. That person and the motives behind this crime will leap from the shadows at us, and we will grab for them."

She checked the street and pulled the car into traffic, enjoying the smooth hum of the engine and incredible receptivity of the steering. Klaus knew how to live, and had shown over and over he knew how to practice law. Nevertheless, she checked again for wayward cars once she got into the flow. She liked to know what was out there. She preferred her shadows mapped.

As she let Klaus out on the curb, he said, "You and I are privileged to be called to practice this great art." And she thought, Forty more years? I'll never make it.

Inside the courtroom, the bailiff called everyone to order just as Nina slipped into her chair. The jury members appeared to have enjoyed their midday repast in the back room. Stefan had spent the break fulminating about Erin. What did Nina think the jury thought so far? What would the newspapers say? How might Erin respond when she read the reports? As a witness, she couldn't be in the courtroom during the trial, and she was continuing to refuse to see him. "I made the biggest mistake of my life, that night, didn't I? I fucked up!"

Nina worked on him, trying to turn his thoughts to what was happening in the courtroom right now. "Don't finger your tie," she reminded him. "Keep your hands on the table, relaxed. Face the court. Look strong, but not conceited. Look at the jury."

He tried. His tie drooped.

"Call Detective Kelsey Banta," Jaime said. Detective

Banta, who had been sitting right next to him, strode quickly, making short work of her journey to the witness box.

A well-respected cop, Kelsey Banta had worked herself up from her initial position as a receptionist into a job as one of only two homicide detectives. It had taken her almost twenty years. Five years before, her brother, a police officer in Campbell, California, had been killed while trying to prevent a bank robbery. Paul had told Nina that Banta had reacted badly, winding up in an alcohol rehab facility eighteen months ago. Since then, her record had stayed clean, though—no DUI's or alcohol-related legal problems.

Busty and long-legged, she had black eyebrows, pink cheeks, deep-set blue eyes, and long bleached blonde hair pulled into a work-time ponytail in back. She wore black pants and a blazer with a lacy beige blouse beneath, one button more than appropriate slyly undone. She didn't seem to have altered her usual style at all for her day in court. Maybe she had been in so many trials she had adopted this low-key uniform for them.

As Banta answered Jaime's introductory questions in a cigarette voice, Nina wondered how well Paul knew her. He had been on the Monterey police force himself, working homicide detail, several years before.

Funny, when she was practicing law at Tahoe, she had never thought about the web of friends and acquaintances Paul would have down here on the Monterey Peninsula. He had been married twice when he was younger, and had always liked women. Right now, she could feel his presence behind her, comfortable in the familiar setting, lounging on an aisle seat so that he could leave when necessary.

Had he and Banta exchanged glances as she came into court? Nina hadn't noticed.

Just as Klaus, who seemed to be snoozing at her left,

had predicted, Jaime took the events of Banta's long shift the night of April 12 through 13 in chronological order, starting with taking custody of Stefan Wyatt from Officer Millman at the station.

Trying to take the hint from Klaus's instructions, Nina took no notes. Like most of the jurors, she just watched and listened. Immediately she realized that Kelsey Banta was a straight-shooter. Banta did not infer anything, but offered precise, probing analyses of the facts. She was a good witness with an excellent memory, who only occasionally refreshed her recollection from her report. Talking about booking Stefan on suspicion after a phone conversation with Jaime, whom she woke up at home, she described how the attorney from Klaus's firm, Alan Turk, had come in for a brief conference with Stefan. He later left, with instructions to Stefan to exercise his right to remain silent.

Not very enlightening yet, but Nina did wonder what sort of legal problem had led Stefan's brother, Gabe, to the firm and Alan. She wrote on her pad, "Talk to Alan Turk," then sat back, folding her arms to listen some more. Banta was answering questions about the search of Stefan's clothing on booking.

"Now, this medal you found on Stefan Wyatt . . ."

"I didn't know what it was at the time," Banta said.

Stefan folded his arms, whispering to Nina, "As if I did!"

"But the amount of dirt suggested it probably came out of the grave," Banta continued. "I scraped off a sample for forensics. I could see the remains of a striped orange and black ribbon and a round metal thing about the size of a silver dollar. There was some engraving on it, but the inscription was in Cyrillic."

"Cyrillic?"

"The Russian alphabet."

"You can read it?"

"I studied Russian in high school. All the renegades from French did." So she had a sense of humor and intelligence in addition to a knockout body, Nina thought. Ouch.

"What did the inscription say?"

"I only took two years, so I'm no expert, but I could tell from the words along with the image on the medal that it said something about Saint George. He's slaying the dragon on the image there."

"Go on."

"I put the medal in a plastic bag and listed it. It went into the evidence locker with the clothes."

"Did you then go out to El Encinal Cemetery?"

"Yes. We arrived at seven A.M., when it was getting light. Officer Graydon, the backhoe operator, and the groundskeeper from the cemetery were waiting outside the tape line Officer Graydon had set up. I pulled on my gloves and went in and looked down in the hole. The floodlights were bright. I clearly saw an arm sticking out of a trash bag."

"What did you do then?" Jaime had a rhythm going with her; he must have taken her testimony dozens of times.

"I got on the ground on a tarp, reached in with scissors, and opened the bags. There were three layers of trash bag. I cut a slit maybe three feet long. There was a woman's body in there."

"And what did you do then?"

"We didn't move her. She was cold. She had been dead for a while. I took photos and put a call in to the pathologist, Susan Misumi, and our forensics technician. While Dr. Misumi was en route we checked out the area. Officer Graydon pointed out some apparent footprints. We took casts.

"When Dr. Misumi arrived, she spent some time with

the victim. She examined the remains in place, taking photos, then she had us remove the body for transport to the morgue at Natividad. By then the sun was well up and we turned off the lights.

"I had called Alex Zhukovsky again regarding opening up his father's coffin. He gave his permission. The backhoe hit the top of the coffin at about eight A.M. and, with the assistance of Officer Martinez, I opened it."

"And what, if anything, did you find?"

"The mahogany coffin had been recently disturbed. The satin lining inside was ragged. There was some gray hair at the top. Evidence of insect activity. Shreds of clothing. The bones, which I would expect to find, were missing."

By now, the gasps had abated to *tsk*s, but they were very unhappy *tsk*s.

"Pretty obvious the coffin had contained a human body, which had been removed, although we couldn't tell when. Dr. Misumi came over and looked at it and more photos were taken."

Surprisingly, Jaime skipped through the details of that hideous early morning find. Nina hurried along with him in her mind, wondering why he was in such a rush to leave the grave, not finding her fissure yet.

"Did you then return to the station?" asked Jaime.

"Yes. I had received a radio message that Alex Zhukovsky had showed up. He'd received two phone calls from us and he wanted to know what was going on."

Salas called the mid-afternoon break and everybody rushed out for enough caffeine to float them through the final afternoon session. Klaus and Nina stayed at the conference table with Stefan.

When they returned, the jury, so fresh and ironed in the morning, had the look of laundry left too long on the line, shirts and sweaters sagging. Weary hands stroked eyes and foreheads. Concentrating for so many hours took a lot of effort, and the golfing lady Klaus had winked at rubbed her leg often, as if to keep it awake or stave off some pain.

During the break, Nina had decided she understood Jaime's strategy—he had seen the break coming and saved the luscious best for last. He would give those jurors something to dream about! Sure enough, he, who appeared as combed and fresh as he had in the morning, leisurely pulled out the forensics photos and transported them back to the graveyard, evoking the fog, the cool morning, the digging toward the victim, all the time questioning Banta exhaustively on the details. By the time he was finished spinning his scene, the dank soil, black bags, and bones had practically taken seats in the courtroom.

After adjournment for the day, before they took Stefan away, Nina asked, keeping her voice down as low as she could, "Stefan, why did you call Alan Turk?"

Stefan said, "Gabe—my brother. Gabe consulted him a while back, had some legal thing with him."

"Any idea what it was?"

"Sorry, no."

"How are you doing?" she asked.

"Only as good as you guys in court. In other words," he attempted a smile, "ups and downs. Like I keep saying, you have to get to Alex Zhukovsky somehow. It's too weird, this thing where his sister's body was found in their father's grave. I mean, he's the link, the only link. Plus, he hired me. He killed his sister and buried her in their dad's grave for his own reasons, or else why lie about hiring me?"

And then why hire Stefan to dig them both up? It made no sense. "We're working on it."

"It doesn't really matter," Stefan said in a pragmatic tone at direct odds with his expression of abject defeat.

"Why not?"

"I'm jinxed. Always have been." He licked his lips and thought about it. "Cursed from birth. I wasn't born to a good life."

"Has your life been so terrible?"

"Erin was my only good luck, and now she's gone." He held tight to the chain he always wore around his neck.

"She may still come around."

"You're a woman," Stefan said.

Nina laughed. "Well, yeah. Mostly."

"Do you think—if someone was in jail for a long time—and maybe he would never get out, how would you feel about him?" The hard work of asking made his big shoulders slump. "Could you ever forgive him?"

If Paul went to jail, and she never knew whether he would get out, how would she feel? The question, one she had never asked herself, made her shiver. Paul deserved jail, at least in the eyes of the law. He had killed to protect her at Tahoe, and she was complicitous in that murder, because she knew and because she said nothing. She shook herself free before the alarming swing of her thoughts knocked her down. Focusing on Stefan's earnest, dark eyes, she said, "You need to ask Erin those questions, Stefan."

"I tried writing to her, but I threw the letter away. Because what could I talk about? The guy two cells over who screams all night, or maybe I could entertain her with stories about the nights I can't close my eyes without seeing that grave. I never saw a dead body until I saw Christina's."

"Stefan, do you believe Erin loved you before all this happened?"

"Yeah. I believe she did."

"Then you tell her how you feel."

"I'm locked up. I have no power. I can't go over there, take her out to the beach where we could really talk . . . And then, even if you pull it off, even if you get me out, would she ever trust me again?" he asked, eyes turning inward. "Nina, I want to marry her. She's my only hope. I'd buy her a house, get a regular job, the whole deal. She could have a baby. I asked her once, and she said she'd like one. I would, too. Cut down on Dart League. No more drinkin' until I'm singin', except on weekends or birthdays." His grimace held the shadow of a smile. "She says I'm a lousy singer."

"Write to her again, Stefan. It's been some time. Maybe she's ready to hear from you." Nina gave him an encouraging squeeze on the arm before they led him away.

Outside, Paul stopped her. "You're doing great in there."

"We need more to work with. You go get Alex Zhukovsky and nail him. Talk to Stefan's brother, Erin, his mom, Wanda, everyone again. I feel like we're missing a layer of meaning here."

"Strange way to put it."

She didn't know how else to describe the feeling, but looking at this case was like looking down a pit without a light. The end remained elusive, and could harbor whales, it was so deep. "Someone knows something. And I need to know everything about Christina Zhukovsky, what she hated, what she wanted from her life. She didn't exist in a void over there in that fancy place on Eighth Street. She had friends, a lover, connections. Important emotional contacts. Find out who they are. We should already know these things!"

He stepped back from her quickly, as if trying to avoid a runaway truck. "Settle down, will you? I'm on it."

She got up on her tiptoes and kissed him. His cheek smelled outdoorsy, like eucalyptus. "Of course you are. I'm just a little worked up."

"Dinner at seven, okay? Bring the kid and the dog if you want, but we need to talk business. I'm not just sitting on my hands all day while you wrap those infernally pretty legs around Sandoval and Salas, you know."

"That's a relief." Nina hustled out to find Klaus and drive him home, thinking all the while she didn't like knowing about Paul's past relationships. She didn't like knowing about his past, period.

Paul doesn't love me like Stefan loves Erin, she thought. He's too experienced, too complicated. And I'm the same. She twisted the ring on her finger, for a moment wishing fiercely that they were some other kind of people.

Paul had never asked *her* if she wanted babies.

8

BOB AND HITCHCOCK, THE BIG black mutt, stayed behind, feasting respectively on canned spaghetti and kibble back at the cottage while Paul and Nina grabbed quick bites at The Tinnery, overlooking the ocean. After they ate, Paul asked her if she wanted coffee so they could discuss what he had been working on.

"A room and a car," Nina said, sighing, looking at Lover's Point beyond the window. "A car and a room. And then comes the night."

"What?"

"I spend all my time inside."

Paul put money on the table and stood up. "C'mon." They walked outside to a summer evening in full swing. A gaggle of bikers swooped past, spandex taut. Twenty cameras clicked. Children dripped ice creams.

"Can you make it down the hill in those shoes?"

"No problem," Nina said, letting the tangy ocean air refresh her lungs.

Like licks of transparent watercolors, sunset darted superreally over the beach, transforming Earth temporarily into Mars. Taking the warning signs on the rocky point seriously, they walked to the back side of the cove, where a rough path wound safely down.

Out on the point, closer to the gargantuan power of the ocean but careless of it, a group of Vietnamese tourists read the beware signs, had a good laugh, and headed down to flirt with danger, arms linked. They clung like barnacles to a rock, in a direct line with the treacherous sleeper waves. Arranging them on the rocks like flowers on a sunny, safe, dining room table, a friend snapped endless pictures. No wave knocked them down, nothing disturbed their placid belief in an innocent universe. Eventually, they clambered back up to the street, illusions of immortality undisturbed.

"Such faith," Paul said, observing them. "Dumb luck?"

"Statistics," said Nina, pushing hair out of her eyes. "How many tourists die every year, getting swept out to sea by these tides anyway? One out of thousands?"

"You let Bob go out on the rocks?"

"He goes when we walk down here. I yell at him," Nina admitted.

"You don't trust the odds, then."

"If I made all my decisions rationally, would I consider marrying again? I mean, it would be my third time." Her first marriage, to an attorney in San Francisco, had ended in divorce. Her second husband had died. "Yours, too. The odds aren't good."

"Good thing we're odd, then."

They laughed and started down the path. "Christina Zhukovsky," Paul said, holding on to Nina's hand as they picked their way, "had a lover."

"I knew it! Great work, Paul! I'm so ready for a break!" Nina's heels slipped dangerously over the wet rocks. She caught her balance just shy of a twisted ankle. They finally landed on the beach, locating a flat rock that commanded a view of a horizon flicking fire over the mirror water, and gingerly sat down, holding hands.

"And she had neighbors, a husband and wife. Too bad they were out of town the night she died, or we'd have our killer wrapped and waiting for us in the kitchen, with a satin bow tying him to the chair. The husband didn't like the looks of Christina's boyfriend," Paul said.

"Don't stop."

The sun sneaked down, coloring the bottom side of the clouds peach.

"The boyfriend's a Russian man named Sergey Krilov. I got a good description from the wife." Paul's voice got high and sweet. "Shiny, scraggly hair, so light it's almost white, greeny-yellow eyes with brown specks around the edges, a chin you could scoop ice cream with, it's so sharp, and a really well defined bod." His own voice returned. "Her husband's description conflicted slightly. He called Krilov an ugly but strong little runt with a nose big enough to park an SUV in, who didn't shave as often as he needed to, with the manners of a mutt. He didn't appreciate his wife's interest in Krilov or in me, and shut the door soon after we spoke to explain why to her in loud detail."

"Any time frame on their relationship?"

"They had seen Krilov hanging around for months, then, in the week or so before Christina died, he didn't come around, as far as they knew. But"——Paul shuffled his position on the rock shelf, trying to get comfortable——"you know Christina organized a conference at Cal State Monterey Bay right before she died?"

Nina nodded. She had seen a mention of it in Klaus's background materials.

"Well, Krilov showed up there. He went after Christina. They argued."

"This was when?"

"About a week before she died."

"Good," she said. "How'd you find out about this?"

"After talking with our young neighbors, I dropped by the company that catered the conference, Thought for Food. The guy who started the business is only in his twenties, Rafe Barker, a natural-food fan and masterful vegan chef. He says he's been working at the university since it started, and has grand plans to create the first campus to specialize in healthy eating. Slow food, as opposed to fast. Something different." The sun slid below the lowest cloud, shooting golden beacons at them.

"Did Rafe witness the argument between Krilov and Christina?" Nina asked.

"No. He overheard two men, one of them Krilov, yelling at each other about it afterward. He got the impression Krilov was supposed to make up with Christina, whatever it took, but she didn't want to get back with him. This other man was pissed about it."

"Why?" Nina asked.

"Who knows?"

"Did Rafe know Christina?"

"Only as a person who gave him headaches bringing 'damn crude foreigners' around who missed their meat, and let it be known to the administration. He heard shouts that day, the second day of the conference. They caught his attention, and confirmed his negative opinion of all things not American."

"How did Krilov react to getting dumped by Christina and then criticized for it?"

"With an undignified lack of decorum, according to Rafe. He smacked the other Russian and turned his back on him."

"Any chance we have a witness?"

"In Russia by now," Paul answered.

"Don't tell me Krilov is, too."

"No record of his departure so far."

"Find him. Please."

"Sure thing, boss." He squeezed her hand. "I'm looking, believe me. Just talked to Rafe today."

"Don't call me boss."

"Okay, my love."

Nina leaned in and kissed him on the mouth. "I like that. This really could be important. I still think Alex Zhukovsky has to be our killer, but now here's a rejected lover who gets in violent arguments. That's an exciting development, Paul. Do you have anything else?"

Paul said, "I wish the sun didn't do that, dipping below the horizon where we can't follow it. I hate to see it go, and I'm not sure it really will come back. Let's walk some more." They picked their way along the beach. "The neighbor lady said Christina loved to talk politics. Russian politics. She couldn't believe how ignorant Americans were, and she would cut out news items for them and bend their ears. They had invited her for dinner once, and once was enough, she said."

"You know anything about it? Russian politics?"

"The Berlin Wall got pulled down, when, in 1989? and the Iron Curtain shredded in '91. The Russian Mafia got big. Big boys took over a lot of the industry. The average Russian looked around and said, 'That's cool, McDonald's in Moskva, now could I please get paid for a change so I can afford a cup of coffee there?'"

"That's my impression, too. What was Christina Zhukovsky's main interest?" Nina asked.

"The future. Post-Communist Russia. Who would rule, according to the neighbors. She bored them to tears, which means I have no idea what was really going on. Not yet anyway."

They climbed back up to Paul's Mustang carefully, the darkness another hazard, but also a refuge.

Back at home and sitting on the couch, Nina surveyed

some notes, then sat with her eyes closed, awaiting enlightenment while Bob tossed a ball around the living room and Hitchcock chased it. She was still gnawing around the edges of the case, not knowing enough to sound authoritative about anything. Like her father, Harlan, king of blarney, Klaus oozed confidence when he wasn't even sure where he was—how come she had to know something to sound knowledgeable?

This Wednesday evening's only enlightenment arrived in the form of a ricochet off the wall beside her that caught her on the head, telling her that ball-playing in the living room, even with a very soft ball, was not to be encouraged. "Homework," she ordered, pointing a finger toward Bob's bedroom.

The trial resumed at nine-thirty, Thursday morning. Sitting in court between Klaus and Stefan, Nina remained uncertain about how to approach the cross-examination, so followed Detective Banta's testimony like any jury member hearing it for the first time.

Banta had added a pink sweater to peek coyly out from underneath her jacket today, and those high-heeled boots would never catch a fleeing suspect. Her laid-back delivery had the jury riding happily along with her.

By ten-thirty Jaime had led Banta to a discussion about the human remains in the duffel bag.

After a few introductory questions, Banta testified that before transporting the bones to the morgue early Sunday morning, she had taken advantage of having Constantin Zhukovsky's son at the Monterey Police Station and had shown him the duffel. Alex Zhukovsky told her that the remains were those of his father, whom he recognized due to an item of clothing that was still identifiable, a yellow sash he had worn diagonally over his jacket, made of a tough synthetic fabric that had mostly survived its long burial.

"I got Mr. Zhukovsky a glass of water—and he asked me, 'Where's his medal? It was pinned to that sash.' Remembering the metal object we had taken from the defendant, I showed it to Mr. Zhukovsky. He told me it was some sort of military medal from Russia. He told me his father was buried wearing it in 1978."

"About what time was this?"

"Almost nine-thirty in the morning by then. I then explained about the other body found in the grave. We hadn't identified it, and I thought it would be worth describing the victim. He became—I would describe him as extremely concerned—and pulled out a cell phone and tried to make a call, but couldn't get an answer. He demanded to see the body, so I called Dr. Misumi and she said to bring him over to the morgue with the duffel and the remains. She met us and Mr. Zhukovsky at the door. The victim was lying on a gurney covered with a sheet. When he saw the victim uncovered, Mr. Zhukovsky became very agitated."

"What do you mean by that?"

"He fell on the body and sort of lay across it, sobbing, yelling. Doc Misumi and I had to pull him off."

"And did he identify the body at that time?"

"Yes, sir. He stated it was his sister, Christina Zhukovsky." Giving everyone time to get that clear, she looked around, then continued. "I took a statement from him. Is that in evidence yet?"

Jaime took a moment to catch up and introduced Alex Zhukovsky's statement into evidence, as well as a number of photographs and police reports. He handed the photos of Christina Zhukovsky's body and the crime scene to Madeleine Frey, who passed them around. Frey seemed to be having trouble this morning. She kept rubbing her leg and shifting around in her seat.

A few of the male jurors stared hard at the photos but showed no visible reaction. One of them, a construction contractor named Larry Santa Ana, took his time. He couldn't get enough of them and passed them along reluctantly. For good or ill, he was one to watch.

A set of the photos lay in front of Klaus on the table. He ignored them. Stefan took his lead and didn't look, either, but Nina was drawn again to Christina's face in one of the photos, a proud face even in vulnerable death, with a strong nose and broad forehead, bluish eyelids finally closed on the morgue gurney. Her neck showed obvious signs of strangulation. You didn't need a pathologist to figure out what had happened to her.

Nina consulted Klaus's notes. Jaime had one more subject to cover, the introduction of the blood evidence into the case. He shimmied step-by-step through the material exactly as though directed and choreographed by the notes Klaus had given her.

"Did Mr. Zhukovsky provide you with information relating to the residence of the victim?"

"He gave us her address, and he gave us his copy of her key. She lived on the top floor in a condo on Eighth Street in Monterey."

"What happened then?"

"I took a statement from Mr. Zhukovsky. Then Officer Martinez and I proceeded to the victim's apartment."

"What time was this?"

Detective Banta didn't need to consult her report. "Sunday morning at eleven-forty-five A.M. Her home was only a couple of miles from the station, near Monterey Peninsula College. It's a four-unit complex. We went up to the third floor, which was entirely taken up by her unit. We knocked and received no answer, and there was no manager on the premises, so we went in."

Nina scratched her chin and thought, Legal issue: illegal entry? Again, Klaus hadn't raised this possibility. She scrolled through the details. The cops were investigating a fresh homicide; they had been given a key by the nearest relative; they needed to enter in case another victim was inside, or maybe a killer, or maybe fresh evidence.

Not a prayer on this one. Klaus had called it right. She kept her mouth shut.

Nothing broke open for her in the next few minutes of testimony. Jaime took Banta through the forensics report. She had supervised the fingerprinting and collection of samples.

Banta reported on the fingerprints without expressing the disappointment she no doubt felt. None matched Stefan's; that was the point Nina would return to on cross-exam. Many could not be identified.

Photos of Christina's apartment now being passed around the jury were snapshots from the life of a cultured woman who sometimes entertained lavishly. Her large, country-style kitchen gleamed with every kind of copper pot and pan. Her dining room table was—had been; the condo had been sold a month before—a long slab of pine ten feet long, incongruously covered with a white Battenburg lace tablecloth. Her taste in art had run to the Russian avant-garde: Liubov Popova, Tatlin, Malevich. The brightly hued blocks of color in the lithographs were precisely offset by the traditional black Bechstein piano that took up one side of the living room.

Christina had been an intense, intelligent person, Nina decided. A cautious person, with two sets of bolts on the door to keep herself safe. Yet this smart lady had let in—no doubt about it; the door had been unlocked from the inside—her killer.

She had kept a crowbar leaning against the wall by the headboard of her bed. She hadn't had time to get it and use it. Nina knew about those bedside bats, golf clubs, rebar pieces, makeshift weapons kept just in case, in the homes of women living alone. Long before, her own father had given her a shillelagh, a knobbed club of Irish origin and real heft. She had brought it with her from Tahoe and currently kept it tucked within reach under her bed at Aunt Helen's.

Maybe she should keep it by the front door.

Jaime moved on to the collection of glass and blood at Christina's Eighth Street apartment.

Banta testified that, although an effort had been made to sweep up, preliminary tests showed the presence of blood in the kitchen. Several tiny broken pieces of glass had been found on the kitchen floor. They fell around a central point of impact—a bar stool pulled up to the central island. A few slivers were found on the broom, and one had also stuck to the dustpan found in the pantry with the broom, although that had probably been washed.

Pay dirt had been struck in the kitchen trash can: the rest of the glass pieces. Nina had a point to make about that, but she decided to save her questions for the forensic technician who would be coming after Banta.

Banta went on in her relaxed, matter-of-fact voice. The glass came from a set of small Czech tumblers found in the kitchen. Traces of cognac from the bottle of Courvoisier V.S.O.P. found on the kitchen counter could be identified on the broken glass in the trash. DNA testing had picked up Christina's saliva.

And no one else's.

Christina had been drinking, but her killer hadn't. Had the killer turned down an offer? Or had she been drinking to buck herself up and not felt friendly enough to offer the same person she had just let into her place late at night a drink?

And the killer had sat informally at a bar stool, not on the red leather couch in Christina's art-filled living room. To Nina, all signs pointed to someone she knew very well. Like her brother, Alex. Or maybe this rejected boyfriend Paul had just learned about, named Sergey Krilov.

Or maybe a new man in her life. Larry Santa Ana, the burly juror, studied Stefan's face, and Nina read his: it wasn't too hard to picture big, hunky Stefan making eyes at a woman. Nina did not like this sort of juror, who fills the holes in testimony with personal life experience. It wasn't too hard to picture Santa Ana making eyes at a woman, either.

"Using all the standard presumptive tests, we searched for the presence of blood throughout the apartment," Banta said, and Nina jerked back to her testimony. "We were able to locate traces of blood that did not match the victim's on a few pieces of glass found on the floor and in the kitchen trash can."

"Indicating what, if anything, to you as a trained homicide investigator?"

"That the victim hit her killer with a glass, cutting him. She probably threw it."

"Did you find blood anywhere else?"

"No."

A hurting Madeleine Frey fidgeted, massaging her left leg. Nina caught her grimacing as Frey crossed it over her right leg. She hoped Frey could pay attention anyway, as Jaime had come to the final and most damning testimony of the day.

"And did you subsequently compare the blood on the

kitchen floor and in the kitchen trash with the blood of the defendant in this case?"

"Yes. The defendant gave his permission to have a blood sample drawn so that DNA comparison tests could be made. Those tests were carried out on May second." Stefan had sworn the tests would clear him, so Klaus, entirely properly, had allowed them without objection. Ginger would be evaluating the prosecution's results, and continued to run new tests.

"Did you thereafter receive the certified state laboratory results?"

"Yes. In late May."

"And what were those results?" Klaus had stipulated that Banta could testify about this, although technically Abbott Lumley, the forensics tech and blood expert, should. Many decisions had been made before Nina's entry into the case, and she didn't agree with any of them. She chewed on her thumbnail impotently. Beside her, Klaus listened intently with his little smile, as though he already knew all the answers and would bring them forth at the proper time.

"According to the report, there was one chance in about three million that the blood did not match the defendant," Banta went on.

"What did you conclude from that scientific result?"

"That the blood in Christina Zhukovsky's apartment had been left by the defendant, Stefan Wyatt." Crowning the moment with a long, level, accusatory stare at Stefan, Detective Banta had just produced the piece of evidence that Stefan couldn't explain, the one that made him look like a liar. Stefan put a hand on his cheek but couldn't hide the anger in his eyes, which wouldn't look good to Larry Santa Ana, who had followed Banta's testimony with trustful approval.

"That test was wrong," Stefan whispered to Nina.

"They screwed up." A lot of lifers had used that line, and Nina hoped he wouldn't be one of them.

Ginger would be testifying all too soon, when the defense had a chance to present its case, and her testimony would convict or clear Stefan, Nina was sure of it. Ginger had called at seven to say she was awaiting final results and to wish Nina luck.

The blood was Stefan's. Then he was guilty, the jurors would be thinking, and they weren't the only ones. The reporters in the seats at the back energetically scratched on pads, preparing to expose his guilt to the world in tomorrow's *Salinas Californian, Monterey Herald, San Jose Mercury News,* and *San Francisco Chronicle.* Of course, while convicting him in the court of public opinion, they would be sure to include a line about innocent until proven guilty.

Not too far from here, a man named Scott Peterson would be tried for the murder of his wife and unborn son. Although the trial had been moved from his hometown of Modesto, the whole country already knew all about the case from the papers. An "unbiased" jury, even in another county, did not really exist.

It worried Nina that Stefan's case kept blowing up bigger in the papers. Each night, the jury was told to go home and avoid the speculation on TV and in the newspapers. Was Larry Santa Ana really able to do that?

Jaime put the forensics report on the blood into evidence and Judge Salas read it over carefully. The previously marked report became an official part of the case, the monster land mine Klaus and Nina would have to defuse later if they were to win.

"You may cross-examine," Judge Salas said after the lunch break and a session in his chambers working on jury instructions.

Nina's turn had come. She stayed at her table, her notes stacked in front of her. She breathed deeply, going for the receptive, open mood Klaus had suggested. "Detective Banta, you have testified that the blood found on small glass slivers at Christina Zhukovsky's apartment matched the blood of the defendant, Stefan Wyatt; is that correct?"

"Correct. Actually, the lab tested more than one sample."

"Did the lab do RFLP DNA testing, otherwise known as restriction fragment length polymorphism analysis, on those samples?" She had memorized the words given to her by Ginger just the night before, and hoped she hadn't scrambled them. Having the terminology correct was important. The jury needed to believe she knew what she was talking about.

"No."

"You know about this method of testing?"

"Yes."

"Isn't that method likely to yield higher statistically individualizing results than the less delicate PCR DNA analysis?"

"Yes."

"Why wasn't that done?"

"You need larger samples than we had."

"You were able to locate only traces of blood on a few minuscule pieces of glass, is that correct?"

"Yes."

"That would be blood in extremely small amounts?"

"In small amounts. Correct."

"Are the bits of glass found at the scene and tested for blood here in court for the jury to see today?"

"No."

"Well, can you help us with this, so that the jury can visualize this. How small were they? This big?" She held her thumb and forefinger about an inch apart.

"Not that large."

"This?" She narrowed the gap.

"Smaller."

"How about this?" asked Nina. She held a pin up.

"They weren't that large."

"No, the samples were about as big as the head of this pin—wouldn't that be fair to say?" Nina asked, knowing full well they were about that big.

"Yes."

"Your Honor, may I approach the jury?"

"You're not going to poke me with that, are you, Ms. Reilly?" said the judge, who didn't approve of her methods but apparently was willing to sacrifice his prejudice in the service of a little humor.

"No. I'm just afraid some of the jurors might not be able to see the extremely small amount of 'evidence' we are talking about unless I bring it up very close."

Some laughter followed her. She enjoyed the attention, and even the jury made an amused show of studying the head of the pin she held. She laid it carefully down on the table and turned back to face Kelsey Banta. "Did you take into account the possibility of contamination of evidence from such small sources?"

"We did. There is always a possibility of contamination if standard protocols for collection of evidence and PCR DNA testing are not followed. However, we were scrupulous." She looked smug.

Nina knew they would have to come back to the evidence on the glass again, but she felt good about leaving it for now. "At the time of booking, did you have an opportunity to perform any sort of physical survey, or did you observe the defendant's body?"

"Yes, I took a good look at him."

"Did you observe his hands?"

"Yes."

"You took a good look at his face?"

"Yes."

"Did you observe any dried blood on his hands, his face, his arms, or any other place on his body?"

The smugness dropped. Detective Banta sat up straighter and removed all expression from her face, hiding behind professionalism, which even Larry Santa Ana, Nina was happy to see, duly noted.

Nina repeated, "Any scabs anywhere on Stefan Wyatt?"

"No."

"So, no blood. But as a seasoned homicide investigator, wouldn't you expect to find evidence of bleeding on the defendant charged with murdering this woman?"

"I suppose."

"You suppose you should find injuries on the defendant, when his blood was supposedly found at the scene?"

"Yes. I would expect that."

"Yet you found none. Isn't that what you stated?"

"There was a small amount at the scene, so the cuts could be tiny. They must've dried up. Or he cleaned himself up, would be my take."

"But at least you saw cuts on him?"

"Not really. No."

"You looked?" This put Banta in a dilemma. If she said she hadn't looked, Stefan might have had cuts. But then the police work would have been shoddy, which might put other evidence in jeopardy.

"I looked," Banta said grimly.

"Ms. Banta, give us your opinion as an experienced police investigator: how could Stefan Wyatt's blood be in Christina Zhukovsky's apartment, without the defendant showing any evidence of a cut on his body?"

"Maybe it came from his nose or mouth."

Every once in a while a witness departed from the expected and rustled up a confounding suggestion like this. Banta appeared amazed at herself. She had apparently just thought of this. At the moment, she probably felt damn cool.

"Do you have any evidence at all it did?" Nina asked quickly, hoping to puncture her confidence.

"Not really, but where else—"

"Detective, are you testifying that your explanation is that Mr. Wyatt had no evidence of cuts because the blood came from his mouth?"

"Where else could it have come from?"

"Let's see," Nina said. "Ms. Zhukovsky throws a glass at him and connects, and he bleeds from the mouth?"

"Well . . ." Banta looked unhappy.

"He opened his mouth really wide and the glass came flying in? I've heard of catching thrown grapes, but a brandy glass? Some shot! Amazing!"

"Objection," Jaime said, drowning out the ripple of laughter behind him.

"Withdrawn," Nina said before he elaborated. "Have you considered that the blood could be old—from a previous occasion?"

No answer.

"Was the blood sample sent to the lab and found on the glass wet?"

"No."

"It was dry. And can it be dated exactly, as to when the blood might have been left in the apartment?"

"No."

"There is no way to say for sure the blood was left that night?"

"No."

She had pushed a few small holes through the wall of

prosecutorial evidence. The jurors seemed relieved to see
the defense acting like contenders.

Driving the Bronco slowly home along Highway 68, Nina
revisited her cross-examination of Kelsey Banta, this time
doing it better, washing away the scenery, the greenery, the
bleak gray evening sky. Windows wide open, she tried to
take in some fresh air after the close air of court but felt
suffocated. She couldn't remember a time a case had
started as dreadfully as this one had, and when one had
seemed so fatally proscribed in advance.

Maybe it was the graveyard scene constantly recalled
to mind, or maybe it was Stefan, hardly taking a breath beside her at the table all day. She had sensed his desperation,
and the jury must sense it, too. He had the attitude of the
condemned, and though he rose to the occasion whenever
she had a minute to talk to him, he squeezed out his re-
marks like a man gripped by a vise, out of contact with his
own innards.

He looked woebegone, like a sad sack, and Americans
don't trust losers. She wanted the jury to know him as she
was beginning to know him, but he couldn't help. He was
afraid. His very presence in the courtroom was working
against him.

Stefan needed a pep talk. Klaus could do that. She
would ask him to do that.

She stopped at Trader Joe's to pick up place mats,
boxed sushi and a bottle of white wine for herself, chicken
taquitos and vanilla soda for Bob along with a salad he
probably wouldn't eat, arriving at the shabby white cottage
in Pacific Grove late for dinner. As always. As always, she
thought of their warm cabin in South Lake Tahoe, and
asked herself if she had done the right thing coming back
to the Central Coast.

• • •

Right after she took the job with Klaus, a few days before Paul had popped the question, Nina and Bob had moved their few things over to the house she had inherited from her aunt Helen, which Nina had been renting out for income.

Paul hadn't wanted her to leave, but having Bob sleeping in his office wasn't working, so he came around and helped them in the end, although now she understood his vigorous objections better. Here he was getting up the nerve to propose, and she was moving out.

While Paul had unloaded boxes, Nina cleared dust balls from corners and cupboards, Hitchcock stuck his doggy snout where it didn't belong, and Bob cut open the small pile of boxes piled on the living room floor. She had tried to stay cheerful and tried to engage Bob in making some future plans about how they would be spending their time here, but the move had been an ordeal.

Coming up the rickety steps, Nina held her case in one hand, and in the other the bag of groceries, which she set on the porch while she found her key and opened the door.

"Bob!" she called out.

"Yo, Mom!" he replied from his bedroom.

Most of their furniture was still at Tahoe, which Nina had left nearly three months before. The couch here was secondhand, and there was no fireplace to cheer the damp coastal nights. Thick area rugs covered the worn hardwood in the living room. Pillows, two easy chairs, a television stand, and a low table made up the rest of the furniture. Cheap vinyl blinds the previous tenants had installed for privacy were the only window coverings.

She put the groceries away and put Bob's meal into the microwave.

The bare bones of the cottage, an old white frame built over a hundred years ago, would be lovely if you could see them better, she decided, maneuvering herself onto the couch with her tray. She poured herself a glass of wine and popped a wasabi-and-soy-sauced piece of California roll into her mouth. The house was ideally located, up a slope and just a block from Lover's Point, offering a glimpse of the deep blue Pacific from its front yard. Various utilitarian renovations had taken place over the years to keep the tenants happy.

Some things would have to change, and soon. Nina was not the kind of person who considered her car or her house an outer symbol of some inner person, but she had her standards. The artificial turf leading up to the carport would have to go.

But why worry about this old place? If she married Paul, they would have to find a larger home that would suit all three of them.

After a few sips, Nina got up again. She set two new white plates on the woven blue place mats she had bought and found silverware and napkins. She set a square candle in the middle of the table and lit it, put the food on, then poured Bob a glass filled with ice and soda, and herself a tall ice water to chase the rest of the wine in her glass. The microwave beeped. From the hallway she called to Bob through his open door. "Dinner!"

"Busy," he said.

"Come and eat," she said. She waited, but getting no further response, walked to the open door and looked inside.

His room consisted of a bed with a wool blanket borrowed from Paul. His closet, gaping open, held a gym bag spilling its contents on the floor and empty metal hangers on the rod above. No posters decorated the bedroom walls; no bonsai tree like the one he had nursed at Tahoe spruced up this barren windowsill. Bob sat at a bare wooden table with his feet up, wearing headphones and an entranced expression.

She walked over to him and removed the headphones. "I hereby command the pleasure of your company at dinner." She didn't make it a question, because that opened up a discussion, and all she wanted to do was to wolf down the rest of her sushi and turn on her precious half-hour news show, which made her forget her own concerns.

"I'm not hungry."

"You ate?"

"Crackers and cheese."

She hesitated, then said, "Come anyway." She led, and eventually, grudgingly, he followed.

He sat down at the table across from her and in front of his steaming taquitos, arms crossed. The late evening sun spilled over the table and over his pinched face. His hair, a dark mop, was getting long.

"So, how was school?"

Eyes as dark as black coffee glowered. "If you really want to know, it sucks."

"Please don't use that kind of language," she said, knowing this was a futile battle, that she should respond to substance not style, but exhausted by the prospect.

"Well, you asked."

"I know it's hard, going to a new school—"

"I want to go home."

She opened her mouth, but nothing came out. She closed it.

"Back to Tahoe."

The final sushi had stuck in her throat, so she cleared it. "High school is always tough. I cried every day for the first three weeks—"

He interrupted. He was not here to listen to her experiences; he was busy fighting through his own. "People here are different."

"How?"

Sometimes lately this boy she knew so well, inside out, put on a face she didn't recognize. Now came one of those moments. "I can't explain, if you don't know. Plus, I never know what we're going to do. I mean, are we staying or going? If you get married, do we move back to that condo with Paul? Can I go live with Uncle Matt back in Tahoe, since I don't like it here? Do I show some guys they can't screw around with me, or let 'em do it because I'm leaving anyway and it doesn't matter? Do I go out for cross-country or will I have to quit? Why bother to join a club, if we're leaving?"

His forcefulness blew her down, typhoon-style. When Bob was a toddler and he cried, she would wrap him up in her arms, kiss his tears away, and make it all better. Unfortunately, that was no longer an option. He was now bigger than she was for starters, and he seemed to have developed an aversion to her touch. "We discussed all this. There will be some changes, but they aren't decided yet, and you will be in on any further decisions, I promise."

"You told me I have to go to school here, so I'm going. That doesn't mean I like it."

"I went to that high school. Carmel High has a good reputation—you have to give it a chance . . ."

"Don't tell me you had a great time, because, Mom, I'm tellin' you, I won't believe it."

He knew she had not. She had rebelled against her parents, given them gray hair, run around, done all kinds of things she shouldn't have done. "Here's the thing I've learned. High school culture is its own world, and you should know the world's bigger than that. You don't have to hook up with that scene. You've been to Europe. I mean, you don't have to wear a letterman's jacket to be accepted!"

He sighed, a world-weary sigh befitting a traveler who was stuck in a culture where many people did view a letterman's jacket as the epitome of achievement.

She got up and began to make herself a supplemental chicken sandwich with chicken from a can, contrarily wishing Bob did want a letterman's jacket. He had once loved sports. "Honey," she said finally, "I can't stand having you unhappy. What can I do?" It was the question she had to ask, whether she wanted to hear the answer or not.

He had an answer ready. As an interim measure, until a final decision was made on where they would live, he wanted to go back to Tahoe and get his belongings. He needed his skateboard, his bike, all his things. "I can't live out of just one bag." He had only the things with him that he had taken on a summer trip to Sweden.

"We'll buy you some clothes if you need them."

"I need my stuff!"

She recognized from when he was little the stubborn yet brittle look that held tears inside. Times like these, she hated being a mother. "After the trial is over."

"Now!"

"Soon. I can't go while I'm in trial, Bob. You know that." She petted Hitchcock, who was the only one who didn't give a damn where they were, who only cared that he was with them and that his food bowl had been filled.

"I'll go without you."

She reacted to the blow by leaping up to tidy. "What?"

"I can take the train to Truckee. Uncle Matt will pick me up from there."

"But—"

"I'm going."

For quite a while, they went back and forth. Eventually, her ability to structure a reasonable argument vaporized in the face of his strenuous desire. Nina agreed to drive him up to the train station early Saturday morning. He would go for the weekend.

Her phone rang. Bob cleared the table and went back to his CDs while Klaus spoke.

"You have the autopsy and material sent from the medical examiner's office?" he asked.

"Of course." She finished off the sandwich.

"Susan Misumi is up tomorrow."

"Right," she said.

"I enjoyed the picture you painted today of the brandy glass flying into Stefan's wide-open mouth."

"Thank you. Did you call about anything particular?"

"I was just checking in," Klaus said hesitantly, and Nina experienced another knuckle-biting moment of doubt. Had he forgotten why he called?

She asked him to talk to Stefan about trying to appear more confident in court, and, with a tolerant sigh, Klaus promised he would. "His courtroom style won't win the case."

She knew it, and she knew very well the pitfalls in trying to control every ineffable in a case, but creating a good impression was about the only contribution Stefan could make at this point, and she felt he should be doing it. As for Klaus, he was an enigma.

Only thing she knew for sure was that second chair in this trial was an active place to be.

Later, from her bed, Nina called Paul. "Wish you were here. I could use your—"

"I like the sound of that," he interrupted. "What are you wearing?"

"A cold compress on my neck."

"Oh, yeah, you sexy thing."

She laughed, then said more soberly, "Detective Banta practically convicted Stefan single-handedly today."

"She's very experienced."

Nina heard the comedy station in the background. "You knew her, didn't you?"

"Way back when. Sure, I knew Kelsey."

"What did you think of her?" Nina didn't know what she was looking for and wasn't sure she wanted to find it anyway.

"Straight arrow," Paul said.

"Did you date her?"

"Why do you ask?"

"She's attractive."

He seemed to find the question amusing. "I like her, and I never knew her to tweak the truth. But no, I never dated her."

"Oh. Okay."

"Nina, she was married. Then, when her brother got killed, she was a secret drinker. Not my idea of a fun date." He waited for her to say something. When she didn't he said, "You there?"

"Just silently finishing my wine here," she said.

He laughed. "Who's up tomorrow?"

"Uh, the medical examiner. Dr. Misumi."

"Susan," Paul said.

The way he said her name, a kind of warm familiarity as he wound his mouth around the word, made Nina sit up in bed alertly. "That's right. Susan Misumi. You know her?"

"Her, I dated," Paul said.

9

DON'T ASK, DON'T TELL HAD been the arrangement between Paul and Nina regarding other recent partners. Even the fact that there was an arrangement had been a don't tell. In truth, they had never talked about it.

Nina admitted to herself now that she had been cowardly. She herself had nothing to tell that he didn't already know, and she wasn't certain how she would react to finding out about Paul's other lovers. She hadn't asked him for any details, had taken the news the night before with admirable lawyerly equanimity.

Then at four A.M. she woke up worrying, not about Stefan or Klaus or Bob, but about Paul, thinking, I shouldn't have moved out of his condo like that, on such short notice, without dealing with the implications first. I could have talked Paul into moving somewhere bigger, where he could have his office and space. Bob could be at the far end of the house with the space apart from us that he needs, too. I should have resolved the marriage issue right away, when Paul asked.

She knew the ostensible reason they had moved here. Aunt Helen's house, Nina's house now, had been available, and she hadn't had much time. But she had lurched gracelessly away from Paul, and she wouldn't be surprised if he held it against her, even if only unconsciously.

Putting the ostensible reason aside, why had she moved so swiftly?

After half an hour of lying in the dark with thoughts stomping heavily through her mind, she gave up and turned on the bed stand light. Her window was open and she could hear the distant bark of seals. The fog moved around in the room with her, like a living presence. In the little room down the hall, Bob muttered restlessly in his sleep.

Paul should give up on me, she thought with a sudden conviction, experiencing an awful mix of fear, insecurity, and loneliness.

After a year of seeing no one but Paul, and years before of seeing him nonexclusively, she should know what to do, but she felt as if she were balanced in the center of the see-saw, unable to move. Either direction, and she would land with a nasty thud.

They had such differences between them, and those differences could be fatal. She flashed to unhappy pictures of Paul in her mind: Paul cleaning his guns; Paul describing various acts of violence he had committed; Paul drunk one night when she had needed him; Paul telling her what to do, trying to push her around, resenting her for being the lawyer employing him as investigator, second-guessing her, not respecting her opinions.

But then: Paul making love to her so sweetly a few nights before. And: Paul's smarts, Paul's jokes, Paul's charm, his devotion over the past years, even when she had been married to another man.

And the moment that had defined their relationship forever: Paul lying in wait outside her house one night, waiting for a killer to arrive and try to break in; Paul killing for her, burying the body God knew where. No one except Bob had any inkling of it. They never talked about it. "I took out the trash," Paul had once told her, and she—she had thanked him.

She loved so much about him, and she believed he loved her. He thought he had proved he would do anything for her, but she could never bridge the distance that the killing had opened between them. He had fearsome qualities that scared her. Ultimately, she did not trust him completely.

I love him, she thought as she had so many times before. I can't do without him. But . . .

She gave up and wandered into the living room. From outside, a streetlight spilled a soft glow over the old couch. She had loaned her cabin at Tahoe to a woman in trouble who had three kids, who now sat on the new brown couch she had bought, used the plates from Mikasa she and Bob had picked out. Another woman lawyer now sat in the Starlake Building office with the orange client chairs Nina had bought at Ric's in Reno one snowy day . . .

What am I doing here? she asked herself. Three hundred miles from Tahoe, where her home and her work were, she existed in a time warp, working for her boss from years ago, Bob not happy.

She answered her own question. She was here for herself and Paul.

Paul, who had told her just a few hours before, "You weren't available at the time, and Susan is an old friend, so we got together a few times. That's all." She had heard the small resentment in his voice, as if it were her fault he'd had to find another lover to fill in the space.

Due to other matters Judge Salas had to take up, court resumed at eleven on Friday morning and was scheduled to run only through twelve, then from one-thirty to three. Nina wore her black suit with the white silk blouse with cuffs. After some hesitation she had also sprayed on some ancient Chanel No. 5 of Aunt Helen's she found hidden at the back of the bathroom cupboard. Two ibuprofen, Rice Krispies, and orange juice sloshed against each other in her stomach.

As usual, all the seats had been taken. Madeleine Frey had brought a cushion for her leg today, and Larry Santa Ana was talking across her to another male juror, who listened attentively. He was a schmoozer, and Nina didn't like networking jurors. Silently, selfishly, she prayed for Ms. Frey's leg to feel better fast, and for Larry to take a header. The two young women she had managed to get on the jury seemed relatively indifferent to Stefan's charm. His perpetually wringing hands and sagging face went beyond the cute-puppy effect, straying into mangy-dog territory, which didn't help his cause with them.

Today, trying to follow Klaus's advice about giving a straight-backed, upstanding-citizen impression, Stefan wore another new suit with squarer shoulders.

Jaime had the staunch posture and sanguine smile of a prosecutor who hasn't been touched yet. Nina wanted to wipe that grin off his face very soon, yet there was little she could do at this phase of the trial, because the police witnesses in general were competent people who had done their job and weren't playing games. Kelsey Banta slouched in her seat next to him, as relaxed as if she were watching TV, the hard work over for her.

Paul sat in the audience behind them, a fence between her and the tough world out there. And Klaus, beside Nina and smelling like a rose, predominated over a court in some faraway universe, peacefully next to Stefan, speckled hands folded on the table, not a thought in his head, for all she could tell.

"Call Susan Misumi." Heads craned. Dr. Misumi was brought in from the hall, where the witnesses had to wait, by the bailiff.

She was no raving beauty, Nina was relieved to see as she stepped into the witness box and sat down, placing her reports carefully in front of her. She wore the uniform of women professionals in California, a black suit jacket with a green, lace-tipped tank T-shirt showing a subtle bit of cleavage, expensive black slacks, and shoes with a slight lift to the heel. About Paul's age, fortyish, reading glasses that dangled from an artistically beaded chain around her neck. She had classic Japanese skin, very pale and fine, bright eyes, and a face that tended toward the round. The feathery bangs probably cost a fortune to maintain.

A smart woman who took care of herself, great, but why would Paul be attracted to her? Nina couldn't help remembering his comment about having dated her. In her mind, Paul's type would be a blonde bimbo, lots of makeup—was *this* Paul's type? This important lady answering Jaime's questions in a measured voice, saying she had in fact gotten her medical degree at Johns Hopkins, received specialized training in forensic pathology at Stanford, and been appointed Assistant Chief Medical Examiner for the County of Monterey some four years before, couldn't be Paul's type. She spent her days cutting open dead people! She did have a nice voice, low and musical, though, and a beautiful mouth, with full cushiony lips.

The mouth must have been what got him.

Nina felt a blurry sea of hot juicy emotion, part anger, part self-dislike, part hatred of this woman, part admiration for her. Sum it up as jealousy, a feeling she remembered well from the days before her divorce from Jack McIntyre had become final.

Klaus was supposed to do the cross-exam, but Nina knew by now not to rely on him, so she began taking notes, though her eyes burned and she found it hard to look at the witness.

Dr. Misumi looked hard back at her. She must know about Nina's place in Paul's life, and she must care.

Misumi went through the autopsy report for the jury. She had been called to the scene, made sure photos were taken of the body of Christina Zhukovsky in situ, and ordered the body taken to Natividad Hospital in Salinas, where the county morgue was. She had also supervised the opening of the coffin and the photos and removal of any leftover bits of human remains.

At the morgue, she had determined from the relaxation of rigor mortis and other signs that the victim had been dead for between approximately twenty-six and twenty-eight hours, making time of death between one and three A.M. the previous morning, April 12. The victim had not been killed at the scene, but had been brought there at some indeterminate time—Nina noted this—and then buried. Stefan claimed he had spent Friday night into Saturday morning drunk, in the arms of Erin, who could hardly corroborate, being drunk herself.

"The immediate cause of death was asphyxia. The jugular veins were pressed, which prevents blood returning from the brain. The blood backing up in the brain leads to unconsciousness, depressed respiration, and asphyxia. She suffocated due to blunt force trauma to the neck," Dr. Misumi said directly to the jury.

"And on what do you base this opinion?" Jaime asked.

"Well, on both exterior and interior evidence. I examined the exterior of the victim, the skin and hair first. The body exhibited obvious contusions on the anterior neck," she said. "The front of the neck." Photos went around the jury. Toughened by the relentlessly graphic photos by now, nobody batted an eye. "I noted one thumb touch pad contusion on the left posterior section."

"Indicating?"

"Manual strangulation. Often only the thumb makes a mark on the neck. The fingers don't press as deeply."

"What if anything did you conclude from this mark?"

"That the victim was approached from behind by a right-handed person who reached around"—she clasped her own neck with her right hand—"and squeezed deeply, fingers against the throat. She was probably being held tightly against the body of the killer behind her."

"Any other bruises?"

"On the neck, there were also two curvilinear abrasions on the anterior neck. The photo marked Exhibit A-twelve."

"Do you have an opinion as to what would have caused such abrasions?"

"The abrasions were caused by fingernails."

"The killer's?"

"No. The victim's. What happened is that the victim put her hands up to try to pry away the fingers of the attacker." She paused and looked at the jury. Madeleine Frey's eyes filled and she rubbed her leg, and Nina thought, This woman is going to be a problem.

"There were also petechiae, small hemorrhages of the skin. They look like pinpoints of red on the skin. They are a sign of asphyxiation."

"And where were these located?"

"I found petechiae in the mucosa of the lower lip. I didn't find them on the neck or anywhere on the external skin, on the conjunctiva of the eyes, or on the deep internal organs. You do look for petechiae there, but their absence doesn't disprove strangulation."

Copies of photos of Misumi's "petechiae" were now

going around. Even the hardened jurors blanched at the one Misumi was now discussing.

"There were also internal signs of strangulation. Here. Exhibit A-fourteen," she said. "I took that photograph at the postmortem."

"And what does it indicate?"

"See the little red spots? Petechiae."

"Located where?"

"On the underside of the scalp. In the picture, the scalp was shown reflected forward over the face"—and this was something even Nina couldn't stand to look at—"which shows the undersurface of the scalp. Petechiae due to strangulation were found there."

"And did you note any other internal evidence of strangulation?"

Misumi picked up her report and read from it. "I did a complete dissection, removing the larynx, including the hyoid bone. It wasn't broken, but it only gets broken in about one third of strangulation cases, so that's not telling. I examined the superficial and deep musculature. Nothing there, no contusions. I examined the laryngeal skeleton for fracture. Nothing. I then opened the cervical spine and examined it for injury. Nothing. So the internal examination of the neck was, I would say, inconclusive, but the external evidence was quite clear."

Jaime had been sitting at the counsel table as he fired these questions. Now he went around the counsel table, sucking in his gut, an imposing, stocky, authoritative figure for the jury to observe. Standing near both the jury box and Stefan, he asked, "Is there any way to tell whether the attacker was a man or woman based on your postmortem, Doctor?"

"You could estimate the amount of force involved,

which in this case was considerable, to leave the thumb impression. But no, that wouldn't rule out a woman. Very little force is needed to strangle someone who is unconscious or intoxicated, especially a small woman like this one. Although the blood tests showed the victim had not been drinking much, even a small force applied in the right place can get past the protective muscles and skeleton."

"And—"

"May I add something?"

"Surely," Jaime said, waving his hand in courtly fashion.

"The amount of force required also varies depending on the amount of neck musculature of the victim. In this case the victim was somewhat frail, with rather less musculature than I would expect. That means less force would have been needed, than, for example, to strangle a football player."

"You're saying it would have been easy for a muscular young man to do the job?" Jaime asked.

"Oh, yes. If she was unable to get away from him."

"Did you try to match the thumb contusion with thumbprints of the defendant?"

"That can be done only very rarely, and not in this case."

Nina noted this, thinking, Maybe Ginger can do better.

"Which leads us to that glass," Jaime said.

"The broken glass?"

"Yes. Did you find any glass slivers in the clothing or on the body of the victim?"

"No," Misumi said definitely.

"Lastly, did you do an examination on the bones that were found in Stefan Wyatt's car on the morning he was arrested?"

"We examined the bones and established that they belonged in the coffin found in the grave below the body of Christina Zhukovsky. After that determination was made, the bones were returned to the next of kin, Alex Zhukovsky, and it is my understanding that all the bones were then cremated." She glanced at some notes. "Oh, let me correct that. The defense forensics expert still has two bones pursuant to an agreement with our office."

"Thank you." Jaime sat down. As he did, a stocky blond man sitting at the back of the courtroom left. Nina felt Paul turning to watch, and she glanced at the man, but quickly returned to her study of Susan Misumi. First, Misumi's eyes studied Paul, who was looking away. He turned back to the front and she caught him with her eyes.

She smiled. Nina, observing her, did not see Paul's reaction, but the smile went on for a significant period of time, about as long as it takes for two smiles to tango.

Then, as Klaus took the cross-examination, Misumi looked disappointed, maybe, as though she had wanted to engage Nina. Klaus had two points to make, and he repeated them several times in different ways—the thumbprint couldn't be matched to Stefan, and no other testimony she had given implicated Stefan in the crime. And Christina could have been strangled by a woman.

Klaus seemed full of energy. His questions were pointed, and he really did have a lot of the old charm, working the jury as he went. He didn't forget what he was going to say next.

He was fine. Nina waited from second to second for a lapse, but there wasn't one. Was he having major problems, or wasn't he?

Judge Salas had been watching the clock. At 2:45 P.M. he began getting restless. The minute Klaus finished, he gave the jury their weekend instructions not to talk to anyone about the case and not to read the papers or watch any TV news.

The gavel rapped. Salas disappeared. All rose while the

jurors filed out, looking as if they had paid their dues today. Then the courtroom emptied fast.

"Chin up," Klaus told Stefan as he was led into the back.

Nina drove them back in the Jag in silence. Klaus rested his head against the back of his seat and closed his eyes, and Nina thought about strangulation and Susan Misumi.

About how she would like to strangle Susan Misumi.

Sandy had already left for the day. Nina returned some phone calls, and when Bear walked past the office, she called out, "Hey, hi, can I talk to you for a sec?"

"Sure."

Bear came in and his bulk filled the tiny office. Nina got up and shut the door. "What's up?" he said.

"I wanted to ask you a question. About Klaus." She saw the big man tense, and thought, He knows. "About how Klaus is doing."

"Seems to be fine," Bear said warily.

"You haven't noticed that he's—sketchy sometimes? Forgetting things? Not quite on the ball?"

"He's old, Nina. What do you expect?"

Nina decided to take the Bear by the horns. "Did you know he wasn't prepared for this trial? His investigator had barely done any work on the case. Klaus didn't file some crucial pretrial motions. He hasn't reanalyzed the blood evidence."

Bear was examining the old law books on the shelves. "Were you able to catch up?" he asked.

"You knew he wasn't ready. That's why you pushed to hire me."

"I have the highest confidence in you."

"The defense in this case is very weak, Bear. I'm not sleeping."

"I'm sorry about that, Nina. I really am. What can I do to help you?"

Nina folded her arms. "That's not the response I'm looking for."

"Okay. Okay." His sheer reluctance halted his habitually antsy style. "I'm going to tell you the truth. When you accepted, I was so happy I would have given you double the pay you asked for."

"That's good to hear, because I'm asking you right now to double my pay, because I'm doing double the work."

"All right," Bear said, humbled. "I'll talk to everyone and get you what you want, although don't expect Alan to be happy. He didn't want the case; he didn't want you; he didn't want the expense. I really feel bad, but I knew you cared about Klaus and could work with him, or around him. Thank you for staying."

Nina sighed. "He did all right today. We're catching up. I have Paul helping, Ginger, Sandy. If I only had another six months . . ."

"This is his last trial, Nina," Bear said. "We're going to have to talk to him after this. But you see, he doesn't realize what's happening. He thinks he's still right on top of everything. Or—I don't know, maybe he does realize, but he's hoping nobody else has noticed. It's humiliating for him. He took on Lyndon Johnson in the United States Supreme Court during the Vietnam War, Nina."

"I know. I'll try to keep him going."

"Sean wants us to bring you in permanently. Would you be interested?"

Nina put up her hands wearily and said, "That's for another day."

"You're supposed to say, 'I'm thrilled.' " He smiled and went out. Nina packed her case and put on her jacket.

In the garage, Alan Turk was just getting into his Ferrari. Nina called to him, "Glad I caught you." Surprised, he turned off the ignition and said, "Yup?"

"You were the first lawyer to see Stefan Wyatt on the night of his arrest, weren't you, Alan?"

"I was. Then I brought Klaus in."

"Did Wyatt say anything to you when you talked to him at the jail?"

The lawyer's lean face looked up uncertainly at her through the stylish glasses. "Say anything? Hell, no! I told him not to talk to me. I wouldn't let him. I wasn't going to be his lawyer and I did not want to know. So—that's it? Because I have a friend waiting."

"I just wondered why they called you."

"His brother, Gabe Wyatt, was my client."

"Oh, yes, that was it. What did you do for his brother? A will?"

"Why, Nina, you know that's confidential."

"We're in the same firm. Is there some conflict I should know about?"

"If there were a conflict, I might not even be able to tell you. The existence of a conflict might be confidential and not in the best interests of my client."

"Just a minute," Nina said. "I know you're in a hurry, but I have to get this straight. You won't even tell me what type of matter Gabe Wyatt was pursuing with you?"

"Sorry, no."

Something about his attitude bothered her. He wasn't just unhelpful, he seemed downright obstructive. "Do you have information from Gabe Wyatt or anyone else that might tend to exculpate Stefan Wyatt?" she asked directly.

"I can't answer that question," Alan said. Nina thought she saw fright in the flecked eyes behind the glasses. He powered up the car, revved it a few times, and backed out. Nina watched him go, her mind racing alongside.

10

AFTER LEAVING THE OFFICE, NINA met Paul and Bob for hot dogs and a sci-fi we-all-die movie downtown. Bob, in good spirits, kept his post-movie critique down to scathing.

"I'm going to Tahoe this weekend," he announced to Paul, full of plans about who he needed to see and what he would bring back.

"Really?" Paul said. "Well, blow me down. What a surprise."

"It was a sudden decision," Nina said. She hadn't told him. Why hadn't she told him? Because she knew what he would say. She spoiled Bob. She gave him anything he wanted. Whatever Paul said, she would feel her jaw clench at the interference. "It'll be a quick trip. He'll stay Saturday night with Matt and Andrea."

"You're not going?" Paul said.

"No."

"Good. Hey, Bob, say hi to Uncle Matt and Aunt Andrea for me," Paul said.

"How much will you pay me?" Bob asked.

Paul cuffed him, but with a smile.

They headed out into the cold night. Paul's car was

parked a few blocks down toward the bay. They walked, Bob beside Nina, Paul offering his arm to her, simply out for a pleasant evening. She thought, Does he compare my body with hers? How could he put those sensual hands of his on another woman's body? How could he? I'm full of self-pity and disaster already, she said to herself, and it's only been one week of trial stress. She laid her head against his shoulder.

Surprisingly, Bob wanted to talk about school. They were studying local history this week, and had gone on a field trip to a ranch in Carmel Valley. "We practiced roping skills. We got to try it in a ring."

"Not on a bull?" Nina asked, grateful for something to think about besides her personal issues.

"A cow," Bob said. "The guy who owns the bull calls him 'Devil Boy.' "

"Best stick with Bessie, then," Paul said. They had reached Fisherman's Wharf, and stood indecisively, the sea lions calling to them, Paul's warm car another block farther.

"Let's walk to the end of the pier," Bob urged.

"Homework?" Nina asked.

"I got it covered." He rushed ahead.

Nina and Paul strolled slowly behind him. "How would you say it went today in court?" Paul asked Nina. He had been out much of the day.

She told him. "Of course, we haven't gotten to our own case. So far, they're seeing only the prosecution's story. We have to be patient."

"I have complete faith in you."

"We've got a client whose blood was found at the scene of a murder. Alex Zhukovsky is hanging tough with his story. We don't know why anybody would want to kill Christina or want the old man's bones. We don't even have a decent theory. We don't have anything," Nina said shortly.

She wanted to stop into a souvenir shop to buy herself a chambered nautilus displayed in the window. They tested the door. The store was closed.

"We will," Paul promised. They caught up with Bob, who shooed them away, having run into some kids he knew from school. From a discreet distance, listening to the sea lions making their evening ruckus for a minute, they searched the calm waters to see if they could spot an otter. Paul said to Nina, "Hey, you didn't mention Susan would be testifying today."

She couldn't decide if he was studiously casual, or just casual. "True."

"Do you think she makes a good witness?"

"Oh, yeah. Just great. Her and her big fat lips."

He laughed. "She's not that bad looking," he said.

"Not surprising you'd feel that way."

He caught her face between his hands and held on gently. "What is it?"

She shook him off. "I don't expect to like prosecution witnesses."

"But her testifying against Wyatt isn't what you hold against her," he said, "is it? You're jealous."

"That's ridiculous."

"No need, you know. The minute I decided to get back with you, we broke it off."

"Did she drop you or did you drop her?"

He wrinkled his nose and sighed. "What's the difference?"

"It matters," she said stubbornly, arms crossed, unable to say why it should matter.

"I broke it off."

"Liar."

"Nina, this isn't like you."

"Yeah, it's me. It's me, in trial. I'm sorry."

He pulled her to him, trying to make up, she could

tell, but she couldn't. She moved away. She felt his eyes on her as she leaned out over the railing toward the water.

A small cruise boat docked farther down, and they watched the rowdy partygoers unload.

"C'mon, let's clear the air," Paul said. "Nina, I'm over forty. I've had past relationships. You knew that. I've had two wives, for Chrissake. And I slept with them. I'll bet you slept with your husbands, too, and there's no question about Kurt, either, now that I mention it, given the fact of Bob's existence!"

He had slept with Susan. She had known it, but the blood pounding in her head told her she had held a vain hope that he hadn't.

"You don't want to dredge up this old stuff," he went on, so reasonable.

The old stuff, as he put it, was already dredged and heaped up high, obscuring her rationality.

" 'Cause, just for example, you'd hate me reminding you about that kid you used to go skinny-dipping with, right? I mean, I didn't know you then or anything, so I have no reason whatsoever to picture you and him swimming on a warm evening out there with the bullfrogs and stars. You buck naked. With him."

Surprised that he was nursing a long-ago, minor mention of herself as a teenager hanging around the rocky pools in Carmel Valley with that wild-kid boyfriend of hers, she couldn't think of anything to say.

"Your clothes tossed behind on the hillside, a little pot in the air. Your hair wet, drifting all over the place. A bright moon. Him some prime example of young manhood. Shit, Nina." He frowned.

She couldn't help herself. She started to laugh. "Yeah, it was just like that, only you left out the poison oak I got, and the tick he got, and the shouting argument part."

"Just tell me his name," Paul said, responding to her,

now on a roll and just teasing. "So if I run into him mind-ing his own business one fine day, I know who to pound senseless."

Pelicans flew overhead and the black water lapped against the pilings and the shopkeepers turned out lights in the stores on each side of the pier. She kissed him. Gather-ing Bob up, they bought saltwater taffy and chewed on it as they walked back toward Alvarado downtown, past laugh-ter and the smell of coffee and grease coming from the crowded fish joints.

Bob skulked along behind them, kicking anything loose he could find on the pavement. "Being back at the old firm getting to you?" Paul asked Nina.

"It's like coming home after going to college or some-where. There's a big brother, Bear, who protects Daddy's image, and a new puppy, Sean, who nips. The dynamics are familiar and sometimes hard. I know they mostly support me. That's the good part."

"The bad part?"

"Progress doesn't usually involve coming home to roost. It's the kind of thing you do after a colossal failure. Now that I'm living here and working here again, I can't help feeling that I'm like a scared person running home. Like I can't cut it on my own somewhere else. Talk of a partnership just makes me nervous."

"A partnership?"

"Bear approached me about it."

"That would be good."

She twisted the ring, which seemed so tight tonight. "That would make Tahoe an impossibility, all right."

He picked at a splinter he had gotten leaning on the railing. "I like having you close."

"Maybe you shouldn't watch—I mean worry about me so much."

"Why shouldn't I try to protect you? You get in the most god-awful messes."

"I can handle my own messes."

"No, you can't." He said this with brutal conviction.

Nina raised her voice. "You're so damn protective, Paul. How long will it be before you try to get me to stop practicing criminal law?"

He unwound his arm from around her waist. "Stop it," he said. "Susan and I are not seeing each other. All right? Get that through your noggin."

"Let's forget it," she said, and she should have apologized again, but she was too angry about too many things and all of them were not about Paul. The best she could do was take his arm.

"What's next?" Paul asked, keeping his voice low with an effort Nina appreciated.

"Sandy set up appointments for you with Alex Zhukovsky; Stefan's girlfriend, Erin; his mother, Wanda; and his brother, Gabe. They'll all be on the stand in the next few days. She faxed you a list of my special concerns about what they might say. And you'll probably want to talk to Klaus's investigator."

"I meant what's next for tonight."

"Oh. We find your car and call it a night."

He nuzzled her hair. "Bob could stay with his grandpa again. He likes staying there."

"Not tonight."

"We need to be together. I've barely seen you, and I've slept with you exactly twice in the past two weeks."

"Don't get mad, Paul."

"I hate sleeping alone. I want you tonight." He pressed against her and she almost changed her mind. But she didn't.

"Soon, I promise."

• • •

Saturday morning, before driving Bob to the train, Nina stopped in to see Sandy at the office. She proofed and signed each paper Sandy shoveled toward her for the next half hour.

"When does Bob go?" Sandy asked.

Nina consulted the clock on the wall. Like everything else at the Pohlmann firm, it had a distinguished but dusty venerability. Outside, a few renegade wildflowers still waved between the weed sprouts of late summer. "His train's at around ten-thirty from San Jose. I wish I could go with him. I could check up on your daughter."

"No need," Sandy said. "We know what's happening. She calls Joseph every night."

How nice that Sandy's daughter liked talking to her father. Nina imagined Joe in the kitchen of their borrowed house at Big Sur, drinking a beer, maybe looking out at the pasture full of horses, the phone to his ear, emanating warm, loving vibes for his troubled daughter. That was the way it was supposed to be with fathers and daughters.

She couldn't remember it ever being that way with her and her father, Harlan. Her mother provided the shoulder while her father straggled behind her, a backdrop to her vitality. He beautifully provided all the practical things—the house, the cars, the bacon—while keeping his distance from her and Matt. Maybe his heart was squeezed tight already by their mother. At the end, when their mother was so sick and he had spent so much time nursing her, when was there time for two needy kids? Especially if you considered his girlfriend, Angie, must have been occupying him, too. . . .

"He keeps his mouth shut and lets her vent," Sandy said, speaking of her husband. "Says it's time for her to decide some things for herself."

"Sounds like a good relationship. Too bad your son isn't a big talker."

"I wish Wish would tell me more. I never know what he's up to. Thinks he's all grown up."

"Boys are hard."

"Bob stopped by the other day while you were in court."

"Oh?"

"He's not doing so good at the high school."

No doubt he had unloaded his closest secrets on Sandy. When had being a parent translated into being a pariah?

"I should go," Nina said, consulting her watch. She picked up part of a stack of paperwork on Sandy's desk and set it down again. "You go home now. Your work's done. We're okay. You need your weekend."

"What time will you be back?" Sandy said, rearranging the stack Nina had upset.

"Twelve-thirty?"

"Meet you here."

Back home, on Aunt Helen's porch, the bald happiness on Bob's face made Nina feel better about her decision to let him go alone. She pulled up to the cottage, but he had run down the front steps and short pathway in front to meet her before she even turned off the car.

"Ready!" he said.

"So glad," she said.

He ran back and hauled his suitcase off the porch. Hitchcock made a frantic good-bye sprint through the orange poppies and overgrown grasses in the front yard before hurling himself toward the back seat.

She had to go inside to make sure the place was locked up. Bob had done a good job. He had remembered to turn off the fan in the living room and lower the thermostat. Even the windows were shut and locked. Sometimes, he was fourteen going on thirty. That would be when he wasn't fourteen going on two, she laughed to herself, find-

ing a heap of wet towels forming a white scar over the hallway's lovely aged oak boards.

North of Salinas, she started to speed to seventy or
seventy-five. But she had forgotten the traffic narrowing
from two lanes to one for construction, which caused
everyone to slam on their brakes and jerk left simultaneously. The Bronco, tippy and therefore not the best car to
maneuver, gave them a minor carnival-ride scare, righting
itself just in the nick of time.

Tall pink oleander bloomed on the sides of the road,
blowing in the hot summer wind. Her usual driving style,
to haul it uphill but drive the speed limit on downhills to
avoid lurking patrol cars, wasn't really an option in the
heavy weekend traffic, so she had time to admire the yellow mountains in all their splendor. The traffic got bad
again in San Jose, at the junction with 280, and they
crawled the rest of the way to the station.

She tried to imagine Paul making the much longer
drive from Monterey to Tahoe over and over to help her
on her cases, as he had so often in the past.

She waited with Bob until the train to Sacramento arrived, then waved him off. He would have to change there,
and had to listen to many instructions about what to do if
there was a problem. She rode back to Monterey wondering what the hell she was doing, sending her boy up to
their home in the mountains while she remained stuck like
dried salt along the coastline.

11

PAUL WOKE UP ON SATURDAY in a rotten mood, not helped by the nightcaps he had drunk the night before.

He had slept alone on the thick new foam pad Nina had bought to soften up his stiff bed. Tossing, unable to sleep, he decided he didn't like the heat the pad created or the cozy embryonic illusion of comfort, so he ripped it off and threw it to the floor. Damn woman, coming in here, changing everything to suit herself and then moving out!

He did not like uncertainty. He lived by rules, such as the first rule he had established when he went into business: if someone was going to get hurt, that someone would not be him. He had just gotten used to her living with him, to her scent and a particular softness of hair. Then her kid arrived, and before he could blink she had gone.

What use was it, having her in Pacific Grove, ten miles away? How was that getting together?

Now, very early, cup of coffee in hand, he stood on the deck watching the sun filling in the morning shadows, the distant line of ocean in the west, and the blue jays flitting around in the eucalyptus trees. He listened to the radio news while he ate, then made the bed and threw the foam pad into the condo Dumpster. He checked his e-mail.

Damn, but the house was quiet and the morning was long.

Wish showed up at Paul's office at eight.

Sandy's son, Wish Whitefeather, towered over everyone, even Paul, and weighed one-forty on a feast day. Twenty years old, he walked into the room with the insouciant glowing health only youth possessed, even if he had spent the night on a pal's floor. His hair was getting long again, just touching the collar of his wrinkled green polo shirt. He was all bone, with a long face with a high forehead, a jutting nose, and a prominent Adam's apple that bobbed as he swallowed the last of his caffeine fix.

"Let's do it, good buddy," Wish said, adjusting his sunglasses. He was wearing his trademark Doc Martens and brown khaki shorts, drinking from a cardboard coffee vat. Evidently Sandy was leaning too hard, because he launched into his problems with his parents, and how he could never escape their watchful eyes. "I leave Tahoe to come here and be on my own, you know? And they follow me!"

"All for a good cause. You're going back soon, anyway," Paul said, picking up Dean Trumbo's shitty investigative report on Alex Zhukovsky and locking his office door behind him. On the landing he glanced down below at the Hog's Breath, always on the lookout for a pretty girl to start the day off right, but the courtyard below was deserted. "You've got nothing to squawk about. You don't have to stay with your parents."

"That's the whole problem. My mom hates letting me

out of her sight." He sighed deeply. "I stay with friends and she really kicks."

"Where are your folks staying?"

"With old friends in Big Sur. They got to know each other when my dad was doing truck driving. They're starting an abalone farm off the commercial pier in Monterey." Wish took the stairs down two at a time, and barely seemed to be working at it, saying, "You wouldn't believe how hard it is to farm abalone." Paul followed at the more sedate single-step pace. "Actually," Wish went on, "since I'm taking a bio course this fall, they've been able to help. They know a lot."

They got down to the street. "We'll take my car," Paul said, leading to the red Mustang parked by the curb.

"Can I drive?"

Paul tossed him the keys.

Wish lectured Paul about the wild ways of abalone, which Paul had heretofore only known as sizzling breaded objects on a plate, all the way up the cottage-lined streets of Carmel. "Don't get me wrong," he said. "I'm still into criminal justice. Bio's important these days because of DNA."

"DNA's our worst problem in this case. You know Stefan Wyatt's blood was found at the scene."

"Yeah. The case." Wish blinked and came back to their mission of the day, the interview of Alex Zhukovsky, Christina's brother.

"If you were on a jury and heard that, you'd think he did it, wouldn't you?" Paul asked.

"Well, it wasn't enough to nail O.J. So Stefan's got that going for him. But between you and me, Paul, ya know, she threw a glass that broke, right? And his blood was on the glass, right?"

"The tests are even more reliable than in O.J.'s heyday," Paul said.

"Nina thinks he's innocent, so we go with that, right?" Paul did not answer, because he wanted Wish to maintain his zeal, but the truth was, Nina hadn't expressed an opinion about Wyatt's guilt or innocence. That could be because she wasn't sure, or thought he was guilty, or he had confessed to her and that was confidential, or simply because she was a lawyer and not stupid.

"What's the first thing to think about, when you want to know who killed her? A single woman, forty-three, not bad looking?" Paul asked instead.

"The love life," Wish said promptly.

"Yes. I go there first myself."

"You lose a woman you supposedly love, well, man, better go kill her! Don't you just love male logic? Oops," Wish said, running over a curb as he made the turn into the college.

"I can't believe you just did that to my Mustang."

"They made this turn too tight."

"No, you took it tight."

They passed under a large brown structure bearing a sign that read, WELCOME TO CALIFORNIA STATE UNIVERSITY MONTEREY BAY. LUNCH IS BACK AT THE GENERAL STILWELL COMMUNITY CENTER.

"Speed limit's thirty here, Wish."

Wish slowed down. "I know. Don't forget, I'm taking an Administration of Justice course here. Just started last week."

Another sign said, WELCOME U.S. ARMY ORD MILITARY COMMUNITY.

"It's a strange association," Paul said, "a college and the military. I'll never think of Fort Ord as anything but a base. Fifteen years ago Seaside and Marina were military towns. Monterey depended on the soldiers. Saturday night at the movies, every skull had a buzz cut."

"Well, they had this huge military reservation, and all

these buildings, and when the military mostly left, they had to do something. I think it's great."

They passed a thrift shop, and a few signs praising the Otters, apparently the university's athletic alter ego. A drab beige corrugated metal building had another sign announcing that it was a "future complex." All around, as they continued along the road into the school, noisy orange machines, expansive dirt lots, dirt piles, holes, and orange fencing hinted at an inscrutable future. A construction guy was lying in the back of his pickup truck on a folding lounger, eyes closed, taking in a little sun on his break. It was cool, though, with fog and ocean never far away along this stretch of coast.

They drove by a field of yellow flowers and trees, striped with pitted strips of asphalt that ended arbitrarily after a few hundred feet. What looked like native coastal scrub stretched east into the far flat distance except for the dirt roads snaking through it. A sign read NO TRESPASSING, and Paul wondered how much live ammo was still out there. He pictured young men and women in uniform, the rumble of tanks, sand flying.

A concrete wall studded with graffiti art celebrated multiculturalism along with FIELD ARTILLERY, and another sign warned visitors to watch out for wildlife. A few girls in shorts walked in a pack toward one of the new buildings, a science center.

"Thousands of military people have passed through here, getting physically and mentally ready to go to war," Paul said. "Now there are these green kids, ready for just about anything else. It's a little like fresh skin growing over a wound."

Weeds popped the asphalt in vast, empty parking lots. They passed by an abandoned guardhouse, and Paul had to look twice at where a faux window had been painted, from which a painted sentinel, wearing a wide-brimmed, World War I–style khaki hat, smiled out.

Wish inclined his head toward the painted guard. "He's the ghost of military guys past."

These students were operating in the midst of an ongoing military attitude. Although the place had the quiet of desuetude, something new and vibrant was sending tendrils here and there, as bright bikes whizzed by and a student waved and shouted at a friend. "Is there any competition between the remains of the military here and the university?" Paul asked.

Wish shook his head. "I haven't noticed any. I would bet most of the military people like what's happening here. There's no more shooting or scrambling through the brush. They're all techies and administrators. Look, this is the building my class is in."

"Looks like a circus tent." The renovated buildings wore coats of raspberry, terra-cotta, yellow ochre, and teal on different sections, a fanatically modern architect's ideal. Stucco covered in strange paint combos apparently meant campus; gray or white clapboard meant military.

Paul decided he liked the place. Tall dunes across Highway 1 hid the ocean, but the air held a sea zest, and the clash of colors, architecture, and cultures suited him.

In spite of Wish's knowledge of the campus, they had a hard time finding the administrative hub. The purpose of some of the buildings remained unknowable. They asked two sets of people before locating a place with a map of the campus. Then, after picking up a parking permit, they set out to find Alex Zhukovsky.

They parked near a temporary building that housed classes in Russian along with several other languages. As they walked over, Paul noticed how quiet the place was. Bugs chittered in the fields around, and almost no cars were parked in the barren lots.

Zhukovsky's office was located in front. He must have seen them coming, because he met them at the main door, which he unlocked.

Deano's report hadn't described him, except to say he taught languages. Zhukovsky was a little younger and shorter than Paul, late thirties, with red-rimmed eyes in a soft face marked by a fine, straight nose and an unhappy expression. He had the well-trimmed beard of a stereotypical academic and the belly of a sedentary type, but might be fitter than he looked. The brown hair was already receding into a *V*. He wore a white dress shirt rolled up at the sleeves, belted jeans, a big emerald ring on his left pinky.

They introduced themselves and exchanged business cards, and he nodded impatiently. Instead of inviting them inside, he pulled the door shut behind him, saying, "Follow me. Let's not waste time sitting around inside."

The three set off, turning up the hill nearby. Zhukovsky's pace was relentless, no trouble but faster than suited decent conversation. They didn't have far to go. He stopped at the student center, and motioned toward the outside tables. "It's better here in the sunshine," he said. "A teacher spends too much time indoors."

Once they sat down, Zhukovsky's foot started tapping. He kept raising and lowering his shoulders, a strange tic. He was hyper, probably. How did he get through his classes? In his own youth Paul had found it unbearable to be stuck at a desk with a soothing voice droning somewhere in the distance, the equivalent of a warm summer day in a flower field, insects buzzing, sun shining, bored out of his skull and sleepy into infinity.

Of course, the instructor could pace around in front, even if he was in the cage, too. And maybe Zhukovsky's fidgeting was a function of nerves. Paul studied him through his sunglasses and decided to be friendly.

"Good of you to see us," he said. Finally, he added

silently. Zhukovsky had stalled Paul for the past two weeks, refusing to meet with him. "I realize you've been interviewed before by someone from the Pohlmann firm."

"Deano, he called himself," Zhukovsky said with a lifted Elvis lip.

"We're not like him," Wish put in hastily, starting up a tiny recorder.

Deano stands alone, Paul thought, king of fools. He was looking forward to running into Deano soon.

"I don't have much time. I teach a Saturday afternoon class for the dedicated and the crazy. I wouldn't have talked to you again. But I have a demand."

"Ms. Reilly—remember her? She's the attorney for Stefan Wyatt and has a few more questions."

"Speaking of crazy, she is if she thinks she'll get Stefan Wyatt off." He said "Stefan" with the accent on the second syllable, and Paul remembered that Wyatt's mother was Polish. Zhukovsky spoke good old American English himself. "First, I tell you what I want. Then, maybe I'll answer some questions."

"Okay," Paul said. He crossed his legs and looked amenable.

"I want my father's bones back. My father, Constantin Zhukovsky."

Paul and Wish exchanged looks.

"Tell me more," Paul said.

"I received my father's remains a couple of weeks ago, and had buried him once. This time the remains were cremated. You can understand why." Paul did understand. The bones had been busy, getting dug up, riding around in back seats, and pawed over by police forensics technicians. "But now I find out two bones were withheld. Do you understand how infuriating this is? How disrespectful?" He jabbed a thick finger into Paul's chest, never a good idea, saying, "I've been informed by the D.A.'s office that your people have them."

Paul held up his hands, to show there were no bones there, but he was aching to jab back, show Zhukovsky what a real jab felt like.

"I want to know why, and I want to know where the hell you are keeping them."

When Paul said nothing, he said more reasonably, "I have a right to know, don't I? He was my father."

"They were considered evidence. The remaining bones are in Sacramento being tested by our expert, a forensic scientist, Ginger Hirabayashi, and they'll be released once the trial is over."

"Tested? What? Why? You have no right! The D.A. never tested my father's bones. They have nothing to do with my sister's murder. I want all testing discontinued immediately. Tell your boss I'll sue her if I don't get them back within a week." He folded his arms, glaring.

"I'll get back to you. I'm a mere functionary in such matters."

"Do that," Zhukovsky demanded. "I don't think you people fully comprehend what I've been going through. My sister is dead, murdered. It's the worst thing I can remember, worse than losing my father. At least he lived his full life. Now she's a spectacle, remembered for all the wrong reasons as the victim of a ghoulish crime." He had Stalin's black eyebrows, which ruined an otherwise rather pleasant face. "It's a shock I will never get over, and then, on top of it, this never-ending thing with my father . . ."

"My turn, now? I'm wondering," Paul said, "how close were you and your sister, Christina?"

"She was older, and, growing up, we weren't close. We became closer as we reached adulthood."

"Were you close enough to know her lovers?" Paul asked.

The foot-tapping stopped abruptly. The shoulders hesitated. This was not a question to ask a brother, Zhukovsky's disapproving face said. "What?"

"Who she was sleeping with," Wish said helpfully.

"Christina didn't confide in me in that way," Alex Zhukovsky said, gathering himself, his agitation showing itself in the rapid eye movements, the shifting of weight, the folding of a napkin. He didn't like this.

"Oh, you probably knew." Wish seemed to be studying the professor. "Even if she didn't tell you."

Zhukovsky said nothing.

Paul flipped through his notebook. "Witnesses say she was having a relationship with a man named Sergey Krilov."

"What witnesses?" The thought of witnesses clearly jarred the professor.

"You know Krilov?"

"I know about him," he admitted. "You're right. They had a relationship for a while. She ended it."

"Was that the day of the conference, or before it?"

"What do you know about that?"

"We know you were there and so was she, along with a bunch of Russian visitors. She was seen arguing with Krilov."

"I believe they broke up before the conference. That day he wanted to reconcile. She didn't. That's all that happened."

Paul felt like a seal breaking through the ice to the surface, finally able to take a breath. Krilov excited him. "I've been looking into Krilov's background and have learned a few things."

"Really?" All the pretend indifference in the world couldn't disguise Zhukovsky's intense interest in exactly what Paul had learned.

"Yeah, you know, information's cheap these days. Anyone can access the Web for the price of coffee in a Styrofoam cup." He waited for Zhukovsky to beg him. He needed the guy engaged at this point, and he wasn't going to let him ice up again.

"What did you learn?" Zhukovsky asked, unable to escape the plan.

Paul smiled to himself. "He's from a family of formerly wealthy Russians who hit the skids when the Soviet Union busted up. He's heavily into politics there, and holds some unusual views, such as, much as he hated the Soviet Union, he hates the current regime more. He hangs with radicals who want to throw out the president and restore a kind of prerevolutionary hierarchy over there. How involved was your sister?"

"My sister—okay, let me tell you the truth about her. She never got over losing our mother and father. She put herself to sleep reading an old book of fairy tales Papa used to read her at night. She never married. She had friends, but her natural reserve kept her from getting really close to people. Her life was—empty, sad. Then this Russian pops up out of nowhere, whispering in her ear, telling her she's beautiful, unique, consequential. Well, can you blame her for wanting to believe him? He gave her life the meaning she needed. She fell in love with him and with the dream of a meaningful existence he offered."

"Did she buy his politics?"

"She wasn't mixed up in any cockeyed, lunatic, jugheaded plans to overthrow the Russian government, if that's what you're implying!"

Whew. Hit a nerve there, Paul thought. So, she had been involved somehow. To give himself a further chance to ponder Alex's overreaction, and Alex a chance to use a napkin to wipe sweat from his forehead, he scribbled in his notebook. "Is Krilov the violent type?"

"Don't try to pin my sister's death on Sergey Krilov.

Believe me, I wish it had been him—but your client's blood was in her apartment! Stefan Wyatt killed her."

Paul wanted to know why Alex would prefer that the killer be Krilov and not Stefan, but the purple map springing up on Zhukovsky's forehead suggested he move on. Zhukovsky would clam up again if Paul wasn't careful. He was feeling guilty about something. A connection with Stefan he regretted?

"You and your sister grew up here in the Monterey area?" Paul asked.

Breathing hard, still upset, the professor said brusquely, "Yes. Our father owned a pastry shop on Alvarado Street. Our mother died when my sister and I were children."

"Was Christina a handful growing up? Anything unusual about her?"

"Everything. While her girlfriends were trading lipsticks, baring their belly buttons, and sleeping around, she was at the library reading. After college, she worked at a preschool and as a recreation counselor for elderly people. Later, she got a job here at the university."

"You worked together?"

"No. There is a big gulf between administration and faculty at most colleges."

"What was her title?"

"Public Affairs Officer. She was in charge of organizing special occasions on the campus."

Low on the totem, Paul thought, for such an accomplished woman. And given her fancy apartment, there must have been family money behind her. He made a mental note. "And you're on the Russian faculty?"

"I am the Russian faculty. I also teach French and German. Unfortunately, nobody around here wants to study anything but Spanish."

"Did your sister speak Russian, too?"

"Yes."

"Impressive," Paul said. "I never learned a foreign language."

"Why should you? You live in this vast land that you consider the center of civilization, and you simply make foreigners learn English. Most of my students are just filling in time or need to have a smattering of language to read technical articles."

"But Christina wasn't like that, was she? She left her work to travel for several months early this year, and nobody could tell me where she went. That's a long time to be living out of a suitcase, isn't it?"

"She was seeing the world," Zhukovsky said shortly. "She was unmarried and unencumbered. Why shouldn't she?"

"Just going from hotel to hotel? I mean, her coworkers didn't even get postcards."

"She kept in touch with me. She had her own money and she wanted to travel."

"Yes, that would be expensive," Paul said. "I suppose your father left you and Christina something."

"That's not your business."

"The probate is a public record," Paul said. "Your father seems to have done very well with his pastry business."

Zhukovsky scratched behind his ear, saying, "Deano didn't bother me with personal questions."

Wish, who had listened patiently, said, "We kind of got that from his report."

"What was she doing during those months she disappeared?" Paul said. "I'm trying to figure her out. She's an enigma." He had an idea about where Christina Zhukovsky had spent those missing months, and he would bet Zhukovsky knew.

"Having fun. I got postcards from all over." A faint red shadow appeared on his neck as he spoke.

Zhukovsky was a liar. But Paul had figured that before even meeting him.

"You know," Paul said, "I have a sister. And she drives me nuts, by the way, but if she disappeared for a month, much less several months, even I would send a posse out to find her." He exaggerated. He would wait as long as he could. She could be extremely irritating.

"I wasn't worried. She could take care of herself." He must have realized how foolish that sounded now because he added, "Of course I would have worried if she hadn't prepared me for a long absence. Is your assistant taping me?"

"Yes."

"Tell him to stop." Paul nodded and Wish turned off the recorder and got out his notepad.

"I understand that before she died, your sister helped organize an important conference on Russian international relations here. Word is," Paul said, "Cal State Monterey as a whole has benefited in terms of prestige and recognition from the conference she set up."

"True," Zhukovsky said. "Christina was very enthusiastic about it. She worked hard to get some big names here."

"What was the subject of the conference?"

Zhukovsky said a long Russian phrase, then, apparently translating, "Post-Communist Russia and the Twenty-first Century."

"Did either of you ever live in Russia?" Wish asked.

"No."

"Did you visit there?"

"What do you think? I am a Russian professor! I studied for a year at a language institute in Moscow."

"Right," Wish said, and wrote that down.

"But your father came from Russia?" Paul asked, taking over again.

"Yes, long ago."

"Whereabouts?"

"St. Petersburg."

"When did he come to this country?"

"In the 1920s." A soft pink crawled up Zhukovsky's neck. "He came from Russia when he was very young."

"How young?"

"Oh, twenty-four or -five."

"How did he end up in Monterey?"

"After the turn of the century, there was quite a Russian immigration to San Francisco and south to the Monterey Peninsula. He came over with family friends."

"Not with his parents?"

"They died in the revolution." His body, until then managing a slow tap of agitation, practically turned inside out as he decided to find himself a better position on the wire chair, failed, and stood up.

"He was a good man, my father," Zhukovsky said firmly. He began pacing the deck, hands in his pockets. "Sociable, well liked. Loved to talk. He could make friends with anyone." A fleeting nostalgic smile died on his face. "My parents had a happy marriage," he went on, tacking in another direction. "After Mother died in 1971, Papa would go to that cemetery. Visit her. He got to know the workers over there. They had their children late in life. Christina was born in 1960 and I was born in 1964."

Paul could see Zhukovsky enjoyed talking about his family history, but he wasn't the only one having problems figuring out how Papa Zhukovsky related to their present-day murder, other than the fact that his grave offered a convenient receptacle for the victim. He wondered, as he had before, if there had been some kind of symbolism in the daughter ending up buried with her father.

Nina's client claimed Alex had something to do with it. He was a logical suspect, considering he knew both of the dead people and had the strongest emotional connection to them, but what kind of a symbol might he mean by the gesture? Paul had thought about it several times, and discussed it with Nina, but neither of them had the slightest idea.

He had lied about Christina, saying he had no idea where she had gone when she took a leave from the university early this year. Why? A normal instinct to keep private things private?

"Getting back to this conference," Paul said, "how many of the participants did you know before they came?"

"These were people from all over the world. Christina knew many of the participants. I knew a few."

"So she did have extensive contacts with the Russian community and with Russia?"

"She was involved locally," the professor said. "We were raised in the American Russian Orthodox Church and have many close ties there. She found people through our church, which is a gathering place for many Russian nationals, and through our cultural association."

"I never know what people mean when they say that. What do these organizations do exactly?"

"The main one that's still active in this area is the Russian Alliance. They raise money for good causes. They allow others with similar heritage to meet and perhaps practice some old traditions."

He was leaning against the railing, and had taken up thrumming with his right hand. Noticing, he put it in his pocket, took it out again, checked his watch, and sat back down in his chair.

Silence fell. Paul had asked about everything but the crucial thing, and he still wasn't sure how to approach it. He took off his sunglasses and squinted out at the windswept sea plain.

Zhukovsky, no fool himself, was waiting anxiously for

Paul to get down to it. He knew what Stefan had told Nina and Paul. Deano had leaked all that months before.

"Professor Zhukovsky, you know that Mr. Wyatt was arrested after digging up the remains of your father," Paul finally said.

"He admits that? He's going to admit that in court? I thought . . ."

"He's not going to testify, I believe," Paul said.

"Why did he kill Christina? Why? I've asked myself that over and over. It's crazy. How did he know her? Has he told you that?"

"He pled innocent to the murder of your sister. But he admits digging up the grave of your father."

"It's all the same," Zhukovsky said with disgust. "I'm sick of this. You're not going to tell me anything, I understand. So what else do you want to know? Let's get this over with."

"On that Saturday night, April twelfth and into the morning of the thirteenth, the night the police discovered your sister's body, how did they know you were related to the man buried in the cemetery?"

"I signed the logbook at the cemetery when my father was buried. I suppose they got my name from that."

"And why did you hire Mr. Wyatt to dig up the bones of your father?"

Alex Zhukovsky drew himself up. All the restive tapping of his fingers on his knee, the twitching of his foot, stopped. His neck—ah, his neck had taken on the hue of a tequila sunrise, heavy on the grenadine.

"As I've told the police and said in a deposition, I didn't. Is that why you came? To drag me into this? Because you don't want to do that."

"Stefan Wyatt collected your father's bones," Paul said. "That's a fact." He consulted his notes. "He says you hired him."

"Yes! Yes! He says that! He's a liar! Does he say I hired him to kill Christina? Because I'll kill him if he has the audacity to suggest such a thing!"

"Calm down, Professor. He only claims that you hired him to get the bones."

Zhukovsky's eyebrows beetled into one. "I didn't. And don't try to claim I did or I'll sue. Tell your boss that. I would never hurt my sister."

"But why bury her in your father's grave?" Paul asked. "That's the thing that keeps me awake at night. There were other graves nearer the street. So why that one? Was he involved in something special, something important, your father, Constantin Zhukovsky?"

"My father was no one, an entirely ordinary man. A baker, for God's sake! Let him rest in peace!" The flush test had stopped working. Zhukovsky was far too excited by now.

"He had been dead for twenty-five years," Paul persisted. "Something or someone made Mr. Wyatt go dig him up. Obviously, there was a point to the exercise. Unless Wyatt's just nuts. Do you think he's nuts?"

"I don't know the man."

"You never met him?"

"Never. I saw him brought into court, that's it."

"No theory about why he would dig up your father, then."

In keeping with his professorial disposition, Zhukovsky could not resist the opportunity to give his sister's death a spin. Paul hoped something in what he said would give them insight into his own motives, which remained tantalizingly elusive. "Christina must have known Wyatt, and took him along when she visited our parents' graves. She always brought cut roses. Sometimes, she cried."

Thus he implied that Stefan might have been his sister's secret lover, Paul supposed.

"And he," Alex Zhukovsky, swept away with his own imagination, went on with alacrity, "that bastard, thought of the grave when he had killed her. And then possibly, while burying my sister's body, when he came upon the casket of my father, he looked inside, saw the medal worn by my father upon his burial, grabbed it, and grabbed the—rest without thinking."

These convolutions didn't seem to convince even the professor, and yet he seemed sincerely puzzled about something, to be struggling to explain the inexplicable. Part lies, part truth, Paul thought, but he couldn't sort it out. Who was lying, Zhukovsky or Stefan?

"Yes, the medal, I wanted to ask you about that," Paul said.

"It was my father's. What else is there to say?"

"What was it?"

He squirmed. "A military honor from the early part of the twentieth century."

"You're an expert in Russian history, correct?"

"I am."

No expert in modest manners, however, Paul noted. "You know your military history, no doubt."

"It's all military history in Russia."

"You weren't curious enough to do some research on this medal?"

"During this last year I've learned it's called the Order of Saint George, First Class. It's solid gold with precious inlays, an original historic medal, with some special features. A Carmel antiques expert appraised it for several thousand dollars. Bad news for your client. I understand its theft constitutes a separate felony.

"My father wanted to be buried wearing it on a sash across his shoulder. He used to say he got it as a kind of joke when he was little for fighting with his teachers. I never knew it was valuable."

"Was your father in the military? Involved in the revolution in 1917, maybe?"

"No."

"Funny how things happened there," Paul said. The naïveté of the comment was rewarded with another snarl. This professor was the fiery sort of intellectual. Paul had no use for intellectuals these days. They made lousy lovers who wouldn't live with you. "Wouldn't the poor old tsar be turning in his grave, seeing how things have turned out for the country that murdered him to make a revolution," he went on, hoping to stoke the fire.

"The country did not murder the tsar! The tsar and his family were assassinated by Bolshevik elements."

"I understand they finally dug up the grave of the Romanovs in 1991," Paul went on, "but two of the bodies were missing. It's a strange parallel."

Zhukovsky made a sound, guttural, untranslatable, but plainly repelled by his comment. Paul had just been riffing, and had never intended to turn the professor off.

"Sorry," he said. "Didn't mean to disrespect your father. It's just—you were talking about the second burial—and the two missing bones."

Zhukovsky had had enough. "You have my card," he said. "I want the remains of my father delivered to me care of that address within one week. I'm dead serious about this."

"He lies, left, right, and center," Paul said. As Wish dodged the curbs, driving them back to Carmel, Paul scribbled. "Let's assume he hired Stefan to dig up the grave, but not to kill his sister. Question is, why? For the medal? It's valuable, and not doing the old man any good under six feet. If Zhukovsky wanted that so badly, then why hire Stefan Wyatt to take his father's remains as well?"

"For a satanic ritual," Wish guessed. "Or, what about this? In Africa they grind up rhino horn for an aphrodisiac and sell it in the Far East . . ."

"The problem with your theory is, once he had the bones back from the cops, he cremated them. We'll check that, but I believe him on that score. I'll grant you, maybe the old man had a horn on his nose no one's talking about that's all ground up . . ."

"You're makin' fun of me."

"Not at all. It makes as much sense as anything I can think up." Paul thought some more, then said, "Maybe Zhukovsky has some genetic issue to explore that he doesn't want anyone to suspect. One of those diseases that hits in middle age? Like we were all worried Arlo Guthrie might get."

"Who?"

"Son of Woody?" Paul stared at Wish, who continued to relay incomprehension. How could he not know these cultural icons? Was Paul, twenty years older, so removed from the current set of urban legends? "Huntington's chorea. Or Parkinson's? I'm not sure which diseases they can find through genetic testing, but I'm making an educated first guess that's what he wanted to find out."

"Then why doesn't the professor just test his own blood?" Wish asked, showing one of his rare flashes of intelligence.

"Good point," Paul admitted.

"His father was dead in his grave for twenty-five years. So what's the big rush?"

"Make a note for me to try to obtain Constantin Zhukovsky's medical records. Alex's will be completely off limits. I want you to Google the Web tomorrow. Look for the Order of Saint George. Write up a report of whatever you can find out and leave it in the mailbox at the Pohlmann office. Nina will be working there Sunday night."

"Check."

"I want verification on what the medal is worth, who gets it, and why."

"No sweat."

"Now, the boyfriend, if that's what he was. The man she spent a lot of time with at this conference."

"Sergey . . ."

"Krilov. Use the ID software on my computer at the office and find out more. Do the same on Constantin Zhukovsky, the father. See if you can find out when he came to this country. Maybe you can find some immigration records. You can get old ship passenger lists on the Web these days. Ellis Island, the whole thing. Check some of the genealogy sites like Ancestry.com. Hell, see what you can find on the whole mother-loving family. Alex. Christina. Give that info to Nina, too. Let's get a copy of the death certificate. Call the county and see what office you have to go to."

"Sure."

"I can't believe Dean Trumbo didn't do any of this work. This is nuts. She's in the middle of trial, trying to incorporate this basic investigative information, tearing her hair out." Paul clenched a fist.

"Didn't Trumbo rent your office last year?"

"Yeah. Deano."

"That's the same face the professor made when he said that name."

"Deano's giving the P.I. profession a bad name, and I think it's time I did something about it."

"Talk to him?"

"Something like that," Paul said.

"Whoa."

"What happened to Christina when she left the good old U.S.A.? A brother is going to know this stuff," Paul said absently. They passed the Del Monte exit, along the eucalyptus-covered grounds of the Naval Postgraduate School. To their right a neighborhood of not-too-spiffy frame houses led to the little strip of sand called Del Monte Beach, where Paul had once had a bachelor apartment on Surf Way.

"I'm gonna say—Russia."

"My conclusion exactly."

"With her boyfriend, Krilov."

"Maybe that's where she met him."

"Playing house or playing politics?"

"That is the question."

Wish adjusted his sunglasses. He said, "I'm getting smarter. I watch you. I'll see if Christina's passport was taken into evidence. So where do we eat? The deli at the Thunderbird Bookstore?"

"Take the next exit," Paul commanded.

"But we're miles from Carmel. This is Monterey!"

"Do it!"

Wish swung off Highway 1 at the Aguajito exit.

"Get to the right."

Wish signaled and moved, setting off a chain reaction of traffic goofs that would be laughable if they weren't so damn sad. These people should put down their mobile phones, quit slopping food around their mouths, quit plucking their eyebrows, and give the open road its due respect, Paul thought.

"Now, as soon as we cross this intersection, there's a tiny entrance on the right. Turn there." Paul scrutinized the row of greenery screening a narrow driveway. "Hard right!"

Wish turned on his blinker and made the turn, squeaking through a narrow, gated entrance. "Cementerio El Encinal," he read.

"Let's take some photos for Nina. Then we'll eat."

12

THE GRAVEYARD AT EL ENCINAL did not feel sad, Paul thought as they wended down the asphalt paths in the Mustang on Saturday afternoon. Here and there, a visitor stood or kneeled near a loved one, and there was an atmosphere of conviviality. Fresh flowers, some wilting, mixed liberally and acceptingly with long-lasting silk. People did not forget their dead, even in these modern times, on a sunny weekend in a resort town. Paul felt heartened by the thought, not that he really gave a damn what happened after he went. Still, it was nice to find people remained sentimental.

He thought of the thousands of people lying under the earth, layers of them, centuries of them, now dirt themselves, recycled, remembered as faintly etched headstones, as bones for study, as ancient cultures, as primitives. He gave their collective souls a nod. If anything, people now seemed obsessed with dredging up historical evidence through bones, looking for clues to what? A broader picture of human identity?

Or was it simply an atavistic urge, like a cat's curiosity, that motivated the scientists? They couldn't help the desire to dig and find things to smell or examine, and so they dignified it with important-sounding reasons.

Wish and Paul drove slowly past one woman in her fifties who sat cross-legged next to a gravestone, plucking at the grass around it, smoothing dirt from the stone, singing a hymn. Crows swooping between a fence and a tall tree nearby cawed along with her. Paul decided to add a list of songs to be played at his wake to his last wishes, songs to encourage weeping, and some to get them dancing. Naturally, he would foot the bill for abundant booze, so necessary to create the proper maudlin mood.

He gave a few minutes over to listing songs that might qualify, while Wish inched along, looking for the Eastern Orthodox crosses that had been described by Nina. "Stairway to Heaven," that was a definite. Played on vinyl, not a CD. Nina could draw him up a will.

They parked the car and hunted for Constantin Zhukovsky's last resting place.

"I never want to die," Wish said, reading each headstone they passed.

"Born to be wild, huh?" Paul said.

"Huh?"

Paul decided if things didn't work out with Nina, he still wouldn't date women Wish's age. Some things a nubile body could not compensate for, such as never having gotten your motor runnin' to head out on the highway.

Happily, according to Wish, most of these dead people were older than Paul, with a few remarkable exceptions. "I mean, not that this isn't an okay place when the time comes. The ocean not too far. Lots of sunshine during the day. Still, I don't plan to die for about a hundred years. A hundred twenty years. Science is making great strides."

Paul wished he were still twenty with illusions that death could be planned or forestalled. "Get those blood lipoproteins buff. That's the latest hot tip for living forever, or so says the newspaper today."

"Okay," Wish said. "How?"

"Exercise and drugs."

"Oh, I'm good then. Paul, I would like to ask you a question." Wish's tone had become formal.

"That would be a nice change," Paul said.

"I would like to ask you if you will hire me full-time. I mean, I'll still take courses and get my degree. But I would like to work for you."

"Well, now," Paul said. "I'm flattered."

"My parents are going back to Tahoe soon, and I don't want to go with them. I've learned a lot from you."

"I don't know if I can afford a full-time assistant, buddy."

"I'll work cheap and help bring in cases."

Paul said, "Okay."

"Okay? Oh, my God. Okay?"

"Yeah, although your first assignment is going to be helping me convince your mom."

"She won't like it."

"One day, you will have an ergonomic chair and a new Glock, like me. And a beautiful young lady holding a baby at your side. And then, when your mom sits down in the rocking chair and holds the baby, she will forgive you. They usually don't until about then."

"What about the Glock? What has that . . ."

"You won't tell her about the Glock."

The fading, golden September day, quiet now, even the insects resting in the slanting afternoon sun, made drama of the long lawns and headstones shadowing the cemetery grounds. Parking not far from where they had entered, they walked up and down the asphalt drives and then along paths between graves, where it was possible. Wish avoided walking right below the headstones, but Paul didn't bother. These people were beyond disturbing.

"Too many dead," Wish muttered, picking his way past a clump of flat markers. He started subtracting dates of death from dates of birth, commenting on those who died around the same age as Paul or Nina until Paul told him to shut up. Unable to find what they were looking for, they split up. Wish wandered toward the street that ran perpendicular to El Estero Lake. Paul made his way to the small concrete building located roughly at the center. He walked fast to ward off the chill that crept up his legs from underneath the damp grass. Before he could reach the door to the building, an elderly woman came out, saying, "Hello. Haven't seen you here before."

"No," Paul said. He gave her a card.

She thanked him and introduced herself as Amanda Peltier. "I'm in charge of the janitorial staff, community relations, and sales. That kind of thing," she said briskly, as if it was terribly mundane, selling graves. Squinting at his card, then pulling on a pair of reading glasses, she said, "Oh, my gosh. Why, you're a private investigator! Is there something I can help you with?"

"I hope so."

Maybe she saw him shivering, although he could swear he wasn't reacting visibly to the cold. Still, the light blue eyes seemed to see right through him, and her voice was kind. "Why don't you come in and sit down. It's warmer in here."

He followed the diminutive figure. Immediately inside the door, he found himself in a room no more than ten by twelve, which held a desk, files, a few big books, two plastic chairs, and a flourishing green plant that on closer inspection turned out to be made of silk. Several framed photographs cluttered the edge of the desk. She motioned him to a chair, then bustled into a smaller room beyond.

He could hear her banging around, although he couldn't see her.

"You take cream in your coffee? Or would you prefer tea?"

"What are you having?"

"Tea."

"Tea, then. Three sugars. No lemon, no cream," he said. He looked around the room. Two dated, large maps of the Monterey Bay area were the only wall decoration. The wooden desk was old, and its leather seat showed the small imprint of Amanda Peltier's trim derriere. She had been here a very long time, he decided. Not even a window broke the wall. The only way out appeared to be through the door. The room was very like a mausoleum, in fact.

The pictures condensed Amanda Peltier's long life into a short visual essay, ranging from an active, beaming girlhood in a wood frame house by the sea, through marriage to a distinguished-looking man with black hair and a stern gaze. The story finished off with Hair 'n' Glare disappearing, and two tanned beach-loving children growing up, marrying, and having three more sand-castle-building young 'uns.

She returned minutes later with a tray, two china cups, and a steaming yellow-flowered teapot.

"You looked like you could use something hot," she said, pouring him a cup and handing it over.

His hand felt better just touching the warm vessel and smelling its contents. "What kind of tea?"

"Earl Grey, of course!" she said. She leaned against the desk without sitting down and pulled a soft green sweater down over her hips. A long skirt led down to immaculate woven leather flats. She had a deeply wrinkled pink face to go with the pastel of her eyes, and a dent creasing the exact center of a stubborn-looking chin. White picket teeth as bright as a freshly painted fence smiled at him. "You're obviously not a big tea drinker."

"No."

"I drink it all day long." She put her head back and took a swig, eager as an alcoholic attacking the first drink of the day, set the cup down on the table, and sighed with pleasure.

Paul tried his. The sugary liquid scalded his tongue. He set the cup down. "I'm looking for a certain grave."

"Of course you are." She nodded knowingly. She walked behind the desk and pulled out a large folded piece of paper, which she laid flat for him to see. The glasses went back onto the tip of her broad nose. "Take a look, here."

They studied a map of the graveyard. Each plot had a letter and a number to identify it. "Constantin Zhukovsky," he said. "That's the name I want."

"Ah, yes. Papa. A popular man these days." She licked the tip of her thumb, and flipped through a big green ledger with oversized pages. "Poor man gets more visitors these days than he did when he first died. That's not the usual trend, you know. I could point you to the general vicinity. He's over there with all the other Russians, but since you're here . . ."

"No computer?"

"Oh, there's one in the back. We have a Web site, of course. My oldest granddaughter helps maintain it. You should have heard some of the ideas she had about what to put on there! Ghastly stuff. Or should I say ghostly."

"I can imagine. Grisly?"

She chuckled. "See, I promise you this is quicker than going through all that rigamarole to turn that darn computer on. People fool themselves, thinking computers are the best thing for every purpose." Her fingers flew through the pages, and within a few seconds she had the page she wanted. "Here we go." She wrote a note on a yellow pad, then ran her finger to a section of the cemetery over by a high fence. "Let me draw you a little diagram. It's close to Pearl Street. Have you found the Russian section?"

"No."

"Their graves are mostly clumped together." She tore the page off for him.

"Thanks."

"You're very welcome. But please, finish your tea. There's no rush. Kostya's not going anywhere today, you know. That was Constantin's nickname." Now she sat down in the chair, crossed her ankles, and drank some more tea.

Alex Zhukovsky had said his father visited the grave-yard frequently. "You knew him, Ms. Peltier? Is it Ms. Peltier?"

"Mrs. Peltier, please. And yes, I knew Kostya. It's a scandal what happened to ruin that poor man's peaceful rest, dug up and carted around like trash. It took me months to go by his grave without feeling terribly sad. Of course, all of us here were upset. We thought of having extra guards at night, but really, graves don't get dug up in the normal course of human events. Dead people aren't worth anything on earth, only in heaven. It's shocking, but not something we could have prevented."

"When did you meet Constantin Zhukovsky?"

"When his wife, Kamila, died in 1971, the same year my Harry died."

"Did you work here then?"

"I did. I was a part-time accountant in those days, and when the manager retired a few months after Harry passed, they asked me to take over. I needed the job, so it was a considerate gesture. Kostya and I were both lonely, and he developed a habit of dropping by. We developed a— kind of friendship during those hard times. Let's see, he would have been just about seventy or so then, already getting along.

"You see, after Harry died so suddenly, I realized he never really knew me. There were so many things unsaid, and so many secrets we could have shared. I guess I thought we'd have longer, or maybe I thought he should try harder. I was devastated. Death is such an abrupt ending to all of life's possibilities. Kostya helped me move on. He was such a sensitive, funny man."

"Kostya came to visit his wife's grave often?"

"Oh, he really loved that woman. Which is why I was so surprised when . . ."

"When?"

She set her cup down, clearly flustered. "Oh, dear. I'm sorry, but I hate gossips! I refuse to play that game!"

"He's dead," Paul said. "Nothing you can say will hurt him now."

She sighed. "His son was here recently so that we could inter the remains once and for all. I suggested Kostya be moved to our new columbarium, but he preferred to keep his father where he was. The columbarium is a beautiful new facility we have over near the lake. Have you seen it yet?"

"Not yet," Paul said, really hoping this was not prelude to a sales pitch for his very own prime spot in the new facility. "I'm curious about something. I've been doing some research and I discovered that in many cases, caskets don't just go into the dirt. They're embedded in concrete. Is that true here?"

"Correct. The law requires that a mortuary prepare the body properly, and then the casket is set inside concrete in the ground. Has to do with keeping things sanitary. Keeping the water table pure, that sort of thing."

"By properly, you mean . . ."

"Embalming," she said serenely.

"That's required by law?" How could this nice lady stand the idea? His flesh crawled at the thought of his blood pouring down a metal drain, to be replaced by preservative. Probably floral scented. Was this the work of some sneaky funeral parlor lobby? Or the manufacturer of embalming fluid, possibly. Or the pair of them, in cahoots. Talk about a powerless consumer group in the grip of forces beyond its control.

"Yes." Seeing his expression, she added, "They're dead, remember. Can't be hurt, as you pointed out."

"But I've been following the trial . . ."

"Oh, what an awful thing."

"I don't recall hearing the Zhukovsky grave was lined with concrete."

"Those were more lax times. The rules have changed since he was buried in 1978."

"Hmm." Paul found her remark obscurely relieving. "What sort of man was he?"

"Kostya?" She looked down at the photographs on her desk. "A family man, like my Harry. Loved his wife and children, of course. A very sociable person, outgoing, gregarious." She laughed. "A big flirt, if you want to know, but it was never serious. I used to make tea for him. He brought his own little jar of strawberry jam to put in it, and we would sit in the back room and chat, or walk the grounds together. He did it to make me feel better, that's all. It came naturally to him, being kind to a sad widow, loving people as he did. Just the most amazing storyteller! He could make me laugh with the wild stuff he would tell me. Half of it just hokum, probably. Physically frail, of course, always very pale. He was getting on when I knew him."

"How often would you say he came here?"

She put the ledger carefully back in its place on the file cabinet with the others.

"Dozens of times, even after . . . oh, heck, I might as well tell you. Who's to protect? This was all so long ago. I was even young then." She smiled, shaking her head. "He did get involved with another woman after his wife died."

"Oh? That's interesting."

"But that didn't stop him from remembering Kamila. He always brought flowers for his wife. The groundsman had to chase him off one time. He was digging away, wanting to plant them! That wasn't allowed even then. Of course, they have to be able to mow and keep things nice. Now her grave and his are mostly gravel, although they were originally grass. You'll see why when you go over there. He had bought a double grave site framed in concrete. It's raised slightly above the other graves, and was impossible to maintain as grass now that they ride the mowers instead of pushing them by hand."

"I'd like to hear what you can tell me about his new lady friend."

She blushed. "He didn't want me to know, because he never said a word, but a woman called here once, trying to find him, and—you can just tell when someone has a claim on someone else, you know? I never saw her or heard her name. So that's my gossip. I've fallen from the path of righteousness again today. Such is my fate."

Paul was starting to really like Mrs. Peltier. She had just handed him a mystery woman to check out. There's nothing like a mystery woman to a detective. "You say he used to tell you stories. What kind of stories did he tell?"

"About his childhood in St. Petersburg, mostly. I guess he was thinking a lot about those days. I think he had some really happy times. And some very bad ones, too. Sometimes, he got absolutely bleak, telling me. But generally, he liked telling about riding horses, learning to shoot, that kind of thing."

"You said he told you wild stories. These don't sound so wild."

"Oh, you know. I hate to pass them on. The whole thing

is probably ridiculous. But"—she shrugged—"nobody's ever asked me before, and I don't really think he would mind if I told you."

"Told me what?"

"Oh!" she said, so delighted she put her hands together in a silent clap. "I even have a picture! I just thought it was so absurd, and nothing he could say convinced me." She started rummaging around. "Let's see. Now where would that thing be?" After searching the central drawer in the desk, she moved down the left side, then down the right, while Paul fidgeted with frustration.

"Let me help?" he asked.

"No, you just drink your tea!" she said. "I know it's here somewhere." She moved to one of the file cabinets. "Could I have put it in here? Over the years, I've been moved to do a little spring cleaning. Let's hope I didn't throw it out. Really, I'm an appalling pack rat, that's the truth. Look at all this stuff." Papers piled up on the desk behind her. A few stacks had settled on the floor. "I simply have to get better organized. It's not as though I have a particularly demanding clientele most days."

Driven to it, laughing with her in spite of himself, Paul drank his tea.

"Maybe I was teasing him back a little," she said, working through the second drawer as if all day and all night lay ahead with nothing better to do, "because he took it so very seriously, and the whole thing seemed just ridiculous. So he brought this picture, which he found in a book in the library. He actually had a copy made for me. He said this would prove it."

"Prove what?"

"Eureka!" she said, pulling out a tatty-edged print. "Thank goodness I'm not at all the compulsive housekeeper Harry always accused me of being. It's just, he never really looked in the drawers. He never really saw all I could pack in there."

She showed him the picture. The fuzzy black-and-white showed an impressive procession of black-booted men in uniform, light-colored shirts buttoned slightly to one side, flat, round caps with brims pulled neatly down over their foreheads. Toward the end of the procession rode a solemn young boy on horseback, dressed like a sailor, with a round white cap.

"These men are prerevolutionary soldiers, the Russian imperial army. Their allies called it the 'Russian Steam-roller.' And that's him," she said, pointing at the boy. "That's Constantin, or so he told me. It could be him." She smiled. "He was older when I knew him." At the front of the marching group stood a man in a tall fur hat, with a neat beard and a heavy, drooping mustache, obviously the most important person there.

"Nicholas the Second," she said to answer Paul's inquiring glance. "The last Romanov tsar. They ruled for three hundred years, until 1918."

"What was Constantin Zhukovsky doing there?"

"He made up so many stories," she said, "but who knows? He claimed he was a page to the tsar. The last one, as he used to say."

Paul asked to borrow it so that he could make a copy.

He left, map in hand, walking the winding strips of road until he ran into Wish. They headed toward a square plot, marked off by a low concrete berm. Inside it, below a spreading shade tree, they found the place where Constantin Zhukovsky had been buried.

"It's a gathering of Russians," Wish remarked, "dead ones." Each headstone there was marked with an unusual cross with two straight horizontal crossbars at the top, and below them, a short slanted one. "Do you think people care if they're hanging with their ethnic brothers and sisters when they are dead?"

"I can't speak for them, but obviously their relatives do," Paul said. "It's just like a community meeting here, only nobody's hell-bent on overthrowing the mayor."

The cross marking Constantin Zhukovsky's grave was made of wood splintered with age. No remaining sign of disturbance in the gravel covering the grave exposed Stefan Wyatt's activities of several months ago. Wish stared at the headstone. "Constantin Zhukovsky, 1904–1978. That's all it says."

"What should it say?" Paul asked.

Wish thought. "It should say, Beloved Father and Husband. Or something. Don't you think at the very least your headstone ought to summarize you somehow? It should mark some special achievement, I think."

"Maybe they hated him and kept it short to avoid embarrassing him."

"I don't get the impression that he was a creep, do you?"

"No," Paul admitted. He took the picture out of his pocket and studied it. What did Mrs. Peltier's story mean? And if it was true, why hadn't the family commemorated Constantin Zhukovsky's fascinating background on his headstone?

13

Sunday 9/21

On Sunday morning, Paul found Erin O'Toole watering a corner plot near the off ramp from Highway 1. While she watered, she crouched now and then to dig up the occasional weed, cut off browning flowers, and check inside her flowers for bugs. She had very long black hair done in two braids that intersected halfway down her back. Her clothes were practical. The minute she spotted Paul, she turned off the hose, and walked lightly toward him.

"Here you are again," she said, pumping his hand. "Never saying die."

Paul enjoyed Erin's energy. You could almost see the billions of molecules bouncing around inside her, pinking her cheeks, pumping those toned legs. He just wished he could get something out of her. He had spoken with her once already, but she had been too upset to say much. Today, she seemed a little more accessible.

"Ms. Reilly's secretary called to let me know you were coming again, Paul. Sorry about last time. I hope I didn't put you off, but I wasn't myself." She lifted her eyes above the frown that had formed. "So let me help you today. What do you need from me?"

"Well, I have some more questions."

"Anything to help Stef." Her voice, with its high, young pitch, held a stalwart firmness in it.

"Is there a better place to talk?" Paul asked loudly, to beat the traffic noise.

"I'm done," she said. "Mind following me home? I'd love to get the sweat situation under control before we get into life stories." The fog had burned off early that morning. Even in Monterey, September could be hot, and unlike yesterday, the day already simmered.

He didn't mind following her. She drove a white van with the name "Green Plant Haven" on its side. They didn't have to go far. She lived in a dinky house not far up from the bay, adorned with flowers. A border along the white picket fence sported a crazed collection of color. The yard had a tidy sprawl to it Paul could not help admiring. Nina's cottage would benefit from Erin's touch, no doubt about it. Erin sat him down in her living room with a can of soda, then disappeared.

When she returned, she gleamed in a dazzling white T-shirt and jeans. She sat down in a striped yellow armchair that tipped into a recliner when she leaned back. "Something to eat?" Erin offered, taking a long drink of her soda. "I've got tuna, even some homemade soup."

"No, thanks," Paul said, even though he was, in fact, hungry. "I just have a few minutes."

"So?"

"So tell me a little more about you and Stefan." He looked at his notes. "You told me before that you met at a restaurant?"

She looked reluctant, but decided to answer. "Yep," she said. "We met at the bar of an old restaurant in Carmel, the Pine Inn. Stef was bartending. This is back when he had a job. They have a cute bar. I used to go there to drown my sorrows," she said, remembering.

"What sorrows were those?"

"Oh, you know. Some guy did me dirty," she said. "My heart was shattered and would never be the same."

"Stefan helped you see differently."

"He helped me so much, at first, just by listening while I groaned about my troubles. I wasn't looking for someone, you know? But there he was, wagging his tail. Lonely, eager, but most of all, he has his own philosophy of life, and a kind of—wisdom. He has a unique take on the world. He's for change, the good kind. Believe in people, give them what they need to get along."

"He was a political activist?"

"His politics weren't the problem," she said bluntly. "His breaking a promise to me was the problem."

Paul nodded.

"Even so, Stef's not a really bad person. People should know him better before they decide he's some generic bad guy and put him away for life."

"What happened to the bar job?"

"He got fired. He wanted to unionize the workers. I supported him in that."

Yeah, you supported him all right, Paul was thinking. Stefan lived his principles, and you brought home the bacon.

"And I support him now, even though we're not together anymore."

"You broke up after his arrest?" he asked, nudging her along.

She nodded.

"Why?"

"I need to trust someone," she said. "I couldn't get my heart broken again by a man who wouldn't be straight with me."

Flame in her eyes, burning, fearsome. If Paul lied to Nina, would she hold it so ferociously against him? No.

They had traveled way beyond hard-and-fast rules. "How long were you together?"

"About two years before he got arrested."

"While you were together, did you ever fight with him?"

"Oh, all the time."

"He ever hurt you in any way?" He had checked and found no record of domestic calls, but many women never called.

"What? Are you crazy? Stefan would never—oh, my God. I see what you're getting at. Did he ever, like, creep up behind me and try to strangle me? No. He never did! He never hit me. He never touched me, except"—she appeared near tears—"tenderly."

"You have your own business?"

She needed a few seconds to blink and change topics. "No. I work for another woman who gets in all the clients. She contracts to landscape and maintain specific commercial properties. We don't do houses, only businesses, which keeps her profits higher. Our clients are gas stations, restaurants, that kind of place. The Monterey Bay area's full of small-business types needing our kind of service," she said. "Sure wish I owned the company. I'd love to buy her out. Stefan and I could . . ." She blushed. "I used to think we'd make a really dynamite team."

"That night that Stefan got caught," Paul said. "Could you tell me about it one more time?" People's stories had a way of changing. He wanted Nina to know what Erin would say on the stand. She needed all the help she could get on preparation for this trial, and had gotten precious little. What a ridiculous situation, Nina taking on yet another lost cause, this time with Klaus, who was speeding into senility, from what he had seen lately.

"We ate out at the Captain's Gig," she said promptly.

"Then we had a few drinks, I think, and just talked. Tequila. It's the devil for sure. I guess I went to bed early."

"You didn't know he went out."

"No."

"You had no idea he was digging up a grave that night," he said.

"No."

"Did you notice what time he left?"

Erin shifted her legs, which had been crossed, to a more rigid position, parallel and aligned. "I didn't notice he was gone at first. I didn't notice until later."

"Which was when?" Paul asked.

"Maybe midnight. I woke up and he wasn't there. And then a few hours later he called from the police station. Talk about a wake-up call. That was bad."

"What do you think of Wanda Wyatt?"

"Stef's mother?" She picked at some loose threads along the edge of a pillow. "He's way more like her than his brother."

A bulb flickered. "But she favors his brother?" Paul said.

"She doesn't have high hopes for Stefan."

"Ah."

"He has potential, but she still sees him as an immature child who never got potty-trained and has accidents to this day. Everything's a personal affront to Wanda, like Stef's messing up intentionally to make her feel bad."

"Messing up, as in lobbing a brick at a police officer?"

She must have heard his disapproval. Her entire body stiffened, preparing for a strong defense. "That cop was beating a friend of his with a stick. It wasn't like it sounds."

"Or," Paul consulted his notes, "getting into a bar fracas and sending another man to the hospital?"

"He was a kid. The other guy picked a fight and he

fought back. It wasn't his fault the guy fell. He hardly touched him."

Oh, this girl was the perfect mate for many, many guys Paul had personally helped put away over the years, back when he had been on the force. What a cheerleader! But what an adorable cheerleader.

"People don't understand him. You don't, and you're supposedly on his side. Let me tell you, Stef's generous, sweet, a real pushover. He does his mother's chores, which his brother would never do. He helped our neighbors, buying them groceries, taking them out to run errands, fixing their cars."

"He's been in jail twice before."

"Yeah, yeah. Repeat offender. That's what my folks call him. Every bad thing he ever did, he got caught and punished for. But he would never kill someone, for God's sake. I just wish—my family is old-fashioned. The truth is, I care about what they think. It's a mess. I couldn't stay with him unless they approved. Obviously, they don't. So who knows what will happen?" She set her cup on the table and ran a finger around its edge. "We need you people to get him out of that place. How can they just lock him up and take away his future? I want him out."

Paul thought about how young they were, and how very long even a few months apart must feel. How long had he hung on to Nina? For years. And he was not getting any younger. Distracted by her hunky young jailbird beau, Erin didn't even bother to flirt with Paul. To her, he must seem out of the running.

"We want him out, too, Erin. We'll do what we can."

She leaned back in the scruffy chair, smoothing impossibly wrinkled jeans. "I had things all planned out for us," she said. "I was going to get him to propose to me, then drag him to meet my family and show them how cool he is, really. Then we would have a wedding on the beach at

Carmel River, with—oh, flags, a pretty dress. Everyone high! And now when those thoughts come into my head, I just put them aside. Either that, or I have to cry. But whatever happens with Stef and me, he's innocent. He shouldn't be in jail."

"He's facing a third strike," Paul reminded her, afraid to enable such powerful faith. How hard she would fall, if Stefan Wyatt turned out dirty.

As they usually did.

"I wanted to talk to you about that. What if I told you—he stayed home that night, and never went to the cemetery at all?"

"I wouldn't believe you. You've been deposed. You've made statements to the police."

"What if I could prove it?"

"How?"

"I don't know. A video with a date on it?" She leaned toward him.

So, she was willing to lie. Love conquers all, including distinctions between good and bad. He guessed he knew that better than anyone. "Did he ever speak directly with Alex Zhukovsky in your presence?"

"Would it help if he did?"

"You want to help him, tell me the truth."

"Then no."

"You don't know anything about someone hiring him to go to the cemetery?"

"I want to help him," she said urgently.

"Erin, what really happened?"

Tears filled her eyes. "I don't know why he went there that night. Damn it! I knew there was something up when he poured his drink in the plant, but he was being so nice. I just thought he wanted to stay sober for . . ." She paused and blushed. "You're a good listener."

"Do you know his brother, Gabe?"

"I've met him a few times. He didn't exactly hang with us."

"How close are he and Stefan?"

"Stef loves and admires Gabe. He's done plenty for him, starting when they were little kids and Gabe was sick. Stef took care of him then, even though Stef was the younger brother. That's hard on a family. Maybe it's why Wanda favors Gabe, because he was weaker physically when they were growing up."

"What was wrong with him?"

"A blood disease. Stefan donated blood or something, and Gabe was cured."

Blood? Paul's ears pricked up, but then he remembered an earlier case: a blood transfusion doesn't change someone's DNA. Rats. "What does Gabe think of Stefan?"

"Gabe thinks he's guilty," she said flatly. "He says the blood evidence can't lie. Have you met him?"

"He was away most of last week and we haven't had a chance to hook up. I understand he works for an agency, Classic Collections?"

"When I first heard the name, I thought, wow, fashion. Maybe he can get me clothes cheap." Her mouth hinted at dimples. "But no, Gabe's your man when it comes to collecting on a bad debt. He's their top agent."

"How does he get along there?"

"He hates his boss. He feels underrespected, underpromoted, underpaid. Wanda hasn't been a good influence, always building him up, praising him for a C on his report card, you know? I think she feels guilty she was a widow, that she couldn't give him a father. Isn't that stupid, as if she could have kept her husband alive when his time came? Have you met Wanda yet?"

"Yes, we've met, briefly." He couldn't think of a case he had worked on with less lead time and more frustrating, abortive encounters. "I'm seeing her again this afternoon.

Any chance Gabe had something to do with putting Stef up to this graveyard job?"

She stared at him. "Why would he?"

"Did Gabe know Christina Zhukovsky?"

"I never heard he did."

"Do you happen to know if he attended a conference that was held at Cal State Monterey last spring?"

"Something about Russians, right?"

Amazed that he finally had a hit, he said, "Right."

"Yeah. He went. I think someone from his work was speaking. Maybe they wanted to open up a Russian office. Weird thought, huh?"

"Did Stefan attend?"

"Why would he? No."

"Does Gabe have a girlfriend?"

"They come and go. You have to be happy in who you are to love and be loved. He isn't."

Paul looked at his notes and asked, "Any idea why he consulted the Pohlmann firm? Because apparently, that's how Stefan ended up hiring them."

She thought, and Paul almost laughed at how intently she screwed her face up, as if organizing the machinery inside her head had to happen before any real thinking could be accomplished. He could see how she might be perceived as flighty or not too bright. Erin wasn't dumb. It had taken him a while to figure that out. She had too much going on inside, and hadn't yet learned to order her thoughts and present them in the way the world liked, strained into a weak juice. "Something about a will. Maybe he needed one? Although it's not like he has any money, or Wanda, either."

Paul got up to leave, thanking her.

"My testimony is coming up," she said. "Shouldn't we discuss that?"

"We just did," he said.

"I mean—what should I say?"

"Tell the truth, Erin."

"I owe him. I want to help."

"That's the way to do it." Even Jaime, not exactly the pit-bull king of all prosecutors, would tear this dark-eyed sweetheart to bits if she tried to pull a fast one.

Paul picked up Wish and stopped for lunch at a corner deli. Breaking his usual rule, Paul ate a turkey on rye in the Mustang and allowed Wish his sloppy salami while driving to Pebble Beach, where Wanda Wyatt lived with her son Gabriel. Paul chatted with the gatekeeper for a moment and followed the directions into the forest, which today looked spectacular in the unusual sun.

"An enclave for the rich and infamous, my mom says," Wish remarked, using one of the pile of napkins Paul had demanded to wipe up a spill of lettuce on his lap.

Pebble Beach had a rep. Golf, mansions, fog, money—but in fact some people managed to live there without much money. Funky cottages like Wanda and Gabe's sneaked between the trees.

A tall, blowsy woman with hair falling almost to her waist answered the door. One hand held a silver barrette, a match for her gray hair. She snapped the clip in place before shaking hands. "You again," she said. "Follow me." Her skin was lined but fresh looking. She was in her early to mid sixties, Paul decided.

They followed her out to a small, clammy patio shadowed by a six-foot wooden fence that enclosed three sides. Two dogs barked and flung themselves at the visitors for a good long, satisfying time before Wanda ordered them away, then settled for giving them the stink eye from a scrap of grass. A mildewy smell surrounded them.

Glancing critically at the dewy grass, Wanda turned off the sprinklers. "You like Lhasas?" she asked.

Wish nodded. He liked dogs, period.

"I like other people's dogs," Paul said. "I don't know Lhasas in particular. Are yours purebred?"

"Mine come from the pound. Rupso," she said, pointing. She was sandy-colored with black-tipped ears and a black muzzle. Small teeth gleamed out of a tangled mass of hair. "I like her overbite. Gives her a rakish air. This little one's Gompa Apso. I call her Bo."

She looked at her watch. "Gabe should be here by now. He knows you've been trying to talk to him." She plopped herself down in a chair in front of a stone table, and motioned for them to sit. "How's the case going?"

"Quickly," Paul said.

"Maybe it seems like that to you, but my son's in jail, so we're real happy to see things proceeding. What happened with the old man? Pohlmann?" she asked. "I thought he was running Stefan's defense. We heard all about his great reputation, and now I hear from Stefan that a woman's doing most of the work."

"Nina Reilly. She's second chair. Klaus is still in charge."

"I hate not being in court. They said the witnesses can't be there."

"Standard procedure. What isn't standard is that you, Stefan's mother, are testifying for the prosecution."

"Look," she said, sounding depressed. "This is an awful situation. I don't want to testify against Stefan. I love that kid, in spite of him wringing the color right out of my hair with his troublemaking!" She touched her head. "If my neighbor hadn't said something to the police, I wouldn't have told them anything."

Her cell phone rang and she answered, spoke, and hung up. Her green eyes, along with Bo's and Rupso's limpid ochres, pored over him. "That was Gabe. You'll have to meet him at work, okay? I'll give you directions."

Paul nodded. "What were you doing out that night, Ms. Wyatt?"

"I just happened to stop by Stefan's house to drop off some leftovers and fresh rolls I made for their breakfast. I made extra for them. That girl of his can't cook for beans. And, more bad luck for my son, I saw him outside."

"What do you know about Constantin Zhukovsky?"

"You mean why my son might want his bones? I can't imagine. It's very, very strange." She did indeed appear baffled.

"Did you know the man?"

"Me? No."

"Did Stefan ever mention Christina Zhukovsky to you?" Paul asked.

She shook her head. "And he didn't kill her, either. When he was a little kid I used to think how much he reminded me of one of his tops, just spinning around knocking down everything that he came near. About as powerful and effective as a gnat," she said. "Any harm he ever did was completely unintentional."

"Stefan was arrested twice before."

"I thought once kids grew up you could get on with your life, watch from afar while they solved their own problems." She petted her dog. "Stupid me. They never stop worrying you. Even when they're adults, you lie awake at night hating that other people hurt and disappoint them, scared they'll do something asinine, which they will. You never escape from being a mother." She sighed. "Stefan's got a good heart," she said dutifully. "I love my son, but he's a hopeless idealist, one of those people who thinks you can change things by making waves in a wading pool. I thought I taught him better. I was involved in all that nonsense when I was young, too, but then I grew up. And what did he get for trying to organize a union? Fired. Surprise, surprise."

Momentarily sidetracked, she turned attention to her dog. "Get down, Bo, or no cookie." Bo got down. "Listen," she continued, "Stefan dug up a grave. I think we all know that. He shouldn't have done it. But he didn't kill that woman. He found her there, just like he said. One thing about Stefan—and this sets him apart from most of the world—he's not a liar. He always openly admitted the cookies he stole: one reason he was always in trouble."

"So let's prove that, Ms. Wyatt. What can you say that will clear him?"

She shook her head, scratching Bo behind the ear with agitated fingers. "Stefan would never harm another soul."

"Ms. Wyatt, did he ever mention that Alex Zhukovsky hired him to dig up his father's bones?" Paul asked.

"Here's what he told me: he said he had a quick job to do, and that he would make enough doing it to buy that girl of his a ring. He said he would have a thousand dollars. So he was hired to dig the bones. Honestly, that kid. How could he not know it was some awful setup or something? Why couldn't God give him a little common sense?"

"More like his brother?"

"Right. Classic mother's lament."

"How do you explain what he did?" Paul asked.

"For the money. I can't explain it any better than that."

Can't or won't? Paul thought, wishing he knew. Classic detective's lament.

"You say you're a widow," Wish said. "What was your husband like?"

"A decent man, but distant from us. He traveled a lot. I raised the boys by myself, pretty much. They hardly remember him."

"When did your husband die?" Wish persisted.

"The boys were very young. Stefan was three, Gabe

was four. Stefan hardly noticed. Gabe was hit hardest. It's funny, he never knew his father well at all, it was more the idea of him. He didn't want to tell kids at school his father was dead. He pretended to have one. I guess I should have remarried."

"What did he die of?"

"One of those breakdowns of the system," she said. "He was old, and he had a lot wrong with him over the years, things that came and went. One day something got him. I was there with him when he died at the hospital." Suddenly, she looked ready to cry.

"What kind of parent was he?" Paul asked hastily.

"Old-fashioned, courtly but conventional in his attitudes about women's roles, in spite of my attitude, which was hardly conventional. But I'll tell you one thing. He loved his children," she said. She petted the pooch so hard its little eyes bulged, and that made Paul want to pursue the topic, but Wanda didn't give much up. "I do believe he did."

"Did your sons get along as kids?" Paul asked.

"Not a bit. They fought dirty." She actually had a lot to say on the topic, many memories, but none of them helped much with the present-day issues. "But Stefan would die for Gabe," she finished. "He proved it when Gabe got so sick."

"With what?"

"Childhood leukemia. They gave Stefan drugs that made him forget the procedure, and promised me there was a low risk of him being hurt, although I felt terrible when they did the spinal thing and took his donation. He was awfully young. But Gabe's paying his brother back now, giving his hard-earned savings to save Stefan's skin. It's a shame. He's worked hard for every dime. Stefan has a lot to answer for. Just—not murder."

"Notice how happy she is talking about Gabe, and how conflicted when she talks about Stefan?" Paul asked Wish as they drove away.

"I'm glad to be the only son," Wish said, accelerating to eighty as soon as they hit Highway 1 going north toward Seaside. "But my parents don't play favorites anyway. No, they're equally conflicted over all of us." He laughed heartily.

"Stefan's the worm; Gabe's the bright, red apple."

"Oldest son, and the striver in the family," Wish said. "Must be a burden for Gabe being her favorite, even though he's got a brother in jail who is definitely no competition."

Seaside, formerly populated almost entirely by transient military families who traded in their thrift-shop furniture to new families when they left, had come up in the world. It had its very own Borders to make up for the bankrupt Kmart. On the eastern fringe of the town, the building housing Classic Collections stood where once acres of artichokes had flourished.

Paul thought he could still smell artichokes, although it might perhaps have been a massive sewer project that had caught his attention.

Wanda Wyatt had directed them to Building E, a small, flat-roofed, asymmetrical building with ominous overhangs some architect had had a blast—no, had been blasted—designing.

The weekend security guard, a small woman stuck behind a desk, excited to have a break from the existential angst of her daily breadwinning, took their IDs, scratched the back of her neck, and wasted a lot of their time making up questions to ask them, mostly irrelevant. Finally, cowed by the brevity of their answers, she called up to Gabriel Wyatt's office. "Second floor," she said, handing back the IDs.

"Thanks," said Paul with what he hoped was a grateful smile, expressing his deep sympathy for the bored. As they waited for the elevator they read off the names of some of the other small businesses sharing the building. This was clearly not a ragingly successful place.

Wyatt met them at the elevator and led them back into offices accessible only to the chosen few with bar-coded cards.

"How's it going?" Paul asked.

"Like it's supposed to." Tall, maybe six feet two, Gabe Wyatt had glossy fair hair, a thin build, and a loose grace as he pulled a chair up to his desk and sat, crossing one leg. A handsome dude, on the ascetic side.

He resembled Stefan, if you caught his right profile, but in a supercharged, glamorous incarnation. He had strong features perfectly sized and shaped, and skin that appeared airbrushed, scrubbed as clean of texture as the face of a computer-generated game hero. If he were a movie star, he would be typecast in romantic leads, and would lose all the good character roles to Nicolas Cage's bird beak and bovine eyes.

"Sorry it's been so hard getting together, but what can I do for you?" Gabe asked. "How's Stef? Holding up? I haven't been able to see him since the trial started, in case I need to testify."

"Not surprisingly, his focus at the moment is getting out of jail. I'm curious," Paul said. "What all do you do here?"

They were sitting in Gabe's cubicle, narrow, with poor lighting, a peculiar mix of executive desk, chair, and a tiny window with a distant view of dunes.

"Need to lean on somebody?" Gabe asked.

"Not at the moment."

"Well, that's what we do."

"What do you mean, lean?"

Gabriel Wyatt laughed. "Hey, I'm your worst nightmare. Ever paid a bill late, even though you were on vacation or the mailman delivered to the wrong address? Well, that's where I come in."

"We're talking phone calls, right? Nothing brutal?"

"Oh, yeah, of course." Gabe Wyatt got comfy in his worn but wide upholstered chair. He obviously spent lots of time with his butt planted there. "It's a hot field. We're the best in the country at collecting. Most people we call aren't the ones that forgot a bill or two, or had them lost in the mail, believe me. Most of 'em deserve a mean spanking."

Paul disliked him instantly. He had talked to Gabe's type a few times. Explanations degraded into weaseled excuses in their world. "What kind of background do you need for a job like yours?"

"I had two years at Monterey Peninsula College, and a semester at Cal State. Studied communications."

"You like your job?" Wish obviously was struggling to keep the astonishment out of his voice.

"Sure." He laughed. "I like dealing with people."

"Things going well for you here, then?" Paul asked, watching Wish, who was desperately trying to come to terms with his first sight of the devil incarnate.

Maybe Gabe, who rubbed his right arm, had picked up on the negativity of their ions. "Hey, I know people hate me for what I do. I work because I have to, and this is not so bad, as jobs go. I'd rather win the lottery. Wouldn't you?" He looked out the window toward the dunes. The sky, feathered with white clouds, looked wintry.

"I understand you first consulted Alan Turk about a will," Paul said.

All the superficial hail-fellow attitude dropped

instantly. "What's that got to do with anything?" Gabriel Wyatt asked. "How will this help my brother?"

"I don't know. I just don't like secrets when our client's freedom is at a high risk of being lost permanently."

Gabe hesitated, finally saying, "I don't want you to think I wouldn't do whatever I can to get my brother out of jail. Maybe my mother told you our father died when we were very young?"

"Yes."

"Well, I consulted Alan Turk about his will."

"He left you something?"

"There were questions. I needed answers."

"Why not just ask your mother?"

"I started there. Our mother wasn't helpful so I went to Alan."

"Okay," Paul said, waiting.

"That's it. You wanted to know. It's nothing to do with Stefan."

"So it seems."

"Anything else I can tell you?"

"Do you like your brother?"

"Funny question," he said. "But I guess I do. He's a nice enough guy. If only he could hold down a job." He said the words lightly, but Paul thought he could detect a slight note of envy.

"Erin, his ex-girlfriend, doesn't seem to feel you respect him much."

He frowned. "He was an angry kid, but I think he's gotten over that since he met her. In spite of his legal troubles, Stefan doesn't need much to make him happy. I guess she notices that I'm always on his case about how he should challenge himself more, make something of himself." He laughed. "As if my life's such a great example. I work too hard for too little. My boss takes advantage of me. Here it is Sunday. Am I out boating on Monterey Bay today? Am I eating ice cream? Stefan would be, if he were out. And I'd be here, working."

"We need to figure out this connection to Alex Zhukovsky. Stefan claims he never spoke in person to the man, and yet he supposedly hired Stefan."

"And you think Stefan's lying."

"Don't know," Paul said, "but we haven't been able to establish a connection."

"Sorry, I can't help you there. Stef never said a word to me."

"Did you get along as kids?"

"We had the usual rivalries."

"He saved your life."

"That's right. And I'm forever in his debt for that, I guess."

"Erin says you believe he's guilty."

Gabe squinted at Paul. "My brother's blood was found at the scene. It's scary. I don't believe in voodoo, and I'm not that big on religion. But blood evidence . . . I wish I could explain it away." He seemed genuinely confused. "I didn't know he knew her. I didn't know he went there. How did this happen, where he ended up burying her body in Constantin Zhukovsky's grave? I've asked Stefan, but he can't explain it. He thinks you should just believe him."

"Everyone says he doesn't lie."

"But—" Gabe said. He picked up the receiver for the phone on his desk and set it gently back into its cradle. "How can you ignore the evidence?"

"Your mom says that as children, you fought a lot."

"What do you expect with two boys in one house? Maybe we got all our animosity out growing up."

" 'Rolled on the floor, kicking each other in the face, dust flying,' she told us," Paul said. "And she says you were the more fragile of the two. Being sick, I guess . . ."

"We're over that," Gabe interrupted.

"Did you know Christina Zhukovsky?" Wish asked suddenly.

"No."

"We understand you attended the conference at Cal State. You know, the one last spring, dealing with Russia?"

Gabe's eyes shifted between Paul and Wish, as if seeking a safe haven and not finding one. "I did, actually."

"Why?" Paul's pen took a rest.

"One of the guys I work with spoke at the conference. I went to see him. It was practically required."

"See, we heard that," Paul said. "Unfortunately, your story doesn't check out. Nobody from this firm spoke at that conference."

Gabe's wheels spun. "Well, he canceled at the last minute. I went anyway."

"Make any good contacts while you were there?" Paul said, not attempting to hide his disbelief.

"Not really. No."

"Sergey Krilov?"

"Doesn't sound familiar."

"That surprises me. You were seen together." No sooner was the lie out than Paul forgave himself.

Gabriel Wyatt didn't seem discomfited, but then, good God. He harassed people for a living, whether they deserved it or not.

"I talked with a lot of people there," Gabe said. "Have a stack of cards a foot high. I might have met him."

"Can I see them? The cards?"

"They're not here."

"Later?"

"I was speaking figuratively. I'm sure I threw them away. Nothing lasting came out of that conference for me."

"You know, Christina Zhukovsky organized the conference. How could you not know who she was?"

"I wasn't looking for her. Look, it's just a coincidence, me going there. I get around. If I'd known she'd be dead a week later and my brother would be accused of the crime, I'd have stayed home."

Paul looked at his notes, zooming in on the one that said, "Call Nina and give her hell for being so distant and sexually unavailable. Make her love you."

"Strange," he said.

"What?"

"People saw you talking to her."

"There were a lot of people there that day!" Gabriel Wyatt said. "I never saw her."

And I'm P. Diddy, Paul thought.

14

Bᵧ ᴛʜᴇ ᴛɪᴍᴇ ᴛʜᴇ ꜰɪʀꜱᴛ cup of coffee kicked hard enough
to awaken her, Nina was already sitting in court, listening to the testimony of the forensics expert, Abbott Lumley. She had not slept at all the night before. After she
picked Bob up from the train station, hit the shower, and
loaded dry dog food into Hitchcock's bowl while he
looked mournfully at her, his way of complaining about
the lack of some kind of gourmet supplement, it was
nearly eight at night. Then Paul stopped by with all kinds
of new information, some so startling she didn't know
where to begin with it.

So, following a long discussion with Bob and an even
longer discussion with Paul, she had sat at the kitchen table
all night long waiting for a clear picture to form out of the
blur. That never happened.

With her lucky pen, she doodled on the pad in front of
her, her way of tuning into the proceedings. She drew the
Russian medal. Stefan looked down at her drawing. What
did the medal mean to him? To read his vaguely alert expression, nothing much. Klaus had started the morning off
with the requested pep talk, which also must have helped.

"Mr. Lumley," Jaime said, "you've mentioned your opinion that an attempt was made to clean the crime scene. What, in your opinion as an expert, was the purpose of that attempt?"

Nina hated hypotheticals but maybe Abbott Lumley would offer her an opening, spinning his yarns. She didn't object.

Lumley, a short, lively, smiling man in his sixties with the plump cheeks of a baby, waited politely for Klaus or Nina to intervene before answering. For all his playful looks, he was a forensics expert who had testified in dozens of murder cases. He knew exactly what to expect in court and what tone to strike. Today, he was apparently going for earnest and helpful.

"Considering the body of the victim was found buried in a grave, I believe the perpetrator hoped that by cleaning the crime scene, he or she would not only hide evidence of his crime, but would suggest to anyone wondering about the whereabouts or safety of Christina Zhukovsky that there was nothing wrong. If her body had not been found, possibly the crime might never have been detected."

"But it was. And your team found broken glass with blood, which has since been identified as belonging to that of the defendant, correct?"

"Objection." Nina thought she had to keep the jury clear on the idea that, no matter what the DNA results, the match was not one hundred percent. "That's an inaccurate statement of the evidence. These are probabilities, not fact."

"Overruled." This kind of probability every court in the land pretty much accepted as fact.

"That's right, the blood on the glass matched that of the defendant," Lumley answered, repeating it just in case anyone had missed the train. "When we first arrived at the apartment, we used light tests to identify the presence of blood. We then used standard procedures for collecting samples. We found blood mixed with glass shards only in the kitchen area."

"How was the glass cleaned up?"

"Swept up with the victim's broom, where we found one of our samples."

They skated smoothly along for a while then, right over where the glass went after it was swept up, and around the fingerprint evidence. Nina made notes, punctuating with fancy asterisks.

"Now, let's go back to the cemetery," Jaime said. Nina thought, Oh, let's not. So much of what had gone before was a replay and confirmation of the testimony of Kelsey Banta. But Jaime was on a roll, back to his favorite setting, recalling the grisly deed, the protruding arm of the victim, the three layers of trash bags that were intended to be the shroud for the murdered woman.

Much of what Lumley said had to do with tying Stefan to the grave site, which didn't interest Nina as much as anything new he might have to contribute about the blood evidence. She knew Stefan had dug up the grave. He had admitted he dug up the grave. Disputing that evidence wouldn't help their case.

With the obsessiveness of a true professional, Lumley lingered lovingly over details. He described matching the bones found in the back seat of Stefan's car to what remained behind in Constantin Zhukovsky's grave. They had found nothing in the garbage bags, other than Christina's body and clothing. A shovel and gloves in Stefan's car contained soil that matched that found in the grave.

Because of rain the previous day, the casts of footprints Lumley made from the area outside the grave showed lace-delicate patterns matching Stefan's Vision Quest canvas shoes. The shoes were irrefutably his, all could see that, right down to the wear marks. Jaime showed the casts and photographs of imprints made from them, then passed around one of Stefan's shoes so that the jury could see for themselves. They passed the plastic-bagged dirty shoe somberly from hand to hand and Nina could feel Stefan's body shaking. The absurd sight of his shoe making the courtroom rounds had gotten to him. She realized he was on the verge of erupting into laughter. To give him something else to think about, she nudged him, hard.

"If I'd seen this coming," he whispered to her, "I'd have worn my new ones to the cemetery. Like wearing fresh underwear in case a truck hits you on the way home. Always best to be prepared." His humor came out at odd times, but Nina liked him better this way than beaten-down and acting guilty.

But the worst was to come, the moment Jaime stuck his extensive collection of blowups onto an easel: photographs of the victim alive and dead, bagged and unbagged; the graveyard; and the deceptively neat crime scene. Lumley took his turn describing them.

Stefan gripped the side of his chair, as if unsteady, and caught on a rocking boat, but from the table up, he viewed the pictures with steely equanimity, as directed. She could smell his sweat.

From the shots of Christina Zhukovsky at work and at home, Nina judged that this had been a woman who didn't emphasize her looks. Behind the glasses her eyes had been a pale blue, and the wide cheekbones gave her character. Her long straight hair had been left to wander where it would. She appeared quiet and smart, ethereal and distant. Not a woman of the body, but of the mind. She had enjoyed the money inherited from her father, Nina could deduce that from the photographs of her penthouse apartment with an ocean view that would look enticing on the cover of a home decor magazine.

But she had never made much of a salary from her past jobs, and—Nina rifled through Paul's notes. Yes, here it was, Alex's interview. His and Christina's father, Constantin, was a baker. None of this had to do with what Lumley was talking about, but Nina couldn't concentrate.

The point was, Christina had inherited money. And money is always worth considering as a motive for murder.

True, the killer hadn't robbed Christina's apartment. Nothing had been missing.

Even so, Nina made a note to have Paul look deeper into Christina's finances.

As Lumley finished up his direct testimony, she reviewed the notes she had made to help her with the afternoon's cross-examination. Judge Salas excused everybody for lunch, and Nina walked out with Klaus.

Klaus, who had worn a milky glaze over his eyes for most of the morning, the better to nap, snapped awake, walking briskly beside her toward the parking lot, suddenly focused, excited about what delicacies they might select from the deli counter.

They bought sandwiches and drinks, and Nina got Klaus squared away at a table by the window. Within seconds, people sitting at a nearby table recognized him, which got them all into mutual reminiscing going back to days before Nina was born. Nina ate quickly, then stepped outside to make calls. She spoke briefly with her father, who wanted Bob to visit that evening to watch a game, eat barbecue, and stay over. She called Paul, but he didn't answer. She wondered if he was catching up on some rest after the weekend, and left a recklessly desperate message she hoped would make him drop any alternate plans he might have cooked up for his evening.

At the doors leading into the courtroom, Klaus stopped her. "This Lumley is very sure of himself. The jury likes him. It's easy to be hoodwinked by the intellectual chicanery of such a convincing advisor. Your duty is to assault his respectability. Ask him who he sleeps with, or whether he knew the victim." He waved his hand. "You'll think of something. But you must throw him off balance. Then you might be able to knock him down."

So, while appearing sanguine and indifferent to this morning's witness, Klaus had been listening. Just when she thought his little gray cells had dried to dust, he fired them up and shot the sparks her way.

Klaus had an awful lot of success in the past with this strategy, attacking the psychology, not the actual testimony of the witness. Opening the door to the court, she reflected that what worked for him would not work for her in this case. As many jurors would hate her as hail her for bringing Lumley down a few pegs in a personal attack. Anyway, that was not the way she practiced law. She liked coercing doubt by letting the elegant framework of the cross-examination do exactly what it was intended to do. She didn't make a good bully, except when it came to logic.

Nina and Klaus greeted Stefan and sat down. Some lingering procedural issues for the judge were dispatched quickly, and she stood up to start the cross-examination.

"Mr. Lumley, in most murder cases, fingerprints provide compelling evidence that a certain person can be proven to have been in a certain place, holding certain items, correct?"

"Yes."

"You've testified at many trials. Aren't fingerprints often the most telling evidence against a defendant?"

"Yes."

"And yet you've made short work of the fingerprints found at the scene of Christina Zhukovsky's murder today. Why?"

He smiled genially. "We found little of relevance."

"Did you find a single fingerprint that would place my client, Stefan Wyatt, at Christina Zhukovsky's apartment that night or at any other time?"

"We were unable to match fingerprints found at the scene with any on record."

"No fingerprints in the kitchen that matched his prints?"

"No."

"No fingerprints in the living room that matched his prints?"

"Correct."

"In fact, in that entire apartment, which is very large by most standards, nearly two thousand square feet, is there any fingerprint evidence proving my client was there?" She didn't want him deviating from the point, bringing up the obvious proof Stefan's blood provided. "Answer yes or no, please."

"No."

"Not even a partial print?"

"No. It's my view that the killer wore gloves."

"And nothing on any of the pieces of glass recovered?"

"No."

"Move on, Counsel," Judge Salas said.

"So the killer wore gloves while he was doing this glass cleanup?"

"That's my opinion."

"Then we have a match, don't we? You found gloves in the defendant's Honda, didn't you?"

"Correct."

"How many pairs?"

"One. Gardening gloves, very dirty." He was holding People's Exhibit 37.

"Made of cloth?"

"A loose-weave cotton."

"And how much glass did you find on the gloves?" Nina turned to the jury, eyebrows raised.

"None."

"They were made of rough fabric, weren't they?"

"Yes."

"And you picked up pieces so small they were almost microscopic off the kitchen floor?"

"Yes."

"So wouldn't you have expected to find glass on those gloves?" She had People's 37 passed along the jury box. The fabric was rough and porous.

"Maybe he had another set."

"Did you look for another set of gloves at the victim's condo?"

"We made a thorough search for anything that might be relevant."

"And no luck?"

"We found no second pair of gloves there."

"What about at the cemetery?"

"No."

"Stefan Wyatt's house?"

"There were several pairs of gardening gloves similar to those found in Wyatt's car."

"Any with glass on them?"

"No."

"Let's see," Nina said. "Your theory is that the killer wore gloves, hence the lack of fingerprints on the broom and dustpan. But they weren't Stefan Wyatt's gloves, because those gloves probably would have retained at least a microscopic speck of the glass, isn't that right?"

They all waited for the response.

"Am I stating your testimony correctly?" Nina said.

"To a point. Maybe the defendant didn't do the cleanup. Maybe the victim did. There were plenty of her prints on both broom and dustpan. Even on the kitchen trash can."

Nina had been waiting for that. "Sure," she said. "Let's follow that theory. The defendant, fearful for her life, threw her glass of brandy at the killer, and the glass hit him and shattered when it hit. With me so far?"

"Yes."

"So then, putting aside her fear, the victim calmly got out her broom and dustpan and carefully swept all the glass she could into the dustpan and put it into the trash. Was this before or after the killer was strangling her?"

"It could have happened. Some period of time could have elapsed between the glass being thrown and the murder."

"Isn't it much more likely that the killer did wear gloves, the killer did attempt to clean up the glass after the murder, and the killer wasn't Stefan Wyatt since they weren't his gloves?"

"Then how come he buried the body at the cemetery?"

"Who says he did? After the body was found, and Stefan Wyatt was arrested, did you also conduct a search of the defendant's home?"

"We did."

"Did you find any evidence there linking him to the crime of killing Christina Zhukovsky?"

"No."

"Any trash bags of the same type used to cover her body?"

"No."

"Any broken glass which matched glass found at the crime scene of the same type in his vacuum?"

"No."

"In his trash?"

"No."

"In his vehicle?" Again, Nina was talking to the jury. She wanted them to know how important this lack of evidence was.

"No."

Very interesting, Madeleine Frey's rapid nod said.

"Now let's get back to that blood. Mr. Lumley, did you supervise the physical examination of my client on the morning of April thirteenth, right after he was arrested?"

"Yes."

"Was there any proof, however small, that he had handled broken glass recently? Any cuts, any invisible shards, anything?"

"No."

"You found no evidence of broken glass on his clothes, in his pockets, on his hands, in his car, or in his home, correct, Mr. Lumley?"

"Objection," Jaime said. "Asked and answered."

"Overruled," said the judge, happy to be exercising his voice again.

She repeated the question.

"No."

"Making it very difficult to imagine how he left blood at the crime scene less than twenty-four hours before, wouldn't you say?" Might as well grab the opportunity to pound that nail in further.

The jury nodded, meditating on the question. How did Stefan leave blood behind in Christina's apartment? They should take this conundrum to bed with them tonight, and work it, Nina thought. Maybe they would figure out what Nina couldn't.

"Mr. Lumley," she said, when he didn't answer. "How could my client, Stefan Wyatt, leave blood behind at that crime scene, when he never bled?"

"I don't know," he said, showing with a deep sigh how disgusted he was that it was so.

15

THE BAILIFF OPENED THE COURTROOM door and beckoned. Nina watched Alex Zhukovsky straighten his tie and follow him in.

On Nina's left and right, people fidgeted, always keen to see a new face. Zhukovsky walked the central aisle, all eyes fastened on him, looking as conspicuous and anxious as an executioner on his way to the hanging. Passing through the low gate, he looked toward the tables on his left and right, defense on the left, Stefan's miserable gaze following him, the jury on the left against the wall. Klaus glared at him. Alex didn't look at the old man but let his own glance catch on Nina, who ignored him and doodled on her legal pad. As if embarrassed by her indifference, he looked at Judge Salas, a head and black-robed shoulders visible above the massive wooden dais. He stopped where directed. The court clerk told him to raise his right hand.

"My name is Alexis Constantinovich Zhukovsky," he said, swearing to tell the truth. He mounted a step and entered a lower, smaller box attached to the judge's dais and turned around to the roomful of faces. He looked toward the prosecutor. The questioning began.

Sitting, not standing, the D.A. asked him a series of

simple questions about his work. Alex Zhukovsky responded, sounding stiff to Nina. "I am an instructor in Russian language and history at Cal State Monterey," he said. "I also teach other courses. I've been there for the past six years." He told the court he liked his job, and was brother to the victim in this case, Christina Zhukovsky, and son to the man whose bones had been disinterred.

"My father was named Constantin Nicholaevich Zhukovsky. Our mother, Kamila Zhukovsky, died in a car crash when we were young. My sister was eleven. I was only seven."

For a while Jaime's questions were simple, and Zhukovsky, required to explain very little, answered yes or no. Then Jaime began asking Zhukovsky about Christina, her life and work.

"How can you reduce a person's life to a few sentences?" Zhukovsky complained. "She had many facets."

He told the court about her work at the university. "Her last job was working at Cal State Monterey in the Romance Languages Department as the Public Affairs Officer. She helped with organizing the conference, and was very involved in all aspects of it. It was one of the largest and most successful conferences held at the college so far. People came from all over the world to attend."

Sandoval gave him a photograph of Christina and, shaking, Zhukovsky studied his sister's image. In this picture, which Nina also studied, Christina, wearing a neat designer suit, smiled proudly, intelligently. Her face wore hope, ambition, and all the glorious things a human face, a living face could hold, when born to optimism. Holding the photograph, Nina felt sad that nobody would ever see her again as she had undoubtedly been, with shiny brown hair and a shy way of looking up at an observer. Nina would bet she used the weak glasses to disguise a driven nature.

"I can't believe she's gone," her brother told the D.A. His voice quivering, he gave the pictures back with a shaky hand. Looking sympathetic, Sandoval gave his witness a minute to get composed, obviously loving this show of emotion and milking it. He wanted the jury to feel for this nice woman with a public conscience, Nina realized. Christina was just like any other friend, family member, or coworker they might call to mind. People could identify with her. She was nobody, just like them.

Except that she had been murdered.

Wasn't this what the psychologists called cognitive dissonance? Christina Zhukovsky was nobody! She appeared so small in the picture, insignificant, and yet she loomed so very, very big in this courtroom. If Nina had known her as her brother did, would she like her as a woman or pity her as a victim?

While the D.A. returned the photo to a file, Alex grabbed for the carafe of water in front of him, poured, and drank. "Yes, I went to the police station." He had been shown his father's body first, what remained of it. He described what he saw, the skull, the eyebrows, the silver hair lying in strings over a dark serge suit. Bones, loosely assembled. Fine shreds of his white collar, tatters that had once been sleeves. Bits of a sash across his chest, bearing the distinctive three black strips on a yellow background, which Zhukovsky said he well remembered. But the medal of Saint George? It was gone by the time he saw his father's body.

All this he confirmed, remembering, wiping wetness from his brow. Maybe he was having a heart attack, Nina thought.

Stefan hardly blinked at Alex Zhukovsky's testimony, even though several of the jurors appeared squeamish at many of the details. What a self-absorbed, overgrown adolescent he must be, thinking this was easy money, Nina thought along with them. Only a fool would have agreed to do that job in the first place.

Holding up the appraisal, Jaime Sandoval started on the medal. Alex acknowledged the facts. The appraiser had assigned a value of at least five thousand dollars. He had discovered the medal was created of precious materials and seemed to be the correct age for an original, first-class war medal. He suggested it might have been privately commissioned as a memento or honorarium by someone of wealth for a courageous member of his staff or family.

The D.A. showed Zhukovsky a photo of the familiar white embellished cross with the blue stone at its center, and the tiny image of Saint George slaying the dragon. Zhukovsky barely looked. "My sister and I saw it many times in my father's study when we were growing up. We thought it was a toy, a replica. We had no idea how he came to own such a thing. As far as I know, he never fought in a war."

The medal and appraisal were introduced into evidence. The prosecutor had to explain why Stefan would steal Alex's father's body after killing his sister, and the medal seemed to be the only motivation he could come up with.

Yes, Zhukovsky reported, after identifying the other body in the grave as his sister's, he had been taken to Natividad Hospital in the early morning hours of Sunday, April 13. He let loose with indubitable facts: his sister's eyes bulged. Her tongue stuck out of her mouth. Her neck had blue marks. He had fainted and his head had hit the steel wheel of a cart, and had required stitches.

He was shown photos of his sister's dead body. "That is my sister, Christina," he said, only his voice betraying hints of his extreme dismay.

Nina watched as Alex wiped his forehead again. Were this witness's reactions entirely within the realm of normal for a grieving brother? Naturally, these very personal, gruesome images were upsetting.

Zhukovsky went on. "I gave the key to my sister's apartment to a woman detective because I couldn't accompany the police to her apartment. I—couldn't."

The judge called a recess.

Klaus had barely moved throughout Zhukovsky's testimony. His face showed nothing of his thoughts, but Nina felt his scrutiny of this witness as rigorous, piercing.

Questioning resumed. Jaime Sandoval wanted to know about Christina's last days. Zhukovsky told some things about the conference, about her mood. He identified personal items of hers—her appointment book, her purse. He told them he missed his older sister.

The D.A. finally stood. He buttoned his coat, preparing himself. Nina could see how Jaime wanted to signify this moment, the heart of Alex's testimony. Alex swallowed as if preparing to live up to the prosecutor's hopes.

"Do you know Mr. Wyatt, the defendant over there?" Jaime asked.

Rustling and muttering burst forth from Stefan's table. Stefan wanted to speak, but Klaus put a hand on his arm, stopping him.

"No."

"Did your sister ever mention the names Stef Wyatt or Stefan Wyatt to you?"

"No."

"You didn't hire the defendant to dig up your father's grave?"

"No, sir."

"Did you pay him the sum of five hundred dollars in cash at any time for any purpose?"

"No, sir."

Nina let her breath out. He had stuck to his story.

Before the trial, when they went over Zhukovsky's

statements, Jaime Sandoval had seemed certain Stefan Wyatt was responsible for killing Christina Zhukovsky. Now her brother had given the jury no reason to believe otherwise.

"Did you have any reason to wish her dead?" Jaime asked.

"My own sister? Of course not," Alex said.

After the break, Paul stood at the counsel table. "You have plenty to attack him with," he said. "Blow him off the stand."

She put her lips together and blew toward the witness box. "Shoot," she whispered. "He's still there."

"Yeah, well, he's no pushover."

Nina stood. Jaime Sandoval, the prosecutor, noticed, then turned his eyes toward the papers spread out on the table in front of him, mad. He had obviously hoped for Klaus.

"Good afternoon, Mr. Zhukovsky," she said. "My name is Nina Reilly and I represent the defendant, Stefan Wyatt."

"Good afternoon," he replied coolly.

She asked him questions about the identification of his father's bones and his sister's body, fairly rapid-fire, but with a logical progression that she hoped made it easy to follow. She cleared up points about how he had offered a key to the police to let them into Christina's apartment. She tried to lull him with a pleasant manner, a singsong voice, a tone that said, And we all know what's coming next, so no worries. She watched for the tension in his shoulders to leave him. She listened for even, unsuspecting breaths.

He answered her quick questions more and more quickly, with less and less premeditation.

And she dropped a bomb upon a dumbly grazing sheep.

"Your father, Constantin Zhukovsky, claimed he was a page to the last tsar of Russia, did he not?"

Alex Zhukovsky's pale, professorial skin whitened.

"Would you like the question repeated?" The clerk read it back. The reporters, aroused, whipped out pens, poising them like arrows.

"He told stories," Zhukovsky finally croaked out.

"When was the first time you heard him tell you that one?"

"I was a little boy. But you know, my father wasn't reliable. I never knew if any of that talk about his early life was true. Here in America, he was a baker, a pastry shop owner. That's the man I knew."

"And he told you he was a page to the tsar of Russia, did he not?" Nina said, worrying him like a ferret worries a rat.

An alarmed Sandoval said, "Objection, relevance." He hadn't seen this coming.

Nina left Alex Zhukovsky to sit like one of Nabokov's moths, pinned to his seat, and approached the bench.

"Objection overruled," said the judge.

"He told you he was a page . . ." Nina prompted.

"To tsar Nicholas the Second, yes," Zhukovsky admitted. "Yes. But you have to understand. He was full of stories, like fairy tales." He was glaring at Paul, apparently having recognized Paul as the source of his present discomfort.

"Did he tell you about how he taught the *tsarevitch*— the young son of the last tsar, Nicholas the Second—how he taught Tsarevitch Alexis to ride a pony?" Mrs. Peltier, having unlocked the most buried of the old secrets, had other, more detailed memories to relate, Paul and Nina had discovered during follow-up telephone conversations.

"A pony?"

"A pony."

A pause. "Yes."

"Being a page to the tsar would have made your father an important man historically, wouldn't it?"

"Not really. A page was a servant, a drudge. There's no glory in that. Anyway, there were several pages."

"But he would have been there near the end, before the tsar's family was taken away to Ekaterinburg to be executed. It's one of the most important historical events of the twentieth century in Russian history, surely something that would interest a professor of Russian. Didn't he ever mention that?"

"The family was first exiled to Tobolsk, to the Governor's House."

"Professor, I stand corrected." She smiled. She had him now, down a path he could not escape. "But of course he told you he was there as the events of the Russian Revolution unfolded in 1917 and right up to the time the tsar's family was arrested and eventually taken to Ekaterinburg?"

Jaime, nettled into pinching his brows together until they almost touched each other, objected again as to relevance. The lawyers returned to the judge's dais to huddle and whisper. Nina won again. The judge told Zhukovsky to answer the question.

"I was told that he was present, yes," he said. "I have no way of actually knowing."

"Did your father's medal, the one our client stands accused of stealing from the grave, come from those days?"

"I don't know."

"Didn't such a medal ordinarily come directly from the hand of the tsar?"

"Objection. Relevance?" This time Sandoval won.

"Did your father retain any other memorabilia from his youth in Russia?" Nina asked Zhukovsky.

"I imagine if there was anything it would have been something small that was sold when the estate was liquidated after his death. His family had fled Russia during the revolution. They spent any savings, I imagine. They traveled to Estonia, then Sweden, then Canada. After all these travels and the deaths of his parents, he had just a few mementoes of his childhood. I'm sorry I can't be more specific. I simply don't know more."

"Did he ask to be buried with his medal?"

"Yes."

"You could have sold it for at least five thousand dollars and possibly much more, did you know that at the time?"

"I didn't know it was valuable. I did as he asked."

"Ever regret that?" she asked.

Sandoval decided to object, and his objection was sustained.

"Didn't you subsequently decide to dig up your father's grave in order to obtain that medal and sell it?"

"No. Certainly not."

"Didn't you hire Stefan Wyatt to dig up that grave for you for that purpose?"

"Not at all."

"Come on, Mr. Zhukovsky. How would Stefan Wyatt know about the medal, except from you?"

"Anyone who attended my father's funeral in 1978 might have seen the medal," he said.

"Was Stefan Wyatt there? He would have been only three years old that year."

"What's this got to do with my sister—*who was murdered*?"

"How did Stefan Wyatt find out the location of your father's grave?"

"I don't know."

Stefan shook his head and sighed. The judge frowned at him.

"You told him where your father was buried, didn't you?" Nina asked.

"No," Zhukovsky said.

"You gave him the five hundred dollars that was found in his pocket, didn't you?"

"No."

"Tell the truth, you lyin' sack of shit!" Stefan shouted from the counsel table, slamming his hand down. Next thing Nina knew, Salas, up to now a picture of proper judicial decorum, ordered the jury to be gone and lost his cool. The yelling took some time. His deep bellows, unleashed, scared the court silent. Stefan balled up into a corner of the table, cowed. Alex Zhukovsky shrank back from the judge's dais, hoping to evade the hurricane.

When the judge had blown enough air to clear the Salinas fog all the way back to the coast, a mid-afternoon break was called.

When Alex Zhukovsky returned, Nina watched one of the young women on the jury come alive to glower at him. Wearing a sympathetic expression, she then turned her attention toward Stefan. So maybe Nina's earlier strategy had paid off. Something about the witness irked this girl, or something about the client engaged her. Either way, it made Nina happy. She had gotten through to the jury. Did they finally understand that Zhukovsky had hired Stefan to bring him the medal? Maybe. Nina sure hoped so.

"Back on the record," the judge said.

"Can I add something to my previous testimony?" Alex Zhukovsky said. "I remembered something during the break." He grinned.

"I object to that," Nina said, perturbed. What was with this incongruous grin? "There's no question pending."

Jaime spoke to the judge, but dithering, plainly wanting something beneficial to the prosecution to emerge from Zhukovsky's testimony, but uncertain about what to expect. The courtroom scraped and scuffled while the judge considered. Finally, the judge said sternly, "Do you remember the question that you wish to answer again?"

"Yes," Zhukovsky said. "Mr. Sandoval asked me if my sister ever mentioned the name of Stefan Wyatt."

"Objection!" Nina said. "That has been asked and answered."

The judge sent out the jury again, who must have been tired of all the back and forth, adjourning court for five minutes. The lawyers followed him and the clerk back into chambers. After a brief, furious fracas, during which time Nina resorted to every trick, every blackmail, every shaky legal antic she could muster, they all returned, the judge red-faced, Nina breathing fast, Jaime triumphant with glee. The jurors fell into their chairs. Four o'clock, the wall clock read. Nina couldn't recall a longer day in her life. She took her place facing Alex Zhukovsky.

"You may supplement your answer to the question," said Judge Salas.

The clerk read it: " 'Did your sister ever mention the names Stef Wyatt or Stefan Wyatt to you?' "

"Yes."

"You may cross-examine on that point."

"Thank you, Your Honor," Nina said, hoping to disguise her fury, but aware that her neck wore its signaling red flag of mortification. She pulled up her collar. "Mr. Zhukovsky, why did you testify earlier that your sister did not mention that name to you?"

"I forgot she mentioned it."

"Did you ever tell the District Attorney's office what you have just testified?"

"No. I remembered during the break. My testimony today—being here—brought it back."

"An hour ago your sister had no connection you knew about with the defendant, and now all of a sudden she does?" She let a smidgeon of her contempt leak into the question.

"I'm sorry," Zhukovsky said, hanging his head. "It wasn't very important at the time."

Right. He's accused of killing your sister, and you casually forgot to mention a crucial fact about that for four months. Well, screw you, Nina tried to convey with her shoulders and the twist of her mouth, you unprincipled creep. "All right, exactly what did your sister say about the defendant?" she asked politely.

"That she knew a guy who did odd jobs. She named him."

This brutal attack on Stefan Wyatt killed all action in the court.

Odd jobs, Nina thought, stunned at this turn of events and the strangeness of Zhukovsky's statement. Well, digging up graves certainly qualified!

"When did your sister say this?" she asked.

Zhukovsky told the court that the conversation had taken place at the end of the first day of the conference.

"What else did she tell you?"

"Nothing. That's why I forgot it until now. But she did say that."

Everyone understood by now. He had linked Stefan with his dead sister, defendant with victim.

Head turned away from the jury, Nina took four quick breaths and gathered all her composure. "So, Mr. Zhukovsky, is it your belief that it was Christina Zhukovsky who hired Stefan Wyatt to dig up your father's bones? Why would she do that?"

He shook his head. "I don't know. Maybe for the medal."

"Isn't it true that your testimony that your sister mentioned the defendant's name is perjured testimony?"

"No."

"Isn't it true that you just thought this up on the break because it casts suspicion away from you and no one can refute it?"

"I had forgotten."

Sadistically wishing she could kick him, she enjoyed the way his knuckles tightened at the question, and a moist sheen of additional testimony sprang up to speak on his balding forehead. She waited until she could sound patient, solemn, reliable. As opposed to him. "For five months you didn't remember your sister mentioned the name of the man you seem to think killed her?" she asked.

"I forgot." He finally seemed to have registered how absurd he sounded, and appeared as disturbed as the jury at the notion.

"You know very well that your testimony is the first link anyone has given between the defendant and your sister, don't you? You know how helpful this is to the prosecution? But you don't mention it for five—"

"Objection!" the prosecutor had finally jumped to his feet.

In a move calculated to coincide with what she was sensing from the jury, Nina openly let her disgust with the witness show. She paced up and down in front of the witness box, clenching and unclenching her fists. She felt the eyes of the courtroom following her, and welcomed their notice.

"She's badgering the witness," Jaime said. He saw what Nina was doing but didn't know how to stop her. He also seemed very aware of the mood in the courtroom, which could generally be described as pissed. Juries hated being confused.

"Sustained."

"Mr. Zhukovsky, why didn't you testify about this on direct examination?"

"I was nervous."

"What made you nervous? Your intent to commit perjury?"

"Objection," Sandoval said. "Your Honor . . ."

"Withdrawn." Nina thought a moment, and just when Alex was beginning to compose himself, said, "So you are saying your sister, Christina, might have hired this defendant to dig up that medal?"

The outlines of Alex's mistake became instantly clear to everyone. He had wanted to connect Christina and Stefan. Jaime Sandoval had begged for a connection, and had in fact looked pleased for that one moment, when the connection caught. But now, if the jury believed Christina had hired Stefan, Stefan might no longer be convicted of the independent felony charge of grand theft for taking the medal, because the defense would explain that Christina had hired Stefan to bring their father's medal to her, making what first appeared to be a theft no longer a theft.

The prosecutor had carefully explained that Stefan could be put in prison for life just for stealing the medal, because it was his third felony conviction and California had a third-strike rule. Now, if Stefan didn't get convicted for murder, he might actually go free.

Along with all the courtroom, Jaime was figuring this out, too. He was not pleased.

"Believe me," Alex Zhukovsky blurted, taking a last stab toward credibility. "Christina wouldn't want that medal any more than I did."

Nina objected, trying to stop him, but he talked over

her, his voice rising to overcome hers. "I expect they got to talking and she mentioned it for some reason, then Wyatt killed her and stole it meaning to sell it. Thinking he'd be rich, from killing my sister. Getting maybe five thousand crummy dollars! Killing her for that!"

The whole time he ranted, Nina shouted for him to stop, but he kept on until he had finished. "Mr. Zhukovsky, you would say anything to convict Stefan Wyatt, wouldn't you?"

"Oh, fuck you."

"Mr. Zhukovsky!" the judge said.

"Sorry! Sorry!"

"Mr. Zhukovsky, even considering the fact that you've demonstrated a faulty memory, let me ask you one final question," Nina said, adamant, knowing Jaime was ready to object, but hoping he wasn't quick enough. "Who is the one person in this courtroom with an irrefutable connection both to the victim, Christina, who was your sister, and to the man lying in that grave, who was your father, Constantin Zhukovsky?"

His face popped, his eyes bulged, his arm muscles contracted, his body appeared ready to leap forward. Why, he was so upset, his body told them all, he could strangle her.

"No more questions," Nina said serenely. She sailed over to the defense table and sat down.

"Wow," Paul said.

"I warned you about him," Klaus said.

She gulped water, overwhelmed, and leaned on her elbows, facing the table so that no one could see her face.

Stefan said nothing.

Klaus's thin fingers wound like a bony claw around her arm. He cleared his throat, which took a very long time.

"A difficult cross-exam, Miss Reilly," he said finally, giving her arm a squeeze. "Yet you exposed that prevaricating blockhead."

"Did I?" She remembered the fight, the clanging of the bell, the mouth guard in her mouth, the shouts from the audience. She just couldn't recall the referee raising her hand in the air, declaring a clear victory.

He slapped his knee. "Controlled, reactive, and powerful," he said. "Masterful."

16

NINA DROVE KLAUS BACK TO Carmel, then drove over to the main library in Monterey. The time had come. One of the characters in this case claimed to be a page to the last tsar of Russia, and what she could remember about the Romanovs from a paper she wrote in high school might fill a paragraph.

The librarian stacked books in front of her, an intimidating pile which she opened one after another. She read. She studied pictures. If she had been at home alone, she would have cried.

The Romanovs ruled Russia for three hundred years, until 1918, when Nicholas II gave up power, and even gave up the rights of succession for his son. The last tsar had failed as a leader, spending too much time leading his troops into massacres, and leaving his German wife in charge of the country. She, Alexandra, had fallen under the sinister influence of a shaman-healer, Rasputin, and all the country despised the situation. Insulted and empowered by Nicholas's frequent, lengthy absences, in the end, rebels forced Nicholas to release his family's ancient iron grip on the leadership of Russia.

The entire family and some of their retainers were sent

into exile, eventually landing in Ekaterinburg. For months they lived an abnormally tranquil existence there, although terror was never far beneath the surface.

And then came their final day at Ekaterinburg, starting with a menacing request: because of unrest in the town, the Romanov family needed to go into hiding in the basement. They were given just over one half hour to dress for the occasion. A boy, his family—four beautiful sisters, a long-suffering mother, a loving father—and a few devoted servants did as they were told.

Alexis Romanov, the tsarevitch, son of the last Romanov ruler of Russia, fourteen years old, described over and over again as a physically fragile hemophiliac, had been learning to play the balalaika. Because of his ill health, his father Nicholas carried him downstairs. His older sister, Anastasia, only seventeen years old, clutched her King Charles spaniel, Jemmy. His mother, Alexandra, suffering from back pain, asked for chairs and they were brought. She and her ailing son sat in the chairs. Her husband and four daughters surrounded her. They were told to line up for a group photograph.

Instead, their Bolshevik executioners filled the room. The fusillade began. First a Colt took down Nicholas II, the last tsar, who was still shouting, "What? What?" at the words read by the leader of the death squad. His wife, trying to make the sign of the cross, died instantly, along with their oldest daughter, Olga, who was taken down by a single shot to the head.

The tsarevitch, Alexis, along with his other sisters and assorted consorts, remained alive as the bullets flew. Marie, Tatiana, and their sister, Anastasia, crouched in front of the wall, arms up, defensive. Alexis, on the floor, grabbed for his dead father's shirt.

Later, the bodies were hauled on a cart, headed for an old mine shaft near an area called "Four Brothers" because of the large pines ringing the area. Eighteen pounds of diamonds which had acted as armor were recovered from the corpses. The Romanovs had realized the seriousness of the invitation to the basement. The gems sewn into their clothing, which protected some of them from the barrage of bullets, at least forestalling their final moments, had also been intended to provide them a future.

In the 1990s, when the bodies were uncovered in that mine shaft in the pine forest, two were missing. One of the scientists involved could not say if it was Marie or Anastasia who was missing, but he could say definitely that Alexis was not among those buried that cold morning. Yurovsky, a man who was present at the executions, wrote that two of the bodies were burned instead.

No sign of the burned bodies was ever found. Did those two Romanovs die? Or did they live?

And what appeared to be an ending was in fact the beginning of a new story. Thus began the resurrection of a new generation of monarchist Romanovs: the pretenders.

Even Nina had heard of one of the dozens of women who claimed to be Anastasia. From 1920 until 1984, when DNA tests disproved her claim, a Polish woman named Franziska Schanzkowska claimed to be the tsar's youngest daughter. Even today, the question of who might be the legitimate heir to the Russian empire was a matter of spirited debate. Grand Duke George, grandson of a cousin of Nicholas II, was a claimant, as was his mother, the Grand Duchess Maria Vladimirovna.

A man in Canada claimed to be the tsarevitch. A man in Finland did, too. One who had been imprisoned in a gulag in Siberia had a really good story. Dozens of wannabe Alexis Nicholaevich Romanovs sneaked into the news on a regular basis.

Some claimed there was no legitimate heir. But a yearning grew up in the hearts of many Russians after the fall of Communism, for the old days and the old ways, and the stories of the pretenders continued.

Did Constantin Zhukovsky know something about the death of the Romanovs? If he did, what in the world did it have to do with the death of his daughter, and her burial in his grave? Did he have some link to a survivor of the carnage at Ekaterinburg?

Nina called Ginger, then Paul to tell him what she had found out, and what she now suspected. Why were the bones of Constantin Zhukovsky stolen? Because someone—Christina? Alex? Sergey?—someone thought Constantin Zhukovsky's heritage was suspect, or useful, and needed the bones to prove it.

Paul had to keep it brief on his cell phone. He was heading north along the coast, in hot pursuit of his suspect.

Up the angular silhouette of California they flew, Paul, in his treasured red Mustang, tailing Alex Zhukovsky. Paul knew his car wasn't ideal for blending in, but figured he could make up for his conspicuousness with his skill. He didn't know what to make of what Nina told him about executions nearly a hundred years before. He tossed the information in with the rest of the wet, involuted salad of facts in his mind.

Dusk brought out the commuters with their cruise controls. The self-absorbed faces all around Paul didn't seem to notice the sand dunes, the glimpses of the Pacific on his left, the seductive air. Zhukovsky, a couple of cars ahead, driving a white Cadillac Coupe de Ville, wove relentlessly through the traffic.

In addition to her unusually moving lecture about the Romanovs, Nina had said, "I don't think I've ever seen anyone with a guiltier conscience than Alex Zhukovsky. He lied on the stand, and, you know what? I think he feels bad about it. Watch him tonight, Paul." So of course, after a quick drink at Alfredo's, the professor headed out of town for points unknown. Paul did have his portable cooler with a quart of orange Gatorade so he wouldn't perish, but he hadn't had time to find Wish. So he listened to Diana Krall's new jazz CD, opened the windows, and tried to enjoy the ride.

At Santa Cruz, Zhukovsky turned onto Highway 17, which meant a trip over the mountains toward San Jose and the San Francisco peninsula. Paul called Nina again on his cell phone and reported in, asking if she needed him to bring home anything from Alaska, in case Zhukovsky kept going, but Nina just said to stay with him. They took the curves fast, but Zhukovsky never made any elusive maneuvers, he just drove grimly on.

Paul merged through one of those exchanges concocted by a psycho highway engineer, ending up eventually on Highway 85. He then turned onto 280 north, at the fringes of the great nondescript metropolis of San Jose, and began feeling an itching deep in his pineal gland, or whatever that thing was deep in his head that sometimes told him he was being watched. A brand-new Infiniti passed on the right, and the driver, a round-headed guy with a blond brush cut wearing dark-tinted driving glasses, gave him a hard stare.

Paul steered straight but his heart lurched from lane to lane. He had seen that round head before, in a back row of Courtroom 2. The guy had been leaning back with his eyes half closed as Paul passed him, just before the Wyatt trial opened. He had also seen him every day in court, and seen him get up and leave suddenly after Susan Misumi's testimony, and again today after Alex's. He had thought the guy was a reporter.

Very interesting. And . . .

He had seen this same car on Highway 1 and again

on 17. The Infiniti pulled ahead, mean and matte, a black light-sucker. A rich gangsta car, Paul thought, and this thought got stronger as he watched it pull back into the left lane, one car behind Zhukovsky.

So now Paul was the tail on a tail. Excellent development. Endless possibilities.

The shadow-caravan whipped past tech heaven along Sand Hill Road and the rural wealth hidden alongside Woodside Road, continuing up and around the dry hillsides, rushing along at eighty miles an hour toward the city by the bay.

Denser housing appeared to the left and right of the scenic highway, the temperature dropped twenty degrees, and the blue sky dimmed as Paul entered San Francisco's outer reaches. Zhukovsky appeared to know the way. He swerved left onto Nineteenth Avenue, keeping a steady pace. They passed Stonestown and San Francisco State University in the usual heavy traffic punctuated by red lights at each and every corner, and entered the Sunset District. Paul could swear the Infiniti driver had not realized Paul was three cars back. Luckily the black car had strange taillights, easy to pick out.

Paul didn't watch for Zhukovsky anymore. The Infiniti driver would do that for him.

The black tree limbs in Golden Gate Park coiled over them like hanging snakes as they cut through. They forked left again onto Twenty-fifth Avenue and rode over a few city hills, past slightly decrepit rows of forties town houses to the lights of Geary Avenue in the Outer Richmond district.

The Infiniti nudged into a minuscule space between two narrow driveways. Paul had to pass it, but the round-head was busy backing up, no problem.

Paul turned left and saw a big church across Geary with an enormous gold onion dome, an Orthodox cathedral, a beauty. It was a landmark he had passed on his way to the ocean many times.

He circled the block and located Zhukovsky's Caddy, but found no sign of him. He parked and walked cautiously back toward Geary, digital camera hanging from his wrist, open and ready to shoot. A couple of girls with dyed black hair wearing tiny plaid kilts walked by arm in arm, laughing. Fog misted the neon signs. This part of town had so many Russian emigrants he could see as much Cyrillic lettering as Roman on the bakeries and coffee places, but the Russians must have been home cooking their dinners because few people were out.

Nobody loitered outside in front of the cathedral, and the big golden doors were locked. Paul zipped his leather jacket and put the camera in a pocket. He started walking the perimeter and passed several gates, all locked. There were more, smaller onion-domed wings, each with its own entry, each locked. The left side of the cathedral connected to a walled school yard.

As Paul turned the corner toward the back of the church, never leaving the shadows, he saw the Infiniti driver lurking against the back fence, and moved smoothly back and out of range.

He flipped open his phone, noting the time was only seven-thirty, and told Nina he had a plethora of riches—several leads, all interesting, to follow when Zhukovsky came out.

"What's he doing in there?" she asked, very reasonably.

"I don't know."

"He's not hiding. You're sure . . ."

"He went straight there. But there's no service."

"It's a Russian Orthodox church?"

"Yeah. More exactly, the denomination is the Russian Church of America. This place has been around a long time. It's called Holy Virgin Cathedral."

"So he's seeing a priest," Nina said as if to herself. "Feeling guilty about all those lies he told us today. The man who is following—any ideas?"

"You ready for a guess? I think he's Russian. I think he might possibly be Christina's old boyfriend, Sergey Krilov. Fits the description of somebody I heard was at the convention. He's been watching the trial. Hang on." The front door of the church opened. A priest came out, elderly, black beard, black robes, looking both ways. Paul shrank into his hidey-hole and flipped off the phone. The priest disappeared and then came back, gesturing with his hand toward someone inside.

Zhukovsky came out. The priest took both his hands in his own and shook them gently, nodded his head a few times, then went back inside and shut the doors. The priest had a funny walk, which reminded Paul of an R. Crumb truckin' cartoon, stomach and legs leading the way.

Zhukovsky went to the light and waited for the green, and Paul caught a glimpse of blond hair down the street. He punched buttons on his phone.

"Where'd you go?" Nina said.

"Zhukovsky's leaving. The Infiniti driver's staying put, but watching. The priest is back in the church. Who do I follow?"

"The Infiniti," she said instantly, and Paul thought, good girl.

"Right." He shut down the phone cover and watched Zhukovsky crossing, the Infiniti driver just a gleam down the street, not moving. Zhukovsky climbed into his car and drove off.

The Infiniti driver waited a minute or two, then came out and moved back toward the church, hands in the pockets of his denim jacket, head down. He paused at the main entry, tried the door—locked tight. Pulling out a pack of cigarettes, he lit up and took a contemplative puff. His pants were too tight, shoes too pointed, hair too groomed—in a thousand ways he made clear that he was foreign. Straight outta Moskva, Paul thought.

Paul followed him to the Infiniti and saw him safely inside, then skulked rapidly back to the Mustang.

Which had two slashed tires, a bashed-in passenger-side window, a stolen CD player, which still must have been hoarding the precious new CD, a gaping glove compartment, and a short note in Cyrillic scrawled on a Post-it, stuck to the dashboard. Paul had a pretty good idea what it said.

He ran back. The Russian was just turning back onto Twenty-fifth. His windows were open, and a singer crooned. He had good taste in music. He liked Diana Krall, too.

17

FATHER GIORGI HEAVED HIMSELF UP from his prayers in his tiny room. He had knelt like this at his bed every morning for his whole life, and he wasn't going to let a stiff knee stop him. Limping, he went into his lavatory. He washed his face and combed his hair and beard. The small mirror above the washstand revealed new creases in his forehead, and a haunted look that all his prayers to Lord Jesus Christ this morning had failed to dispel.

He pulled his robe over his head, attached his belt with the keys and pouch, and walked into the hall. He felt privileged to live right next door to a saint, at least, the room of a saint. Saint John Maximovich had lived and died behind the brown door he was passing. Bishop Vasily, Father Giorgi's superior, had been a member of the committee examining the miracles claimed, and there were many. He had told Father Giorgi that when the saint's tomb was opened in 1994, twenty-eight years after his death, the saint's body had not decomposed, though it had turned a deep mahogany color.

With such a holy neighbor, Father Giorgi had no trouble recalling his mission and the Church's mission. The saint's cell with its iron bed was now a place of pilgrimage.

Or it should be. Few of the faithful actually came, and fewer still were coming to the Sunday Divine Liturgy every year. For so long it had only been elderly women. But then, the change. Freedom had come in Russia. The Church could again freely bear witness to Christ, and a new wave of emigration began arriving in California.

But the newcomers, young and poor, couldn't afford San Francisco, and those who could might come to a Eucharist or a Paschal, but at heart many weren't really good Christians—the Communists had instilled the poison of doubt so strenuously that heartfelt, straightforward faith couldn't get a purchase.

Even the Church could not be faithful to itself. The Church here had basically cut itself off from its mother. Saint John was not recognized in Russia, because the American Church had been responsible for his canonization.

Such a shame. A saint in the house, but doubt, doubt poisoning the Church as it poisoned Russia.

Father Giorgi moved down the nave of the cathedral, greeting a few old people who had come in early to pray in the side chapels, fingering his pouch with the dollar bills inside, thinking about these sad things. The deacons had already lit the beeswax candles and the oil lamps under the ikons. He breathed deeply of the incense smoke, frowned as he noted one of the women wore pants. Kneeling, before God, dressed like a man!

He had been born in America, in Minnesota, but this did not mean he subscribed to the ultraliberality of the American church. His training had been at a strict theological seminary in St. Petersburg, and he had been happy there. He knew what to do and when to do it, loved the liturgies, loved the absolute and ancient nature of the rules of living he had vowed to follow.

But in America—this national church had lost all bearings and fallen into the heresy of ecumenism. He was constantly at odds with authority figures here. They found him stodgy, strange. No telling how long he would last. He just didn't fit in.

Blasphemy is easy when you're so far from your mother, he reflected, lighting a candle that had sputtered out, which was not to say that the Mother Church was without stain. What did she do with her God-given opportunities during the nineties? She sold tobacco and alcohol received as "humanitarian aid"! She slept with Yeltsin for money!

As he did every morning, Father Giorgi opened the heavy entry doors and stepped out. Several of the faithful, familiar with his routine, awaited him on the steps. Patiently, he took their hands and blessed them, but finished quickly and went to the corner light, where he could resume his thoughts in peace.

In the decade since the awful finds at Ekaterinburg, when the photos of the skeletons of the tsar and his family were shown even on American television, Father Giorgi realized that a great hero of the Church had died in the person of Nicholas II. Others felt the same way. He had even heard talk of sainthood for the family. The tsar and his family had appeared on an ikon of New Martyrs circulated around the world.

Yes, they had been true to the Church, and martyred.

Many in this church would not agree. Oh, he had heard what the conservatives thought of him and his radical opinions, those without vision. On more than one occasion he had been asked to consider another career. Fortunately, he knew a few good people and he knew how to hold on to power, however little he wielded in this tiny universe.

His brand of bold idealism begged for attack in these cynical times, so he now operated quietly, missing Christina.

If only she had not died—she had taken his credibility with her. He wanted so much to see the Church in America and the Church in Russia tied again, one undefeatable religious force in the world. He wanted a return to order and authority. Christina had believed in the same cause, or at least some of it. He would help her make contacts and gain support, and then, she would help him.

But the second phase had never come. So many dreams had died with her.

Maybe he should leave the church. In his darkest moments, he knew he probably didn't belong here.

And now along came Alex. Could he be convinced to take up the cause? Could Giorgi convince him, or was this a futile, dangerous exercise that might get another person killed? He had broached the subject the night before, but Alex was not Christina. He didn't have the same yearnings, and he felt no responsibility. He was American through and through, he had told Giorgi, not Russian. And he seemed to blame Giorgi for setting up the events that had led to her death, the decision to hire the odd-jobs man who had killed her.

Could he be convinced? Should he?

Without Alex, the movement would inevitably fail. Giorgi on his own, a small-town boy, an old priest, would never attract the right attention. Puzzling over these thoughts, Father Giorgi crossed the street, his hands behind his back. The car waiting for him honked. He ignored it. He was almost there, and he could sit in his daily refuge for a few minutes now and think about Alex and the confession he had made the night before.

Something had to be done. Was there hope in this confession, or only despair, and an ending? He looked up at the green and white sign, taking a deep sniff of the fragrant elixir he was about to drink.

Ahh. Starbucks.

A tall man with light hair who looked like he hadn't slept the night before got into line behind him, and Father Giorgi's heart sank. Was he—but the man greeted him in reassuring American English. "I wonder if I could talk with you for a few minutes."

"I don't want to be rude," Father Giorgi said, "but can't you come in later, at the church? I'm off duty at the moment." He said to the girl at the counter, "A Grande Vanilla Soy Latte, please. And I'll have, let's see, one of those biscottis."

"This can't wait," the man said. He looked rumpled but not dangerous. "Paul van Wagoner." He held out his hand, and Father Giorgi shook it. Van Wagoner followed him to the tall counter where his coffee would be delivered.

"Would you be kind enough to tell me what this says?" van Wagoner said, thrusting something into Father Giorgi's hand. It was a blue Post-it.

"Is this a bad joke?"

"Supposed to be funny, is it? I can't read it. It was left in my car last night."

"*In* your car?"

"What does it mean?"

"It says, '*Vali otsyuda, mudak.*' It means, ah, something like, 'Get lost, jerk,' " Father Giorgi said uneasily. "Except cruder."

"I see," van Wagoner said, taking it back. He folded it carefully and put it in his pocket.

Father Giorgi's coffee arrived and the man followed him to a table by the window.

"I've helped you. Now please, go away," Father Giorgi said. He had a lot to think about.

"The note was left by a man who was watching you and Alex Zhukovsky at your church last night."

The vanilla soy latte flew off the table as Father Giorgi's hand jerked reflexively. Van Wagoner caught it neatly and set it back on the table.

"Who sent you?" Giorgi said. He looked at the license that was being held out toward him. "Who do you represent?" He looked at the man's hands—not even a wedding ring, at his feet—expensive loafers, and into his eyes—where he saw something tough but not, at the moment, threatening.

"I'm here to prevent the breaking of some more Commandments," the investigator said. "I think the sixth and the ninth have already been broken by Mr. Zhukovsky. I don't have much time, and my car is in the shop, and I had to sleep in a noisy hotel room without so much as a toothbrush last night. So please bear with me if I'm a little brusque."

"What's this about the Commandments?"

"You know. The one that says you shouldn't kill people, and the one that forbids bearing false witness against your neighbor. Mr. Zhukovsky lied in a court of law yesterday. And he may have killed his sister."

"That is ridiculous. What's this got to do with me?"

"He spent the evening with you. Did he talk about it?"

"If he did, I couldn't tell you," Father Giorgi said. "The sanctity of the confession . . ."

The man interrupted, "The Russian following Mr. Zhukovsky—any idea who he might be?"

"I couldn't say." But what crushing news.

Sergey Krilov! Still here, still making trouble!

Alex's confession had been heartfelt. They had stood side by side in front of the Book of Gospels and the Cross, and Alex had said, "I lied to the Court, Father. I distorted the truth." They had talked, and Alex prayed the prayer of Absolution. Then Giorgi made his pitch, and Alex rejected it.

Could Alex have killed Christina? He would have confessed, Giorgi thought; he is a believer. This comforted him for a moment. He sipped at the hot coffee, studying the investigator. Was it nevertheless possible that Alex had gotten rid of Christina out of some subversive desire to take her place?

If so, he would have been more accommodating to Giorgi's plans. No, it made no sense. This investigator must be trying to trick him. Why should he trust this man with those narrowed, flecked eyes? Maybe he was actually sent by Krilov and his gang to intimidate and confuse.

"I can't help you," Giorgi said. He needed to warn Alex, but he didn't want this man to see how flustered he felt. He drank the hot foamy liquid, resenting the fact that he couldn't enjoy it, set it down carefully, and laced his hands.

A complete silence ensued. Father Giorgi was used to silence. He began praying *sub voce*. Holy Mother, send this guy away.

Van Wagoner studied him, then his whole body seemed to relax. "I understand there are things you can't say."

"Right." Giorgi straightened his cassock and took another sip of his coffee. "Now then, who are you?"

"As you saw on my card, a licensed private investigator. I'm working with the defense in the matter of the murder of Christina Zhukovsky."

"You're helping the man accused of killing her?"

"Is there something you should confess to me, Father? I can't believe you would allow my client to be sentenced to life in prison if Alex Zhukovsky confessed to the murder last night."

"He did no such thing; I will tell you that. Your client

must have killed her. His blood was found in her . . ." Father Giorgi stopped.

"You know about the case, Father. Following the trial?"

"Not really. I just—it's a tragedy. A matter of interest to the Russian community in Northern California."

"I see. Why is that?"

Giorgi thought hard for an answer. He could not tell the truth. The pain had dulled after four months of daily prayer, but the greater disappointment remained. All that Christina could have been, dashed to bits by this young American, Wyatt. . . .

"Was Christina a prominent member of the community?"

"Yes, that's it. She was a great organizer. You know about the conference she set up at the college?"

"Yes."

"That conference brought many factions of the community together."

"Were you there?"

"Briefly. I went only the first day. She asked me to be there. I think she was a little nervous."

"How well did you know Christina?"

"From the time she was a little girl. Do you actually believe this accused person might be innocent?"

"I'm working on it. How did you come to know Christina and Alex?"

There seemed no harm in discussing the past, so Father Giorgi said, "A family of the faithful. Their parents always came to the Holy Virgin Cathedral, even after they moved to Monterey many years ago. Their mother passed away, but Constantin still brought Alex and Christina to us. Christina was a—good woman and a true believer. I miss her."

"So you knew Constantin Zhukovsky?"

"Of course, but he died many years ago."

Paul pulled out some photographs. He handed one to Father Giorgi.

"This was buried with Constantin Zhukovsky."

"Yes. I remember the medal. I performed his burial service, as I did for Christina."

"Can you tell me something about it?"

"Saint George was a Christian martyr, and is venerated as sacred in the Orthodox tradition. He represents a valiant, selfless warrior. It's suggested by some scholars that the story of his slaying the dragon is a recasting of the Greek legend of Perseus, who rescued Andromeda from a sea monster. I've seen very old ikons at Novgorod State University dating back to the tenth century."

Actually, he was a good saint who interested Giorgi. He didn't mind talking about Saint George. He just didn't want to discuss the medal.

The tall man listened for a while, until Giorgi veered way off the point and he got exasperated. "So Constantin really was a page of the tsar of Russia. Where else would he get something like this medal?"

Father Giorgi cringed at this turn of conversation. "He used to tell that story, among others."

"He knew them, then. The imperial family."

How many times had Constantin talked about his youth, the incredible last days of Old Russia, the tsarevitch's pony, the padded saddle and stirrups, the excruciating attacks the boy endured whenever he bumped his hand or body, the blood leaking slowly through the capillaries, ballooning into terrifying hematomas. And yet the boy had wanted to play; he wanted to ride, wanted to live.

Constantin had said, "He was brave, but he did cry." The tsarina weeping in the anteroom outside his bedroom. Rasputin, summoned, murmuring unknown things to the boy, passing his hands over the boy's body, while

Constantin stood in a corner, invisible, waiting to be called for any task.

As he recounted these memories of his early life, Constantin would always tear up. He had only escaped the purges by accident, he told them. Then his stories would begin to conflict. Once he said he had fled to Estonia, once to Finland. His parents died in various ways, in labor camps in the thirties, on a farm in Finland, even during the Revolution while still in Russia.

The details never matched, and Father Giorgi had begun to wonder. So many people who had gone through these terrible experiences made up stories to fill the holes in their memories. So many people lived ordinary pasts and embellished them, because who does not enjoy a good story?

What Russian does not have many secrets? What was Constantin's real story? He had tried many times to cajole the truth out of the old man. But the truth had been left for much, much later.

"I never knew what to believe," Giorgi said. The truth. He hadn't, back then.

"Let me ask you something, Father. You know Constantin Zhukovsky's bones were stolen?"

"Another shameful thing."

"Any chance somebody wanted to test those bones because they suspected that this man was somehow more closely connected to the Romanov family? A cousin? Maybe even someone who could claim succession?"

Giorgi laughed. "Look, it's hard enough to believe that the old man was a page to the tsar, isn't it? A typical old man's story, elevating himself beyond his station to give himself a bigger position in the eyes of his family and friends. But if he were a Romanov, why not shout it out?"

"Times have changed in Russia. During his lifetime, it might not be something you'd want bandied about. Now, it's a political free-for-all compared to the Communist era. For all I know, there's interest in restoring the monarchy. Is there?"

"There are a thousand factions and every opinion under the sun when it comes to politics there. My only interest is in restoring the Church," Giorgi said. "I want a government conducive to traditional religion, that's all."

"We've been doing some research. I know there are a number of people who are Romanovs left in the world, and I know the country is—searching for something."

Giorgi forced another laugh. "You mean, to install a new tsar in place of the president? Well, America's done worse, I guess."

Van Wagoner frowned, obviously not liking the political insult. Then he shook it off and even smiled, saying, "Sorry. I've got a lot on my mind today. How about this thought: is it possible someone took the bones hoping to prove Constantin was not the page, or not who he said he was?"

"Why ask me?"

"Okay, then let's go back to Alex Zhukovsky. Why would he lie on the witness stand, invent something that would convict someone else? Unless he murdered his sister?"

"Listen to me. Alex Zhukovsky didn't kill anybody." Giorgi made a big point out of looking at his watch. What would it take to unstick this disturbing tick?

"I'll let you drink your coffee in peace in just a minute," van Wagoner said. "Just a couple more quick questions." The investigator scratched his head and shifted his legs. He seemed to have lost interest. Father Giorgi expelled a silent prayer of thanksgiving.

"You do know Sergey Krilov, don't you?"

How smoothly this was asked, as the man looked idly at a girl standing at the counter ordering coffee. He would never stop asking that question, Father Giorgi realized, and he suddenly felt very tired. "I knew him years ago in St. Petersburg. He doesn't spend that much time in the U.S."

"What does he do for a living?"

"He's involved in his family businesses. He does whatever they need done."

"I'll bet. He follows people, he breaks into cars . . ."

"What?"

"Never mind. Is he blond? Short and built like a brick shit house?"

"He is a big man, but not tall. The Krilov I knew came from a well-known family who managed to make a lot of money during the Communist years, money they squirreled away in foreign accounts. Unfortunately, they squandered it on American biotech stocks and lost most of it when the market fell so drastically a couple of years ago. They are reactionaries who are very unhappy with the current government."

"They miss Communism because it was profitable? That's a twist."

"These people are not ideologues. They want only two things, power and money. They are looking for a way back in. They would happily kiss the president, but he won't let them near. Therefore they would like to see him gone."

"Is Krilov involved in some revolutionary activities?"

"I wouldn't know." He hoped God would forgive him for all these lies. He lied too much; he knew it.

"Christina Zhukovsky went to Russia to be with him, didn't she?"

"Yes."

"While she was there, did he get her mixed up in his politics and put her in danger?"

Giorgi stared at Paul without speaking. "I wish she was here, and could speak for herself. Christina was a woman with her own agenda, her own dreams. Let's just say Sergey was part of her education. In the end, she broke with him, remember that. I thought he returned to Russia long ago, but you say he's here and he followed Alex last night?"

"I'd put fifty bucks on that," the investigator said. "Now will you tell me why?"

"No."

Van Wagoner smiled a little and shook his head. "Your call," he said. "Okay, let's go at it another way. Alex Zhukovsky wanted his father's bones. Did he tell you why?"

"I can't answer that."

"You know, Father," the man said. "This guy Krilov, or whoever the man is who followed Alex Zhukovsky up here and left me this note—he might think you were told pertinent things last night. You should be careful. He let Alex go, and he stayed around the church. I don't know where he is now."

"Don't worry about me." Giorgi squeezed his paper cup and tossed it toward a trash can, missing. He got up to stuff the cup into an opening. "I'm a man of God."

But then he remembered that Alex had told him there were still bones remaining that had not been cremated after their recovery. A woman in Sacramento was testing them. Krilov wouldn't like that. He felt cold with fear. He wished he could ask this inquisitive stranger to help him, but the price was so high. He wanted too much. In the end he decided to say nothing. The man finally gave him a quizzical stare, thanked him, and went out the door.

Giorgi left, too. He hadn't eaten a bite of his biscotti, so he wrapped it in a napkin and tucked it into a pocket for later. He looked everywhere for Krilov on the street, but saw no sign of him.

Back in his room, he picked up the phone and called Alex Zhukovsky.

"Don't pretend you can't see the danger. Whether you

like it or not, you're linked with Christina, as her brother. My advice is, talk to Krilov. Tell him you're no threat."

But Alex was not Christina. He didn't want to talk to Krilov or anyone else. He wanted it all to go away, to have it buried forever with Christina. Hadn't he learned from Constantin's bones that you can never bury an unfinished past?

18

THIS PRIEST IS THE MOTHER lode," Paul told Nina that afternoon, calling on the phone from San Francisco, leaning against his newly repaired car, which he had just retrieved from the nearest garage for the princely sum of sixteen hundred fifty dollars. "I've told you what he said, now let me tell you what he didn't say. What he didn't say is that Alex Zhukovsky spilled his guts to him, and both he and Zhukovsky know something Krilov wants to know. I get the impression that Krilov is going to pick one or the other to go after. And he didn't follow Alex."

"He drove off?" Nina asked.

"Yeah. But maybe only around the block."

"I'll send Wish over to Alex Zhukovsky's place. He lives in Carmel Highlands on Fern Canyon Road. If Wish sees Krilov hanging around, he can call the police."

"What are they gonna arrest him for? Loitering? If he sees Krilov he should tail him, and if Krilov tries a break-in or anything, then he can call."

"I should call Alex Zhukovsky," Nina said.

"And say what? We don't know diddly-squat. It's a feeling. They're all such liars. The priest—what's he up to? He should be ashamed."

"Let's subpoena him, just in case," Nina said. "Do you have a spare subpoena in your car?"

"Sure do. Issued and signed. So what do I do now? Serve his ass and come home? Or stick around?"

"I need you up there. One more night, okay?"

"I'll get a decent hotel room tonight, then. Last night's Travelodge was more like a mosh pit," Paul said. "Hear the bells? He's conducting some kind of service as we speak, so I can get away for a few minutes. Nina. How long should I stay?" A wind had kicked around the corner and he thought longingly about his leather jacket, which of course he had left at the condo.

"We'll decide in the morning. I'm frustrated, Paul."

"Of course you are. You miss my warm body."

Nina let out a laugh, then said, "I mean about the case. Jaime's just as frustrated. He's running this prosecution without two pieces of information that would help it make sense: why bury Christina in her father's grave? And what motive did Stefan Wyatt have to kill her?"

"Alex and his father-confessor know," Paul said. "Driving up here, following him, I couldn't make up my mind. I made Zhukovsky as the killer of his sister, but it's a deep situation, and Krilov could be a professional."

"Because he broke your window?"

"Because of *how* he broke it. Quickly and without a second thought. Leaving me a note, for Pete's sake."

"Be careful, Paul," Nina said. "I-I'm thinking of you."

"I'm always careful, honey." He closed the phone and walked back, thinking, Man, are we ever tiptoeing around our situation. He and Nina seemed to have arrived at an implicit understanding not to deal with their relationship right now, but Paul was damn lonely these days and sick of it. They needed to clear the air somehow soon.

Across the street from the cathedral he spied a bakery with signs in Cyrillic. Inside, he bought himself a roll and coffee and sat at a small table watching the golden doors while babushkas came in and went out with bread in their shopping bags, as if he had just been transported via magic carpet to Novgorod.

The bells rang again and the people came out of the cathedral, older people mostly, Father Giorgi doing his thing with the bowing and the chatting and the hand holding. The big doors closed. Traffic roared up and down Geary, and the wind blew litter down the wide avenue.

"Got a paper?" Paul asked the bored woman at the counter. She produced one that said "NpaБГa," or so it seemed to Paul. *"Pravda,"* she said. "Truth. You read Russian?"

He passed on the news, although a little truth wouldn't have gone amiss. It was going to be a long afternoon.

At five, another church service inspired what appeared to be the same people going in and out, and a different priest. Paul entered, inhaling the incense, standing with them for a few minutes as the prayers went on. He saw no sign of Father Giorgi. He felt jumpy. You needed two to stake out a tango for more than a few hours. He needed exercise, a chase, something.

Otherwise, left with only a heavily thumbed real-estate throwaway and his own thoughts to amuse himself, he would brood about Nina, which he didn't want to do. She would never believe he could give her the room she needed to be herself, and in truth, he wondered himself sometimes. He did fight a wolf urge to gobble her up. He wanted to protect her, which she hated. He had done awful things for her, which he did not regret, but which had left permanent, unfortunate stains on his soul. How many times had he asked her to marry him now, three? More?

She had the ring. He had worked the script. But Nina

didn't answer. Time barreled along, and still she did not answer.

And maybe he didn't have the heart to hear her excuses anymore.

Man, he was tired of being a good boy all the time. He had tried and tried with this woman, and all he got was yanked, mostly not in a good way. In his younger days, he might have stopped into a bar looking for a healthy, all-out brawl, just to remind himself who he really was. He was in that frame of mind.

Disgusted at his lack of progress on every front, he went back outside, crossed the street again, walked down to Anza to check on his car, and found a ticket.

Now he needed a bathroom. The street grates didn't look too inviting. He walked rapidly back to Geary and down the block found a sushi place where he ordered *ebi* to go and took care of his human needs. Bearing his white paper sack of sushi, he headed back toward his observation post.

The bakery closed and the bar next door opened, and Paul found a place by the street window. Traffic increased, then died away as dusk came and the streetlights came on. By now Paul could have drawn the cathedral by heart. It was inordinately beautiful, sublime, and a saint had lived there. How comforting to have all the rules divinely received, so you didn't have to question and test and doubt ever again.

He began to ponder his own upbringing as he drank his Coors. His parents still lived nearby, and so did his sister. He should give them a call, go see them while he was in town, but he knew he wouldn't. No time, on a job, all the old reasons. Excuses.

He had been raised in the Mission District, just down Geary and a few miles south. His parents had insisted he attend Sunday school. The dusty room reserved for children of the faith contained a blackboard, some frayed books and missionary magazines, a stack of Bibles, and a map of missionary activities, which Paul studied with the obsessive interest of one confined in a place one does not want to be. Sunday after Sunday he puzzled out the names: Celebes, shaped like an octopus; Sumatra; Burma; Cebu; fabulous jungly places he would go to someday.

It had been a long time since he had thought about those youthful stirrings of travel fever, and longer still since he had been a believer. He considered the stops along the way, and thought on the whole he could never go back.

A black Infiniti cruised by. Krilov! Paul ducked, then took a cautious look out the door. Nothing new; parked cars, the restaurants spilling out customers, the cathedral domes gleaming in the streetlights.

He gave Krilov a couple of minutes, which he was later to regret, before venturing across the street and up the stairs to the main door, which was locked again. Hastening his steps, he went around the corner on the right, but the subsidiary doors looked locked, too.

Again Paul gave it time. He didn't want to be standing in the open if Krilov was still parking half a mile away.

From far away, Celebes maybe, he thought he heard a shout. No, it was from inside the church. He made a sudden decision and started trying the side doors, but they were all locked.

Then he saw a floor-level window, the rusty grillwork pulled aside, glass shattered along the asphalt beneath. Krilov was unbelievably decisive and fast. Paul pulled off his sweater and wrapped his hand and probed around the dark hole, decided it felt big enough and safe enough, and snaked his way in.

Blackness, some sort of small room. He smelled the pungent church incense, bumped into a hard cot, and found the light by the door.

He was in a tiny cell-like space containing a cot, a plastic-topped desk, and a wooden chair. On the wall above the bed he saw a double silver cross with the same curious slanting line at the bottom, the cross of the eastern orthodox churches. Some black robes hung on a hook. On the table two lit candles illuminated tin cans full of flowers. Incense burned. Propped on the table was a large photograph of a heavily bearded man wearing thick glasses, and a gold-rimmed black ikon of the Virgin Mary.

"Sorry," he muttered to the dead saint in the picture. He pulled on the sweater—the room was deathly cold—patted his shoulder holster, and listened.

Sobbing, coming from deeper within.

He turned the doorknob and found himself in a long dark hall with shabby carpeting, some sort of light at the end where another door came in. The sobbing sounds came from there.

Paul edged down the hall, thanking whomever for the carpeting that muffled his footsteps. At the edge of the open door at the end he hesitated briefly, then stooped and very swiftly looked in and back out again.

Father Giorgi was doing the sobbing, a quiet, resigned kind of crying. Kneeling, he faced the door, eyes closed, beard sticking out, head pulled way back by Krilov, who held a long wicked knife to his throat. Krilov spoke in a low insistent voice, the voice of one who is extorting information, but the language was Russian and Paul had to stop that knife. He pulled out his Glock, stepped in, and said, "Drop it!," holding the gun in both hands, in position, ready to blow Krilov away if the knife moved.

Krilov's lips parted and his eyes widened. Father Giorgi's eyes popped open and he flung himself back convulsively, knocking Krilov off balance. The priest leaped up and flung open a small door on the other side of the room and ran for his life, Krilov only steps behind him, and Paul tearing along behind Krilov.

They ended up in an alley between the school yard and the church, but by the time Paul found the two other men again, Krilov had slammed Giorgi against a wall. Without pausing he leaned down and reached a muscular arm around the priest's neck and pulled him tightly to him. The knife was back in place before Giorgi could let out more than a surprised grunt and before Paul could get a clear shot.

Krilov dragged the priest to his feet, Giorgi's bulky body covering all but four inches of his round head, white-blond hair, one eye, a glimpse of a once-broken nose. He began edging the priest toward Paul. Paul didn't move, but Giorgi jerked again, resisting, and the knife sliced smoothly across the priest's throat.

The priest's eyes widened. Then they closed and he sagged. Blood flowed from the long slice, down the neck and onto the black cassock. That was good, it wasn't spurting, maybe he hadn't hit an artery. "Back off!" Krilov yelled from behind the priest. The light was bad and Paul couldn't take the chance. He lowered the gun. Krilov pushed Giorgi at Paul. Paul caught him, and Krilov ran for the street, disappearing around a corner, fast and low.

Where the hell was help? Paul let out an enraged yell, realizing he couldn't follow. He let Giorgi down gently and took off his sweater. He pushed the two flaps of neck skin together first, then wrapped the sweater around Giorgi's wound. Pushing against it with what he hoped was enough pressure to keep Giorgi alive, but not enough to strangle him accidentally, he called for an ambulance on his cell phone.

Giorgi was coming around. "Hang on, Father," Paul said. Paul got him up, propping his head against the wall, thinking a better position, gravity, hell, what did he know about all this blood except that neck wounds could bleed profusely, and he had an idea that Sergey might not have nicked the priest if Paul hadn't startled him. As the sirens got loud, Giorgi opened dry lips and said, "Am I going to die?"

"Relax. The ambulance is here." From somewhere in the cassock the priest's hands produced some beads and he began mumbling prayers. Finally, another priest came rushing out of the church. Wailing at what he saw, he pushed Paul away to attend to Giorgi. Giorgi was now fully conscious and Paul saw to his relief that the bloody sweater didn't seem to be getting any more catastrophically soaked.

Paul and the other priest stayed at Giorgi's side as the paramedics slid him into the ambulance, the one thing that whole day that Paul did absolutely right, because just before they shut the doors, Giorgi pulled off his oxygen mask. "Warn her," he said, voice gurgling on his own blood.

"Who?"

"The woman with the bones."

"Who? What do you mean?"

"She kept samples, Alex told me. I had to tell . . ."

"I'll take care of it, buddy."

But Giorgi didn't hear. His eyes closed and the doors closed, too.

Dr. Ginger Hirabayashi returned from her eight P.M. appointment two hundred dollars poorer, with her newly rhubarb-red waif hair a quarter inch shorter than it had been, soft around the face, with stiff spikes that radiated like sunbursts from her skull. She admired it in the reflective glass doors leading into the boring building in North Sacramento where she ran her forensics lab.

"Hey, Doc," the security guard at the desk said, checking her out. "I like it, although my wife might feel moved to give you a word of motherly advice about that color." A retired cop, he still had the brush mustache he had worn in younger days, only the originally firm brown jaw had a fleshier edge, and the once-dark hair was a spongy white. He pushed a clipboard toward her to sign.

"Hi, Phil. Tell her my mother does that for her." She signed, then kissed her palm and flipped it toward the video camera screwed into a high corner near the elevators that faced the doors. "You awake up there, Dick?"

A long pause. The image of a young man with tousled black hair and whisker-bruised cheeks appeared on the monitor on Phil's desk. "Of course I'm awake," said the tinny speaker. His slow words echoed off the marble walls in the darkened atrium.

Phil and Ginger rolled eyes at each other. "Finish that paper on Milton yet, Dick?"

"Turned it in this morning."

"Ever consider studying a real subject, the kind of thing that might get you a real job someday, like, say, pathology?"

"The smells coming out of your lab say it's not for me." The video clicked off.

"They ought to fire that guy," Phil muttered as she pushed the clipboard back toward him.

"Helps to be the landlord's son. Anyway, we've got you, Phil. He's just dressing." She didn't care if Dick was listening. He hated the job, and didn't mind saying so.

"What you doing in so late, anyway?"

"What do you think?"

"Hard to imagine what's so goldang urgent about dead people," he said, "that it should keep you up at night."

Ginger walked past his desk, hit the elevator button, and waited, listening to the elevator moving through space without giving a hint of its whereabouts. A clunk, and the doors opened abruptly. She got in. More mirrors inside gave her a chance to adjust her blue denim miniskirt. She liked it riding low. Although she worked in a lab, she had never owned a white lab coat. Most of the consultants who shared facilities on her floor, all forensics experts who had formed a consortium a few years ago, did wear a uniform, however: jeans and T-shirts, jeans and dress shirts, jeans and blouses, jeans and tank tops.

Her concession to pragmatism was to wear a red faux-leather apron, the better to keep herself clean as she went about her messy business.

She didn't like working late but her new girlfriend kept strange hours, and hadn't been home when she called. She could give Nina's case some extra time. She touched her new gold ear cuff, which hurt more than her other piercings, and reminded herself to douse it in alcohol when she finally did get home. She knew only too well what an infection looked like when it got to tearing through a body's system.

She might be here for hours. She stepped out of the elevator into the hall, where she had hung a jolly painting by an artist named Hans Bellmer who liked to mix up female body parts.

Ginger was a forensic pathologist, not a priest or a detective, but it was human to seek explanations, and curiosity had kept her awake a few nights since that meeting with Nina, when her lover hadn't. If Nina's client had in fact committed the murder, the crime scene made sense. If he hadn't, the evidence was somehow misleading them. With the certainty of a person who relied on science and reason for explanations, she felt illumination lurked inside those bits of DNA in the blood from the victim's apartment, but after two weeks of looking she still had no answer to her questions.

She was supposed to testify for the defense within the next few days, and she had nothing for them yet.

Unlocking the door to her lab with a key, she decided that was exactly why she liked Nina's jobs. When Nina worked a case, she took the dross nobody else found interesting and, with the fire of a fanatic, made it fascinating, whether you believed or not. So she wasn't going to let the little matter of an old man's dry bones stop her from figuring out whatever there was to figure out.

Her lab was large, about eight hundred square feet, which she couldn't have afforded if she was on her own. She shared it with several other people: Jimmy, the HPLC wizard; Carol, the toxicologist, who did chromatography on suspect drugs and used tissue samples to find traces of poison or drugs; and Kevan, their resident blood-man. He did ELISA's and radio-immuno assays to determine blood types and find useful proteins that might be present in a sample. She flipped on the banks of color-corrected overhead lights, illuminating slab benches made of black epoxy with a matte finish in varying states of disarray.

Jimmy had her beat in sheer weight of shiny chrome machinery, but only by a little. Ginger's bench held a clutter of equipment including the thermocycler, which looked like a hot plate or waffle iron, and sat on a toaster-sized computer. A matrix of little holes in the top held bullet tubes that replicated the molecules of DNA. Over one whole wall a narrow strip of windows, black now, looked out into the night. The other walls were an assortment of glass-closed cupboards and open shelving with lips to prevent the chemicals stored in brown glass bottles from jumping off the shelves in an earthquake.

From the wall hung a blue Calder mobile, kept turning by the awesome air conditioning, and on the back wall by the bathroom she had hung another painting, this one by a visionary named Alex Grey who painted human bodies sans skin. Like the Bellmer, it combined technical virtuosity with art, which was exactly what Ginger saw as her goal in her work.

She replaced a bottle of ethidium bromide on the shelf, pushed the thermocycler back, and tidied other miscellaneous things away, making room. On her bench, the two Zhukovsky bones lay neatly on white paper, like museum relics. She flipped on the radio and pulled up a stool and began to work.

She heard a key in the lock, and wondered who else had decided to work late. It could be any one of them. All four were night owls. "Jimmy?" she said, but there was no answer. He probably was wearing his headphones, which the group had insisted upon once they heard the maniacal screeching he called brain candy. She turned back to her notes. What was she missing? Somewhere in this sheaf of material, was there a message that would direct them to an understanding of what occurred on that April night?

Nina believed her client. Ginger believed her evidence. The blood of Stefan Wyatt matched the blood found on the glass fragments. Her tests confirmed it.

As for the bones, the DNA profile of the old man held no unusual medical facts or mysterious anomalies. He was normal, and he was dead of natural causes.

What else was there to find out about him? She put the two sheets side by side, staring at the black-and-white grids until her eyes pulled them together into one stereo image.

Somebody was behind her. Ginger, tuned to danger through countless classes in self-defense and a violence-speckled childhood only another Japanese-American girl who preferred girls to boys could fully imagine, felt her undefended neck prickle. She whipped around, bending a leg back at the same moment, didn't like what she saw, and kicked with boots on.

19

Thursday 9/25

NO TRIAL IS COMPLETE WITHOUT its disaster dreams, and although Nina kept a clamp on her anxieties during the day, even acting downright cocky whenever she came upon Jaime Sandoval on the stairway, her dreams humbled her, reminding her that she was mortal, that they were all mortal, even Judge Salas, whom she had killed off at least once, and also that showing up in court was not good enough; she needed to be dressed.

Between nightmares, she did not sleep much on Thursday night. Paul's presence in her bed would have helped, but Aunt Helen's house was small. After the first night they were all together there, Bob had complained, "The walls are so thin. I can hear him—sneeze. He's really loud. You're loud, too." Nina knew what he was hearing, and it wasn't fall allergies. Bob was fourteen, too smart to pacify with white lies and too young to leave at home alone all night, so most of the time she was left to her ruminations, conscious and unconscious, and her insomnia.

On this night, Thursday, she had fought with Paul. He had told her about San Francisco, ending with Giorgi's ambulance ride. "I had to stay with him. Couldn't leave," he fretted.

"You did the right thing. But now things are getting really rough, Paul."

"Krilov's gone, and if he went to Sacramento to find Ginger, he's way ahead of me."

She knew Paul. What made her afraid made him furious. "That's what phones are for. Have you tried the lab?"

"An after-hours recording."

"And you left a message on her cell phone, I assume."

"What exactly do you think I've been doing up here? Weaving baskets?"

"How about her family? Have they seen her?"

"I've spoken with people who haven't seen her skinny, tight leather ass in years! Where the hell is she?"

"Calm down . . ." It was probably just as well she couldn't decipher the words that followed her suggestion. "Maybe you should come back here tonight."

"Right. I'll hide under your bed. Smart thinking, Nina."

"Maybe you should call me when you get over yourself!"

The phone clicked, and he was gone.

About three o'clock in the morning, after driving off a bridge at Big Sur and finding it difficult to open the windows once the car was submerged in the Pacific, Nina gave up her nightly battle for rest and made herself a cup of coffee. She pushed open the creaky living room window and looked out at the empty street, smelling the salt of the ocean and listening to its whispers.

The phone rang.

A phone ringing at three o'clock in the morning is not like a phone at any other time of day. It bawled through the house, more frightening and piercing than a child screaming in distress, a siren announcing imminent calamity. She stumbled, running to stop it. "Hello?"

"Ms. Reilly? This is Carol Elliott. I share a lab with Dr. Hirabayashi."

"Ginger?"

"I know she's been doing some time-sensitive work for you, and I thought I should call. Also, I didn't want you hearing about it in the media tomorrow without some warning."

"Hearing what? Where's Ginger? Why isn't she calling?"

"She can't. I'm calling from the hospital. Someone broke into the building where we work. He stabbed the guard on duty, stole his keys, and ransacked our lab. Ginger's still unconscious."

Nina touched the scar on her chest, cold, remembering. "Was she stabbed?"

"No, although I wasn't sure at first when I found her. She put up one hell of a fight. The lab's wrecked." She must have realized how frightening this sounded, so she went on hastily, "He hit her in the forehead with something and knocked her out. She's had a mild concussion. She has a cracked rib and a black eye. But she'll be fine."

"Thank God. How's the guard?"

"He took some serious cuts on the arms and hands, but he'll make it. Another guard saw the attack happening and called for help right away. Unfortunately, nobody came quick enough to catch the guy that got Ginger."

Horror tugged at Nina. Ginger could have been killed. "Who did this? Do the police know?"

"They don't know who and they don't know why. They seem to think maybe someone was looking for drugs. There's a surveillance video but the police said it wasn't helpful. He was wearing a mask."

"Were any drugs stolen?"

"Nothing that we could determine."

She puzzled over the information. "Was anything taken?"

"Nothing of value, although it did look like her bench had been swept clean."

"What was on it?"

"As far as I can remember, bones. Labeled as being from you. That's why I called. I'm assuming the bones were taken by this intruder. I told the police and gave them your number."

Bones, again. What was the story on these damnable bones? "When can I talk to her?"

"Tomorrow morning. They want her to rest."

"Should I come up? I'm only a few hours away."

"No, really, you can't do anything. I wish I could tell you more, but I just got here."

"You've heard something," Paul said, once he was awake enough to answer his phone. Nina explained about Ginger. When she was finished, he said, "Shit. This is my fault."

"You couldn't have prevented this."

"She was up against a pro. Amazing that she survived."

"She practices karate three times a week. She fought like crazy, probably kept herself alive. You're sure it was Krilov? The Russian?"

"It was the Russian."

"The bones, Paul. Why would Sergey Krilov take them? Why are they worth a guard's life, a priest's life, a doctor's life? He's gone on some sort of rampage. I'm calling Alex Zhukovsky again."

"I think the rampage is over," Paul said. "He wanted the bones, and he has them. Have the Sacramento police call me too when they get in touch. I can't believe I let that bastard touch Ginger."

Friday morning Nina made a few calls, then got Bob off to school, which wasn't simple.

"I hate this school. I hate all the kids."

"Why don't you make more of an effort?" she said. She was making his lunch, slapping blackberry jelly and peanut butter on wheat bread, tossing a bag of chips and a milk carton in the brown bag. Ordinarily, he made his own lunch, but when he was this contrary, he would go without rather than compromise. "Join a club. Get involved in fund-raising for the cross-country team. People are the same everywhere, you know. It's not a regional thing."

"I disagree," he said, folding his arms. "Here they are all the same. They wear the same stupid Carmel clothes. They like the same jerk music and the same lame movies. They grew up together and I'm a freak and I hate it, Mom."

He would not go, he informed her, refusing to eat, re-fusing to dress, and finally, refusing to get into the car until she threatened him with various punishments, and one fi-nally caught his attention. "Get in that car now," she said, "or I will take away your music. I will take away your com-puter and I will dump it in a ravine!"

One thing she had done right with him. She never made promises she didn't fully intend to keep, and he knew it. He dragged around, but he got dressed and made it outside.

All the way there, while he maintained a silence as noxious and pervasive as the fumes spewing from the garbage truck up ahead, she agreed with him in her heart. For sensitive souls, such was high school. But if he was that kind of boy, it would probably prove just as hellacious at Tahoe.

After she dropped him at the school, forcing him to lean in for the kiss he was still just young enough not to refuse her, she parked on the street and tried calling the hospital. They found Ginger right away.

"Hey, you," she said. "They shaved a perfect bald square very neatly in the hair above my forehead so they could dress the cut," she said. "Normally, I might consider it a serendipitous style-statement, but I just got a really good haircut, damn it."

"How are you?"

"Leaving as soon as they unhook the IV."

"The guard's doing okay."

"I heard. Phil fought back. And the funny thing is, this kid, this loser, the other guard? He was quick enough to get people there that got Phil help, and interrupted the attack on me, without risking his own skin. Phil's saving for a houseboat so he and his wife can spend their golden years floating around on Lake Shasta, drinking mai tais. Right this second, I'm motivated to join them."

"What happened, exactly?"

"I knocked the knife out of his hand, I do remember that, but there were too many potential weapons in our lab, turns out. He whacked me on the head with the ezda, I'm told, although I jumped away and avoided serious damage. I hope I got his nuts good, at least."

"The ezda? What's that?"

"That bum, Kevan, talked us into buying an ESDA a couple of months ago. It's an electrostatic device that detects indented writing on questionable documents. It's as big as a portable copy machine, so this guy is strong."

"Did you get a look at him?"

"No. He had a ski mask on. Somebody ought to outlaw those things, or at least register the name of any purchasers. I wish I knew who it was, because I consider our business unfinished. And I don't like pending business."

"We know—we think we know who attacked you, Ginger."

"Great. I've got a pen. Just give me his address and I'll take care of the rest."

"His name is Sergey Krilov. He's involved in our case, although I'm not sure how. We don't know where he is. Anyway, you leave him to the police, Ginger."

"Speaking of that, the police asked Carol to make a list of what's missing from the lab, and it's pretty clear what Krilov wanted, Nina, since he took every single thing on my bench."

"He wanted the bones."

"Yep."

"And he got them."

"Yep." But Ginger sounded almost blithe, and Nina thought, she must be on Vicodin.

"Shit," Nina said. "Now I'm more sure than ever—"

"Don't fret, baby, he didn't get everything. Just before he arrived, I decided to do another marrow extraction. I took fresh samples. I stored them in the fridge. I asked Carol to check this morning. Still there, frosty as they ought to be."

"Really?"

"No shit."

"That's a great break!"

"The son of a bitch missed 'em. Yippee! We still don't know why the bones are important, but it's more obvious than ever that they are. I have new test results. I wish I could tell you what they meant. I can't. Yet."

"Right." That meant Nina should cancel the appointment she had rushed to make this morning with Jaime. She had thought, with the bones missing, there was a chance she could get some time out of him, more time to develop their case. Since they still had marrow, that wouldn't play.

"Ginger, this is important. Don't tell anyone you have the marrow. That's between you, me, and Paul."

"And Carol. She's cool. I'll need new copies of the

DNA profiles for our defendant and victim from you. They're gone."

"Done." She made a note for Sandy to send copies immediately.

"I've run some new tests on the marrow, and I'm getting some good ideas. Sorry I can't say what yet. I'm not sure I even remember. But the results weren't lying on my bench, they were on the counter by the fridge, and Carol has 'em safe. Is that cool or what?"

"That's very cool. Do you feel able to stay on the phone with me a few more minutes? I have a strange little angle we're working." Nina filled her in on what she and Paul had been thinking, that there might be a Romanov link. "Is there any way you could compare his DNA to that family?"

"Maybe if I had several months, a translator, and a bunch of politicians smoothing the way."

"Oh. I didn't know it would be so hard."

"One of those pretenders to the throne has been trying to compare his DNA with the DNA of one of the Romanov family dukes for years," Ginger said. "It's a political thing."

"I guess the Romanovs are getting sick of all the Anastasia descendants out there."

"Something else strange," Ginger said.

"What's that?"

"I'm forgetting something important. It's a creepy feeling, like old age sneaking up on me. I had a thought and lost it."

"You have a concussion," Nina reminded her.

"Maybe—maybe even an insight. Damn."

"It'll come to you." Nina heard rustling on the other end of the phone.

"The IV's out," Ginger said, "and I am out of here. I'm

going back to the lab to survey the damage. I'll call you later."

"Is the doctor there? Did the doctor say you could leave?"

"Nobody's here except me."

"You took out the IV yourself?"

"See, that's why I work with dead people. They are so much more patient than the living."

Paul met Nina in front of the Salinas courthouse at nine. "He's been following the trial," he said, after moving in for a kiss and receiving a distracted peck on the cheek.

"Who?"

"Krilov. He left the minute he heard there were still bones out there."

Nina set down her case and adjusted one elegant shoe. "I suspect a political connection to Russia, Paul, and he's our link. He was Christina's lover; Father Giorgi knows him; he comes from an important family. We've got to find him."

"Oh, I'll find him."

"Let's assume Constantin was a page to the royal family, as he claimed. Maybe he knew something—important. Maybe he knew something about their deaths. Maybe he was a witness? And Sergey's family—but why would any of this matter all of a sudden? This all happened nearly a century ago."

"I hate to admit it, but I don't know much about Russian history."

"Take a look at my research, okay?" she said, checking her watch and smoothing her hair. "Sandy has copies. What I told you is a little sketchy. I've got to go."

She turned and left, forgetting to kiss him good-bye. What a relationship, Paul thought. How could she leave without that last kiss? They might never meet again. She should be able to tell the news media, when he croaked that day in a high-speed crash, I told him how much I loved him.

Paul paid a king's ransom for a large cup of coffee, stopped by Nina's office to pick up her handwritten research notes, then went to his office, once again conducting an exhaustive study of the paperwork in the case. He reviewed the old reports, and sure enough, found a mention of Sergey Krilov in the report Dean Trumbo had filed with Klaus several months before. At last, he had an excuse to track the bastard down.

He found Deano playing an early racquetball game at the Sports Center in downtown Monterey. In a large glass booth, grunting and sweating, he took on his competition, an athletic sprite who flew from corner to corner, returning every volley, smacking every serve like a pro. With pleasure bordering on the sadistic, Paul watched Deano lose big.

Seemingly undisturbed, Deano shook hands with his partner, even giving him a little congratulatory pat on the arm. Well, you had to expect it. Show me a good loser, Paul thought, and I'll show you a loser.

"Rotten luck," he said as Deano caught sight of him, raised the racket for protection, and turned as white as a boiled egg.

"It's y-you," Deano said.

"I'm here on business," Paul said, not wanting to scare him off. The last time they had met, Paul had been compelled to beat Deano almost senseless for trying to steal his business. Judging by the fresh layer of sweat boiling up on his forehead, Deano hadn't forgotten the encounter.

Deano recovered his cool act fast. "Follow me," he

said, jerking his head toward the locker room. As tall as Paul but dark, with a trim, square jaw and black curly hair, which women found compelling but Paul found effeminate, he led the way, his stride consciously casual but his towel getting a workout on his brow.

"Work going good?" Paul said, adapting his stride to Deano's anxious one.

"Great! I mean, fine. I've got a few pans frying."

"Such as the one with Klaus Pohlmann's firm."

"That job's finished. I heard you picked up the investigation."

"Yeah, Klaus told me he had hired a second grader when the graduate was unavailable."

They reached Deano's locker. Dean spun the combination lock and opened it. Clothes smelling like dead, wet fur hung on pegs. Pulling out the clothes and setting them into a neat pile on the bench, watching Paul for any sudden moves out of the corner of his eye, Deano said, "You really scared my mom, calling her like that."

Paul thought about the last time he and Deano's mom had spoken. He had been pretending to be an IRS agent.

"She thought I was in trouble with the government. Wouldn't talk to me for months. Was terrified I was gonna get arrested. Thought it might reflect badly on her." He glowered.

"Now, why would she think you'd be in trouble with the government?"

Deano slammed the locker shut. "Let's just leave it that you got even, okay? Now what do you want?"

"It's this report you prepared for Klaus Pohlmann's firm, Deano," Paul said. "You mention a guy named Sergey Krilov."

Deano took the report and skimmed it. "Oh, yeah. He's nobody."

"He was Christina Zhukovsky's lover."

"Really? I guess that makes sense."

"How do you know that? You don't say here."

"Stands to reason. She went to Russia to be with him. Lived in his apartment, or whatever they call an apartment over there. He followed her back here, at least for a while."

"I don't see anything about Christina's trip to Russia here, Deano."

He leaned over Paul's shoulder and shrugged. "Huh. Guess I didn't put that in there. It was deep background, not relevant. Remember that time she was gone? She went there. Her cleaning lady told me. I don't think I got around to writing up those notes."

"What was she doing there, Deano?" Paul asked.

Deano blew air from his mouth, but decided to humor Paul. "Screwing Sergey Krilov, obviously."

"She followed him there, or she met him there?"

"She met him here. I guess you missed the cleaning lady. Oh, right, Genya was just getting ready to go back to the Ukraine when I talked to her."

"So did Genya tell you why Christina went to Russia in the first place?" Paul asked.

Deano took his shirt off, revealing a nicely muscular torso gleaming like a spritzed model of youthful perfection. He leaned over the report, studying it. "Well, I don't say why, do I? Hmm."

"No. You don't." Paul swallowed his anger.

"Guess not, then." Deano pulled back. From a duffel bag, he extracted a comb, shoes, and fresh socks. "So, why did she go?"

"Deano, how much did the Pohlmann firm pay you? A thousand? Two?"

He looked cagey. "Oh, that was months ago. It's hard to say."

"More than you deserved for two hours' work, wouldn't you say?"

"Hell, no. I spent at least a day on this." He appeared truly offended.

"What did Christina Zhukovsky do while she was in Russia? I mean, aside from sleep with Sergey Krilov?"

"I think she was political," Deano said. "According to Genya the cleaning lady. Genya was a beauty, but what a talker. Talked my ear off." Paul hadn't run across any Genya. Months had gone by; Deano had interviewed an important witness, but hadn't made a report or even noted her name or her interview, and Genya was probably gone for good. It rankled.

Deano sensed criticism in the air. "Genya didn't know diddly about the murder," he said. "She was visiting relatives in San Fran when it happened. All she knew was general background."

"Sergey Krilov is in California. I want to know where he is, Deano."

"Well . . ." Deano thought. "Not with Father Giorgi."

"He's connected with Giorgi?"

"They know each other, but I don't think they like each other. Christina ended up tight with the priest and told Sergey to fuck off. Genya really enjoyed eavesdropping on that conversation. She loved listening to Christina on the phone." He took his stinky socks off slowly and stowed them in the outside zip compartment of a black gym bag.

"Why would Krilov stay?"

"Here's the thing," Deano said, pulling his pants off to reveal things Paul never wished to see. "These people aren't like you and me. They take no pride in their government. They have no money. They don't have nice houses. They can't afford health clubs, probably don't even give a damn about being buff." He pushed back his hair, looking astonished at the thought. "They amuse themselves by griping about two things, the scarcity of alcohol and the dirty

politicians. Well, you can't blame them. What else is there
to keep a person sane in a godforsaken place like that?"

"Where does Sergey Krilov stay when he's in California, Deano?"

Deano stepped into the shower and turned his innocent, unlined face up to its flowing waters. "I haven't got a
clue, my man." He shrugged and rubbed soap into his
armpit, giving Paul a roguish look. He had decided that
Paul was not going to pound him this time.

He started to sing the song Paul hated the most in all
the world. " 'Cherish is a word I use to defi-hi-hi-hi-i-i-i-
ine—' "

Paul said, "Give my regards to your mother."

"What? Sorry, my man, this water—"

Paul grabbed him by the throat with his left hand. He
just couldn't help it. With his right hand he turned off the
shower.

"Hear me now?" he said.

Deano, a lover, not a fighter, tried to nod his head, his
eyes bulging.

"Don't ever take a job from the Pohlmann firm again."

Big nods.

Paul released Deano, who fell back into the shower
and pressed himself against the wet wall.

"Read your spam," Paul said. "There are a lot of cures
out there for conditions like yours."

Paul drove over the hill to Carmel. Hungry, he decided to
stop off next door at the Hog's Breath for lunch before returning to his office. He ordered a turkey sandwich on rye,
flipped open his phone, and called the Sacramento police.
He spoke with a lieutenant there, Martin Gross, who was
working on Ginger's assault case. The Sacramento police
had a great interest in the bones that were stolen, and Paul

filled him in as well as he could. Even with this strange
background, they were working on the premise that this
must have been a drug theft gone bad.

Did Ginger or her associates keep useful or illegal
drugs on the premises? Paul had asked.

No, they didn't. But why else break into a lab? The
suggestion that the bones might have motivated someone
made the lieutenant chuckle at first. Then he wanted to
know the reason for the suggestion, then grilled Paul for
details, asking many questions about Krilov, although remaining somewhat unclear on the connection. He kept
Paul on the phone for a long time, trying to collect information.

Maybe they would find Sergey Krilov for him, Paul
thought, hanging up, but he wouldn't count on it. He finished his sandwich, punched in the number for San Francisco General, and asked to speak with Father Giorgi.

"Sorry, he doesn't answer," the switchboard reported.

Did that mean the priest was sleeping, or did it mean
he was gone?

"No one has checked out of that room," said the helpful girl on the phone. "Want me to page him on the hospital intercom?" She did, but he didn't answer the page.

"Get me the nurse on duty," Paul said.

She did. The nurse on duty confirmed that Father
Giorgi was in his bed, sleeping.

"He needs to call me," Paul said. "It's urgent."

"I'll make a note of it," the masculine voice said dubi-
ously. "But I'm off-shift in a couple of hours, and he's been
badly hurt."

Paul considered the chances of one of the nurses remembering to tell Giorgi to call, and even if that happened, the chances of Giorgi calling. Then he estimated
how long a trip to San Francisco would take. He paid the

tab and walked back out to the Mustang. He could make it by night.

He could think of one place Krilov might be. He might be near the hospital, waiting to finish the job. Although he had notified the police that Krilov might come back, they hadn't put a guard on Giorgi's room, just warned hospital security. But Giorgi knew dangerous things, and maybe he'd be ready to share them now, with Paul, before he had to share them with Krilov.

20

Friday 9/26

K LAUS," NINA SAID BEFORE THEY entered the courtroom, "I'm concerned."

"Are you?" he said serenely.

"We are losing this trial."

"That kind of thinking will get us nowhere."

"I'm concerned that too much is slipping by us. While I'm straining to get us through each day in court, you seem—hardly here."

"That's the young, untried Nina talking," he said. "Not the skilled lawyer who can handle anything. Naturally, when you have a failure of nerve, you attack. In fact," he said thoughtfully, "that's good strategy. You see, you're smarter than you think, and are certainly well able to assist in this case."

"Don't try to flatter me. You had months to prepare for this trial. I had two weeks. You sit there and you make little comments, and now and then you participate, but the whole thing has fallen on me."

Klaus cupped his hand to his ear. "Do I hear a whining sound?"

"I don't care that it's hard, and I'm not properly

prepared. I care that you aren't giving it everything, and that our client will suffer for it."

His thin shoulders raised up and lowered. Suddenly he was just a fragile old man, doing his best. "I'll take over," he said. "It's no problem, if you don't feel ready."

"That's not what I meant!" she said, exasperated. If anything, she had finally seen a definite need to take over herself. "I just want you to be . . ." *Awake* is what she was thinking, but before she could say more, Klaus had opened the door to the courtroom.

"Yes," he said mildly, introspectively, "time for me to take over."

"No!" she said, too late. She followed him into the courtroom.

Erin O'Toole took the stand, got sworn in, and sat down, tucking a loose end of her blouse into black slacks with fold marks. She obviously didn't wear them often. Her long black hair was held back in an orange scrunchie, but wisps framed her pretty face. Beside Nina, Stefan's glumness deepened. "This sucks. If only she didn't have to go through this."

"She can handle it, Stefan. She's tougher than you think."

"I wish . . ." he said, but Jaime Sandoval had begun his direct examination with innocuous questions, like the ones you gave to polygraph subjects before dinging them with the real deal.

"If she ever takes me back, I'm getting her that ring," Stefan continued to whisper while Erin answered tedious questions patiently. "The one she always looks at in the window on Alvarado. I'll sell my car. I'll sell everything."

"Maybe you should wait on the ring," Nina said, finding her own in place on her finger, still feeling awkward, and thinking possibly he should think first about finding out if Erin loved him the right way, and enough.

"Don't be so hangdog!" Klaus leaned toward them both, whispering. "We need absolute confidence."

They all sat back and listened in astonishment to the story Erin was concocting.

"We were drinking tequila that night," she said. "It wasn't Stefan's choice, but I like it. I got into it back in the old days at Northstar with the ski crowd. I used to waitress, and they always ordered tequila. To me, it's a classy drink." She laughed deprecatingly, and to Nina's surprise, so did the audience behind her. "If potent."

"He was drinking?" Sandoval asked, clearly flummoxed by this unexpected line.

"Yes," she said. "Things got wild. I mean, we were in love, you know what I mean?"

Stefan spoke close to Nina's ear. "She's confusing that night with the night before, you know. When I didn't go to the graveyard. She waylaid me," he said, apparently unaware of the choice of words, "and I didn't make it to the graveyard."

Was she confused? Nina didn't think so.

"Ms. O'Toole, are you claiming he drank a lot that night?" Sandoval asked.

"More than usual. And we went to bed early."

"Are you claiming that Stefan Wyatt did not leave the house that night?"

"Absolutely." She nodded. "He was busy with me."

"And . . ." Jaime began.

"And—it was memorable!" She lowered her eyes. "Don't tell me you want details."

"Ms. O'Toole. Please tell me you are not claiming that he stayed home that night."

Her head bobbed. "Oh, but he did. He was in bed with me the whole night."

"You say you were drinking."

"That's right," she said, wary. "But I can handle my liquor. I wasn't flat out or anything. I noticed who was in my bed with me."

"You say you loved each other."

"Yes."

"Isn't it true, you'd say anything to get Stefan out of trouble?"

"People who lie are weak. It's cheap. I don't like it."

Stefan, sighing on Nina's left, certainly knew that to be true.

Jaime knew the answer was unresponsive, but saw Erin had a lot of empathy going with the jury. Rather than alienate them by taking her to task, he said, "You wouldn't lie even if someone's life was at stake?"

"If I knew that person was innocent," she said carefully, "I would be tempted."

"So, whatever you say here is subject to that higher purpose."

"I didn't say I would do it," she countered. "I don't have to lie when I tell you Stefan's basically an honorable person. Whatever they say about him that's bad, it isn't true. Somebody needed to come up here and say that. Speak in his defense. He never gets a break."

"You would do anything to save him?"

"Anything?" She sounded disgusted. "I don't have to. He's innocent. He didn't kill that poor woman. It's easy enough to prove. I mean, I couldn't have drunk that entire bottle by myself or I'd be dead."

"Do you drink often?" Jaime asked.

"I'm not sure what you mean by that."

"Say, three times a week."

"Sure, if you include wine or beer in the equation."

"She doesn't give a damn how she comes off. What a woman," Stefan said, voice brimming with admiration.

Yes, Nina thought, damn.

"I mean, with a meal, or at a barbecue. We like to socialize. Who doesn't? Stefan's a popular guy."

"Erin's the popular one," Stefan murmured.

"How much would you say you drank that night?" Sandoval continued.

"Oh." Wrinkles formed on her forehead. "Maybe four drinks?"

"Over what period of time?"

"Fast," she said. "Maybe in an hour."

"How much do you weigh, Ms. O'Toole?"

"I don't have to say that here, in front of all these people, do I?"

"Answer the question," Judge Salas insisted.

"I have to tell?"

"Yes."

"Okay, well, I'm five feet three inches tall and I weigh, um, oh, this stinks. I weigh a hundred twenty. Okay, I weigh a hundred thirty-two. If you're trying to establish that I ought to consider a diet, I admit it. I could stand to lose a few pounds, okay? You got me, copper."

A few people on the jury tittered.

Jaime Sandoval brought a chart out. "I have here a chart put out by the DMV suggesting how many drinks a person of your height and weight can drink before being considered legally drunk. According to your own testimony, you were intoxicated."

"But Mr. Sandoval," Erin protested. "I never drove anywhere that night."

"Please wait for a question," the judge said, studying the chart.

"You were out of it that night, were you not, Ms. O'Toole?" Sandoval asked.

"I didn't drive anywhere."

"Does alcohol make you sleepy?"

"Yeah, a little."

"Were you sleepy that night?"

"Yes!" she said, triumphant. "We headed off to bed, and after a little bit, we went to sleep. Slept through 'til morning. Nobody went anywhere."

"How many drinks would you say Mr. Wyatt consumed that night?"

"I can't really tell you."

Nina could see she really didn't know what to say anymore. Was there a right answer? Erin O'Toole did not know.

"You can't say or you won't say, Ms. O'Toole?"

"I can't."

"Ms. O'Toole, is it fair to say you were dead drunk that night, and not really capable of knowing whether Mr. Wyatt left?"

"Not fair at all."

"Are you aware that when Stefan Wyatt was arrested the next morning, a few hours after midnight, he was tested for alcohol?"

"I didn't know that."

"And that the test showed negligible amounts?"

For the first time, Erin looked toward Stefan. He looked guiltily back at her.

"He looked like he was downing beers. Several."

"So you assumed he was drinking even though he wasn't. And you thought he stayed home, that's what you've said, isn't it? In that case, how do you explain your signed statement to the police?" He waved it in her face. Then he marked it for identification and had her read from it ("I think maybe he went out for a while"), then he moved to have the statement admitted, and finally he started grilling her like a slab of fresh tuna at Trader Vic's.

"I made a mistake signing that paper."

"You were lying when you signed that paper? Or you're lying now?"

She didn't answer.

"Miss O'Toole?"

"I shouldn't have signed it," she said.

Jaime Sandoval smiled. "So you've said. Your witness," he said to the defense.

"Let me handle this, please, Klaus," Nina said, starting to stand, but the old man, suddenly spry, was on his feet and talking. "Ms. Wyatt," he began.

"I'm not married," Erin said in a soft voice. "My name is O'Toole."

Stefan winced.

"Pardon me," Klaus said, discomfited. "Hmm."

Silence stopped everything cold until he remembered what he was doing. "You've described Stefan Wyatt as an 'honorable' man," he said finally. "Will you tell the court why you would say that about him?"

"He's decent and kind. He helps people when they're in trouble. You can depend on him," she said, foolishly adding, for the belated sake of exact accuracy, "usually."

"How long have you known Stefan Wyatt?"

"Two and a half years."

"In that time, has he ever been violent with you?"

"No."

"He hasn't hit you?"

"No."

"Put his hands around your throat, or even threatened you, anything like that?"

"No."

"Would you describe him as hot-tempered?"

"On the whole, no. He's easygoing, like me."

"As far as you know, did he ever know, or have even

casual contact with the victim in this case, Miss, um . . ." Again, Klaus seemed to lose his thread.

"He didn't know Christina Zhukovsky," she said. "He would have mentioned her to me." But although Erin tried hard, she was tired and her exhaustion showed. She had already made a full-steam effort and lost the race, and she knew it.

Klaus dragged the cross out for quite a while, but his points were few and far between, and whatever strength they had lost potency under the weight of the irrelevancies preceding them. Erin continued to testify like a little kid with one hand in the cookie jar, chocolate on her cheeks, and a big fat juicy lie on her lips. The jury appeared sympathetic but unconvinced.

Klaus returned to his seat with a nod to Nina that said, All's well that ends well.

Stefan put a hand on her arm. "You have to love Mr. Pohlmann. He really knows his business, doesn't he?" he said, punctuating his hopeful words with a desperate look. Nina was far too busy kicking herself for her weakness in attacking Klaus to say anything.

This whole fiasco was her fault. She could have steered Erin back to the truth. She would have asked her to talk more about their relationship, and why she felt it was necessary to do something, anything, to save this man she obviously still loved—but what was the point, thinking these things? It was too late.

Jaime made short work of Klaus's attempt to rehabilitate Erin, effectively blowing away any molecules of credibility that might hover in the courtroom air. Then, out of the jury's hearing, he asked that Erin be arrested for perjury. Salas should have done it. To Nina's amazement, he turned Jaime down. Maybe he had a daughter Erin's age, or maybe he was just tired of filling up the jail.

Some people just catch the breaks. Maybe lucky Erin could keep Stefan's bad luck at bay.

Wanda Wyatt appeared next as an adverse witness. After Erin's high-pitched sweetness, she smoldered, low-voiced, deep lines sinking around her mouth. She wore a sober brown skirt with a few stray dog hairs attached, and sensible heels, her long gray hair defiantly free down her back.

"You are the defendant's mother?" Jaime asked.

"That's right."

"Remember back, please, to the night of April twelfth of this year. That was a Saturday night, correct?"

"Yes."

"You told the police you took a ride that night."

"Yes."

"You went out?"

She pulled the words out. "I did."

"Where did you go?"

"I drove over to my son Stefan's house in Monterey."

"You drove to your son's house at what time?"

"Late. I can't say exactly what time."

"Why did you go over there late at night?"

"I knew they were usually up that late on a weekend night. I had cooked a big dinner and had leftovers. I just thought I would drop some by."

"When you arrived at your son's house, what did you see?"

Wanda became silent.

"Mrs. Wyatt?"

"I saw my son loading things into the trunk of his car."

"My own mother," Stefan moaned to Nina.

"She doesn't have any choice," she whispered. "She can't deny it, Stefan."

"What kind of things?" Sandoval asked.

"It was dark! I'm not sure."

"And yet the next morning, didn't you tell your neighbor, Donna Lake, that you saw your son loading gardening implements . . ." He took up a piece of paper and read, " 'A shovel, a pick, that kind of thing'? And isn't that what you admitted to the police?"

"I didn't know what I saw," she said stubbornly. "I couldn't see what he was putting in there."

" 'It was bizarre,' you said. 'I couldn't imagine why he'd need a shovel at that time of night.' You did say that to your neighbor before you heard your son had been arrested, didn't you?"

Wanda glanced at the audience, at Nina, and finally, at Stefan, then shook her head, sighing. What could a mother do with such a beetle-headed son?

Klaus did a little better on the cross-examination this time. Nina couldn't decide if he was aware of how badly he had done with Erin or not, but with Wanda, the old-gentleman game worked. He had her relieved and nearly smiling by the time she stepped down. She had told the jury what a basically good boy Stefan had been, and she had shown she loved her son in spite of any doubts she might harbor about his judgment. The defense, at this point in the prosecution's case, with all the evidence in the world showing her son was guilty, could hope for no better.

21

"I NEED YOU TO MAKE PHONE calls and do some computer work from the office," Nina told Paul on Saturday morning. He didn't like Nina telling him to do things he didn't want to do, but he inferred from the inflexibility of her tone that he wasn't going to be set free to go find the Russian.

He sat across from her desk in the tiny office in the Pohlmann building. For once the day had dawned clear and brilliant, so the light could pour down on her brown hair, which seemed to have come straight from bed to the office without a stop at the brush station. She was wearing tight jeans and a black sweater, and with her pale skin and red lips she looked like some elfin beatnik from the fifties.

"The defense case starts on Monday and we have to get as much of the grunt work in as we can at this point. Dean Trumbo didn't do the job, so . . ."

"Klaus didn't do the job," Paul said. "Look, honey, Sergey Krilov is important. He's probably the killer. He's a pro."

"And he's back in Moscow or someplace right now, thinking he's got the last pieces of poor Constantin

Zhukovsky," Nina said. "Lucky for us, Ginger has the samples she took just before the assault."

"I talked to her. She shouldn't have taken the guy on."

"She came out of it better than Father Giorgi."

Paul thought about his wasted trip to the hospital the night before. The priest's face, as he argued with a nurse about how much medication he needed, had a kabuki pallor. The nurse said his injuries were superficial. He had a broken finger, some slight cuts to his chest, and a shallow neck wound that would heal nicely. He was doing fine. Paul supposed medical people had a looser definition of "fine" than he did.

After thanking Paul for saving his life, Giorgi had begged off any further conversation. Paul spent the long drive back home from the city hashing over each not-too-bright move he had made. Giorgi had been subjected to two-bit torture, all in two minutes. Every time he thought about the way the Russian had efficiently slit the man's throat, just so Paul would have to stop and he could get away, he burned. He would never forgive the attack on Ginger. How gratifying it would be to find the guy and . . .

"The Russian chose not to kill him, or else Giorgi would be dead. He knows his knives."

"Yeah," Nina said.

"It's my fault. I need to find Krilov."

"Prepare the defense now, take revenge later," Nina said. "It's an excellent working philosophy."

"But he's the killer!"

"Just a minute ago we were thinking the killer was Christina's brother, Alex," she reminded him.

"Look. We start poking around in the dirt in this case and we turn up a pit viper. We can't just let Krilov crawl away."

"He's already gone, and we only have a few days left," Nina said. "We have to figure out why he wanted the bones, I agree, but Paul, we won't find out by finding him. We'll find out from working the people and facts that are sitting right here."

"Well, what does Ginger say?"

"She has no idea. We were kicking around some ideas. Maybe Constantin wasn't really Christina's father. Ginger's going to check for paternity."

"So what if he wasn't?"

"There's a money aspect. He left a million bucks to each of his children," Nina said. She showed Paul a probate file. "I got this from the county clerk's office at the Monterey courthouse right after court." Paul flipped through the old man's will. He had given the contents of his stock accounts at Charles Schwab to his children Christina and Alex. He had also left a trust fund in the amount of three hundred thousand dollars to his housekeeper of many years, Wanda Wyatt.

"Wait a minute!" Paul said. "Wait just a doggone minute! Wanda Wyatt? Stefan Wyatt's mother? She was Constantin's housekeeper?"

"Fresh off the presses."

"Incredible!"

"How to use it to help Stefan is the problem," Nina said. "It makes Wanda a liar. She said she didn't know the Zhukovsky family. Well, she did. By the way, Alan handled the Zhukovsky probate. He also handled the transfer of an annuity to Wanda Wyatt. He knows both families. He could have helped me link some of this up."

"Alan Turk? Anal Alan? Have you talked to him?"

"I called his house at eight this morning. He sang the usual song. It's all lawyer-client privileged information."

"But this firm represents Stefan Wyatt!"

"So we have to avoid the appearance of impropriety and not share information. Alan wouldn't talk to a lawyer from another firm about this probate, and so he can't talk to me."

Paul tapped his fingers on his thigh. He couldn't get any of it straight. "Okay. A will. Big money to Christina and Alex. Right?"

"That part is public record," Nina said.

"You're thinking Christina was killed for her money?"

"Not directly. I'm trying to link up the money with the theft of Constantin's bones. Let's say Constantin wasn't Christina's father. Then she would not be entitled to the money, conceivably. Alex would get her million. So Alex has a motive to dig up the bones and have a paternity test done, Christina tries to stop him, there's a struggle, and it adds up to acquittal for our client."

Paul nodded. "I like it. It's the first thing I've heard that ties up the bones and the murder. But the father died in 1978!"

"I know. I know. Why would Alex wait? I haven't got that worked out."

"Maybe he just got suspicious all these years later. Somebody told him something."

"Maybe," Nina said. She shrugged. "The other problem is that the estate was settled years ago. Ordinarily after the acceptance of the executor's final report and distribution of the property, no one can come back and complain. But there's one common exception."

"Which is?"

"In a case of external fraud."

"So Christina knew, but didn't tell?"

"I don't know," Nina said. "Anyway, we'll find out soon. Ginger's calling about paternity as soon as she gets any results."

"What a passel of information to get hit with in the middle of a trial," Paul said. "Good thing you're brainy and can figure all this out. I want a beer, and it's nine in the morning."

"I'm doing legal research today," Nina said. "I need to see if I can break the confidentiality privilege with Alan. He must know something about this situation. Also, Wish says he got the death certificate on Constantin, but I've looked and we don't have it. I think he forgot to drop it by, so get that. The other important thing is Wanda."

"Wanda the housekeeper," Paul said, nodding. "He left her a whale of a lot of money. She never mentioned it when I interviewed her. She acted like she'd never heard of the old man."

"Maybe she was afraid if that news came out it would connect Stefan with the Zhukovskys. The prosecution would sure like to know this, Paul. I didn't bother calling Wanda yesterday when I realized she hadn't told you, I just went over to the jail and talked to Stefan. He says his mother used to do housework for people before she got married, but he doesn't remember the name Zhukovsky ever coming up. He swears she never mentioned that name to him."

"You believe that?"

"It's a hell of a coincidence, but then again, this isn't a huge metropolitan area, Paul."

"Zhukovsky left Wanda money, then Stefan went to dig up his bones and found Christina's body," he said slowly. "I can't get my mind around it."

"We-e-ell," Nina said, "you mentioned before it was a lot of money to leave a housekeeper, no matter how good she was at vacuuming up dust bunnies." She gave him a wicked smile.

"They were lovers?"

"Maybe. Though where that thought leads I do not know."

"I'll talk to Wanda today."

"First do your paperwork, big boy. Not here. It's too distracting having you around." She handed him a list of items.

"So you feel something, too? A certain—urgency?"

Nina laughed. "Let's just get the work done."

"But tonight, tonight the champagne will be waiting on my coffee table. We'll take a walk with Hitchcock and I'll make you supper."

"That'd be great, but sorry, Paul. I just can't. I'm cooking for Bob, and I'm going to be getting up early on Sunday and it's just too much."

"Too much?" Paul said. "Okay, change of plan. I'll provide take-out, Bob can come, and I will give you a massage and make sure you're asleep by ten. In my bed, of course."

"And Bob will be where?"

"He's fourteen years old, for chrissake! I'll drive him home while you lounge on the couch."

"Bob has issues," Nina said. "I have to spend some time with him. I'm really sorry."

"I have issues, too," Paul said, rather loudly. "What the hell did you move down here for? To practice law and live with your kid in a new place? You're doing the same thing to me you did up at Tahoe! Doesn't that ring on your finger," he grabbed her hand roughly, "mean a thing to you?"

"Come on, Paul. Don't be that way. I didn't know Bob would come back from Sweden so early. He hasn't adjusted to all this. He needs time, too." She extricated her hand gently, but her firm jaw pushed out and her eyes got steely. She might as well have said it quite clearly, *Bob comes first, buddy,* and Paul suddenly felt sick of it, all of it, and he blurted, "I'm not going to be third best to your kid and your work anymore, hanging around for when you have a minute." He felt terror at what he had said. It sounded like an ultimatum.

Then he felt good. It *was* an ultimatum.

Nina's thumb went to her mouth. She tore the nail to the nub. He waited for more from her and didn't get it. Finally she hugged him. "We'll talk later," she said. It wasn't enough, not at all, and she must know it, but she didn't seem to have the spirit to go any further with it.

Paul left her in the office, where she was already picking up the phone, having stuck him into that compartment in the back of her mind where she put inconvenient, time-consuming things.

Although he wanted to, he didn't call her all day. She didn't call him, either. She was busy. She could have given him a quick call, but no, he was last on the list. She didn't want a man, she wanted an on-demand escort service.

He hit some gold, too, on the computer, but, perversely, he decided to wait for Sunday to report it.

At six, Paul packed it in and went down to the beach for a run. On this cool bright September afternoon, with surf massing like storm clouds and kelp floating in enormous beds just offshore, most of the remaining tourists had found other places to visit. The beach by Thirteenth Avenue was almost deserted. Taking his shoes off, Paul rolled up his pants legs and ran up and back down the mile-long beach, then flopped down to catch his breath and the last shoots of golden sunshine.

A fog wall on the horizon awaited night. The sand felt cold, and he shivered. He said good night to the old yellow lady who was heading off to bed, and watched the half-moon creep above the fog, ready to party with the stars. Clouds flowed in from the east. Fall had arrived in Northern California. It was a time to take stock, a time for new beginnings.

Saturday night, and me and Sam Cooke ain't got nobody, he thought, depressed. He drove home and showered. Almost out of booze, in the back of the fridge he found a couple of Stella Artois beers, which he downed in five minutes. An unopened bottle of slivovitz his uncle had given him years before called from the freezer. He opened it, downing a couple of shots of Slavic white lightning. Then he turned on ESPN and went over to the phone to call for pizza.

The message light blinked.

She had changed her mind. He still felt angry, though, and wasn't sure at this point he even wanted to see her.

"Paul?" Another woman's voice spoke, furry, uncertain. "I just called to say—I've been wondering how you're doing. If you're free, I'm home tonight. Give me a call. Bye."

Susan. Rubbing his lips, Paul blinked a few times. He hadn't seen Susan for ages. He was in love with somebody else, yeah, that was right, had to save himself for the Loved One, had to be lonely for the rest of his life and give up this hot woman who was thinking of him, missing him, and had taken the time to call him and tell him so.

He went out onto the deck and leaned on the railing. A coyote cry sounded in the hills. He couldn't see the stars through the clouds gathering up there. The neighbor next door, Mr. Mitts, had company tonight and Paul could smell teriyaki. Tight-lipped Mitts with his cat and his knitting had a friend visiting.

Meantime I'm saving myself like a virgin in a medieval romance, he said to himself. He felt unmanned thinking about Nina, and then there was Sergey, who he couldn't do anything about right now. He would like to break the Russian's skull. He would like to teach him about justice in America's wild wild West, if only he could find him.

He went back to the phone and pressed the callback button.

"This is Susan."

"Hey. Remember me?"

"Do I ever," Susan said in a voice rich with pleasure.

"It so happens that I am home tonight."

"What a coincidence. I also am home. Alone."

"Two such fine citizens should combine forces."

"That would be—fine."

"Would you possibly be in the mood to drive over here? I've had a couple and I can't come to you."

Susan didn't ask any questions. She was free at the moment; he was free; they didn't plan things. That was how it had been with them in the brief time they had hung out together. She just said, "How about an hour?"

"Chinese sound good?"

"Sure."

He had the best local take-out Szechuan waiting on the kitchen table when Susan arrived. She threw her jacket on the couch and took the shot glass of slivovitz he offered. The red tube top over jeans left her shoulders bare and undefended-looking.

"Up yours," she said, smiling up at him from under the black bangs, and drank it down, then sputtered. "What the heck is that?"

"Something my uncle cooked up," Paul said. "Hungry?"

"Always." They sat down at the kitchen table and started talking as if a lot of time and a lot of events hadn't passed. Susan said, her mouth full of noodles, "I met Nina."

"Right. In court."

"The circumstances weren't conducive to developing a friendly relationship."

"Do you need to?"

"I guess not. In fact, I didn't like her one bit."

"Oh? Why not?"

"Too pretty. What's she doing tonight, by the way?"

"I don't know."

"Well. Let me have another shot of that stuff. It'll break down the hoisin sauce in my stomach so thoroughly I won't absorb a single calorie."

Paul laughed. He leaned over the table to give her another one.

"You, too," she said.

"But that would be excessive."

"Isn't that the point?"

"Good point."

"Drink up, then," Susan said. "Very good. I like the way you throw your head back when you drink. Don't ever cut your hair. May I ask you a question?" She took his hand lightly. "Remember the picnic at Point Lobos? I guess it was in August last year. And afterward? At my place?"

"You have red curtains," Paul said. "When the light comes through them, the bedroom feels like a nightclub. I do remember."

"We were getting to be good friends," Susan went on. "I don't have many friends here. I work odd hours, I don't have family around, and I don't go to church. If it wasn't for e-mail I'd pass a lot of evenings feeling pretty lonely."

Paul looked at her, really looked, and saw a woman, a sweet woman with a sense of humor, brought up well, straight A's in med school, her parents' darling. All alone in America. Her parents hadn't liked California and had gone home to Japan. Her mother probably wrote her once a week: "Come back." But Susan was forty-one and liked the U.S. "You're very pretty," Paul said. "Very nice. Not like . . ."

"Not like your idea of a pathologist who cuts up corpses for a living?" Susan said. "It can put people off, if you know what I mean. Just ever so slightly. I suppose if I worked the line at the slaughterhouse I might be less popular."

"Well, why are you in this town, then?" Paul said. This string of beach towns surrounded by lettuce fields, a hundred thirty miles from San Francisco, not exactly a hotbed of intellectual vigor or cutting edges, although you could probably find them if you searched. "Why do you stay?"

"Fair question. I came for the excellent job after my divorce, but I do wonder if I should stay. Some nights I walk around my place, Paul, and there isn't a sound. Everything is just where I left it. There's no disturbance, no action, no life. I won't be going on much longer like this. So now I get to my question."

"You want to know why I stopped calling," Paul said. "Just when we were getting on so well. I'll tell you. Nina called and I answered, then recently, she moved down here to be with me."

Susan looked thoughtful. Ignoring the pile of food Paul offered, she poured them both shots. The kitchen, post-Nina, looked as it had looked pre-Nina. Raising her eyebrows, she got up and stood at the doorway to the living room and studied the scene. Paul knew she was searching for the woman who was supposed to live there. She downed her drink, standing at the doorway, and said nothing.

"She moved out," Paul said.

"Left you flat."

"No. We still see each other."

Susan came over to Paul, seeming to slip and tumble softly into his lap. She put her arms around his neck and her lips close to his ear and whispered, "I miss you. Can we listen to some music? Let's just relax. It's so great being here." She took the bottle.

Paul had just bought a digitally remastered recording of Coltrane's *A Love Supreme*. He knew every note of the music. He hadn't had the heart to play it yet, he realized now. Music wasn't right if two people weren't listening. He inserted a disk into the little Bose and let the first seven notes open his soul, saying, "Did you ask your question yet?"

"Soon. You know, Paul, it feels so good just to have someone to lean against. Just your physicality next to me. I liked being friends with you. That's why I called." The heat popped on, and Paul's living room, with the prized old Tibetan rugs and the beat-up leather chair, the books piled on the dining room table he never used, all seemed to wake up, come alive.

How lonely he had become. He felt an acute sadness, understanding suddenly that he had begun to give up on Nina. God, he was sad. Not confused, not drunk, just damn sad. The sax flowed out of the Bose straight at him, the tone one of longing and desire.

"I'm with her, Susan," he said, sitting down, leaning back and closing his eyes. "I'm . . ."

"And here comes my question," Susan said. Softly, her fingers touched his hair and began to stroke his forehead. The alcohol, the music, and this tender stroking let Paul slump into complete relaxation for the first time in a very long time.

"What I'm wondering is, well, could I stay here tonight? Just as a friend, a lonely friend. Would you do me that favor?"

Paul turned and held her. She smelled like roses and her body steamed with heat. "Don't talk that way," he mumbled. "Like I'd be doing you a favor. It's the opposite, in fact."

"It's just that I feel so good right now."

Turning out the light, he carried her into the bedroom and placed her on the bed, listening to Coltrane playing his joyful and tender sax. She took off her clothes; he could see her in the half-light, sitting up, naked now and slipping under the comforter. Outside the half-open balcony door, foggy wisps drifted on a wind. He pulled his shirt over his head, sat down with his back to her, and let her fingers caress and appreciate him. He lay down, overwhelmed, overtaken, overjoyed. Damn sad.

Then Susan pressed her body to his, and she had her own loveliness, her own ways. He could give her everything she needed and take from her all he needed.

He kissed every inch of her, caressing her body until she moaned, murmuring "please," and "more," and when he finally let her have relief, the pleasure was so intense they both cried out. The old bugaboo, loneliness, skulked out the balcony doors to blow away on the wind, while they held each other that whole long, life-changing night.

22

SUNDAY. SUSAN HAD SLIPPED OUT early. Neither of them had wanted to talk. Paul showered, ate three fried eggs and most of a package of bacon, and drove to his office.

He worked hard that Sunday morning, not in any hurry to think about the extraordinary shift in the universe that had occurred. One minute Susan wasn't there, and then she was. Should he keep her secret? He sure didn't feel like talking about her, or trying to define things for anyone.

He decided that until he had sorted things out, he didn't have to say anything. He would see Susan now and then. He wasn't really engaged. He wasn't married. He didn't even live with anybody. He had no commitment. With Susan, he felt like his old self, in control, central. He also felt—vivid, yeah, vivid, like he had brightened up, been given a shot of pure life.

He wasn't going to think about Nina right now, except as his employer. She remained the Boss, around whom the schedule revolved. He got on the phone.

Phone company employees weren't paid enough to secure their honor along with their daily toil, Paul concluded, having successfully bribed one who had put up no more than token protest. Old records? Price tag: fifty dollars. Several old records? Double that. The hardest part had been figuring out who to direct the money toward. About eleven, the e-mail came with the phone messages as a Word attachment.

He had to laugh. Dean Trumbo could have done the same thing many months before. The connection Nina had been looking for was right there in the April statement. Paul made meticulous logs on his computer. One could say he was playing at the serious professional, making sure his documentation was both accurate and thorough. Or one might assert that he was not ready yet to call Nina with the information, because the thought of calling Nina made his face twitch. And because he didn't want her theory of the case to be correct.

He went downstairs to the parking lot in back, got in the Mustang, and drove down Highway 1 to Carmel Highlands. Paul parked on Fern Canyon Road across the street from Alex Zhukovsky's house and called him.

Nina would say, See if you can get a confirmation. "I'm just looking at a few notes and wanted to check to make sure I'm not going astray here," he said when Zhukovsky answered his phone.

"Listen," Zhukovsky said, "the only thing I care about at the moment is that my father's remains are still floating around somewhere. I told you people I'd be speaking to counsel. I meant it. You'll be hearing from us."

"But we no longer have them," Paul said, not being true to the letter of truth, since they still had bits of them, but doing the spirit thing. "I thought Ms. Reilly called you. They were stolen from our lab."

"She didn't tell me that. She did call me about Father Giorgi, though. I appreciated that."

"Yeah, well, it happened on Thursday night. Our

pathologist was assaulted and robbed." He didn't expect sympathy from Zhukovsky and he didn't get it.

"Robbed?" Zhukovsky said. "Of my father's bones?" The word "scandalized" didn't do justice to his already savage-sounding mood. "What are you talking about? Someone broke into your expert's lab and took my father's bones?"

"Right."

"Who?"

"The Sacramento police are looking into it," Paul said, glad to have fall guys in case Zhukovsky needed to lodge formal complaints or something. "But I know who did it." He watched through a massive plate-glass window in the redwood house that probably had a superior view of the ocean and saw the professor pace to the window, holding the phone to his ear. He seemed to be wearing an old bathrobe.

"What's your idea?"

"Sergey Krilov. That guy you keep telling me you don't know."

Over the phone, you could not really hear a silence the way you could hear it in real life, but Paul felt certain that this time he knew what he was hearing in Zhukovsky's quick, and quickly arrested, intake of air. "You do know him, Professor. I wish you'd stop lying about it."

"No."

"You know him. He's been following you. He hurt Father Giorgi because of you."

"Don't blame me for that."

"How is he connected to you? Why is he after your father's bones?"

Zhukovsky didn't hem or haw. He merely held his place on the phone, each breath as carefully calibrated as a ventilator. He seemed to be pulling himself together, and he had decided to keep quiet while he was at it.

"Okay," Paul said, "you're a bystander. You don't have a clue who would kill your sister."

"Stefan Wyatt killed my sister. The police found his blood. My sister knew him."

"Well, if he did kill her, it was after a long talk with you. I happen to have here a record of your calls during the month of April."

"I'm sure your method of obtaining such a thing was illegal," came back the restored busy, brisk voice of academia. "I have a right to privacy."

"You called Stefan Wyatt."

"Never."

What pseudo self-assurance! But he was forgetting computers knew all, and sometimes people found out a few things, too. "You called him twice, and one of the calls was on the day after your sister died. The phone company says so, and what they say goes. Anyone who ever tried to dispute a monthly bill agrees with me, by the way." When the professor didn't say anything, Paul added, "It's a toll call, you know, Carmel Highlands to Monterey. Only a few miles. Doesn't seem right, but that's American business for you. They'll stone you and then they just say 'good luck.' "

"It's a mistake," Zhukovsky now said in a sagging-shoulders sort of way.

"Thirty-two minutes on this statement say otherwise. You hired Mr. Wyatt, and you've never admitted it. Well, now we have proof." Paul almost felt sorry for him. Four months had gone by without the defense doing anything. Zhukovsky must find all this last-minute fact-finding most unfair. Besides, Paul didn't think Zhukovsky had the guts to kill his sister. He wanted the killer to be Sergey Krilov.

"Others besides me have access to this phone."

"Like who?"

"Anyone who has been into my home."

"The chimney sweep didn't call from your home,

because Wyatt doesn't have a fireplace," Paul said. "We can pretty much check him off the list. Who else might call?"

"I have no idea."

Paul let out an aggravated sigh. He got out of the car and walked to the foot of Zhukovsky's stairway, still holding the phone. "Tell me where Krilov is, and all is forgiven, even your protecting the asshole who really did kill your sister."

"Don't say that. Don't—ever—say that."

Paul mounted the stairs and rang the doorbell. Zhukovsky flung it open, glasses askew, robe open enough to exhibit a sable farm's worth of hair on his chest, long feet bare, mouth open in amazement. Paul handed him the subpoena. "Avon calling," he said.

After this phone call and meeting, which Paul felt ended on a fairly bitter note, he drove back to Carmel and began another search on his computer. He plugged into the main Monterey County sites, then some genealogical sites like Family Tree Finder and ancestor. com, and pulled up a few city records. After a good two hours of false leads and endless list-browsing, he came upon a good source for the information he was seeking.

Giving up on the site's search engine, he scrolled through the years he thought might be relevant. Meantime, the radio yakked in the background. Another professor, this one of biology, was promoting his new book. He theorized about why man, of all the animals, had a sex drive that operated all day, all night, and all the time. Well, well, well! Justification, always very welcome, Paul thought. "The beasts," the professor said, "do not engage in bestiality. Only man is driven to have sex with pubescent boys, little girls, dead women, dead men, horses, sheep, donkeys . . ." It all came down, according to this expert, to a fundamental, beyond-all-reason craving for immortality.

Wasn't that a nice rationale for his transgression? Transgression—that word would have to be thought about. Had he transgressed? What had he transgressed?

And male attempts at monogamy had to do with the same inexorable compulsion, the voice went on. A man needed a long-term connection to a woman and by extension his children, or who else would remember him? It was a symbolic complaint, Paul realized, since the longevity of his genes was the ultimate goal, but in that case, why had Paul never felt the urge to procreate, merely to inseminate? On the other hand, he had indulged himself in the urge to merge a few times, married twice, and tried for three with that baffling boss of his.

The scrolling stopped as Paul hit a couple of names from the case, tied together in some county records from the seventies. Whoa!

He shook his head at what he was seeing on the computer screen, got up and ate a banana, spun in his chair for a minute, and said to himself, Why, Constantin, you old dog.

A few blocks away, Nina toiled at her desk, the dull orange late afternoon sun out the window hovering on the periphery of her own inner fog, unable to penetrate. She liked the familiarity of Sandy tapping away in the outer office, but she would be deaf not to hear the phone calls that came more and more frequently over the past week, upsetting them both. Sandy, who had never brought her personal life into the office before, seemed unable to avoid it this time.

"He can't do that to you," Sandy said into the phone now, sounding as firm and in control as ever. She listened for a moment. "Poor idea. Uh-uh. Even worse one. Okay, listen, that's it. I'm sending Joseph back. He'll straighten that boy out." She replaced the phone in its cradle with a solid thunk, then appeared in Nina's doorway. She was wearing a corduroy skirt and jacket with a lot of turquoise today, her long shiny black hair pulled back into a beaded clasp. Her broad face looked as impassive as usual, but she pulled on her lower lip, a sign of massive inner turmoil.

"Everything okay?" Nina said.

"No."

"I'm sorry, Sandy. Is there anything I can do?"

"Move back to Tahoe."

"What?"

"You asked; there's your answer."

"Is—you said your daughter's family was staying up at your ranch. Is everything all right up there?"

Sandy nodded, then, contrarily said, "Not unless you consider a divorce in the family all right."

"Oh, no."

"Joseph can go up for now. I'll go up next weekend. We'll straighten them out."

"I'm sure you will."

"Let's hope the trial's over by next weekend, because we don't want to come back. The animals need us. I want to take Wish home with me, but van Wagoner's got his mitts on him, too, so he'll be staying. For the moment."

"Can't your daughter's family take care of the animals for you?"

"Not the mare. She's got the vet scratching his head. Not the geese. My daughter's afraid of them. She can't take care of her own husband, much less the animals."

Earth fell away from Nina's desk. She placed both hands palm down to steady herself, and said, "Sandy, I know you're upset, but I need you here! You said you'd stay through the trial."

"I'll stay through the trial, but the minute it winds up,

I'm gone." Sandy then did something rare. She sat down in the chair in Nina's office across from her desk. "Is there a chance you'll come back to Tahoe? Because ring or no, I'm wondering."

Nina scratched her head, trying to think of how she could persuade Sandy to stay on. "Paul and I haven't planned that far into the future." She twisted her romantic, twinkling ring. The pragmatic issues stuck to the edges of those many-colored facets were not only murky, they were piercing. "Would a raise help?" she asked. "I realize this is stressful for you, not being at home."

"A raise is always good, but I don't live here. I need a real job in Tahoe that's going to be around next week. I have the ranch, and Joseph is basically retired, you know. Besides, the air isn't right down here. It's thick. Congests everything." She sniffed. "Can't think straight."

"I was born here, Sandy. It feels good to me."

She nodded. "You're adapting to this altitude, and that's right and good, if you're staying. But up there, the sky is closer. You can see farther. Down here, it's soft. Everything's fuzzy. You can't even see the Milky Way at night."

"You're right about that much."

"I have to go back."

"I don't want you to go."

"Even my daughter admits that sometimes I know something. We were doing good up at Tahoe. We had our own setup. You picked your own cases and saw 'em all the way through. You had a career. Now look what's going on. You're babysittin'. The case is a mess 'cause we got here too late."

Nina had never heard Sandy sound so severe. Sandy was unhappy, and without her, Nina was going to be even more unhappy. She looked at the files on her desk. "Sandy, let me get through this trial. Then we'll talk about all this. Promise me you won't make any other commitments."

"I have a life, too. I have to move on." Folded arms. They stared at each other for a moment, and Nina realized how important Sandy was to her. How could she keep her?

Hauling herself to her feet, Sandy adjusted her jacket. "If you love him, you're just going to have to get with the program. He's here; you're here. Deal with it."

The phone rang in the other room. Sandy closed the door on her way out. But it wasn't her daughter again, it was Nina's family getting into the picture now.

"It's your sister-in-law," the firm's obsolete intercom stated flatly.

"We miss you and Bob," Andrea said, after greeting her. "People with three kids never go anywhere. You were our social life. Even Matt's complaining."

Nina told her about the ring.

"Well, isn't that wonderful!" Andrea said, only it sounded more like a question than a statement. "Does this mean you aren't coming back? Because the woman who was using your place is gone. Your house is empty again."

"Thank God."

"But—will you and Paul be keeping it? I could help you find someone to rent, if you want."

"Oh, Andrea." Nina felt choked up, and put her hand up to her face to press her cheek, holding in the emotion.

"Are you okay, Nina?"

No wonder Andrea was so successful in her work at the women's shelter. Eventually, even the hardest core cracked and revealed all. The silky warmth in her voice made Nina want to climb through the phone and sink into her arms. Instead, she told her everything, about her problems with the befuddling case, about her confusion about Paul.

"As soon as you finish the trial, come for a visit," Andrea urged. "We'll help you sort things out."

"Oh, I don't know. It's wonderful to hear that our

house is ready for us again, but Paul and I have a commitment to each other. We're working on moving back in together. So don't go looking for me. On the other hand, I don't want to make any decisions about the house up there yet, okay?"

"I guess you'll want to consult with Paul about it, decide whether to sell," Andrea agreed. "Gee, I can't imagine you without Sandy."

"Neither can I. And, as happy as I am with Paul, I'm afraid of all the changes. But I never let fear stop me."

"Matt and I will keep a close eye on things. Just come when you can."

"How're the kids?"

"Well, Troy's trying out for basketball at the junior high tomorrow. He's stressed out. Brianna's good. I'm teaching her to sew."

"How do you find time? With the baby?"

"She's a good little thing," Andrea said, and Nina could imagine her reaching out to touch her daughter June.

"You're astounding. You do it all with such—such élan."

Andrea laughed. "Funny you should say that. We're having roast élan for dinner. Take care of yourself."

The afternoon wore on. Paul had turned off his cell phone. Nina was having a hard time concentrating due to Sandy's announcement.

At four, Nina called the attorney who had taken over her practice at the Starlake Building in South Lake Tahoe. As she expected, Carly Ann Moffatt was at the office on this magnificent Sunday in September. It is the way of my people, Nina thought.

"Hi!" Carly Ann said brightly, launching into a progress report. The cases were going very well. She had just finished the dissolution hearing on Mrs. Rennsalaer, and the client would get her share of her husband's pension plan after all.

"Good work," Nina said. "That case dragged on too long."

Carly Ann had brought in twenty thousand bucks already this month, settling half a dozen small personal-injury cases, and one of the P.I.'s had brought in her brother yesterday. The brother was on crutches and in obvious pain. He had police reports and medical records, and the driver who had hit him was a drunk with deep pockets! A potential bonanza!

And the ladies down the hall were so nice. Carly Ann had lunch with them every day, and she wanted Nina to know she didn't need to worry about a thing, Carly Ann had everything under control. She was loving it, in fact, and wondering if, well, Nina would let her buy Nina out.

"I'd pay you monthly, and just take over the practice, Nina! Isn't it great, you can set up down there with Paul and you won't have the practice hanging over your head!"

"Wait a minute, Carly Ann. Slow down."

"It's been months . . ."

"Just the summer . . ."

"Whatever. I can't work on salary forever. I'm doing all the work up here, getting some super settlements. I thought you'd be ecstatic!"

"Maybe I am ecstatic," Nina told her. "I'm glad you're doing well. I'll consider your offer."

Hanging up, she sipped her tea, wondering where Paul was. She had a sudden strong desire to run over to the condo to see him, but she really had to work. She took a break and walked down misty Eighth Street to the Tuck Box, a tiny establishment with the curving shingles usually associated with rural England. One cottage pie, a steaming

Darjeeling, and an hour later she was back at the shack, the office rather, bending her head over Ginger's report.

Stefan's blood matched the blood found at Christina's. It was unlikely such tiny amounts of blood had been planted. Ginger had some tests pending.

Stefan must be lying. The blood evidence had gone through the state's lab and Ginger's lab. He had to have gone there, a glass had to have been thrown. Had Alex Zhukovsky hired him to kill his sister?

But he swore he'd never been there, and he didn't even know her.

Then there was the complete blank on Constantin's samples. Yes, Christina was his daughter; that was about all Ginger could establish. What was so important about the bones? Why were the Romanovs haunting her case almost a century after their tragic ends?

"Hello, Ginger."

"Just a minute." A wheeze of machinery. Ginger got back on the phone. "How are you doing?"

"Tired."

"I'm really sorry."

"That's okay. I'm always tired on Sunday. So you're working tonight, too," Nina said.

"My night doesn't start till midnight, my workaholic baby," Ginger said, "but I'm glad you're on the case tonight. You wouldn't be as good as you are if you weren't working all weekend. Never go to a lawyer who golfs or can talk to you about the latest movies, because those are sure signs of a procrastinator. Plus, I know you do it out of a sense of responsibility. I do it out of a sense of money, so I don't get as many points. Did you get my bill?"

"Not yet."

"Hold on to your baseball cap. It's big. Figured out what day I'm testifying? Is it Tuesday or Wednesday?"

"I'm not sure yet. Ginger, I'm not sure about you testifying at all. You're not helping us on this case."

"I can sound dubious and talk at length about the unproved type of testing the state is doing, the rat-infested labs—wait a minute, I guess they want the rats there—but the news on the blood is bad. I got the second round of panels back this afternoon. I was just going over them one more time, trying to find some mistake I'd made. Bummer. My work is impeccable."

"Then he did it," Nina said, closing her eyes. She let a wave of exhaustion blank out her brain for an instant.

"He left his blood, unless the sample isn't really from her apartment at all, and the cops are pulling something."

"I've gone over the chain of custody. It's solid. Thanks anyway, Ginger. Did you get anything from the bone samples?"

"There is something."

"Judging by your voice, I'm not sure I want to hear it."

"I have no idea if this will be a help or a hindrance to you. I know for sure it's puzzling. Remember there was something I couldn't remember the night I was attacked?"

"Yes."

"Well, here's what I was doing. I had the electrophoresis results for Constantin, Christina, and Stefan jumbled together on my bench, just kind of lying there side by side."

"Electrophoresis?"

"It's a way to separate out large molecules, like DNA fragments, from a mixture of similar molecules. You pass an electric current through a medium that contains your mixture. Each kind of molecule makes a trip through the medium at a different rate, and separates out. You get a picture that looks like a bar code in the supermarket, different for each person. Then you can compare them for similarities and differences."

"I know you've explained it before. Someday I'll go

back and study chemistry and I'll remember from one moment to the next. But I think I get the picture. You have bar
codes that are different for each individual that you compare, and there are details you can read from those codes.
Fifty-nine cents versus two bucks. Pringles versus Doritos.
Check."

"Right. Now, Nina, are you sitting down?"

"Why?"

"They're related."

Nina felt impatient. "You told me the paternity
checked out—"

"They are all three related. The parallels are unmis-
takable."

"Who?"

"Constantin, Christina, and Stefan."

"No."

"Im-peccable. No doubt." Nina's mouth was hanging
open. She just couldn't take it in.

"You're saying . . ."

"It's a close relationship. Christina was Stefan's half-
sister, I would say. Constantin was his father."

"It's all one family?"

"The mothers are probably different."

"Of course! Of course!" She thought about Wanda's
money from Constantin. Wanda would have been in her
mid-thirties between 1971, when Kamila Zhukovsky died,
and 1978, when Constantin died. And—Gabe had been
born in 1974, Stefan in 1975.

"So Constantin and Wanda were lovers!"

"And had two children, I'm thinking," Ginger said.

"But—what did Stefan know? Did he knowingly go
there to kill his own sister and then dig up his own father?
Could he want the money from her inheritance?" They
talked all around the subject, speculating on the repercus-
sions.

"Try to give me twenty-four hours notice on the testimony thing, if you decide to call me," Ginger finally said, "so I can get down there from Sacramento. I'm leaving my calendar as open as I can. Look. Why don't I drive down right now and take you out to a fashionably late dinner. You must be feeling like shit with the case in the dumper, and Paul . . ."

"Paul?"

"You don't have to act all brave with me, babe. This is Ginger. Go ahead, cry on my shoulder. Or maybe you're not crying? Maybe it's okay? Which is it?"

"Which is what?"

"Who's on first?" Ginger said, and laughed merrily, then went on in a kindhearted voice, "You know, I think I mentioned, there aren't that many Japanese-American gal pathologists in California. In point of fact, there are only three of us. We keep in touch, tell autopsy horror stories late into the night and stuff. As I said, I know Susan."

"You know Susan Misumi."

"She told me she's in love today."

"With Paul? Well, he's taken," Nina said.

Ginger seemed to have dropped the phone. There was that rhythmic, awful, machinery wheeze again, like some monster coming to rip Nina's heart out . . .

"Babe, I am about to become the bearer of seriously majorly bad tidings," Ginger said. "Because you have to know, there's no way I'm going to let you walk around with a foolish grin on your face. And I'm warning you right now, it's going to blow your work tonight."

"Don't be so dramatic," Nina said. "Get to it."

"Okay. Susan spent the night with Paul last night. She's in love. She couldn't wait to tell me. She's been alone a long time, and she's dead earnest. So that puts you somewhere brand-new. I don't understand why two smart babes like you let Paul do this to you. And I liked Paul, too, in spite of my reservations. I took him for basically cool. Nina?"

Nina said through her tears, "What?"

"Let me come down there."

"No. I have another three or four hours of work tonight."

A pause. "You sure?"

"I'm fine."

"Liar, liar, pants on fire. Look, call me tomorrow. I'm going to stay up late in your honor and figure out this blood evidence thing. It's the least I can do. I'll think of something."

At nine P.M., Paul came to the office. Nina went out front and let him in. He looked sporty in a red windbreaker and new white shoes. Relaxed. Happy.

"What happened to you?" he said, examining her. "Your eyes look like someone jabbed them with a poker stick. And did you know your phone's off the hook?" He followed her into her office. "That looks an awful lot like Klaus's special Napoleon brandy on the desk. Almost empty, too."

"It is."

"Well, I've got news worth celebrating," Paul said, sitting down in the chair opposite the desk and putting his feet up on it. He smiled brilliantly. "Sit down, honey, and let me get to my report."

"Your report," Nina said. She sat down.

"Two breaks, Nina, big ones. Number one: we've caught Alex talking to Stefan on the phone right before the murder. I already subpoenaed the bastard. Maybe you're right, maybe he did hire our poor schmuck of a client to dig up some bones and leave his footprints around. Anyway, he's a perjurer, and you're gonna rip him apart."

"Rip him apart," she repeated.

"What's that look? You sick?"

"Yeah, I'm sick."

"Well, this'll make you feel better. I got a hit on Wanda Wyatt. Ready? Constantin Zhukovsky engaged in holy matrimony with Wanda Ruth Wyatt on May twelfth, 1973. After his first wife died, he married his housekeeper."

"Huh."

"You don't seem surprised."

"It's a little anticlimactic."

He stared at her. "Well, I can't figure out what it all means, but man, look at the birth dates on the Wyatt boys. Wanda's a liar, for one thing. Dominoes, Nina. The bones could be Stefan's father! Let's get Ginger right on it. She'll prove the relationship."

"No need. She already did."

Startled, Paul paused. "You knew? Well, what do you think?"

Nina got up, came around the desk, and pushed Paul's feet off the desk. "I think you should make an appointment when you want to come into the office and report. I think you should keep your freaking shoes off my desk. That's what I think."

Panic flickered in Paul's hazel eyes. "What's got into you?" he said.

"I have court tomorrow at nine-thirty and we are starting the defense case. I didn't sleep much last night and I don't plan to sleep much tonight. You have just given me two crucial pieces of information, and I'm trying to incorporate them into a mind that is already at the bursting point."

"Oh. Is that all?"

"That's all I can stand right this minute. Now. The phone record. Zhukovsky."

"What's our strategy?"

"Get the truth out," Nina said. "Zhukovsky did hire Stefan, so we give him a chance to tell the jury why and save himself from his previous perjury. And maybe we start understanding why Christina was murdered."

"What's he gonna say? What do you think?"

"No idea," Nina said briefly. "But he's not going to implicate Stefan any worse than he's already implicated. He's not going to say he hired Stefan to do the killing, I promise you that. I know it's never good to ask questions without knowing the answers, but you've talked to him twice, and the witness stand is where he belongs. Is Wanda subpoenaed?"

"Not yet. I—"

"Here's another issued subpoena. Go get her. Right now. I want her back in court tomorrow. Stefan is Constantin Zhukovsky's son. I believe he doesn't know it."

"His brother, Gabe, too, who may know. He's closer to his mom."

"Which makes Christina and Alex Zhukovsky—assuming the rest of the story is true and they had a different mother—half-siblings with Stefan and Gabe."

"Yes. It connects Stefan to Christina directly for the first time."

"Which is bad," Nina said, "extremely. There may even be a money angle, someone trying to get some. The two older kids got all of it. Maybe that's where the consult to Alan ties in. Well, the only person who can fill in the background is Wanda."

"She'll be there. But be careful, Nina. You sound frustrated. Don't make any mistakes tomorrow."

"Right. No more mistakes," Nina said. She opened the door. "Better get going."

"Can I drop you at home on my way to Wanda's?"

"I have my car."

"How much of that brandy have you had?"

"I'm not going home for a long time yet. I'll be fine."

Paul hung in the doorway. Nina went back to her desk. She read phone records and took notes.

"No kiss?" he said finally.

"We're in the middle of a trial. Let's keep things on a business footing, okay? It's easier right now."

"If that's the way you want it."

"That's the way I want it."

"You're the boss."

"Then get going."

She heard the Mustang roar to life on the quiet street outside, dropped the records, and put her hands on her cheeks and her elbows on her desk.

She had seen it in the shifting of his eyes and felt it in the distant politeness of his body. Paul had been with another woman.

But Stefan was depending on her. She had to concentrate on the case. Talking with Paul would incapacitate her.

She put him out of her mind. She had to.

23

Russians," Klaus said with satisfaction. He folded his hands on his paunch and snuggled back into the soft leather passenger seat of his Jag. Nina had just told him about the connections Paul had found, and updated him on Ginger's evidence. "Everybody east of the Danube. All the same."

"How do you mean?" Nina asked abstractedly. Nine o'clock on Monday morning, court starting up in half an hour, and now that she had safely navigated them both to the courthouse parking lot, she was polishing off lukewarm liquid in the travel mug she had brought from home. Bright marine sun glanced in at them. Klaus was resplendent in navy blue and high spirits.

"I will take Wanda," he said. "Yes, indeed."

"Do you know something I don't know?"

"Put a couple of Slavs in a room," Klaus said. "Two minutes later, you will have a conspiracy. That is what we have in this case."

Klaus would have been in his prime in the fifties. He probably had a photo of himself and Stalin tucked away in a box. His idea of Russia was antiquated. "Who's in this conspiracy?" she asked, setting the brake. "What's the purpose of it?"

"We will find out. The ball of kite string is rolling free and the kite is flying off into the blue."

"I've got Wanda worked out," Nina said. She handed Klaus the papers outlining her cross-examination strategy. He folded them neatly and stowed them in his jacket pocket.

"The copy of her marriage certificate is there," she reminded him. "Sandy had it faxed this morning."

"We do not need it. She will tell us." He leaned his head back and fell into a light doze, his eyes fluttering. Nina thought about getting out and leaving him to carry out his courtroom warrioring in his dreams, but he was not really asleep, he was thinking.

"So we have a big family here. The Zhukovskys. Two wives, four children, ties to ancient royalty, however tenuous. The makings of classic tragedy. The Tolstoyan unhappy family."

Nina hung her purse off her shoulder and put the Jag keys in the flap pocket. "We'd better go. We need to talk to Stefan. This is really two families with the same father," Nina said. "Wanda, Gabe, and Stefan. Constantin's first wife, Kamila, and their children Christina and Alex. Look. I made a diagram with birth dates."

Klaus took it. "Thank you," he said. "You have done well."

She felt an absurd sense of gratitude for that acknowledgment. "The problem is that connecting Stefan to the Zhukovskys will make him look even more guilty."

"At first."

"What if he is guilty? What if he's part of this conspiracy you're talking about?"

"Miss Reilly, you have talked to him now how many

times? Half a dozen? Can't you trust your own eyes, your own heart, your own brain?"

"No," Nina said. "I've been lied to and I've believed the liar. I've watched cases put on by other lawyers, first the prosecution, hugely credible, then the defense, equally sturdy. I believe both of them. I hope I'm never a juror."

"Hmm. A little more experience and that will never happen to you again."

"I hope it never will."

"Well, let me assure you then. Stefan is as innocent as the fuzzy head of a baby. Let us go and talk to him."

Staring into space, Stefan sat at a conference table in the prisoners' waiting room. He hadn't shaved very well, which gave him the slightly dissolute look of a blond Enrique Iglesias, not too bright but oh, so tight. He jumped up when Nina and Klaus came in and pumped the old man's hand. "Ouch," Klaus said kindly. "Please sit down, my friend."

When they were settled, with the rolling file cases parked in the corner, Klaus looked around the ceiling, as if searching for a bug before commencing. Finally he said, "What do you know about your father?"

"My father?" Stefan scratched his head. "John Wyatt was an insurance salesman. He left us when I was, um— three, that would be twenty years ago, man, long time. Gabe was five. He died back East. We barely knew him. Our mom raised us."

Klaus leaned over, shaking a finger in Stefan's face. "Lies," he said, in a quiet voice as startling as a shout. "Your mother lied to you, don't you know that? Your father was Constantin Zhukovsky!"

"Huh? He was a salesman for Occidental Life . . ."

"Your mother has a big photograph of him on the piano?"

"She was upset when he left—she didn't keep photos."

Klaus pulled the marriage certificate out of his pocket. He stabbed it with his finger. "Look."

Pale, Stefan read the document.

"Yes. Constantin Zhukovsky was your father," Klaus said, with the look of a man who had seen plenty worse.

Stefan turned to Nina, a hundred questions flying in his eyes.

"Your mother was married to him, all right," Nina said. "From 1973 to 1978. You were born in 1975, right?"

"What in hell's going on here? First my mother testifies against me—I know, she had to—but now you're telling me she's been lying about our father for our whole lives?" He seemed truly distraught. "And you're telling me I dug up my own father's bones! Shit! What is this craziness?"

"Calm yourself," Klaus said. "No need for that kind of language."

"Sorry," Stefan said, pushing a hand along his forehead.

"We'll find out more this morning," Nina said. "Your mother's taking the stand."

But he couldn't let it go. "How could she lie like that to me and Gabe? She never said—she was always like that. Secrets. Always tucking letters away when I came in the room, always hanging up the phone fast when I came in. What was she doing?"

"Russians," Klaus said. "Secrets."

"She's Polish. Wait a minute. But that means— Christina Zhukovsky. We were related? She was my half-sister?" His skin paled down to the white roots of his blond hair. "I saw her dead body," he almost whispered, "wrapped in garbage sacks. And I put her back in the dirt. Oh, this is so bad."

Nina said, "Stefan, how did you meet Alex?"

"I told you, he called me. He said he heard I did odd jobs."

"Yes, but how did he know that?"

"He just said he heard. I never asked him why he called me. He didn't want me to ask questions. If only I'd turned him down, but five hundred bucks—I couldn't. Oh, my God. Listen, does this mean I'm related to him, too? Me and Gabe? I need to talk to Mom." He pounded a fist on the table. "I'm so helpless in here!"

"Stefan, we need you to hold on. I know how hard it's been, but this isn't over. We need you strong." Nina looked at her watch. "Maybe at lunch. She's testifying in about ten minutes. Klaus, are you ready?"

Klaus got up, straightening his starched cuff. Patting Stefan on the back, he said, "Be patient, my friend. You are in good hands." They left Stefan wilting at the table like a nutrient-starved plant, waiting for a guard to whisk him away.

In the hall, Wanda Wyatt and Alex Zhukovsky book-ended opposite sides of a long hard bench. They spoke quietly to each other. Wanda, in a beige knit pantsuit, looked agitated. She crumpled the subpoena Paul had served on her between twisting fingers. Zhukovsky frowned. His legs were crossed and the raised leg wiggled nervously. The courtroom doors opened. People filed in, leaving the hall empty except for witnesses.

Nina felt like a hunter, barely holding back a desire to pounce and tear the truth out of their throats. Klaus's confidence had spread to her.

"I thought I was finished on Friday," Wanda complained. "Why did you do this to me?"

Klaus approached her, goatee bobbing with indignation. "You, dear lady . . ."—that stabbing finger again, which Nina remembered from her law clerk days—"are going to tell the truth this time." Alex Zhukovsky turned to watch, annoyed.

Wanda's chin trembled. "You don't know what you're doing!"

"You would let your own son be convicted . . ."

"I can't help Stefan!"

"If you lie in court this morning," Klaus said, "I will bring you back in the afternoon. And tomorrow. And so on and so on. Until you tell the truth."

"Leave her alone," Alex Zhukovsky said, standing up to step between Wanda and Klaus.

Klaus's chin lifted higher. Shorter, older, physically no match, he didn't budge. He looked up at Zhukovsky. The men stood chest to chest. "And you," Klaus said, "our Russian professor with the execrable memory. Here you go again. You must have known about her all along. You must have remembered her working in your house, and you would know that information could be crucial to figuring out what happened to your father. You make a poor excuse for a son."

"Hey, today was the first time I recognized this lady, sitting right out here on this bench. I haven't seen her since I was a kid, and we're talking once a week over twenty years ago. Anyway, you should talk! A senile old man, a poor excuse for a lawyer," Zhukovsky said. "You ought to be playing canasta and watching daytime TV. Yeah. Eating cabbage and kasha."

Klaus's face reddened. "You two-bit teacher from nowhere. How did you protect your sister? What evil came looking for her and what did you do about it? Coward! I knew you the minute I laid eyes on your stupid face! I will take care of you soon! Just wait! I will—I bet that beard isn't even real . . ." Klaus reached up and gave Zhukovsky's beard a sharp tug.

"You don't know what you're doing!" Zhukovsky said in exact imitation of Wanda.

Nina pulled Klaus away. "We're late. We have to go in." She managed to get him moving, but he screeched over his shoulder in a high voice, "Call me senile, eh! We will see! We will see!"

Paul was sitting a couple of rows back. He gave Nina a friendly wave. She lowered her head and went on to the counsel table.

As she laid the files out, poured the water, and found a comfortable position in the old wooden chair, she thought: We're going to break this case wide open.

The jury came filing in, Madeleine Frey limping and Larry Santa Ana, who was going to be their loose cannon for good or ill, telling a story to another male juror. The two young women chatted quietly. Nina gave them all a respectful smile, and a couple of them smiled back.

Judge Salas appeared on the stand, sitting down ritual-istically, adjusting his robe and glasses and tidying his pa-pers. Nina had found out one important thing about him during the trial: he might act injudiciously biased and emotional on occasion in proceedings outside the presence of the jury, but he stayed careful when they were seated. Deliberate and calm in his speech, he never exhibited any sign of the favoritism toward Jaime Sandoval that Nina had noted in her previous dealings with him.

He might actually turn out to be a good judge. Any-way, he was a bastion of impartiality at the moment. For that, Nina was grateful.

She looked over at Jaime at the next table, powwowing with Detective Banta. He caught her look and gave her a brief smile. We're professionals, his look said. Nina thought, Whatever happens with Paul, I could practice law com-fortably with this judge and this D.A. for a long time.

The day before, while she sat wedged behind her desk,

Bear, accompanied by Sean, his earnest second, had come in to up his offer. A permanent position with the firm, a fast-track partnership, and a nice signing bonus. The money was an enticement she could resist, but a decision to resist could not be casual.

She had worked so hard for so long, and she was hitting her stride at last. The drive into Salinas in the morning, the scent of fields and growing vegetables, the sleepy streets and soft morning sun, the pillars and gargoyles and the old wooden chairs the lawyers sat in—it all had seemed civilized, manageable, easy, not as craggy and challenging as at Tahoe . . .

Then she thought of Bob, unhappy; their house at Tahoe, empty; her practice up there, waiting; and Sandy, leaving. And Paul, perfidious but loved, still loved. He lived here.

Klaus's mood remained rambunctious. He talked loudly, aiming oblique insults toward Jaime, who thought Klaus had no business practicing law anymore. Well, maybe Jaime was right. Did Bear and the others view her as merely a baby-sitter, just skilled enough to keep Klaus active for another year or two?

She turned her head. Paul stared at her with an unfathomable expression. He gave her a thumbs-up. She turned back to the judge.

Who was saying, "Call your first witness."

Klaus rose, all trace of his tantrum in the hall erased.

"Your Honor," he said, "the defense calls Wanda Wyatt to the stand."

"Now then, Mrs. Wyatt. When were you born?"

"In 1937."

"And where?"

"Where was I born?" Wanda looked at the judge. She

had put on bright plum-colored lipstick that gave her angular white face a garish look.

"It's a simple question."

"In Poznan. Poland."

"You speak Polish?"

"Yes."

"Sprechen Sie auch Deutsch?"

Wanda said, *"Ja."*

"You learned these languages as a child?"

"That is right."

"Vui govoritye po-russky?"

"Da," Wanda said in a thin voice. "Pretty well."

"And where did you learn Russian?"

"I—I learned it from someone. An employer."

"Oh-ho. An employer. And who might this employer be?" He had sneaked up on her sideways like a crab, and like a crab he was waving that expressive claw of his already.

"Constantin Zhukovsky."

Madeleine Frey looked astonished. Larry Santa Ana nodded happily, as if watching a piece of metal clicking into place in a car engine, satisfied with this turn of events. The young women, along with most of the other jurors, simply appeared puzzled.

"You were Mr. Zhukovsky's housekeeper, that is right? During what years?"

"For a few years in the 1970s, starting about 1972."

"Ah. During the years your two boys were born, that's so, isn't it?"

She appeared to have given herself over to the goateed devil gesticulating in front of her. Without resistance, she said, "Yes."

Klaus's finger slashed downward several times as he said loudly, "Why did you lie to the court about your relationship with Constantin Zhukovsky!"

"Why did I . . ."

"You never told the jury that you were married to the man whose bones were in that grave, did you?"

"Nobody asked."

Nina looked over at Jaime, who scratched his nose and tapped his pen against his file.

"So it is true? You married Zhukovsky in 1973, after the death of his first wife, Kamila. You became his second wife?"

"Yes." The word forced itself out of her.

"That is better," Klaus said. "Now, then, tell the jury why you kept your marriage a secret even from your children." Jaime could have objected on foundational grounds or because Klaus was badgering Wanda, but the other counsel table held to a conspicuous silence. Apparently, Jaime thought Klaus had swerved off on some pointless tangent. He didn't mind letting Klaus waste his energy in idle pursuits.

Wanda's eyes flashed.

"Answer!" Klaus said.

"There's no simple answer."

"Then we will hear the complicated version."

"Okay." She thought. "I worked in his house starting right after his first wife died. He was lonely, and I was . . ."

"You were lonely, too?"

"Not exactly. I was in my mid-thirties. I had spent all my twenties into my early thirties sleeping around, having fun, using birth control, you know? It was those times. I was a free spirit, no ties, just a party girl. And what happened was, I saw him, and how much he loved his kids. I wanted children." She shrugged. "I was worried I would get too old, and there he was, needing affection. We got close. I loved him."

"By his kids you mean Christina and Alex?"

"Yes."

"And then?"

"I got pregnant. When he found out, at first, he was upset. I was his servant. Eventually, he got over himself and married me. He wanted our child to be legitimate. But we never planned on a conventional family scene. That was okay. I just wanted kids so much."

"So your first child, Gabriel, was born in 1974."

"And my second," she turned her head toward Stefan, "came in 1975."

"How did Constantin take the births?"

"He understood I wanted them. He accepted it."

"Yet he never lived with you?"

"His daughter, Christina, was very attached to her parents, more than normal, I would say. When her mother died, she broke down, needed counseling, the whole nine yards. The son—Alex—hardly talked to anyone for the first year after his mother's death. They all missed her. Constantin's first wife was very cultured. Her children knew me as just this low-life hippie housekeeper."

"This Constantin was a snob, eh?"

She clearly hated this question. "Kind of."

"What about your children? Gabriel and Stefan? Did Constantin come to visit, bring little toys? Bring hugs and kisses on his visits?"

"When they were babies, he did. But he got sick and aged fast—he let go."

"He treated them like unwanted illegitimates, it seems."

Her face gave them an answer.

"He left money for you in a trust?"

"When he was failing, there at the end of his life, he told me he wanted to give some to us. I thought that was great, really generous."

"How much?"

"Three hundred thousand."

The jurors appeared shocked.

"Sounded like a lot to me then, too," Wanda said, "but it amounts to only about four hundred a month. A lot of it goes to pay for health insurance. I still clean houses, and sometimes the companies I work for have bad coverage or none. The rest bought our groceries. We ate a lot of noodles."

"His other children inherited much more, didn't they?"

"I didn't know about that. I thought he was a baker. I didn't know he had much money. He didn't act like it."

"Why keep your marriage secret?"

"He wanted it that way, and so he put it in the agreement. I didn't care then. Now I see some of my decisions weren't so smart. I dropped out of high school to get a job so I could leave home, and later I got arrested at peace marches from here to Washington, D.C." She frowned. "I posed nude for a girly magazine for a few bucks back in my twenties, too. I can't justify my life, except to say I did what I wanted mostly." She pulled on her gray ponytail. "One thing right was having those boys."

Stefan wiped at his eyes with his hand until Klaus handed him an immaculate handkerchief.

"I only wish for their sakes I had never agreed to keep my marriage secret, but I did, so I stuck by the terms for a long, long time. Does my telling everything here in court today mean I'm giving up that money?"

"Maybe not," Klaus said. "What you testify to as a subpoenaed witness can be protected."

Jaime was taking fast notes. Nina assumed he was beginning to realize the testimony could be used to hurt Stefan. Klaus rocked back on his feet a moment. Oh, no, she thought, he's forgotten what he was talking about.

A pall fell over the courtroom. "Klaus," Nina whispered.

"A moment, Your Honor." Klaus walked unsteadily back to her.

Nina handed him a sheet of legal paper. He read it, nodded. "Thank you," he said with great dignity, and asked Wanda Wyatt, "Which of the four children found out?"

Judge Salas looked sharply at Wanda. Nina heard murmurings in the audience.

"Tell us," Klaus said, gathering steam again, like an aged locomotive that has just had a fresh load of coal dumped into its boiler.

"Gabe saw me looking at something Constantin gave me," Wanda said. "Crying over it, if you must know."

"Now we are getting somewhere. What was this something?"

"A copy of a photo from a book. Constantin as a boy, dressed in a sailor suit."

"Acting as page to the last tsar, Nicholas the Second."

"So he always said."

"He must have come from a good family."

"Yes. He told me they were nobility but they all died during the revolution."

"Your son Gabriel caught you weeping over this picture, and so you told him the truth at last."

"Yes."

"When?"

"Several months ago."

"Do you remember exactly when?"

"No."

"You told him, although you risked losing your monthly stipend?"

"Gabriel missed having a father, more than Stefan ever did."

Sitting beside Nina, Stefan winced. His mother had hurt him many, many times with her opacity, Nina suspected.

"Gabe is so like his father in his character and his appearance," Wanda went on. "I used to look at him, seeing

Kostya's nose, Kostya's eyes. He deserved to know. I didn't want to keep it from him anymore. The unfairness of it—it eats at your soul, Mr. Pohlmann. I started thinking, I should tell him. He would have an example, he would understand himself better if he knew."

"So you told Gabe."

"And it did help him," Wanda said. "Now he knows that he comes from a good family."

"And then Gabriel told Stefan? Or did you?" Klaus said. No, no, no. That wasn't what they wanted to elicit, that Stefan knew! In spite of her resolve to remain impassive, Nina flinched. Jaime loved it. He shuffled papers, cleared his throat, and practically did the rhumba to make sure the jury paid special attention to the answer.

But the answer didn't help him after all. "No one told Stefan," Wanda said. "I swear it. Gabe promised he wouldn't tell."

Stefan whispered to Nina, "And I swear my mom can tell the truth when she really wants to."

One of the new school of lawyers who prefer to save their feet, or maybe don't think on them very well, Jaime didn't rise from his chair for the cross-examination. Bad sign, all that relaxation. Klaus drank water, smacking his lips, his job done, well done, as far as he was concerned.

"What astounding news that would be for a person to hear—that he had two siblings and an entirely different family history. How do you know Gabriel didn't rush off to share this information with his brother?"

"I asked him not to. I couldn't see the point in confusing Stefan with information that wasn't relevant to his life. And Stefan had a girlfriend. He's not the type to keep secrets. He would tell her." His mother didn't even give Stefan a nod of recognition when she said these hurtful things, she just continued blithely on. "Gabe swore he wouldn't tell Stefan. He keeps his word."

"You considered the information not relevant, eh? Well, it's certainly relevant today," Jaime said.

"Objection! This is improper," Nina said. "Not a question." She sputtered on for a bit, hoping to soften a little of the harm he had done.

"Sustained."

"Now, Mrs. Wyatt," Jaime said. "Mr. Zhukovsky purchased a small annuity for the support of you and his children. Did he leave you anything else?"

"A small souvenir or two."

"Nothing valuable?"

"No."

"Was this all set up in his will?"

"No. The trust was set up outside the will. So Christina and Alex . . ."

"Right. Couldn't let the other kids know. What did he leave them?"

"I don't know. I never saw Kostya's will."

Jaime stopped to think up some new questions for which he already knew answers. He didn't like fishing. Clearing his throat finally, he decided he had gone as far as he could safely go. "Nothing further."

"We'll take the morning recess," said the judge.

Salas gave the jury a few instructions and they filed out. Wanda went out into the hall. She had shifted the trial toward a new place where both sides wanted to go, but neither knew how to get there without crashing. Jaime gestured to a trial deputy in the audience and held a quick, whispered consult. Nina nodded to Paul, who came up immediately. "Out in the hall—keep an eye on Gabe Wyatt. Don't let him get away."

24

Monday 9/29

As soon as Salas's gavel went down, Nina flew out the door. Sandy had left a message, so Nina called her at the Pohlmann office. "Ginger wants to talk to you. She's driving down with some stuff to show you."

"Okay."

"Her ETA is about noon."

"Tell her to meet me at the courthouse in Salinas."

Nina went back in and whispered her worst fear to Klaus, who hadn't budged from the counsel table. "Maybe Stef knew. He was upset at Christina, maybe because of her money from her father. Jaime can insinuate a lot when his turn comes."

"But it doesn't explain the hunt for Constantin's bones," Klaus said.

His preternatural calm struck her as discordant under the circumstances, which Nina considered dire. "I want to call Alex next. I want to handle that examination."

"He is mine."

"You don't like him, Klaus. He upsets you. That won't work." But she saw that she had riled him again. His mood shifts were becoming a big problem. He veered so quickly into anger that she couldn't see it coming.

"You don't think I can control my temper? Your attitude tells me that you have as many doubts as that vexatious prosecutor. I wonder why I allowed Mr. Cunningham to hire you."

"I thought it was you who hired me." He had hurt her.

There was a pause, during which Klaus pursed his lips and turned his eyes upward. And just as suddenly as it had arrived, his anger departed. He laughed. "Let us join our prodigious forces to get this lying bastard. You may take the lead, but not because I cannot."

"Thank you, Klaus. So—how do we stop the lies?"

"Don't try to intimidate him. That makes him stubborn. Ingratiate yourself, and then appeal to his pride," Klaus said. He didn't offer any specifics on that topic, though, and by the time the session resumed Nina was reduced to scribbling more diagrams on her legal pad, not notes. Father Giorgi linked to the Zhukovskys; the Wyatt family now linked to Christina and Alex; Alex hiring Stefan; Sergey Krilov linked to Christina; and on top, hanging over them all like a confounding angel, Constantin Zhukovsky. What links did they still not know?

"Call Professor Alex Zhukovsky," Nina said. The professor was brought in, puffing as though he had just arrived, told he was still under oath, and asked to state his name again.

"Alexis Nicholas Zhukovsky."

Klaus gave a great start in the seat next to her. He half rose, his chair falling over behind him, clutching at his chest, trying to speak, his eyes wide and staring.

"Klaus!" Nina cried, half supporting him. The bailiff rushed over and Salas said, "Call nine-one-one," to his clerk.

"No!" Klaus cried in that silly high old man's voice that had so disconcerted her in the hall before court. "I am fine, no problem." The bailiff picked up his chair and Klaus toppled into it. "No problem," he repeated, waving the bailiff away. He noticed the people from the audience standing, craning their heads, and said, "No show today." The jury sat back in their chairs and shook their heads.

"Are you sure you can continue, Mr. Pohlmann?"

"Quite sure, Your Honor." Klaus began to smile, but it still looked like a toss-up as to whether a hearty laugh or unconsciousness would follow. He fanned himself vigorously with a file. "Miss Reilly will examine the next witness." He leaned over to Nina and whispered, "Listen carefully: European boys are often given the name of their grandfather."

Nina nodded. She had no idea what he was talking about. His breathing returned to normal and his color was restored, but an impish smile stayed pasted to his face.

She stood up, wet her lips, and said, "Good morning, Professor."

"For you, perhaps."

Now, that was not a good beginning, but it told her what she wanted to know, that Alex Zhukovsky knew what had been going on in the courtroom. "Have you engaged in a recent conversation with Wanda Wyatt this morning?"

"Yes." A scowl.

Aha. "What, if anything, did she tell you about your family?"

"She told me she had married my father. She explained fully."

Salas's face darkened. He told the bailiff, "Go see if you can find Ms. Wyatt. I want to speak to her in my chambers over the lunch break. Continue, Counsel."

"Did this information surprise you?" Nina asked.

"I had no idea."

"How did you feel about your father, Professor Zhukovsky?"

"I loved him. He was my father."

"Did you think he was an honest man?"

"On the whole. My father loved telling stories. Anyone could tell you that. But at heart, he was good."

"You admired him?"

"Yes. He had been through a lot in his life, and had managed to find peace in his later years."

"You were proud that he was your father?"

"Of course."

"Where is this going, Counsel?" Salas asked.

"Just one more question along this line, Your Honor," Nina said, keeping her eyes on Zhukovsky's eyes, holding him there. "Are you proud of him today? After what you have just learned?"

He hesitated. "I'll always be proud of him. I don't know why he kept this from Christina and me, except that we were selfish brats who went kind of nuts when our mother died. But we were children. I feel sure he would have trusted us eventually, had he lived longer."

"When you hired him to dig up your father's remains, you had no idea Stefan Wyatt was your half-brother?"

Jaime started to object. He had several grounds for objection, but he changed his mind and choked them off. He had calculated that the answer would only add to the idea in the jury's minds that Stefan had a definite and strong connection to Christina.

Nina turned back to Zhukovsky, who was ruffling the sides of his cheeks with the backs of his hands, making up his mind once and for all. He knew they could get legally obtained records of his call to Stefan entered into evidence, and he should be worried about perjuring himself further at this point. Salas waited. They all waited.

"You're right," Zhukovsky said. "I need to change my

testimony in that regard. I just—I was afraid that it could be thought that I had something to do with my sister's death. I didn't."

"It's about time," Nina said. A deep fatigue drifted along inside her, tempering the relief. They'd had to keep at Zhukovsky. She had feared he would never capitulate. Jaime could make use of the information, too, as he could with Wanda's testimony. But they could make no progress, discover no further truth, until this moment when Zhukovsky sat up straight in the box and pressed his eyes shut as if in a moment of prayer.

Nina said, "You hired Mr. Wyatt?"

"Yes."

"You asked him to dig up a grave at El Encinal Cemetery and told him it was your father's grave?"

"Yes."

"You offered to pay him five hundred dollars to do it?"

"Yes."

"Thank God," Stefan said loudly enough for the jury to hear. He held his hands over his eyes. Klaus put an arm around his broad shoulders and whispered to him.

"When was this?"

"Two days before Christina was murdered."

"Did you know what day this job was to take place?"

"I asked him to do it on Friday night, April eleventh."

"The night your sister was murdered."

"I didn't know she would die that night! The two events are unrelated, I promise you."

"But we know he didn't dig up the bones on that Friday night, don't we?"

"When I went to pick up the bones and they weren't where they were supposed to be, I called him again. He said he hadn't gotten around to it. As if I had asked him to mail a letter or something! He promised to do it Saturday night instead. April twelfth."

The jury, provoked out of lethargy at hearing lies exposed, leaned forward, looking eager. Even Nina felt eager. At last, a breakthrough with this obdurate, deceitful witness. How long they had waited for this information. "Now, you have claimed your sister, Christina, gave you Stefan's name, haven't you?"

"Yes."

"You had no other personal knowledge of Mr. Wyatt?"

"No. I didn't recognize his name. I know that a woman named Wanda cleaned house for us occasionally a very long time ago." Disquiet and amazement sneaked into his voice. "But I had no reason to connect things up."

"All right. Now let's hear it, Mr. Zhukovsky. Why did you want to dig up your father's grave?"

He gave her a look he might give his surgeon on the morning of a root canal, like a man anticipating severe postoperative pain. "To persuade my sister not to do something incredibly foolish," he said. "To protect her from public humiliation. To save my father's name and myself from ridicule. To protect her from crackpots. I wanted his bones dug up for the sake of my sister."

The jury looked as puzzled as Stefan, but Nina felt again that aggressive joy as the case opened in front of her like a croc opening its jaws and showing her its big teeth. She couldn't wait to wrestle with it, clamp the massive jaw of it, get it under control now that she had finally identified what kind of animal it was. Klaus tugged at her sleeve and she bent down. "Ask him: who was he named for?"

She didn't know why he wanted this, and she didn't want to do it, but Klaus had that look, and she realized she would not be able to escape what amounted to an order. "By the way, Mr. Zhukovsky, who were you named for?"

"So," Zhukovsky said. "You knew all the time? Christina made a lot of it. She considered it another good piece of evidence." He said something in Russian.

"I couldn't get that down," the court stenographer interrupted.

"Sorry," Zhukovsky said. "It's a long story, and an incredible one. We've kept quiet about it for such a long time . . ." He stopped to fumble with a handkerchief, which he used to wipe his hands. "Should I go on?"

"Be my guest," Nina said, hardly able to hear her own voice over the roar of her tension. She wanted to jump up there and squeeze the whole thing right out of him. She couldn't wait another minute. On the other hand, she was fully aware courtroom surprises were sometimes dangerous, even lethal to a case.

Everyone in the courtroom sensed the importance of this moment. The room got noisy momentarily as people repositioned their bodies for comfort, settling in for a good quiet listen. Klaus held Stefan by the arm, whether to steady himself or to steady Stefan, Nina couldn't tell. The judge's eyes narrowed to turtle slits. He would let things in a little at a time, and cogitate at his leisure. Jaime, as anxious as she was, sat back in his chair, arms behind his head, a picture of confused hope. He was holding himself in check, secretly praying for a narrative that would present him with an opportunity for ambush.

"This all started several years ago. Christina met a man . . ."

A phone rang in muted tones on the bailiff's desk. He spoke softly into it. Then he was out of his chair, whispering to the clerk, then the judge. Salas pounded his gavel. "Clear the courtroom immediately. Stay calm and proceed outside. We have a bomb threat."

Like a deer smelling hunters on the wind, Salas took flight, leaping down from the dais to rush past Nina. The astonished audience rose with him and pushed for the doors. The bailiff ran over, weapon in hand. He pushed Stefan facedown on the table. Somehow he cuffed him, then pulled him up again by his shirt and joined the crowd pouring out the exit. Nina helped Klaus up, grabbing the crucial files. They were at the back of the crowd.

Paul pushed up until he was next to her. She took Klaus's hand. They spilled outside, herded along with hundreds of other people.

The entire courthouse was cleared. Bewildered clerks clustered along the street at a safe distance from both the parking lot and buildings. People who had gone in to pay tickets, lawyers, and the family involved in the custody hearing next door all poured out. Police cars skidded up and uniformed cops jumped out and started directing the crowd.

Nina, Paul, and Klaus took up positions across the street. "I left my purse!" she said. She felt through her briefcase and, relieved, found her wallet there. Klaus, crimson-faced and bleary-eyed, was breathing too hard. "Should I call a doctor?" Nina asked.

He waved her away. "No, no. I'll sit down." Paul helped him to a spot under a tree.

Nina looked around. On the courthouse facade, the concrete faces looked stolidly down upon the chaos. Stefan had disappeared with the bailiff. Paul was scanning the street alertly. By now they were several hundred feet from the courthouse, watching, waiting for it to blow up. Their eyes strained as the fire trucks came down the street and bullhorns came out. "What's happening?"

Paul squeezed her arm in a familiar gesture. "We'll know soon." He got on his cell phone.

Nina bent over Klaus. "Are you sure you're okay? How are you feeling?"

"He never answered the question," the old man said, stroking his beard as though he was still sitting at the counsel table.

Paul snapped his phone closed. "They got a phone-in

bomb threat. That's all anyone seems to know at this point. A bomb squad's on the way."

"Miss Reilly. Mr. van Wagoner."

"What is it, Klaus?" Nina said.

"There's no bomb. It's perfectly safe. We can walk right back in there. Sit in Salas's chair and render half-baked judgments on his behalf until the official all-clear comes and he skulks back."

They stared at him.

"Don't you see, they're after Zhukovsky!"

"Who is after him?" Nina asked.

"The Russians? Possibly them. Possibly someone else."

"I think I have some fresh water here somewhere," Nina said, feeling around her briefcase for the bottle she thought she had put inside it that morning.

"Don't patronize me, girl! Call the police! Where are your brains! Think!"

She found the bottle and offered it to him. He pushed it away. "He was about to tell us!" Klaus screeched.

"It *is* a quick way to stop a trial, Nina," Paul said, "calling in a bomb threat. And the timing was . . . opportune. He seemed on the verge of saying something really big, didn't he? Did you see Zhukovsky leave the stand or see him on the way out?"

"No," Nina said. "Are you saying this bomb threat was to shut Alex Zhukovsky up? Klaus, what is going on?"

"Haven't you been reading up on the Cossacks who became royal pages, on the murder of the Romanov family at Ekaterinburg, and how those bones were dug up but some were never found? Haven't you paid any attention at all?" Klaus said, struggling to get up. Paul took his arm, practically lifting him from the ground into a standing position.

"Of course I have. But none of it seems very relevant. I mean, Constantin was a page, but . . ."

"Haven't you figured out yet who you had on the stand just now?"

"Who?"

"Son of the tsarevitch! Of all the Russias!"

"Oh, my God," Nina said. The old man, the legend, had finally cracked. She dithered. Did they need an ambulance for him, or should they just run for Paul's car and take him themselves?

"Mr. van Wagoner! Tell her!"

"Okay," Paul said, "but first you're going to have to tell me what you're talking about."

People ran by. Sirens wailed. Klaus leaned back, putting his weight against a telephone pole. He started to laugh, then cough. He broke up, first gasping, then giggling. "Ha, ha! Buried right there in old Monterey! He has been under our tushies all these years! It's perfect!"

"Paul, we have to do something for Klaus," Nina said.

Klaus held on to the phone pole, helpless with laughter.

25

A T ONE-THIRTY, IN A STATE of monumental ire, Judge Salas called the court to order once more. Alex Zhukovsky did not reappear in the hall outside Courtroom 2.

The falseness of the bomb threat was almost as tormenting as a real bomb would have been, Nina reflected. Judicial processes shot to hell, people standing around on hot sidewalks, judges sent scurrying, police standing helplessly around—it made fools of them all.

And yet, Zhukovsky's absence was one real and cautionary result. The jurors had been kept corralled at the Honeybee throughout; the reporters weren't going anywhere; Stefan had eaten his tuna salad sandwich at the police station. Zhukovsky was the only one missing.

Nina and Paul debated what to do. They had spent the interim calling Klaus's wife, Anna, a sensible psychoanalyst who sent a minion over to take Klaus home for a long nap. He had been overexcited and maybe worse than that. He only agreed to go after Nina promised him faithfully that she would get him a copy of Constantin Zhukovsky's death certificate. Paul was at the office of Vital Statistics taking care of that long shot right now. Under pressure from Sandy about his decision to stay in Carmel and work with Paul, Wish admitted he had forgotten to get it.

Nina decided not to ask for a recess. Salas would not like that, would perhaps implode at such a request after having lost so much status. His hard-won rituals shattered, he was seething with male hormones and Nina knew she would have to soldier on.

Just as Salas said forbiddingly, "Call your next witness," Ginger Hirabayashi strode through the doors in a flurry of black leather and Grinders boots, to resolve their dilemma. Her Hermès briefcase gaped open and she pulled papers out as she walked. Limping and wearing a matching black neck brace, she seemed not at all embarrassed at being the main object of attention. She went straight to Nina and whispered, "Huge break. Am I on?"

"We have to talk first," Nina whispered back. "Our first witness isn't here, so you can go on, but I have to know what you're going to say."

"Okay. Take five."

Nina stood up and begged the time. Salas wouldn't even dismiss the jury. She and Ginger had to consult in hisses in the hall.

"How are you?"

Ginger said, "Me? Oh, you mean the Russian. I'd like to thank that asshole. He got me thinking even harder. I'm fine."

"But—your neck."

"Listen, are we going to spend the time talking about me getting a little beat up?" She ripped the collar off her neck, wincing. "There. Better?"

"You're sure you're ready to go? I don't like not having time to . . ."

"Jump right in," Ginger said. "Just put me on. On the blood evidence. I had another panel percolating in the back of the lab that took the comparison of DNA right down to the quark level, and it took time. But look what I found."

She talked so quickly Nina barely had time to nod, punctuating her statements with, "Do you believe it?" Nina got more and more excited. She bit her thumbnail and said, "Okay. You keep one copy of your report to refer to on the stand. Give me the other copies and the original and I'll introduce it right now."

"I can't wait to get a paper out on this. Medico-legal history."

"I really thought Alex Zhukovsky killed Christina. I think you have given us the real killer, Ginger. But I still don't understand the crime."

"Is he subpoenaed? Put him on the stand after me."

"I'll do that. Anyway, congratulations. As always, you're a prodigious intelligence."

"Same to you, baby. You pestered it out of me."

Paul's head appeared on the landing as he came up the stairs. He saw the two women high-fiving in the hall and said, "What'd I miss?"

"Come on in and watch the show," Ginger said.

"Here's the death certificate on Constantin." Paul held it out to Nina, but Ginger grabbed it.

"Let me see that." She read it, read it again, and said, "Huh. I'll be damned!"

"What?"

The door opened. "The judge is ready," the bailiff said.

Nina said, "Ginger, you'll be damned in what way?"

"Destruction of the world as we know it on a volcanic scale! Yeah, this is living!" Ginger said nonresponsively as they marched back into the jungle. The natives were already getting restive in the back pews. The jury looked hyped-up after the bomb threat. They expected some action.

Nina didn't waste another second. "Call Dr. Ginger Hirabayashi."

They spent some time going through Ginger's stellar curriculum vitae, her medical degree, her certifications, her years as a chief medical examiner, her long experience as an expert. Jaime had offered to stipulate that she was an expert in the field of forensic pathology, but Nina wanted the jury to have an exact knowledge of the worth of her testimony.

"You asked me to perform DNA testing on blood evidence found at the scene of the crime, to determine whether the blood found there matched the blood of various other parties in the case." The main party, of course, was Stefan, who had asked Nina what was going on the minute she came back in.

"Trust me," Nina had told him, "all the way to the end here. I think you're going to be okay."

Plainly wondering where "okay" could possibly enter into this equation, he swallowed twice and clutched the edge of the table. Then he scrutinized Nina's face for clues. He knew that the blood was the single most damning evidence against him.

Nina asked open-ended questions, and Ginger began discussing the work she had done in the case. She had performed one set of tests comparing Stefan's blood with the blood found on the glass shards, she testified.

"The result was a match with Stefan Wyatt's blood sample," she said.

Expecting something different from this witness who was supposed to save him, Stefan let out an appalled gasp. Jaime smiled tightly. He seemed to have decided to humor the daffy defense, which was doing a lovely hatchet job on itself.

A complete set of Ginger's lab records was provided to Jaime and the judge, confirming her testimony. Ginger authenticated the records and, holding her breath, Nina asked that they be accepted in evidence as defense exhibits. She knew that Jaime had a legitimate objection to make— he had the right to examine them first and discuss them with Susan Misumi and others.

But the results so far were attractive to the prosecution. Nina was dangling a good chance for a conviction and hoping Jaime would be too pleased to take the time to see around it. It reminded her of playing chess with her brother Matt. She beat him now and then by sacrificing her queen. Matt would get so excited about grabbing it that he wouldn't notice her sneaky rooks setting up the checkmate from the other side of the board.

Behind the professional mask, Jaime's eyes glittered triumphantly. He rubbed his back against his chair as if he was itching to finish destroying Stefan on his cross-exam. "No objection," he said. "Subject to cross, of course."

But wait, as the infomercials always said. The Nina and Ginger act was just getting started.

"I also asked you to perform a second series of tests, didn't I?" Nina asked.

"Yes. You provided me with the left femur and hip bone from the remains of Constantin Zhukovsky. You asked me to run a series of tests on the bones and also to obtain a DNA profile on the bones."

She felt Jaime's eyes narrowing behind her. What was this? Those bones were old news. Weren't they? "And what were the results obtained from those tests?" she asked quickly.

"Well, several things. I wasn't sure what we were looking for. I found no sign of poison on the standard tests for toxins. Physical examination of the bones didn't show anything. I ran the DNA panel, didn't find anything unusual. I took some bone-marrow samples and stored them the night I was assaulted and the bones were taken." Briefly and without hand-wringing, Ginger described her fight with Sergey Krilov.

"That night, I noticed a resemblance between the two samples, one from the bones, and one from your client. They were related."

"Your Honor," Jaime said, but he seemed dubious, "that's established." Maybe he shouldn't be objecting? He didn't have enough time to decide.

They were invited to speak to the judge up close.

"I'm going to show that the blood found at the crime scene did not, in fact, belong to Stefan Wyatt," Nina said, "if I can have a few more minutes. It's science, Your Honor. It takes time. It takes a few logical steps."

Jaime said, "You just showed the blood was your client's. Now you want your expert to contradict herself?"

"She'll explain her finding."

Salas said, "Don't get us into some inexplicable dither. I won't let you confuse the jury."

"I'll keep it simple. Even Jaime will understand," Nina said.

"Do it in ten minutes," Salas said. They went back to their seats. Ginger stretched out in the witness box, enjoying herself. Nina, on the other hand, had sweated right through her silk blouse to her jacket. She had thought she could let Ginger run through her findings with just a few questions, but she wasn't sure she was helping much.

Ten minutes to revolutionize the case. Get to it.

"As I was saying, in establishing paternity, I ran a number of additional tests on samples obtained from the bones," Ginger said. "The results were so subtle, I would have missed them if I hadn't been looking. As I said, I compared the two samples and saw that there was a close blood relationship between Constantin Zhukovsky and the owner of the blood found at the scene of Christina Zhukovsky's murder."

Jaime leaned forward, puzzled. They knew this. Stefan was his son.

"I went back to the original evidence sample found at the crime scene and compared it with results from a blood test performed on Stefan Wyatt," Ginger said, "and discovered I was getting a very few sort of rogue cells, not Stefan Wyatt's. It was weird. I wasn't satisfied. I discussed my findings with a colleague who runs a company called Blood-Tech in San Francisco."

"And what, if anything, did you do next?"

"Based on that conversation, I ran a special battery of tests, PCR-based assays analyzing polymorphic STR markers to try to detect what those rogue cells were."

"STR markers?"

"Short tandem repeat systems. It's a sensitive and rapid way to analyze DNA."

"And what did you learn by using this very sensitive technology?"

Ginger smiled broadly, revealing an outstanding veneer job. "I found a situation called mixed chimerism. The blood found at the scene of the crime was a mixed chimera sample."

Nobody appeared enthusiastic at this pronouncement. Yeah, so what? juror Larry Santa Ana's expression said. Nina had no idea what Ginger was talking about, either. The examination was out of control, but Ginger was an intelligent lady and on their side.

Nina asked Ginger to spell "chimera," then asked, "So what is this mixed chimerism?"

"It's named after a mythical monster with a lion's head, a goat's body, and a serpent's tail. It poetically describes a mix that can occur after a bone-marrow transplant." Good old Ginger, she knew to turn back to the jury and speak earnestly.

"Now, is this the same thing as a blood transfusion?"

Nina remembered Paul mentioning that Erin had told him something about one.

"No, although laymen might not realize the distinction when speaking casually about medical issues. A bone-marrow transplant is a widely used treatment for various blood diseases. It has only been available for that purpose since the early seventies. What a marrow transplant is—there's a donor and a recipient, the sick person. The recipient's marrow is killed with radiation or chemotherapy, and the donor's marrow is introduced and begins to grow normal platelets. In the best circumstances, the underlying syndrome is cured."

Salas kept looking at his watch. Now or never.

"And what does a bone-marrow transplant have to do with this mixed chimerism?"

"The crime scene blood sample was not a perfect match for Stefan Wyatt's DNA. It showed a few cells that came from someone else. It's as if the sample was the melding of two people. Apparently, there weren't enough of these original recipient cells to make the owner of the blood sick again, just enough to show up on this advanced battery." She folded her hands, looked at the judge and jury, smiled again.

She was a scientist. She thought they understood now, but nobody understood a thing.

"Let's try to summarize this," Nina said. "The blood sample from the crime scene showed something unusual on further testing?"

"Yes."

"Something called a mixed chimera effect?"

"Yes."

"Showing that the person who left the blood in Christina Zhukovsky's apartment was not, in fact, our client, Stefan Wyatt."

"Correct."

"This person's blood held Stefan Wyatt's DNA profile, but showed anomalies that proved to you it belonged to someone else?"

"Right."

"Did you identify this person?"

"Yes, I believe so."

"How did you do that?"

"Simple. With permission, I obtained Stefan Wyatt's medical records and learned that in childhood he had been the donor in a bone-marrow transplant."

The courtroom was quiet now, getting it.

"And who was the recipient of this bone marrow of Stefan Wyatt, the one whose blood was found in Christina Zhukovsky's apartment?"

"According to the medical records, that person was his brother, Gabriel Wyatt," Ginger said, with one final, definitive flick of a finger through her spiked hair.

26

THE JURY MEMBERS LOOKED LIKE they were still trying to take it in, but everyone seemed to recognize that suspicion had been directed at someone else, and that this was a surprise. The peanut gallery buzzed.

Gabriel Wyatt should still be outside in the hallway waiting; he often came along with his mother. Nina hurried to the counsel table and grabbed her form and a pen. She passed through the attorneys' gate and headed down the aisle, tossing a question over her shoulder. "Your Honor?" Salas inclined his head and his bailiff moved along behind her, hand on the butt of his weapon.

Nina found Wyatt in the hall, lolling innocently on a bench, a dog-eared paperback in his hand. A glance at her, and another at the bailiff standing sternly behind her, was enough to make him drop his book, spin on his heel, and take off running. Eddie, the bailiff, ran after him, but there was no need for haste. Paul had Wyatt squeezed in a hammerlock before he could reach the stairway.

Skidding to a halt, Nina tucked the paper she had grabbed into Wyatt's shirt pocket. "Sorry about the short notice," she said. "You're under subpoena. Due in court right now."

"I changed my mind. I don't feel well and I don't want to testify." He worked one arm free and threw the subpoena to the ground and stepped on it, grinding away at it as if pulverizing a cockroach. Paul held tightly to his other arm.

"Stay right there, sir," Eddie said. He spoke into a phone. Within seconds two more bailiffs roared up, excited by this break in their day, and uncertain what level of threat to anticipate, therefore anticipating the worst. Their guns were drawn. Gabe was breathing hard, and Nina, blocking his way in front, saw resignation forming there. His shoulders slumped. Paul and the bailiffs read his body language immediately; some of the tension dissipated.

"Let go of me," Gabe said to Paul. "Who is this guy to manhandle me anyway?" At Paul's nod, Eddie took over. "Now let's just mosey on back to the courtroom," Eddie suggested in a polite Southern accent, picking up the discarded subpoena. "You don't want to keep the judge waitin', do you? 'Cause let me tell you, he looks sweet, but he ain't."

They returned to the courtroom, Nina feeling like a baton twirler leading the parade.

"Ladies and gentlemen, we have to work out some matters out of your hearing," Salas told the jury. "We will resume as soon as possible." He gestured with his chin again. One of the additional bailiffs escorted the jury out.

"Mr. Wyatt, come forward and bring that subpoena with you. Now then," Salas said, "we are on the record." For a man who hated disruption, he had controlled the situation admirably. Buoyed by the judge's decisiveness, Nina felt as though he understood that the job was to get the truth out, not follow process to the dead letter. She had been wrong about him. He was the first Mexican-American judge in Monterey County's long history, and she had thought last time around that he had a chip on his shoulder that might weigh him down forever.

He didn't. Nina was thinking about sending him roses when the trial was over, whatever the result. A bigger bouquet if they won, of course.

"Am I under arrest?" Gabe said.

"No, sir. I'm keeping you here while we sort some things out. Ms. Reilly? You wish to speak?"

"Thank you. I have no further questions for Dr. Hirabayashi at this time. I wish to call Mr. Wyatt here as my next witness. He is under subpoena. I request that the court caution Mr. Wyatt as to his rights before any testimony is taken."

"I feel sick. Can't I go, Judge?" Gabe asked.

Salas ignored the question. "Mr. Sandoval, what is the State's position as to the defense motion to take testimony out of order?"

"We oppose it. The defense case is in disarray. The jury is confused and that's not good. The defense called Alex Zhukovsky, and then Mr. Zhukovsky didn't return after the bomb threat. I agreed to withhold my cross-examination due to the confusion while he was located, and I did not request a continuance. So Dr. Hirabayashi was actually put on out of order. The defense surprised me with a new expert report and I did not object to the taking of testimony regarding that report. That was my mistake, since Dr. Hirabayashi took advantage of my cooperation by making wild accusations during a disorganized direct examination.

"Now it is suggested that instead of my cross-examining Dr. Hirabayashi, she be allowed to step down and we put Mr. Wyatt on the stand. The defense wants us in a state of uproar, and that's a setup, Your Honor. Next, she'll ask for a mistrial on grounds that the whole trial is compromised by the confusing way the evidence is being presented."

"Ms. Reilly?"

"Counsel is right in most respects, Your Honor." She saw surprise flit over Jaime's face out of the corner of her eye, but the judge just listened. "I admit that the defense case has not run smoothly thus far, and I apologize to the Court and counsel. But there is no intent to ask for a mistrial. Sometimes the evidence—the evidence runs off with the case, Your Honor. It may mean that we are pursuing the wrong line of inquiry in this trial. In any case, the Court has inherent power to make adjustments in the order of presentation of evidence in the interests of justice. Section 1385 of the Code of Civil Procedure."

"Mr. Sandoval, if you let her put this witness on, I'll give you tonight to prepare a cross-examination of Dr. Hirabayashi and order her to stay over," Salas said. "I'll also make sure you have a full and fair chance to do the cross on this witness."

Jaime gave him an incredulous look. "I don't think it's appropriate," he said. "I'm going to be surprised by this witness's testimony, too."

"He's on the witness list we supplied several weeks ago," Nina interrupted. Judge Salas looked through the court file for this token correctness and found it.

"He is," he told Jaime.

"Does it say he's going to testify about the blood evidence?"

"The description is so general he could testify about Mao Tse-tung. You could have filed a pretrial motion objecting to the vagueness of the description."

Of course Jaime hadn't done that, because his own witness list, provided to Nina on the last possible day, had also featured vague descriptions.

"I object to putting Mr. Wyatt on out of order," Jaime

said grimly. "I move for a continuance to allow me to prepare a cross-examination of Dr. Hirabayashi." He had decided to stand on procedure. Nina couldn't fault him for that, but she had a strong sinking feeling that if they recessed now, Gabe would find a way to be absent in the morning.

Before she could protest some more, Salas told Jaime, "Your motion for a continuance is granted. You may have until tomorrow morning to prepare an examination of Dr. Hirabayashi."

"I didn't mean that—I meant, we should adjourn . . ."

The judge ignored his flustering. "Your objection to putting on this witness out of order is overruled. Mr. Wyatt?"

Gabriel Wyatt, who had been following all this with the shocked expression of a seal in the mouth of a shark, said, "Me?"

"You. I am going to bring the jury back in. We'll take your testimony at this time. However, it has come to my attention that you need to be cautioned, and I am going to tell you about certain rights you have at this time." Salas pulled out a card to let Wyatt know that he could take the Fifth Amendment if at any time he felt his testimony might be self-incriminatory, and told Wyatt he could have time to consult a lawyer if he needed one.

When he finished, Gabe's expression remained the same—stunned, resigned, and maybe just a little cagey. During a long silence he thought about his rights. To Nina's vast relief, he finally said, "Oh, let's get it over with."

She turned and walked decorously back to the counsel table. When she got there, she squeezed Stefan's hand so hard he said, "Ow!"

She took a deep cleansing breath and exhaled it. She would have to fly by the somewhat worn seat of her pants a while longer, which was okay. Somehow, she felt more comfortable in that position.

She only wished Klaus was there to see.

Then again, this streak of Tahoe gambler's luck couldn't keep up much longer. Judging from Gabe Wyatt's face, he had no plan to confess. Jaime was conferring with Detective Banta. The jury filed back in and the judge muttered to his clerk, looking not a bit perturbed by the rash of on-the-spot decisions he had just had to make.

"You may step down," Salas told Ginger. Ginger passed Nina on her way out to the hall where the witnesses had to wait. She leaned down to whisper, "Am I cool or what?"

"Stick around outside. I didn't get half your testimony."

"Don't forget to check out that death certificate for Constantin. We should definitely discuss that when you get a second."

"Okay, thanks." Nina shuffled through her paperwork to find the certificate, then looked down at her legal pad, which held a few Q and As and a comic-booky series of sketches showing a glass thrown, connecting, shattering.

She called Gabe Wyatt to the stand. He was sworn in, giving his name in a strong enough voice. She imagined that he would have dressed differently if he had known he'd be giving a show today—the khaki pants weren't pressed and he wore a green polo shirt. Examining the back of his head as he swore to tell the whole truth, he looked a lot like Stefan, but better.

"You are the defendant's older brother?"

"Yes."

"How much older?"

"One year."

"What is your occupation?"

"I'm a junior executive at Classic Collections."

So let the jury think he had friends in fashion. Nina didn't care. "Where did you attend school?"

"Pacific Grove High, then Monterey Peninsula College for a while."

"Did you graduate?"

"Yeah, from high school. My family wasn't well off," he explained. "College was a luxury we couldn't afford." He nodded as if to himself and Nina realized with a stab of joy that he wanted to tell a story, was dying to tell it. All she had to do was get out of the way.

"You and Stefan lived with your mother, Wanda Wyatt?"

"In a two-bedroom shack we rented. Our mother worked as a maid most of the years we were growing up."

"You've done well," Nina said.

"I don't like my work, but I work hard. I'm paid enough to get by."

"Where was your father while you were growing up?"

"That's the question, isn't it?"

"He didn't live at home?"

"My mother told us he left us, and died somewhere else. She told us a lot of lies about him."

"How do you know that?"

"Recently, she told me the truth."

"When was that?"

"Last spring. I stopped by the house. My mother was looking at an old picture of the old man she had worked for before we were born. She'd had a few."

"Do you remember your father?"

He shook his head. "I don't. I guess he must have come around sometimes, but I don't remember him. Neither does Stefan." He sounded resentful.

"What truth about your father did she tell you?"

"She said my father was Constantin Zhukovsky."

This much Nina knew from Wanda's testimony, but

now she wanted to go further. She let her own curiosity lead her in her questions. If Jaime wanted to object, he would.

"What was your reaction to that?"

"Anger. He died in 1978. I was only four, but she told me that, other than when I was an infant, he wasn't around. He must have been ashamed of me and my brother, ashamed of our mother. He had married her, though, I saw the marriage certificate. We were his legitimate children, but he was fixated on his first two. The father's name on our birth certificates said John Wyatt. Our mother told us he was an insurance salesman who died when we were young."

"The 'first two' children you're referring to are Christina and Alex Zhukovsky, is that correct?"

"Exactly. They had not been told, either. I decided to check into the whole situation."

"The situation being your father's marriage?"

"The situation being my whole fake childhood. The situation being the deprivation he let us grow up in. The situation being how the first two got coddled, while Stef and I couldn't—didn't have anything." Envy and bitterness flavored his words.

Nina let them spread over the courtroom, then asked, "And how did you go about checking into this?"

"First, I looked at the death certificate. I saw how and when he died."

Nina brought the copy of the certificate for him to examine. "Is this it?"

"Yes."

It was entered into evidence.

"According to this, your father, Constantin Zhukovsky, died in 1978 of a syndrome known as thrombocytopenia."

"That's right. I did some reading on the topic, and questioned my mother some more. Turns out, he had a blood disease, aplastic anemia, which led to a syndrome, thrombocytopenia, that had made him sick off and on for years, especially toward the end. That got me thinking. After all, I had aplastic anemia that led to a serious blood disease, when I was a child."

"So you came to believe what your mother had told you?"

"It was a weak link, but yeah, I believed her. By then I was hooked. I took a look at my new siblings. I found out where Alex was teaching and I shadowed him for a few days. I knocked on his door in Carmel Highlands one day when he was out and the cleaning people were there, and I saw his furniture. Roche-Bobois sofa and chairs, rug worth a fortune. He drove a new Coupe de Ville."

"And what was the purpose of this shadowing?"

"Curiosity. I wanted to see what he was like. I wanted to see if he had money. Then I did the same with Christina."

"You checked her out?"

"She got up late, sat on her balcony making phone calls, ate lunch at nice restaurants in town. She dated now and then and had friends over to lavish spreads. She was working on some kind of Russian conference at the college, but there was something more going on. She drove a Caddy, too, an Escalade SUV. Any idea what those cost?"

"Why don't you tell us, Mr. Wyatt."

"Fifty grand stripped down."

Nina said, "Were you jealous of how well your new siblings lived?"

"Hey, no. I prefer my mom's hand-me-down Taurus to her Escalade. I like going forty-five because it won't go any faster on hills. Of course I was damned jealous."

"What happened then?"

"This conference happened. The Russian one that Christina organized."

Nina continued to ask open-ended questions. Gabe went on with his story.

Gabe Wyatt went to the conference on post–Soviet Russia at Cal State. In spite of what he had recently learned about his father, he didn't care about Russia. He had a different agenda, to follow Christina. Unlike their father, she was alive. He understood Alex. Now he wanted to understand her.

He had ruminated upon the fact that she had grown up with their shared father, and that she and her brother were somehow the favored ones, being legitimate in the eyes of the world, while he and Stefan were the ugly secrets. It was almost worse than before, when at least he could fantasize that his father loved him.

The lack of money mixed in with the lack of love. Too late on the love front. Maybe he could still get some of the money, do something big with it, something important. He had waited all his life for a break. Maybe this was it.

At the opening ceremony, Christina introduced the keynote speaker. From the second row, Gabe studied her, listening for a familiar note in her voice but discovering none. He looked at her blue eyes, and thought maybe they looked like Stefan's. Certainly, nothing about this woman reminded him of himself. She was a complete stranger who had gotten between Gabe and his father.

Getting antsy to see if she recognized something in him, he tested her a few times, trying to catch her eye, walking close by that first day. During lunch, he sat down beside her on a bench briefly while she ate. But she didn't notice anything unusual. She didn't seem any more connected than he did. She faded into the woodwork after the duty of introductions, a forceful but quiet intellectual woman.

"So you followed her around without her knowledge at this conference?"

"Right. I got kind of obsessed. I couldn't figure her out."

"Did she have any repeated contacts with any of the attendees?"

"Sure. A Russian Orthodox priest, Father Giorgi. Plus her brother Alex was there. She spent a lot of time in little sessions outside with both of them. And a man I figured for an ex-boyfriend, judging by the way she reacted to seeing him lurking around. Very blond. He figured out I was watching her, but he didn't do anything."

"And did you learn the name of this man?"

"Sergey Krilov, supposedly an economist from St. Petersburg, at least that's how he was listed among the participants. He didn't know a euro from a hole in the head. I knew something was up, and it didn't have anything to do with the Moscow stock exchange."

"Did you come to realize what this something was?" Nina said.

"Well, Christina was such a busy bee, hitting people up for money, secretly meeting with this priest from San Francisco. She talked to Krilov, but didn't look happy about it. Then she'd sneak off somewhere to talk to her brother."

"So you were suspicious that the conference was— what?"

"Rigged. A front."

"For what?"

"She organized it to raise money for a pet cause of some kind. I never got details, because they were very discreet, but I think it had to do with some scheme she had . . . and then Christina was attacked. It was late in the first day of the conference. She had just left a presentation and walked by herself toward her car with a heavy briefcase. I followed her. It was getting dark. To tell the truth, I had made up my mind to talk to her. I was starting to feel foolish, and I had a lot of questions. I—"

"Hold on. You say she was attacked?" Nina asked.

"A heavyset bald man, big as a grizzly, came around the corner and took hold of her from behind. I didn't have time to think, much less do anything about it. If he had really meant to kill her, I couldn't have gotten to her. He held her tight and whispered something into her ear, something that scared the hell out of her. Then Krilov popped up, jumping him from behind. I don't even know where he came from. He did something to this man's neck that made him scream. He dropped his hold on Christina and took off. Krilov dusted off his hands like he'd been handling something dirty and tried to talk to Christina, but she wanted nothing to do with him. She brushed him off."

Nina took a second to go to the table. Stefan wanted information, but she shook him off with a finger to the lips. She drank water and tried to think. A big bear of a Russian man? She didn't know if Gabe was telling the truth or inventing folk tales to distract attention.

But the jury members were listening. Just as she did, they wanted to know who in hell had killed Christina Zhukovsky. Maybe not Sergey Krilov, if he had been so keen to defend her from attack. She decided to let Gabe run with his story until somebody, the judge or Jaime, shut her down.

"That's quite a tale, Mr. Wyatt," she said, putting the glass down, looking at the jury. Santa Ana definitely didn't believe a word of his testimony so far.

"You know what? I've been wanting to tell what happened," Gabe said. "But I was afraid. You'll get why in a minute."

"Do you know who this attacker was, as you sit here today?"

"No. Although later I overheard more about him."

"What did Christina do then?"

She was tough, Gabe gave Christina that. She talked sharply to Krilov, sent him away, then she walked uncertainly a few more steps to an old wooden building and made it inside, but reappeared soon after with her brother Alex. Gabe stood back behind the building, watching them, listening.

"I tried, but couldn't hear anything in there, but they came out after a few minutes and stood by his Cadillac, and she told him everything, why she was attacked, why she went to Russia, the whole thing."

The judge leaned over, saying, "Mr. Wyatt, do you know where Alex Zhukovsky is?"

Up to now, Nina had taken in Wyatt's story like a computer spreadsheet took in data, making lists in her mind: this goes here; that goes there; now how does it add up? Salas had other concerns.

"I remind you of your rights," Salas persisted, not specifying them again because of the jury's presence.

"No idea," Gabe Wyatt said. "None."

"All right. Continue, Counsel."

"What exactly did you overhear at that place and time?" Nina said. Jaime and his assistant scribbled furiously.

"Okay. Alex was really worried about her injuries. Christina said, 'I knew this was a dangerous game to play, stalling them, putting them off. They can't stand it that I'm my own woman now, and I won't be a puppet. It's time, Alex, time for the world to hear about me. Tell the papers. That's the only guarantee I'll be safe.'"

"Did she explain exactly what the world should hear?"

"She said . . ."—he smiled as if embarrassed—"she was heir to the throne of Russia."

One of the jurors giggled.

"I laughed at first," Gabe said.

"Go on," Nina said.

"She said, 'Our father, Constantin Zhukovsky, was the tsarevitch, the only son of Nicholas the Second, the last tsar of Russia.' "

"How did her brother, Alex, respond to the information?"

"He flipped. At first he just asked her what kind of brainwashing they did on her while she was over there. Then, when she wouldn't back down, he said she was talking like a madwoman. She needed psychological counseling. I agreed with him, by the way.

"Alex said, 'So Krilov was just using you.' I think that upset her a little, like he wouldn't have gone for her otherwise, but she did agree. She said she broke with him when she found out Sergey wanted her to get in with some people he knew, not because they could do good for Russia, but because they could make money with her as a figurehead, or even just as a backer. That it was greed, not the power to do good, that motivated him and his group.

"Meanwhile, Alex had been thinking. He told her that if she went public, their family would be humiliated, meaning him, I guess, since she didn't seem to care. He said that without proof she was putting herself in harm's way for nothing, that everyone in the world would hear about it and if they weren't laughing too loud, they might feel threatened by her, thinking she was making a power grab. She would put herself and Alex in danger for a ludicrous pipe dream.

"She said it *was* a power grab, in a sense. She had dreams of a better Russia, a new regime. They argued. He said that Constantin never claimed to be anything but a page. She said the people who took their papa out of Russia swore in an affidavit—that Krilov showed it to her—that Constantin was, in fact, really the young tsarevitch, son of Nicholas the Second.

"Then she asked, 'What about what I told you—how when I was young, Papa showed me a little blue egg.' "

Another giggle from the jury box came from someone who found all this silly. Nina, trying to catch with both hands the information flowing out of Gabe fast as mucky rainwater down a gutter spout, couldn't look around. "An egg, you say," she repeated, feeling as idiotic as she sounded.

"A jeweled egg. Blue. She described it, saying she remembered it and had found a picture of it on the Web. She called it the tsarevitch egg." He looked apologetic, recognizing how preposterous it all sounded. "Said Fabergé made it especially, when the tsarevitch was very young.

"Alex said where the hell was this mystical egg, then, and she told him that their papa must have lost it or sold it or something.

"He told her she had a sick attachment to the fantasies of their father, and then begged her not to talk about any of this until they did some tests. He said, 'We'll get the bones analyzed. Constantin's bones. We'll compare his DNA to the Romanovs, but you have to promise me you'll dump the crazy scheming if there's no match.'

"She didn't want to do it, but eventually agreed. He said he'd make the arrangements."

"They agreed to dig up Constantin Zhukovsky's bones?" Nina asked.

"Kind of. Alex said he wouldn't do it himself, but yeah, in essence."

"They would get the bones to prove Christina was a member of the Romanov family?"

"She was a stubborn fanatic. Alex hoped the result would shut her up."

"Objection," Jaime said.

"That last statement is stricken as speculation," the judge said. "The jury will disregard it."

"But here's the thing I should tell you," Gabe said.

"Go on, Mr. Wyatt," Nina said, watching for a reaction from Salas, who gave her only his attention.

"I looked into the whole thing, you know, whether she could be the heir? Well, she wasn't."

The audience in the courtroom, already agog, backed off like a low tide. So, the story really was a fantasy. What a relief to return to reality, and how sad that reality always turned out to be so mundane.

"Why do you say that?"

"I looked into the history. The tsarevitch had hemophilia. People born with hemophilia back then never lived into adulthood. Christina really was whacked-out crazy."

"Move to strike the opinion," Jaime said, although he clearly agreed with it. The judge ordered it done.

Nina said, "This conference, this attack on Christina, and the conversation with Alex took place when?"

"In April, about a week before she died."

Friday night, April 11, before it was dark, Gabe had arrived at Christina's door, a fresh business card in hand, curiosity eating away at him. She answered after he knocked twice. "Uh-huh?" she said. She appeared tired and careworn. The cotton shirt she wore looked slept in. In the space behind her, he could see slick mirrors, views all the way to the ocean, neatness.

"I'm in an awful business," he said.

"What?" She seemed a little more alert.

He thrust a card at her, then stepped back. "I can see this is a bad time," he said. In Gabe's experience, women liked his hesitation. It instantly defused their very natural caution, and insulted them just a little.

"Not at all," she said defensively. She took the card and read it. "A home-security business? I've seen you before, haven't I?"

"I picked up your card at the Russian conference. I was there talking to a couple of clients and, you know, networking. We install a system called The Bodyguard because it's so effective. Nobody's really safe these days. You read the paper."

She nodded. "Well, it's not a bad idea. I'll think about it."

"Sure." He let his shoulders fall, and put on his disappointed face. "But this is a one-time offer, a hundred bucks for four hours, top to bottom. Not just some useless analysis of your security needs. No, I'll install our foolproof system."

He could see that although she had a cautionary air, she liked his eagerness. A gratifying light appeared in her eyes. "I should probably think." She started to close the door.

"I don't blame you for being afraid of me," he said quickly.

The door cracked wider. "But I'm not."

"I'm a stranger. Why should you trust me?"

"Good point," she said, but she was smiling.

Within a few more minutes, he had an appointment.

He showed up the next day with a plan of action for her apartment, which mainly consisted of a few motion detectors and a cheap alarm that was supposed to blow if anyone fiddled with the front-door lock. He had fun fiddling with wires, looking experienced. She stayed around while he talked. She listened, growing progressively more paranoid as he fed her stories, some real, some made up, of break-ins, attacks, and other unsavory local activities.

"Best thing," he said, screwing a white box into the ceiling of a small hallway that wouldn't do much, but had an official look about it and was supposed to blip in certain unlikely events, "is to defend yourself aggressively, not be passive and sit back and let them take you down."

"Yeah," she said. She wore blue jeans and a blue sweater. While he worked she swiped a mop around on the kitchen floor. "That's my plan."

He took a second to admire the apartment and to consider that this woman, who lived in this very elegant penthouse apartment, was his half-sister. Again, he couldn't see much family resemblance, but then, they were only half-siblings. Was it really possible, this story about their father?

He had been reading his Russian history. He knew that most of the last tsar's family had been found, but that the young tsarevitch's body had never been recovered. So intriguing. And there had to be millions buried behind that story somewhere, in the jewels they tried to take with them when they escaped, or in money smuggled out before the revolution. How much had the tsarevitch made off with? Had their father managed to hide some away? How much did she have, anyway?

"Women need to be able to protect themselves because men won't anymore. I believe in bearing arms," he said.

"Me, too," she said.

And then the conversation got around to what kind of gun, and what she would carry, given a choice. They groaned about the difficulty perfectly honest people had getting guns for their own protection.

He offered to get one for her.

She thought that was a great idea.

27

MAYBE HE WAS TELLING THE truth about all of it. All of it led up to the night Christina Zhukovsky had died, and they were returning to that night in the words of the man who had evidently killed her.

Let him talk. From Salas's rigid shoulders and Jaime's intent eyes, Nina saw that they had no intention of inventing obstacles. Immersed in the testimony, the entire courtroom seemed to vibrate.

"What did you do after approaching Christina Zhukovsky in the guise of a home-security salesman?"

"The next day, I went to a lawyer. Alan Turk. The lawyer who handled Constantin's estate."

"I want every nickel accounted for," Gabe had told the lawyer. He had dressed carefully in dry-cleaned navy blue slacks and a light blue dress shirt. He didn't want to show up at a law office looking poor, like he was begging for something. Look powerful, be powerful. Across a shiny desk, Alan Turk played busy man, rearranging the orderly paperwork stacked in front of him, beside him, and behind him on a credenza.

"I've got a right to know the terms of my own father's will, don't I? As a member of the family."

"Of course," the lawyer said. He had listened to Gabe's story about spying on Christina, about the theory that Constantin Zhukovsky had something to do with the Romanovs, and about how Gabe had offered Christina a gun in order to meet her, with an expression of complete disbelief. Then he had taken the 1973 copy of the marriage certificate of Wanda Sobczyk and Constantin Zhukovsky and read it word for word. Turk didn't look very interested or very encouraging when he was finished. The lawyer held a folder up, like he ought to be thanked for achieving the bureaucrat's eureka, the relevant closed file. He opened the file and read. "Hang on. My apologies," he murmured, "just a second to review." He scanned quickly.

Gabe looked around the office, at the Chinese vase on its carved pedestal, the silky rug, the display case of netsuke figurines, thinking he would have gone to law school if he'd had the money. He had cracked a few law books recently, since his mother's little revelation and Christina's blockbuster surprise, and he could understand most of it. You just had to want to know something.

He examined the books in cases against one wall. Yes, he could imagine himself, glasses on his nose, a client across from him needing his help, leafing through one of those red tax books, slapping it shut with satisfaction.

The lawyer looked up. "Tell me, Mr. Wyatt, why did you come to me?"

"Pretty obvious, isn't it? I want to know the terms of his will, which I was left out of. This is California. My mother, who was legally married to the guy, was entitled to half the estate, wasn't she, at least whatever he made while they were married. Well, she got gypped."

"Ah," he said. "I contacted your mother after you called, because I had a few questions, too."

Well, in that case, Gabe thought, annoyed, why the big show about reading his notes again? He must have read them before calling Wanda. Maybe he was the forgetful type. Or maybe he was stalling Gabe for some reason.

"I was not aware Mr. Zhukovsky had remarried. However, he and your mother signed a prenuptial agreement. They weren't that common in those days, but apparently it was something he had drafted by another attorney. She was kind enough to send me a copy. It's all very aboveboard."

"Secretive bastard didn't even want his own lawyer to know about my mother," Gabe said. "Either that or he didn't trust you anymore." He laughed.

The way Turk's jowls hardened showed he did not find Gabe's little joke funny at all. He was younger than Gabe's mother, maybe in his middle to late fifties, not too wrinkled, but with a receding hairline he tried to disguise.

Turk tapped a pen against the edge of the desk, arched his back, and got comfy in his leather swivel chair. "I'd like to know more about your interest in the will, if I could."

Inside, Gabe laughed at the language. He could do that too, push people around with a delicate hand. However, unlike this fancy attorney, he didn't have to. "I don't see why," he said. "Obviously, I have a right to know."

"This will was written and probated more than twenty years ago. Naturally, I'm curious."

Gabe got it now. He might not appear aggressive, but old Turk wasn't going to give until he understood the scene. Well, Gabe considered, what would it cost him anyway? Nothing. This guy couldn't tell anyone about what they said in this room. Gabe didn't have to go to law school to know that.

"I only recently found out my mother was married to the guy, okay? Otherwise, I promise you, I would have stopped by earlier."

"You had no idea?"

"None at all. My mother kept the information from me."

The lawyer nodded. "It's straightforward," he said. "He wrote the will right after he married your mother, but before you or your brother were born. Other than a few small bequests to charity and to his church up in San Francisco, your father divided his estate between his first two children, Christina and Alex Zhukovsky."

"How much did they get? Exactly."

Turk's nose hid behind the file for another minute. Then he put it down and stroked it with his hands. "I can't say exactly. That is not in the will, of course. Assets are calculated after debts are paid, holdings are sold, and so forth. But I believe, at least, if memory serves me, each of the heirs received roughly a million dollars."

"Each."

"Yes." He kept his hands on the file as if holding tight to something precious. They looked cold, and the buff color of his skin roughly matched the manila folder.

"That's a lot of apple pie."

Turk shrugged. "I don't know how he made his money. He must have invested wisely over many years."

"You know what my mother got?"

"Three hundred thousand dollars, invested in an annuity with certain restrictions that passed outside the estate."

"Four hundred a month to take care of her for life. I bet she thought that was some chunk. What a laugh by comparison, huh? She's always had to work, you know, for as long as I can remember. While that— Ever seen Christina's apartment?"

The lawyer said nothing.

"Well, I have. It's a penthouse. Must have cost her a bundle. Maybe she owns the building. In those days, back in the seventies when he died, two million bucks was worth something, wasn't it?"

"That's certainly true." The lawyer smiled slightly. He was still trying to figure Gabe out.

"There's another issue."

"Oh?"

Gabe couldn't help laughing. "Well, I told you about this Romanov connection. Somehow Christina latched on to the idea that her father, our father, wasn't just a page to the last tsar of Russia. She thinks he was his son."

Alan Turk let out a snort of disbelief. "His son? His *son*? You mean, like the Anastasia stories?"

"She went to Russia and met some people and came back believing it. And she's ready to go public with the idea, too."

Gabe enjoyed the flabbergasted look on Turk's face. "She must have some sort of psychiatric problem!"

"Yeah, delusions of grandeur," Gabe said. "But even my mother says the old man talked more and more about Russia before he died. He said he couldn't tell her all of it. He said he had decided when he came to America to keep his secrets."

"You mean Christina's going to say that she's some sort of heir of the Romanovs?"

"The heir to the throne. She was the oldest of Constantin's kids, and even though she was a daughter she thought she could be recognized by the Russian church, then the people. She thought she had a shot at it."

"At what! There hasn't been a monarchy in Russia since 1918!"

"Don't ask me," Gabe said. "Maybe she just wants to cause an uproar. Or the people behind her do. But here's what I'm thinking. I know it's a long shot, but maybe it's true."

"You're joking!"

"Kind of, yeah. But. If it's true—one chance in a million, I know—well, then, the old man might have escaped with more than the shirt on his back, you know what I mean? That's why I think we need a thorough accounting."

"I performed a thorough accounting. I'll make you a copy of the Inventory and Appraisal filed with the Probate Court twenty-five years ago."

"I'll demand another search of that house he lived in. You didn't know about this theory. We ought to search the chimney and under the house. And check if Christina or Alex grabbed anything they shouldn't have before you did your inventory."

"That's assuming you have a claim."

"Isn't there a claim here?" Gabe said, looking the lawyer right in the eye. "I've been doing some reading. Our mother's agreement with Constantin Zhukovsky doesn't mention me and it doesn't mention my brother." He motioned toward the file Turk clung to so fondly. "Go ahead. Review away."

"That isn't necessary. You're right. The agreement doesn't mention you or your brother."

"When people write wills, they are often advised by their lawyers to use a kind of general bequest—like, 'I leave my estate to my children,' unstated meaning, all of them, born or unborn, named or unnamed, right? But my father's will didn't mention us at all, did it?"

"The only heirs are specified. He was adamant."

Protecting himself from any accusation that he did a piss-poor job, Gabe thought. A lawyer worth his salt would plan for the chance a child could be born or adopted after the will was written. "Therefore . . ." He was playing a little game, waiting to see if the lawyer was just testing him. Maybe he thought Gabe was dragging things out but knew nothing. "Come on. Help me out here."

"You want to know if you and your brother have a right to some of the money your half-siblings inherited under your father's will."

"I wouldn't have said it quite like that," Gabe said. "No, I would have used the term 'pretermitted heirs.' "

Turk stared down at the file as if reading something on its blank surface. When exactly was it that the pleasant, affable fellow who had greeted him at the door to his office just a short while ago turned so homely? Gabe decided he was one of those sorry men who looked best when smiling. Unfortunately, in his business, he probably didn't smile all that much.

"You've been doing your research," Turk said.

"Right." Gabe folded his arms. Now it was his turn to be smug. "So, tell me, Mr. Turk. What's our position?"

"You're right. There is a California statute that protects pretermitted heirs, that is, children who have been left out of a testator's will. It's conventional thinking that a testator would have made provision for his or her children if he had given it some thought, which is the reason so many wills do leave a 'class gift,' including all heirs, named or unnamed. Obviously, Mr. Zhukovsky didn't do that."

A "class gift" had a ring to it. "He didn't leave us out intentionally, right?"

"You know, Mr. Wyatt, it's my belief, after talking with you and your mother, and remembering his insistence on the wording of his will, that he did, in fact, leave you out intentionally. I don't know why."

"But what I mean is, he didn't say so in the will, did he? He didn't say, 'I'm leaving Gabe and Stefan and any other future kids out because I'm a dumb-ass.' He didn't leave us ten bucks or his Lionel train collection so he could get out of leaving us money."

"That's right."

"Don't I have this right? The law assumes it was an oversight, his not mentioning us. So, we can make a claim against the estate."

"Mr. Wyatt . . ."

"Why not?"

"You don't have a case."

"Why not?"

"The will was executed and probated many years ago, over twenty years ago. A judge has already ordered the assets distributed. The paperwork's done, signed and sealed. If your father had died without a will, your claim might be stronger."

Gabe shook his head. What was with this guy? Didn't all lawyers love meaty money cases? Where was the greedy glitter in his eye?

Turk was still talking. "An objection might be made that your mother had an obligation at that time to secure or protect your rights."

"If," Gabe said, striving for patience, "we had been old enough to figure out what was going on when the man died, or if our mother had the sense of a finch and had consulted a lawyer at the time and staked a claim, then what would have been our share?"

"There's a formula. Quite simple really. You take the amount of the estate left to any children, and divide it by the total number of children."

"A million each, in 1970s money."

"Actually, probate was concluded in 1980."

"Still. In those days, I'll bet a house in Monterey could be had for fifty grand. And in these days, what with interest and all, what with accounting for inflation . . . our share would be significant, wouldn't it? Way more than a million. Double that, maybe. Or more."

There it was, a gleam emanating from the lawyer's brown, reliable eyes, focused directly on him. "Not exactly. It's very complicated. You're determined to pursue this?" he asked.

"Do you need a retainer for something like this, or is it a contingency deal?"

Turk smiled, but it wasn't a warm one. Probably still pissed about failing to put a class-gift clause into the will in the first place, which would have saved them both a lot of trouble.

"This firm can't represent you."

"Why the hell not?" Gabe had just been getting used to the plush office with its black-shaded lamps.

"Even if there was something to dispute, there's a possible conflict of interest. I handled the probate. I distributed the money. I attended the man's funeral. In a sense, I represented the named heirs. Their interests are in direct conflict with yours. Therefore, it is my feeling that it would be unethical for me to handle your case."

"Then why did you let me tell you the whole thing? You were curious?"

"It's all pretty curious, but don't worry. This conversation is privileged. I will never discuss it without your authorization, even if I am called into court."

He stood. "Just for your information, I think it's too late after a quarter of a century to reopen the probate. That's not a legal opinion. I can't advise you. I'd just hate to see you waste all your money on a court case that's destined to go nowhere."

"Well," Gabe had said. "Thanks anyway."

Gabe asked for a glass of water. Salas called an afternoon break, and then they resumed. The jurors showed no sign of the usual afternoon yawns.

"What did you do after seeing Mr. Turk, with regard to Christina Zhukovsky?" Nina asked him.

"A couple days later, I went back to Christina's apartment on Eighth Street. We had made an appointment, and when I came back, I brought along a few motion-detecting lights, that kind of thing. Told her I didn't have the gun, but I could bring it on Friday."

"And when was this?"

"Thursday."

"Why didn't you just tell her the truth?"

"That I was her half-brother? I wanted to have another lawyer lined up and know exactly how we were going to proceed. I wasn't ready."

Nina shook her head. "What did she say when you told her about the gun?"

"She was impatient. She wanted it right away. We agreed I'd bring it over that Friday."

"The eleventh of April, the night she died. And did you bring her a gun that night?" Nina asked, praying to herself, please, no interruptions, let him go where he's going now. . . .

"Yes."

"What time did you arrive?"

"About ten. She opened the door right away. Dumb move. I could have been anybody."

"You say, about ten?"

"I think so, yeah."

"You had brought a gun?"

"I borrowed one from a friend of mine. It was just to get in and try again to look around. The first time she had watched me like a hawk." Again that bitter smile. "I didn't care about her stories. I didn't care if she was stark raving mad. What I cared about was her money. Her and Alex's money. But I decided to use the story to get to her. I wanted—I'll be honest—I wanted to get into her place and look for documents."

"Why?"

"I wanted to find out exactly how much money she had."

The atmosphere of the courtroom closed around

them, a mixture of sweat and too much stale air. Although it was nearly four o'clock, there was none of the usual coffee-deprived shuffling. It was a good jury.

Nina said, "What did happen?"

"She offered me a glass of brandy. I said sure, and she went into the kitchen. When she came back, I was looking in her desk drawer. My timing was off."

"You say you touched her desk drawer?"

"It was a cold night. I was wearing gloves."

"How long were you there before she came back in?"

"Coupla minutes."

There seemed to be no limit to his cooperation. He was digging a grave like Stefan, only it was his own. Had Salas cautioned him properly about his rights? She hoped so. But Gabe barreled on, throwing the memories out as if he were projectile vomiting. He had a queer expression of distaste on his face now.

"She caught you?"

"Yes."

"What happened then?" Nina asked, looking directly at the jury, not at Gabe.

"You know what? Her brother Alex was right. She was nuts. She way overreacted, got mad and, I think, scared. She didn't ask what I was doing, but went back into the kitchen. It was as if she'd known all the time I wasn't really there to help. I followed her. She threw a glass of brandy at me, connecting with my scalp. It was some thin little glass, so it hurt and shattered. Couldn't have been worse. I put my hand up and I was bleeding. The situation was out of control. She screamed at me to get out before she called nine-one-one. I was so surprised that when she yelled at me to get out, you know what I did?"

"No," Nina said. "What did you do, Mr. Wyatt?"

He seemed unaware of the impact of his words on the courtroom. Even the court reporter waited hungrily.

"I left. I just went like a kid obeying his mom. She slammed the door behind me."

What, no murder? No hands around her neck? No struggle? All the air seeped out of the bloated balloon of anticipation in the courtroom.

"Your testimony is that you immediately left?"

Gabe spread his hands. "I swear it."

"Did you then return?" Nina asked.

"No. I was bleeding. I went home and took care of myself. I gave my friend his gun back the next day."

"You didn't return later that night?"

"No."

"You didn't sweep up the glass?"

"What? No."

"Mr. Wyatt, why did you run when we approached you in the hallway a few minutes ago?"

"I had a damn good reason. You people put my brother in jail on blood evidence. I knew my blood was there, too. I thought maybe you had found it finally, and would put me in jail, even though I had nothing to do with hurting that woman."

"You're trying to tell us," Nina said, "that you were alone with Christina Zhukovsky late at night on the night of her murder. By chance, you were wearing gloves. The situation became violent. You were injured by her. You were jealous of her and searching through her private papers, but you didn't kill her? Is that what you claim?"

"I don't claim anything," Gabe said. He nodded. "I didn't kill her. It was my blood on that glass, that I admit, but I never touched her. She was alive and hopping mad when I left, but when I heard she had been killed, I knew how it would look. I broke down. I sat down at my house, waiting for the police. But they didn't come. They arrested Stefan instead. They said he left blood there, too. I couldn't figure out what was going on."

Nina felt dizzy. The intensity of the last hour had drained her. Too much information bombarded her, too fast. Did they have enough from this brother who appeared willing to say anything except the ultimate thing, that he was guilty, guilty, guilty?

The blood! The most important thing! Confess or don't confess, pal, she told Wyatt in her mind. You're going to clear your brother. She turned briefly toward Stefan at the counsel table. Their eyes met and she tried to keep from giving him an encouraging nod.

The case against Stefan was starting to fall messily apart. But Stefan blinked at his brother's testimony, trying to take it all in, frightened. He didn't want it to be his brother.

"All right. Let's get back to that blood you left in Christina's home. Are you aware of Dr. Hirabayashi's testimony earlier in this courtroom?"

"No."

The judge allowed a brief explanation, which Gabe followed with amazement.

"I heard his blood was found at the scene, and there was nothing said about my blood. I assumed he went there after me that night. I couldn't understand—"

"You suffered from leukemia when you were young. You were the recipient of a bone-marrow transplant?"

"Yes. It cured me."

"Who donated the bone marrow that cured you?"

"Stefan was the donor."

"Isn't it true that you knew your brother, the defendant, shared the same blood as you?"

"Wait a minute, I had no idea. How could we still have the same blood? The transplant was so many years ago, I assumed by now I had my own blood, you know, that it came back."

"That's not how it works, Mr. Wyatt," Nina said.

"Objection."

"Sustained. Strike that last statement by counsel."

Nina walked back to the counsel table and picked up her notes. The courtroom was waiting, on her side. Salas actually rubbed his hands together, a sign that he was excited. She knew exactly what question to ask now, what the answer had to be.

"How did Christina Zhukovsky come to have your brother's name and phone number?"

"She asked me at one point if I knew anyone who could help her with odd jobs. I was trying to get close to her. I wish to God I hadn't done it."

Bingo! And Christina passed Stefan to Alex! A huge hole in Stefan's story was filled in.

"How helpful of you. Isn't it—"

"Objection!"

"Sustained. Counsel, do not comment on witness testimony. The jury will disregard the comment."

Nina knew that she was too excited. Moving away from Gabe Wyatt, she got as close to the jury as she dared, hyped up, angry, outraged at what he had put Stefan through. She made sure her voice carried to the back rows as she asked, "Isn't it true that you planned to kill Christina Zhukovsky and set your brother up as her killer?"

"No!" His voice softened. "I'm embarrassed to admit, I really thought Stef must have done it. He's always been the one who screwed up. This time, I thought, he must have gone in way too deep. I never wanted to be the one who connected my brother directly to Christina. I tried to protect him."

"But all along, it was your blood on the glass, Mr. Wyatt. You killed her, didn't you? And then you told lies to protect yourself. This is your chance to make things right for your brother. Tell this jury the truth."

"I *am* making things right. I'm telling the truth. I didn't kill her."

"You spied on Christina. You were at the scene of her murder in the time frame of her murder. You admit to a violent confrontation. Your jealousy and hatred of this woman, who had grown up with your father's love and been given his money, got the better of you that night, didn't it, Gabe?" Nina said.

"No! Somebody came there after me! If it wasn't Stef, then—I—"

Nina turned to the jury.

"Expect us to believe that?" she said softly.

"Objection!" Jaime roared.

"Withdrawn. I am finished with this witness, Your Honor."

28

SALAS ADJOURNED IMMEDIATELY AFTER GABE Wyatt's direct examination. What a hell of an endless day. They all needed to go to their offices and homes to cogitate and reflect.

Jaime could reflect on how he was losing his murder case. Another lawyer might care deeply about that and try to bring the case under control, at the expense of the truth. Jaime couldn't help himself. He wanted the truth, too. Sitting in her little office in the Pohlmann Building after hours that night, Nina thought, He's gonna end up on the defense side. He has a bad character flaw for a prosecutor; he hears both sides.

Nina drew pictures on the pizza box on her desk: a big young man falling off a giant fishhook, Stefan a Christlike figure with his arms out. Most of the pizza reposed in her stomach right now, along with a healthy infusion of red wine. She looked at her watch.

Almost ten P.M. Bob was home alone at their house in Pacific Grove; Paul had left a message that he'd be back very late; Klaus, feeling better, according to his wife, rested in his bed in the big house on Peter Pan Way in Carmel Highlands; Sandy packed up suitcases in Big Sur.

A massive deconstruction was going on.

Meantime, Stefan was innocent, she was positive of that now. There were still problems. What seemed clear to her wasn't necessarily clear to the jury. Ginger's testimony had flashed by like a telecommunications satellite, too high to grasp except as a bright moving point in a sky of confusion.

And Gabe hadn't sounded guilty enough. Nina could hear it now. At least one jury member was going to use the word flimflam.

She tried not to think about the evidence, but instead to concentrate on the people. Stefan, a young man in love and in jail, wanting only to marry and create the happy family he had never had. Christina, a shy woman who transformed herself to live a life she finally found purposeful, pursuing a dream.

Father Giorgi, hearing all his prayers for the old Russia come true when Christina came to him, and watching them fade when she died.

Sergey Krilov, Christina's lover, still something of a mystery, but likely another hopeful wanting to cash in on Christina's potential.

And Gabe, forever aggrieved, seeking his share of whatever it was that his father had given to Alex and Christina, but never able to attain the love he so desperately wanted.

He must have done it.

Nina picked off a piece of pepperoni from the single piece of pizza swiftly turning rancid in its cardboard box. Her door was shut and she was alone in the building. To avoid the creepy feeling night fog always gave her, she had closed the blinds. She clicked back to Google on her computer and searched for some more of the Russian Web sites. So many things were still unexplained. What had brought Sergey Krilov to the U.S.? Where was he? What relationship had he had with Christina?

Yawning, Nina pushed her hair back. She had reached that bleary place beyond simple exhaustion, where you can go on forever.

What a story Christina could have told, if she had lived. Romance, Russia, assassination. An alluring fabrication, unfortunately, like Anastasia's story, like the stories of all the pretenders to the Empire of the Russias. It would have made a lively press conference, though.

Even immersed in her fantasy, how could Christina explain to herself the one obvious fact that made it all impossible, that all the Web sites with their escape theories had to acknowledge? Constantin Zhukovsky could not have been a fourteen-year-old tsarevitch in 1918, for the simple, well-known reason that, aside from the fact that he was almost certainly assassinated at Ekaterinburg along with the rest of his family, the tsarevitch had hemophilia.

Alexis's mother, the tsarina, Alexandra, had brought Rasputin in, hoping he could help cure her chronically ailing son. Ultimately, that relationship was one of the biggest factors in the downfall of the Romanovs. The Russian people, already reeling from the suffering caused by war, drew the line at being ruled by this haughty German woman and her wild-eyed lover.

"Hemophilia/tsarevitch." Lots of sites. She scrolled down a Web page about a tsarevitch pretender who supposedly had come to Washington State via Estonia after escaping the bullets of the Bolsheviks. This particular site was chock-full of colorful theories. She read down the page, her head aching.

Then her eye stuck on a word. She went back and looked.

Thrombocytopenia.

"It is always said that even if the tsarevitch escaped the assassinations he would have died soon after from hemophilia. But maybe Alexis did not have hemophilia. He may have suffered from a similar condition called thrombocytopenia, a medical syndrome referring to a hemorrhagic condition which is underlain by another disease, such as—"

Had she read it right?

"Such as aplastic anemia."

She stared at the page. Gabe Wyatt had just testified that afternoon that he had been diagnosed with aplastic anemia, which had led eventually to leukemia. She hadn't known Gabe's symptoms could include hemorrhaging.

Strange to have such a rare illness pop up twice in one day.

Where was that death certificate? She found it eventually, sandwiched between two sets of pleadings.

She had remembered correctly. The treating physician had listed the cause of Constantin Zhukovsky's death as "thrombocytopenia."

Associated cause of death: "aplastic anemia."

Confused, Nina went back to the Web site. The site went on to quote an anxious letter from the tsarina in the early 1900s referring to Alexis's bouts with fever. "It's possible the diagnosis for his illness was in error, since hemophiliacs do not suffer fever during their attacks," the Web page said.

She called Ginger. "You up?"

"Always."

"First of all, is there any possibility Constantin Zhukovsky really was the tsarevitch? Was he misdiagnosed with thrombowhatchamacallit, but really had hemophilia?"

"I would have to examine his medical records to be sure," she said, "but I would have to say no. He was born in

1904, before there was an adequate treatment for hemophilia. I don't think he could have lived into his seventies. He would certainly have been an invalid from an early age. No, I don't think it's possible. He died of thrombocytopenia, which is also a hemorrhagic syndrome, but some of the symptoms are different."

"Okay, then here's something else. I've been doing some reading about hemophilia. This Web page says hemophiliacs don't have fever during bleeding spells. Is that true?"

"Let me check. I know a lot, but not every single thing." Ginger's phone clunked down.

Nina rubbed her head, trying to move the aching from one side to the other while she waited for Ginger to return.

"It's true. Fever isn't associated with hemophilia in general, but Nina, people with that disease can get a lot of associated problems, infections, all kinds of things that might cause fever."

They hung up, Ginger returning to her nocturnal lab ramblings, and Nina returning to the tsarina's letter. So maybe the tsarevitch was a sick hemophiliac with complications that caused fever.

Or maybe the Web site was right and the tsarevitch was the one who was misdiagnosed, way back at the turn of the century. He didn't have hemophilia, but had thrombo—thrombo—whatever.

His body was not buried at Ekaterinburg along with the rest of his family. Maybe he escaped.

Maybe Constantin Zhukovsky really was Alexis Nicholaevich Romanov. Then Christina had been heir to the tsar all along. Then Alex, then Gabe, and, ultimately, Stefan.

The doorknob twisted. Wearing a striped cardigan over a white shirt, white hair rumpled as if he had been napping, Klaus poked his head in. "How did it go today?" he asked as if it weren't almost midnight.

"Did you drive here?" Nina asked.

"Still playing baby-sitter." Klaus sat down heavily opposite her. "I am annoyed with you, Miss Reilly. I did not enjoy being hustled off to the doctor like a sick person. My wife got alarmed unnecessarily."

"You didn't seem well. I'm sorry."

"Pizza?" He picked up the slice and ate hungrily. "Excellent. So. I hear you have implicated Mr. Gabriel Wyatt in the murder of Christina Zhukovsky."

"Stefan never even went to Christina's," Nina said. "I think we'll get an acquittal. Jaime still has a lot of cross-examining to do, but after he's finished I think we should rest on the defense side and let the case go to the jury."

"Very good. However."

Nina felt her insides clench. Pizza or Pohlmann? "I can summarize the closing argument for you right now," she said. "I don't know exactly what happened after Gabe Wyatt got into her apartment, but I don't have to know. He was there, he was jealous of her, and they got into a fight. He killed her. He's a slimeball. He let his brother go through the arrest and trial, and probably would have let Stefan spend his life in jail."

"Perhaps."

"What? What, Klaus?"

"What happened to the egg?" Klaus said. "Constantin's little blue egg? He seems to have been very proud of it. That is why I hauled my ancient body out of bed tonight, left my warm wife, and drove my car back here, even though I have no business driving. I want to look at the Zhukovsky probate file again."

"The egg?" She didn't ask, Are you crazy? So much craziness skulked around the fringes of this case, she couldn't fight it anymore.

"May I have the file?"

Nina pulled it out of the stack.

Klaus pulled his chair up to the opposite side of the desk, bowed his head, and started looking through it. Bits of mozzarella clung to his white beard. "Here's the inventory and appraisal for the estate," he said. "Note the absence of an egg. Any egg, even a reproduction of a Fabergé egg."

"Maybe Constantin sold it. Christina hadn't seen it since she was a child."

"He wouldn't do that. It was his proof."

"It proved he was the tsarevitch?"

"Yes. No need to get cranky, my dear."

"You've been on the Net."

"I twiddled my digits all afternoon. I went to the very same page you are on right now," Klaus said.

"These people with their stories. There were doubts about the diagnosis. The tsarevitch escaped from Ekaterinburg with a friendly family to Vladivostok, then Japan. Or Vienna to Paris. Estonia to Washington. Finland to Monterey, California. Maybe he did, maybe he didn't."

"Do you think I have lost my wits? Gone dotty?" His eyes were on her, rheumy to be sure but extremely sharp at the moment.

Nina decided the time had come for honesty. He deserved that from her. "I think you have trouble with your memory, and I wonder about your judgment," she said.

"Then I'm wasting my time with you." Klaus got up. "Good evening. I will see you in court in the morning." The door closed.

He had taken the sheets from the probate file, and Nina was afraid she would never see them again. She got up quickly and looked out into the dark hall.

Klaus hadn't left. He had skittered down the hall to

Alan's office. The door was closed, but she could hear drawers opening and closing, see light under Alan's door.

The connection was obvious. Alan had handled the probate and Gabe had consulted him. Klaus was going to read the privileged file made after Gabe's consultation.

What a wicked old man! But what a good idea; unethical, but good. They could always put the papers back exactly as they had found them and never tell anybody.

Pushing the door open a crack, Nina crept down the hallway. Klaus had already made a mess: Alan would never leave papers on the floor.

Klaus bent down in the corner, pulling up the rug.

He had truly fallen off the deep end. Nina entered the room. His back was to her. Crouching on the floor, he pulled mightily at the corner of the heavy rug. He had moved Alan's prized reproduction gilt Louis XIV client chair aside.

"Need help?"

Klaus reared up, falling backward. "Miss Reilly! Do not do that ever, ever again!"

"I just thought you might need assistance with your completely unethical prying through Alan's files. What are you up to?"

Klaus had gone back to his tugging. "Come help me."

Together they pried up the corner, folding back a three-foot square.

Installed in the floor, black, about a foot square, was a safe. "He uses it for sensitive files, original wills, probate items he hasn't distributed yet, that sort of thing," Klaus told Nina.

"You know the combination?"

He nodded. "I have the information in case something happened to Alan. Although I have never tested them before, I assume my numbers are correct. Do it for me, please, my dear. My knees ache."

Nina bent down and, using the numbers Klaus gave her, heard a click. She pulled on the handle and the door opened.

"Let's have a look," Klaus said. "Open sesame."

"But Alan . . ."

"Are you in or out?" Klaus challenged her. Nina almost laughed. "All right then," he said.

Inside, one compartment held files, the other, a few wrapped packages. She pulled the files out. "Ferrari," the top one was labeled in Alan's neat hand. The next one said "Pickering Will." Then "Chavez Estate," "Monte Rosa Will," "Matter of Egler," "My Will." Nina said, "Nothing," leafing through the files.

"Let us check the rest."

"We are so bad."

"In for a penny, in for a ruble. If you are having scruples, get out of my way."

"I'll do it." She pulled out the boxes. They looked like valuable items from probates Alan was handling, just what they ought to be. She opened a box marked "Monte Rosa," and found a mass of diamond and gold jewelry piled inside. Two other marked boxes contained jewelry and coins. She had been down the hall from a lot of money and hadn't known it. Alan should have kept this stuff in a safe-deposit box at a bank, but apparently he liked to keep an eye on things. The floor safe *was* a safe, after all. There was no rule against it.

A smaller box caught her eye. Unlabeled, with an old red ribbon circling the long end, it was made of carved wood. She raised an eyebrow at Klaus, who nodded. They were both sitting on the rug like kids opening Christmas presents. Slipping off the ribbon, she opened the box. Inside, she found something wrapped in yellow silk. It glimmered blue in the light of Alan's green banker's lamp.

A jeweled egg. Sapphires, they had to be. Nina held it in her hand. "I don't believe it," she said. "It can't be."

"The tsarevitch egg," Klaus said. He whistled.

About three inches tall, it was encrusted with precious stones and gold filigree. Nina opened it. Inside, a frame of diamond filigree surrounded a tiny painting.

"Holy Mary," she said. "It's him. The tsarevitch."

The little boy in the picture smiled. He had sandy, almost reddish hair, and wore a sailor suit. The picture was only about an inch square.

She was holding history. Gently she set it down on its blue-and-gold stand.

"Alan was holding on to it. But for who?" Nina said at last.

"I believe I will call him," Klaus said.

"It's after midnight!"

"You don't think this is important enough?" Holding on to the desk, Klaus pulled himself up, bent to and fro a few times to get the cricks out, then lowered himself into Alan's leather chair and picked up the phone.

"We have violated your safe," he said to Alan. No beating around the bush, his tone said; it's late. "Yes, at the office. We found the egg." He listened for a moment. "I understand. I will explain everything. But first you will tell me about the egg." Another flood of indistinct words emanated from the phone. "Very well. We will be here."

Klaus hung up. "I have worked with Alan for decades," he said, "and still he surprises me. He is on his way down to find out why we are meddling with his wills and estates."

"Where does he live?"

"Carmel Highlands. Fifteen minutes away."

"Then we'd better finish up our meddling."

"My sentiments exactly. Check everything you haven't already checked," Klaus said.

"What are we looking for?"

"Like a lady in a hat shop," Klaus said, "we are just looking."

But there was nothing else of interest in the safe. Its precious contents lay spread around Nina, but the center of it all was the blue egg.

No word other than "glorious" would do.

She sat back on her heels. "Let's figure this out. This could be a real Fabergé egg. Presumably it's the one Constantin showed his daughter, in which case, either he stole it from the Romanovs or he was a Romanov. But how would Krilov know that?"

"Somebody helped Constantin escape. Perhaps they left some record. Perhaps the Russians knew all the time, and only now felt it would be politically expedient to bring back a hint of a Romanov. Someone they could control."

"If I'd known about the egg, I think I would have dug up my father's bones, too," Nina said, so unhinged she had to stand up and pace around. "Alan must have some file relating to this. Maybe he mislabeled one of these files on purpose."

Klaus pulled on his beard. "Check," he said.

"He's going to shut us down as soon as he gets here."

"Yes."

Nina sat down in the ornate client chair and opened the Pickering file. One of the heirs, a young woman, had filed for extra temporary support from the estate while it was probated, due to a sensitive psychiatric condition. The doctors' reports were in the file. "No," Nina said. She laid it aside.

She picked up the Monte Rosa file. The estate had been probated ten years before. Nina leafed through the paperwork. "Why put this one in the safe?" she asked. "He's got three diamond necklaces. Maybe he's still looking for the heirs?" She went to the inventory of the estate.

Funny. The necklaces she found nestled in their boxes did not exist on the inventory.

"Klaus?"

Head on the desk, Klaus snored lightly. Nina didn't have the heart to awaken him and ask for his thoughts. She looked again at the inventory and at the box labeled "Monte Rosa."

She turned to the Matter of Egler, a conservatorship for an elderly lady. Her daughter had taken over her possessions. Reading the list of items carefully, Nina looked again at the box of gold coins and diamond rings marked "Egler."

No match. The items in the box weren't listed in the inventory in the probate file. Puzzled, Nina closed that file. Klaus stirred, and Nina heard the sound of Alan's Ferrari pulling up outside. He would find them here, and she no longer cared.

She touched the superb egg again. Fantastic. Why hadn't it been listed on the inventory in the Zhukovsky probate? A dreadful realization spread like a cancer into her brain, making linkages, expanding and tying up loose ends, and making her hold her head as a jabbing headache took over.

"It's late," Alan said. In spite of being rousted from bed, he wore dark slacks and a Burberry trench coat. He looked prepared to take a meeting. His chin was dark, though, and his eyes . . .

"Oh, Alan," Nina said. "Isn't it beautiful? I can almost understand."

Alan glanced at his peacefully sleeping boss. Dropping

to the floor beside Nina, Alan picked up the egg and caressed it. "It's really something, isn't it?"

"It's—historic, Alan. It could have been Christina's proof."

"But it's mine, mine for twenty-four years. Adverse possession."

"You kept it here in the safe?"

"A good spot, don't you think? I loved having my clients sitting right on top of it. And I could look at it now and then." He admired it. "When I listed Constantin's assets for probate, I found it in the false bottom of a dresser drawer. I could never have afforded it myself. It's worth millions."

"Does this mean—was Constantin . . ."

Alan shrugged. "Who knows? Who cares? The Soviet Union didn't care. Constantin didn't want it known, or he would have made it known."

"Christina cared."

"Silly woman. Another Anastasia. Doomed for a rout. Who would believe her? She could hardly keep her hair combed, no offense."

Nina pushed at wisps. "What about Mrs. Monte Rosa's children?"

"My God, you know everything?"

"It's a huge embezzlement, Alan."

"And too late to fix now."

"You've damaged the firm, maybe irreparably."

"No, you did that by finding out."

For the first time, Nina felt afraid, in the presence of a murderer. "What about Klaus?" she asked, hesitant. "This could kill him."

"You brought us here tonight, Nina. The egg was— I never intended to sell it. I just wanted to have it."

"Well, our client suffered because of it."

"How would it have helped your defense? Knowing

about the egg?" Alan said. "Clue me in, Nina." He cast a wondering look through his eyeglasses.

"If I'd known you committed the murder, I could have defended Stefan better," Nina said.

Alan closed his eyes as if to obliterate the idea.

"Alan, why did you bury her in her father's grave?"

"Oh, it's a long sad story, Nina, and it's late."

"Please. Tell me."

"Nothing's going to help me. There's no excuse. None. But I'll make a deal with you," Alan said. "I explain and then you give me a couple of hours to leave town."

"You'll be caught."

"I won't."

Maybe he wouldn't be caught, but by now she wanted to see Alan arrested. She shrugged. "Go ahead."

Alan smiled from one side of his mouth, as if he was well aware that she wasn't making any deal with him about anything. "I followed Gabe Wyatt that night," he said, "thinking I'd have to do something. He wanted to resurrect this old business. Somebody, somewhere was bound to figure out what I'd done if he managed to reopen the probate. I found myself outside of Christina's apartment, and I heard an argument. She threw a glass at him. He ran out.

"I knocked, telling her I was her father's lawyer who had come on urgent business. She was cleaning up the broken glass she had thrown at Gabe. At first, she was very reluctant but she vaguely remembered me, and I spend all my time persuading people to do things they don't want to do, don't I?"

Nina had no answer for him.

"I told her there might be more money coming and she should let me in. I told her that Gabe had come to see me and that he was her half-brother. I tried to convince her to drop this insane dream about resurrecting some bullshit Russian monarchy. I warned her of the danger. I told her fame attracted craziness.

"She was irrational. She said I was lying about Gabe. She told me that at that very moment, someone was digging up the remains of her father, and that those remains would prove she was no crackpot, but was a Romanov.

"I panicked. You've known me for a long time, Nina. I'll bet you didn't expect me to panic." He picked up the egg and stroked the side with his finger.

That was all he had to say about strangling Christina Zhukovsky.

"I wasn't sure where to put her. In the ocean? Bodies come in on the tide. In a ditch somewhere? Hikers would find her. I remembered her saying someone was digging up her father's grave that night. I thought—what a perfect place. The cemetery was less than a mile from her apartment. I'd been to the funeral and thought I could find the grave. The soil would be loose, and an empty coffin waited for her there."

"Oh, Alan."

"I waited until whoever was digging up the grave could finish. I wanted to feel sure nobody official took note of the event, so I hid Christina's body in the trunk of my car until it was almost morning. Then I went to the cemetery. It was a hell of a job. I was surprised at how hard the soil was. I never even made it down to Constantin's coffin.

"I love this office," Alan said, his eyes roving around, stopping on his paintings, his plants, his barrister's case with old leather volumes of California cases. "I love being a lawyer. It's just that in my work you come across things that other people won't miss, beautiful things. I hardly ever sold things, Nina. I only stole a few times, precious things that nobody else would miss. I mean, it's been twenty-five years! Nobody cared about having that egg, except me."

"And then Gabe came."

"He probably wanted to screw Christina and Alex. His motives were selfish, like mine. He told me Christina was going to send out some kind of press release announcing she was the heir to the throne of the Romanovs. He just wouldn't quit, and she seemed just as determined. I didn't think I could handle the scrutiny. The estate would be re-opened."

"So you decided to kill Christina and implicate Gabe."

"I never decided to kill her. It just happened. And then I thought Gabe would be arrested, not his brother. Stefan ran into some bad luck there."

"It just happened?"

"I was excited, not thinking too straight. I went in to tell her she was a fool," Alan said. "My fingers went around her neck. In a way she committed suicide. The Romanov heir? She was a nobody who got carried away wanting to be somebody."

Nina breathed fast. She got up, but Alan held her wrist. "Now give me my chance," he said. "Your client got his acquittal."

She couldn't escape his viselike grip. Cravenly, she said, "I told you it's a deal."

Alan let go and she took off, throwing open the door, running down the hall. All she needed to do was get outside and— But Alan spent his mornings jogging around the neighborhood in his expensive running shoes. Grabbing her around the neck, he pulled her back just as her hand touched the knob of the front door.

They heard Klaus behind them. "Let her go!" he said in the high voice he used when he was distressed and angry. Alan didn't even turn around. He had the front door covered.

Now he would have to kill Klaus, too. Sickened, Nina struggled for her life, but he lifted her clear off the ground.

Alan was still holding Nina when an explosion tore through the room. He turned around so that she stood in front of him, both of them looking at Klaus, who held a large pistol in his hand.

"I have a safe, too," Klaus said. "I never trusted you enough to tell you."

"Shoot and she dies." Alan held Nina tight. Her body blocked him from Klaus. Only part of his curly black hair showed.

"Tch, tch," Klaus said, appearing to be thinking. Raising the gun, he shot Alan's ear off. Nina felt the bullet whiz past an inch from her own head. With a scream, Alan slapped his hand over his bleeding ear. Nina ran behind Klaus.

"Nine-one-one," Klaus said matter-of-factly.

Nina called and offered details. "Klaus," she said, finding her voice, "what on earth are you doing with a gun?"

"Handy for shooting myself. I decided it was that or retire."

29

THE NEXT MORNING, FIRST THING, Judge Salas dismissed
the charges against Stefan Wyatt. A rumpled Alex
Zhukovsky had reappeared in the hallway, apologizing for
his absence without explaining. Jaime had spent the night
interviewing Alan Turk, and had the amazing grace to join
in the motion.

Paul tried to catch up with Nina after court, but after
answering just a few questions for the press and posing
with Stefan as two big smiles, she lit out and had probably
hit Highway 68 going west toward her office in Carmel
before he could work his way through the crowd. She was
smaller, and had her little ways of avoiding traffic, human
and otherwise.

The reporters engaged in an orderly feeding frenzy,
sticking huge microphones into any face that happened
nearby. Salinas was an interesting town, sleepy and quiet as
aromatic fields growing on the one hand, and full of bois-
terous, drunken, sometimes fatal trouble on the other. It
must be a slow news night because everyone plus his uncle
Dave was looking for action at the courthouse that afternoon.

When he got to the Mustang, Paul considered going

back to Carmel, too, but he didn't want to go back to Carmel. In Nina's book, Alan's confession ended things. He, however, had some unfinished business.

He drove up Highway 101. From Salinas, in unobstructed traffic, the trip took a little over two hours to San Francisco, and he got lucky, spotting no highway patrols, catching the tailwind of a harebrained Mack truck driver who was illegally hogging the left lane most of the way up. He cut over to 280, wound through Golden Gate Park, and found a spot for the Mustang on Twenty-fifth Avenue.

Father Giorgi, wearing clean, fresh bandages on his face and neck, working in his office in a side wing off the main cathedral, was not glad to see him, but he was astonished to hear the news about the resolution of the case.

"Congratulations on your rapid recovery," Paul said. The priest looked much improved.

Giorgi touched his neck. "A few stitches. A broken finger. A lot of blood and fright, though. I never really believed it was Stefan," he said. "Do you know that a lawyer from Monterey contacted me? Christina had been doing some fund-raising for a nonprofit. She requested that I be left in charge in her stead." He couldn't hide his pleasure at the news. "There's a board, and they've agreed."

"The money she raised at the conference?"

"Yes. It's been sitting in a bank, losing capital, I might add. These days, they charge you to hold your money and invest it for their own profit."

Paul didn't want to get into that particular conversation with Giorgi, who had quite an interest in money and its interest, he also noticed. "What will you do with it?"

"Christina had a lot of ideas, some not so realistic. Universal health care, a true democracy in Russia. I think the money should be used to promote the Mother Church."

Paul didn't doubt Giorgi would do what he wanted

with the money. In fact, he had many ideas, and wanted to expound on them to Paul. He wanted to justify his shift in philosophy from Christina's way of thinking to his. Paul listened for several minutes, then said, "I'm here for Krilov."

Giorgi sighed. "It's a matter of honor?"

"Yes."

"You don't intend to kill him?"

"Only if necessary."

"Ah. Hmm. I don't like the sound of that." Nevertheless, he reached into his drawer, pulled out a book, and began to make a few calls. "I know everybody," he said, "and most of them owe me favors."

Paul wondered if he had the favors marked in there, too. It wasn't long before they had the information he needed.

Krilov was holed up in a single room in the Tenderloin, a nasty San Francisco neighborhood full of theaters, strip joints, bums, and all the other colorful creatures of the earth that thrived under an alternative value system. Paul arrived in the afternoon, when the early birds were scratching and hitting the streets and the late ones continued to slumber. This sun-filled day exposed all the globs of gum on the sidewalk and the shabbiness of clothing. Transformation would come with the darkness, when neon signs splashed the streets with colorful illusions.

He told the clerk where he was going, and after the man assured himself Paul was not the cop he appeared to be, he let Paul go up without calling ahead.

Krilov opened on the first knock, bleary-eyed, coughing like a cat with a hairball, obviously just coming off a drunken binge. Paul didn't wait to be greeted. He punched him twice, once in the stomach, and next in the ribs.

Unprepared, and without the spark of battle lust to inflame him, Sergey crumpled to the floor, not letting out a sound.

Paul kicked him, but not hard enough to bruise him. "I don't like people getting hurt on my watch."

Sergey, dewier than Paul by maybe six years, had the sickening, rebounding ability of youth on his side. He stood slowly, then sat himself down on his littered bed. He coughed, picked up a glass of water, and drank it to the bottom. "Is there more?" he asked. "Because I'm very busy right now."

"You want more?"

"No."

"Okay."

"But if you came to beat me, you'll have to hit harder, for longer. I was a soldier, you know."

"I didn't."

"Before I met Christina." He pulled a packet of brown, foul-looking cigarettes out of a pocket and lit one, which smelled brown and foul. "Ooh. I'll die young," he said, breathing smoke through his nose.

"What a shame," Paul said. "Meanwhile . . ."

"Meanwhile, what the hell. When Christina died, I thought I should continue on, you know. Follow the DNA trail. That's what I came here to do. Stop anyone who might feel the need to continue the farce we had started and allowed to get so badly out of hand. That's why I went to the lab."

"You almost killed Father Giorgi and the guard."

"Unexpectedly, that coward Giorgi flinched, and the guard fought hard. I never meant to hurt them badly, if it matters."

"It doesn't."

"But in my favor, note that I did not kill that strong Japanese woman in the lab, the one with all the bones laid out like doilies on those granite counters."

Paul examined the pile of junk on the bed and said, "You're leaving?"

"Yes," Sergey said, looking at the ticket Paul had spotted. "Tomorrow."

"Going to Vancouver on the train, I see."

"Unless stopped at the border. I guess you could arrange that. I suppose I'll have to change the ticket now." He blew smoke thoughtfully.

"Where are the bones?" Paul said.

"Bones?"

"You know what I'm talking about."

Sergey dragged so deeply that Paul could picture the black tar adhering to his lungs. "You mean Constantin's? That's what you're here for?"

"Right. You stole them in Sacramento. I want to know what you did with them."

Like a kid searching for goblins, very tentatively, he reached underneath his bed. "You want them?" He held the two long, dusty bleached bones in his hands. "Well, enjoy."

Paul took them from him. "Won't your pals get mad if you don't come back with them?"

"I was supposed to destroy them. Then I thought they might continue to offer some financial possibilities and considered keeping them myself. But I've grown tired of these games." He held out a pack of cigarettes. "Want one?"

"No, thanks." Paul looked around, found a towel on the radiator, and wrapped the bones in it. Krilov watched impassively.

"Sit down. I've got no one to talk to in this frenzied country since Christina died."

Paul remained standing, but did let himself rest against the door frame.

"We don't want any more pretenders to Russia's throne creeping out of Monterey," Krilov went on. "If there is any hint of that, the rest of them will probably be murdered. I myself was instructed to phone in the bomb threat to stop Alex Zhukovsky from testifying. I was supposed to kill him, but I just picked him up when the people came running out and rode around with him for a while. You might say he convinced me he had no interest in bringing up old histories."

"I might say that you just didn't feel like killing him," Paul said.

Krilov laughed and coughed. "True. I thought, after him, there's the next brother, and then the kid who just spent months in prison. It just seemed like needless butchering, like the Bolsheviks shooting and stabbing the little daughters. The rest of them are harmless. I think Christina was—unique. What a shame she defected over to Father Giorgi's faction, a bunch of radical religionists. We wanted to make her a tsar, or at the very least, give her a beautiful power. Make her famous. Get her picture in magazines around the world."

"You wanted a masthead for a phony monarchy you would run from behind the scenes. When Christina figured that out, she dropped you. At least Giorgi might have helped her do some social good."

"She was an experiment that failed."

"That sounds damn cold, from what I know of your relationship. You were lovers, weren't you?"

Krilov shrugged. He didn't seem to care about anything anymore.

"What happens when you go back to Russia?" Paul asked him.

"Oh, I won't go there again. My death would be slow. I think maybe Cuba."

Paul nodded.

"What will they do with the bones?"

"Cremate them." Paul would have a little talk with Gabe, convince him.

"Fine." Sergey dropped his cigarette butt into a cup, where it sizzled. "We're all victims of tradition, even in America," he said. "Bury the dead, all that kind of thing. Death."

"Closure," Paul said.

"Do we have any other business?"

"I'm afraid so." Paul pointed his weapon through his pants pocket at Krilov. "It's a Glock," he said. "My beautiful power."

"You're going to turn me in? They'll never prove anything. Giorgi won't talk."

"They'll deport you back to Russia," Paul said. Krilov jumped up and ran at him, low, dangerous because he was willing to take a shot, but Paul's big hand with the gun came down hard on his neck.

"*Mudak*," Paul said. He opened the door and invited the cops in.

30

Thursday 10/2

STEFAN COULDN'T BELIEVE, COULD NOT believe, that he had agreed to return to the cemetery, but here he was, going, dressing in one of the suits he had worn daily to court, which seemed appropriate, given the occasion.

At the door, he said good-bye to Erin, but she wouldn't let him go right away. She took him by the shoulder, forcing him to admire the ring on her finger, the chip of a diamond, really, no more than another promise, but one that he would keep.

The weekend after they let him out of jail, on a windy Saturday, he had invited her to a picnic at Carmel River beach. They walked down toward the ocean and found a place on the sandy slope where they could watch the clouds fly over the water. They talked for hours. He apologized. He begged her to forgive him; then, when the sun had gone down, and Erin was shivering, he had bent down on one knee and proposed. She cried, and then she took the ring. "I'll be able to get a bigger one eventually," he had told her. But she swore she loved it, and she loved him. He didn't deserve her, he knew that.

"One more kiss," Erin said, holding onto him. "I never

knew one heart could hold so much happiness," she whispered in his ear.

What luck! He drove back to El Cementerio Encinal, music up loud, this time in blazing sunlight, same scrungy Honda Civic, but without a broken taillight, and nothing in the back seat to make a bored beat cop say what the hell.

When Alex had called to ask him to come, Stefan spent most of the conversation thinking about how guilty Gabe must feel, and how mad he was at his brother, and how sorry he was about the whole damn mess. If it wasn't for Gabe's consult with that lawyer, Christina might not be dead.

But Alex had told him Gabe wasn't responsible. "Christina and Alan Turk were infected by the same sickness. They placed an inflated importance on anachronisms, nobility, royalty, divine destiny. Alan killed to claim his personal piece of royal history, and Christina died because she wanted to claim hers. You know what's sad? The newspapers won't let this story drop. She got the fame she craved so much, but she had to die to get it."

Today, taking in the salty wind, Stefan would say hello to a brother he had never known and good-bye to a sister and a father he had never known. Erin accused him of being too sentimental lately, but in jail he had squeezed back so many feelings, he now welcomed tears when they came. Singing to himself, feeling alive, smelling the sea air and loving the warm sun on his left arm, he turned into the narrow gate of the cemetery, open this time, and went straight for the Russian headstones.

Alex Zhukovsky and Gabe had already arrived. They stood talking quietly beside a small, fresh mound of earth below the double cross with its slanty wooden stake planted awkwardly below. Stefan parked behind another car, trying to get off the pavement a little in case someone wanted to get by him, but unwilling to intrude too much on those unfortunate dead with positions too near the edge.

"Hey, Stefan," Gabe said. "Meet your big brother, Alex."

Alex held out a hand. "Hey, Stefan," he also said, smiling, getting the accent wrong on Stef's name, saying it like a foreigner.

Stefan took his hand, thinking about how Alex had looked in court, so hunted, and how today, he looked relaxed, maybe even a little happy. "I brought bouquets," Stefan said, showing them. "Erin made them."

His brothers nodded. Even though Alex was shorter, older, with much less hair than Gabe, the two men looked remarkably similar.

Stefan looked down at their father's grave, the full force of their history bearing down on him. He and Erin had been reading about the last tsar. "We'll never know, will we?"

"Oh, come on," Gabe said. "We know. Where'd the egg come from, and the stories? Not from some flunky baker or page. Let's stake our claim. Say it out loud just this once. Our father was tsarevitch Alexis Nicholaevich Romanov, who lived a quiet life in a small place, right here in Monterey."

"But say it only today," Alex said. "Like I told that crazy Russian who kidnapped and almost murdered me, this is a final burial. We don't want to be haunted by this part of our past any longer. We don't need crazies coming after us. We don't want anyone messing with our father's remains or our bones for that matter, not if it means death threats and assholes who want to kill us coming around."

"We abdicate," Gabe said, and Stefan, smiling, nodded.

"I don't know if Gabe has told you yet," Alex said, taking one of Erin's bouquets and laying it on the fresh dirt mound. "We sold the Fabergé egg to the Russian who bought the Forbes collection, and along with the settlement we've agreed on, we'll be splitting the proceeds three ways." He stood close to Gabe, and as he spoke, put an arm around him in a careless way, as if he knew him, as if they had grown up together. Gabe, prickly old Gabe, grinned. "Did Gabe tell you he quit his job?"

"You did?" Stefan asked.

Gabe nodded.

"What'll you do? Travel?" Buy a castle and play lord of the manor? Stefan thought, but didn't say.

But this brother he thought he knew inside out had some surprises in him still. "He's been working with the Leukemia and Lymphoma Society for a long time," Alex said. "He quit to work there full-time."

"One thing I'm good at," Gabe said. "Squeezing money out of people. I don't want any more kids to die and never live to see a day like today." He picked up a rock and threw it toward a tree. "And I'll have more for you rich boys on that topic later, when our ship comes in."

"Gabe, wow. Count me in." Stef forgave him everything in that instant, every bad thing he ever did. So what if Mom liked him best? Maybe he deserved it.

"Papa would be so proud," Alex said.

"I sometimes think I remember. His mustache tickled," Stefan said, rubbing a finger along the letters on his father's headstone.

"I think I remember his growl," Gabe said.

"I'm sure he was happy to have two more sons," Alex said, "but Christina exerted such influence over everyone, including Papa. She never listened to anyone except him, and he listened to her, and was her hero." He sighed. "I regret you'll never know them, and maybe come to forgive them both."

"What was Christina—our sister—like?" Stefan asked.

And Alex, unleashed, filled them with stories about

their childhood, stories that showed a younger brother's admiration for his smart, dreamy older sister. "She loved the story of the snow maiden. I often think it was because she felt an affinity for this character who went all the way, in spite of the danger she certainly saw coming, who wore that mark of being special, and who died because she couldn't settle down and accept a smaller, happy life."

They threw dirt on their father's final resting place. They had cremated the last bones, and burned the DNA results. Only ashes lay in the grave now.

Christina's grave was next to her father's and mother's. Stefan left her a bundle of bright fall leaves and flowers. Gabe contributed irises. Alex put down one yellow rose.

"Our big sister." Gabe ran the sounds around in his mouth. "Well, she would appreciate a good toast. I know she could throw a glass." He reached behind himself, bent, and brought out a bottle of vodka and three small glasses. "To our Christina," he said, "almost tsar of all the Russias."

"Za nashu sestru," said Alex, raising his glass. "To you."

31

Friday 10/3

PAUL ASKED NINA TO GO dancing. There weren't too
many places to dance, but he found one in a hotel with
a band and a wooden dance floor. He wanted her to come,
so she did.

The dancing, mindless, absorbing, physical, was about
as perfect as it could be. Sweat flew off his forehead, and
she stomped until her knees hurt and her clothes stuck to
her body. The music carried them along, and the evening,
had it been a first date, would have been perfect.

Except it was a last date.

Exhausted, ready for a little champagne and bruschetta, they collapsed at a table beside the action. Paul
toasted her: "An amazing, courageous, crazy, sexy, cool
woman. A winner."

And she toasted him as her love.

The waiter poured them second glasses, but Nina was
thirsty, and drank ice water from a cold, slick glass instead.

Paul downed his champagne, head tipped back, hair
too long, neck of the thousand kisses exposed. He was
watching the dance floor, flashing lights flicking color on
the writhing bodies, and Nina could see how responsive he
was to the movement, to the raw physical power out there.

"Paul, we need to talk."

"Damn. And things were going so well," he said with a smile.

She took the ring off and put it gently in his hand, where it lay looking sad, unwanted.

"So, this is the answer I waited for so long to hear," he said slowly. "Mama always said you should be careful what you wish for." He turned the ring over a few times. "You heard about Susan, didn't you?"

"I don't want to talk about her."

"I should have said something at the time, but you were involved in that trial."

"Please, let's not get distracted."

"That's what she was, a distraction." He took her hand. "If anything, she put my head back on straight, made me understand that I'd do anything to have things right with you, Nina."

She couldn't resist engaging. "And anything includes sleeping around?"

"It wasn't like that at all."

"I didn't want to get into this with you, Paul. She is not the problem. We are the problem."

"I thought you were a big girl. I thought you would understand. You hurt me, Nina."

"I know. I should never have accepted your ring and then strung you along like that. I'm sorry."

"Well, I'm sorrier." He drank some water. "I want to ask why, then."

She didn't want to get into explanations. They were always self-serving, and they never explained, but she wasn't ready to go the next step, either. She needed time to stop shaking, and get her heart beating right. "This case . . ."

Plainly, he expected something different, because he interrupted impatiently, "Talk about a distraction."

"See, I don't see my work that way. It doesn't interfere

with living. It doesn't fit in between other things. It is my life."

He took a breath as if to steady himself, and asked, "Okay, what about the case?"

"It was all about a woman who found her way. Christina finally found her place—it was crazy, maybe, but she felt right. She felt useful."

"Okay, so this is relevant how?"

He was trying to stifle his impatience, but she heard it in the brusqueness of his words. It firmed her resolve. She was doing the right thing.

"When you offered me that fantastic ring," she said, "I wanted it so much, I took it. But I shouldn't have. These past few weeks, I've admired it so many times. It's so balanced and graceful. I wish I could live up to it. But I'm not balanced. I'm driven and obsessed and sometimes I sleep better alone. I have a place where I belong already, and it isn't as your wife." She didn't want to watch him take it all in, so she watched the people on the dance floor dip and spin. "I hate this. I'm not graceful, either."

He broke off a piece of bruschetta and ate it. "I really hoped the ring would clinch it. I thought we needed the ring, both of us. It was a mistake. Another one among several I've made with you, lately."

She didn't want to ask but she wanted to know for sure. "You slept with her, didn't you?"

He nodded.

Nina tried to speak again quickly, to keep up the pace, but she felt a rock lodged in her throat. She worked to clear it, but nothing came out. Garth Brooks was singing about being sad and in pain, but how he still would have done the dance no matter what.

"Nina, I'm a proud man."

She couldn't trust her voice yet, so she nodded.

"On the whole, I like myself. You love me, but

sometimes you don't like me. I get no respect, and honey, I deserve it. Remember how, when you met Collier, you married him a minute later?"

Her "yes" came out like a croak.

"Well, I was there before him and I was there after him, but I never managed to swoop down and fly away with you like he did. I guess I figured out what was really going on with us when you wouldn't answer a really simple question a few weeks ago. But you've danced with me, yeah, and you're a really fine dancer." He took her hand. "You are graceful."

"I am?"

"Even in those impractical shoes you wear. Nina, I love you."

"Oh, Paul," she said, her heart breaking with such force, she hardly thought she could live through the violence. "We're saying good-bye. I can't. This is too hard."

"Let me help you then, just this once." He grinned at her, same old Paul, full of tease, hazel eyes twinkling, same as always. "It's over, honey," he said. He put the ring up so that they could both watch its million colored lights radiate. Then he popped it into his pocket and kissed her hand. "But don't believe that bullshit they feed you about men and women never being friends. I'll always be yours. I'll always adore you."

She stood. He stood, too. She prepared herself for a run to the car, where she could be noisy in peace, but he took her hand, squeezed it, and led her back to the dance floor.

"One last time," he whispered.

The band eased into a slow tune. He pressed himself tightly against her, closing his eyes. Swaying slowly, they relaxed into each other, into the painful, familiar-feeling rhythm, his hip slides, her hip slides, their hips slide together.

Finally, he let go. He walked her to her car. "More stars

up in Tahoe than in Monterey," he said, looking into the murky black sky. "You can see the Milky Way up there. I know you miss that."

"Good-bye," she said.

"See you." He smiled and disappeared into the darkness.

Bob had them packed within two hours the next morning.

"Hitchcock misses Tahoe," he said. "I talked to Uncle Matt this morning and he says our house is in good shape. Snow's coming soon. Hitchcock has to prepare, get that thick coat growing."

"I need a thick coat, too, come to think of it," Nina said. The thick skin she also needed wouldn't come along for a while.

She had turned down Bear's offer. With Alan gone, they would have to find a new partner, but there were a million fine lawyers. They could find a replacement. Mostly, she would miss Klaus's retirement party, but the old man seemed to understand when she called him. "Were you really thinking of shooting yourself?" she had asked him.

"I wouldn't have done it," Klaus had said. "My wife would not have approved. Miss Reilly . . ."

"Yes?"

"Good work."

"You, too, Klaus."

Bob was smiling happily. "Plenty of snowboarding this winter, according to the almanac. Troy and Brianna are both really good. Plus, Aunt Andrea makes the best turkey. Plus, we'll get to hang with baby June. You know she's already smiling?"

He packed boxes while she paced, and when she got too overwrought, he said, "Hey, Mom, follow me."

Stupid, bulging with silent tears, she followed him out to the carport and the artificial turf they had never replaced. She looked around. "Why are we here?"

He pointed up to the rafters above the car. "See that?"

She looked and saw her old surfboard, a long one, bought based on her weight and height, one she had used as a teenager and left with Aunt Helen more than a decade ago.

"Well, September's the warmest month for the water. The waves are good today. Just look out for sharks."

She put on her old wet suit, too tight, dusted spiderwebs off the surfboard, and stuck it into the back of the Bronco.

"Are you sure you don't need the car so you can pack it?" she asked Bob, worried.

Her son stood on the rickety porch, face beaming bright as the late September sunshine. "I'll stack the boxes out front."

She drove down the hill to Lover's Point.

The wave rose behind her, a silk sheet, rippling and folding, the blue and gold of a Fabergé egg, collecting the sunset colors. With a sudden heave, it gathered in strength.

This would be the one, Nina decided, admiring its perfect lift, and the hint of a perfect curve to come.

She paddled toward shore, mindless, pushing against the pulling tide, waiting for the right moment, before the wave broke, when it arched in fierce momentum, before it began its wild roll toward shore and its own destruction.

She paddled, breathing, waiting to get caught up by its massive, invisible power. It swelled behind her, a low hump, rising to a hill, surging into a mountain of water. She let go of her hold, and she took it on, standing up on her board to ride all the way in. The shore rushed at her, hard golden sand, soft foam, and churning sea water, and she fell back into the cold world.

AUTHOR'S NOTE

A man who claimed to be the last page to the last tsar of Russia is, in fact, buried in El Encinal Cemetery in Monterey. He said he taught the tsarevitch to ride a pony, and knew Rasputin. Our character and his descendants, while inspired by this story, are entirely fictional.

The facts regarding the Romanov family's execution at Ekaterinburg and exhumation of the remains of only five of the family in the 1990s are true. Alexis and one of the princesses were allegedly cremated, and their deaths have continued to be hotly disputed over the decades that followed, as no evidence of cremation has ever been found.

It's an unusual fact that a bone-marrow transplant gives the recipient, permanently, the blood DNA of the donor while the skin and hair DNA remains that of the recipient. Our thanks to Deej Dambrauskas for these facts.

Others, especially on the Web, have advanced the theory that the tsarevitch did not have hemophilia. He suffered from high fevers as part of his attacks, which is not characteristic of hemophilia but is characteristic of thrombocytopenia.

The last tsar of Russia, Nicholas II, loved to give unique, elaborate Fabergé eggs as gifts to his family.

ACKNOWLEDGMENTS

As always, grateful thanks to our exceptional publisher at Bantam Dell, Irwyn Applebaum, and our insightful editor, Danielle Perez.

We owe too much to our agent and friend, Nancy Yost of Lowenstein-Yost Associates Inc., to express in a few words, but hey, thank you, you terrific woman.

We thank Dr. Ellen Taliaferro, co-founder of Physicians for a Violence-free Society, for related ideas. We consulted research on strangulation by Dean A. Hawley, MD, George E. McClane, MD, and Gael B. Strack, JD. (All errors are our own.) John Farrelly, cemetery coordinator at Cementario El Encinal, kindly shared his memories.

Pam would particularly like to thank the talented writers who taught, entertained, and kept her going during the writing of this book, all to be found at The Critical Poet's Final Polishing site (http://pub8.ezboard.com/fthecriti-calpoetsmessageboarfrm12): dmehl808 (Dave Mehler), Drgib, Ashersimeon, jaxmyth, posthumous, cyberwrite, antidora, arabianlady, kdkaboom, eliashoi, ameuc, and all the rest.

Kudos to the members of Windward Oahu AAUW, who help so many; and to the unique characters in the Ladera Book Club, who provide such amusing intellectual distraction.

Thanks and love to the family and friends who sustain us: Andrew, Ardyth, Nita, Elizabeth, Brad, June, Connor, Cory, Stephanie, Joan, Meg, Patrick, Sylvia, and Frank.

ABOUT THE AUTHOR

PERRI O'SHAUGHNESSY is the pen name for two sisters, Pamela and Mary O'Shaughnessy, who live in California and at Lake Tahoe. Pamela graduated from Harvard Law School and was a trial lawyer for sixteen years. Mary is a former editor and writer for multimedia projects. They are the authors of ten Nina Reilly novels: *Unlucky in Law, Presumption of Death, Unfit to Practice, Writ of Execution, Move to Strike, Acts of Malice, Breach of Promise, Obstruction of Justice, Invasion of Privacy,* and *Motion to Suppress.*

Don't miss the next thrilling novel
to feature Nina Reilly

CASE OF LIES

Coming in hardcover from
Delacorte Press in July 2005

PERRI
O'SHAUGHNESSY

CASE
OF
LIES

CASE OF LIES

On sale July 2005

A fresh mug of Italian espresso in hand, stockinged heels riding the edge of her desk, Nina stole a moment to reflect.

The long workday had begun. On the drive down Pioneer Trail that morning toward the office, Nina had watched the bicyclists and joggers with even more than her usual envy. They were out grabbing the last glories of fall, so damn happy, smelling the fresh tang of high snows and watching fluttering dry leaves while she contemplated her day, the bitter child-custody battle coming up, along with two grisly settlement conferences, all to be conducted in the windowless courtroom of the irascible Judge Flaherty.

Long ago, when law began, the advocates and judges must have met in tree-shaded glades, toga-clad, birdsong the accompaniment to their work, courtesy and dignity their style, and—

—And of course, as a woman, she would have been pouring the wine from the ewer, not arguing the case. But one could fantasize at seven forty-five in the morning while watching birds and squirrels chase around the autumnal marsh that rolled out toward a distant, twinkling Lake Tahoe.

After several months in Monterey, she and her son Bob had returned to Tahoe. Sandy Whitefeather had returned to her domain in Nina's office in the Starlake Building and was drumming up business before Nina had time to put her cup down on the desk. The young woman lawyer who had been handling Nina's cases found a job in Reno, and left open files and a busy calendar of court appearances.

In spite of the time crunch, Nina found just enough space in the morning to pour Hitchcock's kibble and Bob's cereal, and to enjoy the short trip up Pioneer Trail to her law office.

When evening came, after she and Sandy locked up, Nina would drive home through the forest to the cabin on Kulow Street, noting hints of the winter to come in the dry pines and parched streams. The cabin still basked in early evening sun. Inside, she would kick off her shoes, pour herself a glass of Clos du Bois and watch the world news, make dinner and dog Bob into finishing his homework and bath. Once a week she called her father, and once or twice a week she and Bob went to her brother Matt's house for dinner.

September and October passed in a flurry while she reestablished her routines. The fees rolled in and she paid off her debts.

The judges accepted her back. She had a pretty good working relationship with most of the local lawyers, and she finally knew what she was doing.

The small office suite in the Starlake Building on Lake Tahoe Boulevard, right in the heart of town and less than five miles from the Nevada state line, now felt like home, but some part of her was still restless. She had gone from Carmel to San Francisco, to Tahoe and back to Carmel and then back to Tahoe again in the past few years. She was beginning to ask herself, uncomfortably, if she would ever settle down. Bob deserved stability, and she was going to have to stay put for a while.

She wasn't even sure why she had returned to Tahoe. She might just as well have stayed in Carmel and joined the Pohlmann firm, which had made her a very good offer.

And she had made one other uncomfortable discovery since returning to Tahoe.

Her ex-lover, Paul van Wagoner, and his new flame, Susan Misumi, had quickly moved in together down in Carmel. Fair enough, since Nina had ended it. The why of Susan Misumi, her black bangs, her humorlessness, escaped Nina, but it wasn't her business anymore. Nina and Paul still checked in on each other. They managed to stay friendly because they had been friends before they became lovers.

Nina had moved on. She went out, danced, ate good food, had a few unexpectedly intimate conversations. But she had discovered that she didn't expect much from men anymore. She didn't want to try for love.

That feeling had been growing in her for a long time, and she sometimes wondered if it even had something to do with the breakup with Paul. Finding a partner seemed impossible, based on her experiences, so she put it out of her mind.

Men and places. The restlessness would come over her, and she'd feel a need for another place and another man. Other people followed their life lines. She careened along too fast, not able to see her own.

But she would always have two constants to ground her: Bob and her work.

Today, we persevere, she thought. With the last gulp of coffee, she threw two ibuprofen down her throat.

The phone buzzed. Nina swung her legs down, sighed, and picked up the phone. Sandy must have come in. Her desk was only ten feet away, through the closed door, but Sandy didn't like getting up.

"He's here, and so's she. Your eight o'clocks," Sandy said.

"And a fine morning it is."

"Hmph. You have half an hour."

The man stood with his back to her, hands in his pockets, looking at one of Sandy's decorations, a Washoe Indian basket on the shelf. He wore a green and black plaid lumberjack shirt tucked into a well-broken-in pair of jeans. The belt, a leather craft affair, must have dated from the sixties. Work boots, a body used to physical work.

A conservative local, Nina thought, pegging him almost before he turned around. Nice wrinkled tan face. Grim expression. Plenty of gray-brown hair on both head and chin. A belly, that was a surprise.

Behind him, clearly trying to fade into the white wall, pretty Chelsi nodded. She was taller than her uncle. She wore her hair down today and it fell straight and satiny. Something had turned off the smile.

"Hi. I'm Nina Reilly," Nina said, looking the man in the eye, holding out her hand.

"David Hanna."

"Please come in." After ushering Chelsi in too, Nina glanced toward Sandy, resplendent this morning in a heavy turquoise necklace and a denim jumper, who seemed to be writing something in the appointment book. Sandy gave Nina a swift look back, one eyebrow cocked.

Look out.

Now, that was an interesting take, since Uncle Dave looked harmless, but Sandy's first impressions had to be taken seriously. Sandy knew where clients hid their guns and buck knives; she knew if the Rolex was real or faux; a few words to her in the reception area revealed if a new client was resentful, desperate, or suicidal. Recently they had installed an emergency button hooked up to the local police under her desk, and a thick, intricately carved walking stick propped behind her desk only doubled as a decoration.

Such is solo law office life in a gambling town. Prepare for Uzis, Sandy frequently said.

Nina closed the door and Hanna pulled an orange client chair away from the wide desk. He sat, crossing one leg at the ankle, stroking his beard, looking out the window behind her desk toward the steel-gray lake, but not focusing, just gazing. Chelsi sat in the chair next to his, back straight.

Nina took her time getting comfortable, arranging a few papers on her desk, adjusting her chair. Let them get used to her.

"I don't know why I'm here," David Hanna said finally.

"Because you need to be," Chelsi said.

"I'm not working much. Money's tight. Chelsi and her dad, they've offered to pay for your services, but I just don't know. It doesn't seem right. I hear Chelsi's already told you about the case."

"A little," Nina said.

"Rog was Sarah's brother. I know he can't help wanting to do something. What I can't figure out, what I haven't been able to get my head around all along, is what good it does, suing someone. My wife is gone."

"What's your brother-in-law's name again?"

"Roger Freeman." While Nina made a note on her yellow pad, Hanna watched, squinting. The tops of his ears were flushed red, like raw meat, and looked sunburned too. Either he spent a lot of time outside, or, as Chelsi had suggested, less healthy indoor pursuits heightened his natural color. "What's your usual line of work, Mr. Hanna?"

"I'm a carpenter. Used to be a firefighter."

Nina looked at her Client Interview Sheet. "Placerville's a great town."

"It's a long drive up Fifty to get here. I don't come up the Hill much anymore since it happened. Chelsi said this conversation right now isn't going to cost us anything?"

"Free consultation," Nina said. "We have half an hour and you came a long way, so how can I help you?"

Hanna shrugged and said, "That's the point. I haven't got a fucking clue."

When Nina didn't bridle at that, he added, "Like I said, talk won't bring her back."

"But you're already involved in a lawsuit. Isn't that right?"

"There's this lawyer in Placerville? Name's Bruce Bennett. Two years ago, after Sarah died, Roger contacted him and had this lawyer file a civil suit against the motel where it all happened. I wasn't sure about the whole thing, but Bennett got us in his office and oh, he talked it up, how much money we were going to hit them up for, how they were negligent. They let the bastard onto the property. No video camera and the clerk off somewhere. The lawyer talked us into suing the motel. Why, he practically had us convinced that the motel owner, who by the way wasn't even around that night, did the shooting."

"Sounds like he was trying to put on a very aggressive case on your behalf."

"I guess." He shook his head. "It never sat right with me, blaming the motel, but Roger was so gung-ho. We used up some of Sarah's life insurance to pay Bennett, but when the money ran out he filed a substitution of attorney form and left us flat."

"I guess that didn't leave you with a very high opinion of lawyers. I know Bruce. The lawsuit stayed active?"

He shook his head. "I really don't know where things stand with it."

"You couldn't pay Bruce Bennett, so he quit?"

"Basically."

"I would think carpenters were in big demand around here. I can never get anyone to come out and fix my porch," Nina said.

"I don't work much lately." He sighed. "I have problems."

"Problems?"

He chewed on a thumb, as if the question demanded

arduous consideration that was beyond him. Scanning the room as if he might locate a swift escape route that wouldn't require him to pass Sandy, his eyes landed on Chelsi.

"Uncle Dave's been sick," Chelsi said, taking her cue. "Like I told you."

"Hmm," Nina said. "Well, I understand you were going to bring me the court papers to look at," she went on neutrally.

"Right." He reached inside his wool shirt and pulled out a battered envelope. He set it on the desk, the hand revealing a slight tremor. Nina looked at him carefully, noting the thin burst of broken capillaries in his ruddy cheeks, the tangle of red veins around the edges of his eyes.

He hasn't had the hair of the dog this morning, she thought, and he misses it. No wonder Sandy had given her a warning eyebrow. Sandy didn't like drinkers.

On the other hand, wasn't it a positive sign that he had held off to talk with her? Maybe there was still hope for him.

She opened the envelope and pulled out several legal documents in the Wrongful Death and Negligence case of *Hanna vs. Ace High Lodge and Does I-X.*

The complaint Bruce Bennett had drafted was on top, followed by some unserved summonses, an answer filed by the Ace High Lodge, and a set of pleadings filed recently by the Lodge's attorney, Betty Jo Puckett of South Lake Tahoe. While Nina skimmed through the pleadings, Dave Hanna slumped in his chair, never taking his eyes off her.

Chelsi had displayed a good grasp of her uncle's legal

situation. He was about to have his case dismissed on the motion of the Ace High Lodge, because he had done nothing to bring the matter to trial for almost two years.

Bennett had done a workmanlike job laying out the facts in the complaint. The Hannas had been celebrating their tenth wedding anniversary by spending the weekend at Lake Tahoe, at the Ace High Lodge, one block from Harveys and the other Stateline casinos. They had gone to a show at Prizes and walked back, then stepped out to the second-floor balcony of their room.

There, according to the dry legalese of the complaint, "They observed an armed robbery in progress." And, in what seemed to be a case of being in the wrong place at the wrong time, at thirty-nine, third-grade teacher Sarah Hanna had been shot once through the heart. She was three months pregnant.

There were few traces of the gunman or other witnesses. The motel clerk, Meredith Assawaroj, had heard the shots from an adjoining property. She had missed seeing the killer, but had provided the South Lake Tahoe police with a fair description of the three motel guests who had been held up, young people who had packed up and left before the police arrived.

The clerk's descriptions of these three led nowhere. The gun hadn't been left at the scene.

Now the Ace High Lodge wanted out of Hanna's lawsuit, which alleged that its clerk should have been in the office, that the motel security should have been better, and so on and so on. Hanna might have had some sort of case on the merits if he had pursued it, but leaving it to languish for so long had exposed him to Betty Jo Puckett's Motion to Dismiss.

Puckett's work looked good. Her law was solid. Statutory limits restricted the ability of plaintiffs to file a lawsuit and then do nothing, as Dave Hanna had done.

Puckett had apparently advised the motel owner well—to lay low for as long as possible and then attack Hanna for failure to prosecute. Nina hadn't met her, but the courtroom grapevine said she had an effective style.

She looked up. Hanna's cheeks flamed, but his eyes were sunken into the sockets. He looked like a big, healthy man who had developed some wasting disease that was ruining him. Nina wondered how long he had been drinking way too much. At least he was sober at eight in the morning. She found it painful to imagine what he'd gone through, how bitter he must feel now.

She cleared her throat. Setting down the Motion to Dismiss, she said, "Your wife seems to have been the classic innocent bystander."

"Did you know she was expecting?"

"Yes."

He shifted in his chair, like the seat hurt him.

"What do you plan to do now?" Nina asked him.

"Slink away, I guess."

"The Lodge wants attorney's fees."

"I might get socked with their lawyer fees?"

"Perhaps."

Dave Hanna put his hand on his heart and said, "Let me get this straight. They want *me* to pay them? How much money are we talking about?"

"I don't know. I could guess, from the amount of work I see here, possibly several thousand dollars."

"If I do nothing, what will happen?"

"You'll probably have to pay their fees."

During a long silence Hanna deliberated about whether to—what? Confide in her? Walk out on her? "Well?" he asked finally.

Nina raised her eyebrows.

"What do you think?"

"It isn't hopeless," Nina said.

"There isn't a damn thing I can do to stop them. Is there?"

"You can fight the motion. The Code of Civil Procedure does require that a suit like yours be dismissed two years after service on the defendant with no action. But it hasn't been quite two years. It's still in the discretion of the court."

Hanna blurted, "Look, lady. I understand you need to drum up business. Maybe you hope we've got a stash of dough hidden away. I hate to say this, but we don't. Bennett demanded a hundred fifty dollars an hour and five thousand up front, and called himself cheap. I don't want to bankrupt Roger and Chelsi. And I'm broke, like I keep telling you."

"We'll take care of the money, Uncle Dave," Chelsi said.

"I will need a retainer," Nina said, thinking of Sandy, who would hold her accountable. She came up with the lowest amount she could manage. "Two thousand, billed against my hours. I also charge a hundred fifty an hour. There may be expenses. If we manage to keep the case going, those expenses could mount up fast."

"Done," Chelsi said, whipping out her checkbook. Hanna bowed his head, looked at the rug. "It's not for revenge," Chelsi said. "It's not for money. It's for my aunt. You know?"

Nina nodded. She pushed the button, as though Sandy hadn't left the door open a crack and been listening the whole time.

After Hanna had signed an agreement and left with Chelsi, Nina adjusted her suit coat and hung her new briefcase over her shoulder.

"You think we can make money on this?" Sandy said. She reposed like a Buddha in her Aeron chair, detached, hands folded calmly on the desk over Nina's notes.

"I do. Fast money. That's if we can get past this motion to dismiss. The motel clerk should have been in the office. The area should have been less of an ambush invitation. There may have been other incidents—this kind of crime occurs in clusters. Maybe the motel should have been on notice."

"The client's unreliable."

"Yes. But his relatives seem to have him in line. I think some money might help him, Sandy. Rehab. Grief counseling. Whatever. I trust Chelsi to steer him right."

"Where do you want to start?"

"Let's get the police reports and check to see if there were similar crimes reported in the area a couple of years ago. File a notice that I'm in as Hanna's attorney and send a copy of the notice to Betty Jo Puckett. She represents the Ace High Motel."

"Betty Jo Puckett?"

"You know her?"

"I met her. She has a problem in the tact department."

Nina smiled, saying, "Report anything else you hear."

"Before you go, what else do you need?"

"Get the file made up. I'll get going on drafting the Response to the Motion to Dismiss after court. There are a long line of precedents regarding innkeeper liability for inadequate security. Sandy, remember Connie Francis?"

"The singer? Nineteen-sixties. 'Lipstick on Your Collar.' That wasn't even her biggest hit. But even now it strikes a chord with me." Sandy's husband Joe and she had broken up for many years and only recently remarried.

"She won an early motel-security case. The damages award was in the seven figures. I don't think it was in California, though. The trial took place in the mid-seventies. See if you can locate the case on Lexis."

"She was robbed?"

"She was raped. During the early seventies, I think, while staying in a hotel room. It was brutal. I think it ended her career."

Neither woman spoke for a moment. Then Sandy said, "So some turkey fired off a wild one during a stickup and killed a third-grade teacher. Do we go looking for him, or just nick the motel?"

"We go looking."

"Good."

"We get started, at least."

"Shall I call Paul?"

"He's tied up."

"You'll need an investigator, and he's the best."

But for many reasons, Nina did not want Paul van

Wagoner involved. She did not wish to see his handsome face, his flirty manner, his sexual vibrations. She was over him, at least for the moment. Someday, Paul could enter her life neutered into professional cronyism. Until then, he needed to stay filed in the Great Memory file.

She said with emphasis, "Do not call Paul."

"Okay, okay. I heard about another good investigator who might be available."

"Good. See what you can do." Nina trotted down the hall and climbed into her old Bronco. Five minutes until court. She bumped off the curb into the street.

There's an advantage to small-town law. She would make it to court right on time.